best sports stories 1977

best sports stories 1977

A PANORAMA OF THE 1976 SPORTS WORLD
INCLUDING THE 1976 CHAMPIONS OF ALL SPORTS
WITH THE YEAR'S TOP PHOTOGRAPHS

Edited by Irving T. Marsh and Edward Ehre

E. P. DUTTON / NEW YORK

Dedicated to Mark, Laura and David Welborn and Gregory and Lisa Denny. Play Ball!

Library of Congress Cataloging in Publication Data [Library of Congress Catalog Number]

ISBN: 0-525-06623-3
Published simultaneously in Canada by Clarke, Irwin & Company Limited, Toronto and Vancouver

10 9 8 7 6 5 4 3 2 1

First Edition

CONTENTS

ILLUSTRATIONS

THE PRIZE-WINNING PHOTOS

Best Action Photo

Best Feature Photo

OTHER PHOTOS

PREFACE

A year ago the editors of *Best Sports Stories* were taken to task by a woman's libber who contributed one of her efforts to the book as the only lady sports writer included in *Best Sports Stories–1976*.

Well, we think she'll be a little happier with *Best Sports Stories–1977*. For of the 45 pieces in this thirty-third annual anthology, four are by female sports writers, a good percentage considering the small number of women employed in the fun-and-games department of the nation's newspapers and magazines.

More, one of them has captured one of the three awards of $250 offered by this annual: Jane Gross, of Long Island's *Newsday*, winner of the news-feature prize for her story on the sex change of Dr. Renée Richards. "A bizarre [story]. . . . carried off with amazing delicacy of touch," says one of our three judges. Further, she is only the third woman to have gained an award in the 33 years of the competition, the other two being Carol Hughes of *Pageant* in 1945 and Joan Flynn Dreyspool of *Sports Illustrated* in 1957. Both took the magazine prize.

Ms. Gross is the daughter of Milton Gross, late sports columnist of the *New York Post*, himself a frequent contributor to this anthology. The winning feature was the first story ever submitted by Ms. Gross to the annual anthology.

Both of the other winners have appeared here before and for Shirley Povich, sports columnist of *The Washington Post* ("The Great Yankee Stadium Holdup"), this is the second news-coverage award. He won the same prize in 1957 for his story on Don Larsen's perfect World Series game against the Brooklyn Dodgers for the New York Yankees at the Stadium. Yankee Stadium seems to be an inspiration to Mr. Povich, who was once named Woman of the Year by a woman's organization.

Mark Jacobson, winner of the magazine award for his story "Rebound for Glory," which appeared in *New York* magazine, made his *Best Sports Story* debut a year ago with "Trying Out with the Jets," which also appeared in *New York*.

The panel of judges—John Chamberlain, King Features columnist; John Hutchens, member of the selection committee of the Book-of-the-Month Club; and Jerry Nason, retired sports editor of *The Boston Globe*—named 20 of the 45 stories as point-winners.

As in the past, the stories that were sent to the judges went to them "blind." That is, they were identified with no indication as to the writer or his or her publication. Three points were given to each story for a first-place vote, 2 for a second place, and 1 for a third. You may note that's how the stories are identified by the judges in the box score and in their comments, which follow.

THE BOX SCORE

News-Coverage Stories	Chamber-lain	Hutchens	Nason	Total Points*
Boxing [The Great Yankee Stadium Holdup by Shirley Povich]	2	3	2	7
Wimbledon [The Hatchetwoman Called Crissie by Bud Collins]	3	—	3	6
Connors [Connors Puts It Right on the Line by Ted Green]	—	2	—	2
Rose [The Reversal Story by Joe Hendrickson]	1	1	—	2
1st Series [An Easy Victory, If Not an Artistic One by Mike Gonring]	—	—	1	1
News-Feature Stories				
Renée [Tennis Isn't the Only Issue by Jane Gross]	3	—	1	4
Nadia [Nadia is a Perfect Angel by Stan Hochman]	—	—	3	3
Joe [Where Have You Gone, Joe DiMaggio? by Will Grimsley]	—	3	—	3
Little [Little League Umpire by Leonard Shapiro]	—	2	—	2
Floyd [The Anticlimactic End of the Masters Golf by Edwin Pope]	2	—	—	2
Jenner [King of the Decathlon by Dave Kindred]	—	—	2	2
Alston [The End of an Era by Wells Twombly]	—	1	—	1
Dorothy [This Was a Night for Perfection by Monty Montgomery]	1	—	—	1
Magazine Stories				
Ronnie [Rebound for Glory by Mark Jacobson]	3	—	3	6
Money [Baseball's Money Madness by Pete Axthelm]	—	3	—	3
British [How We Blitzed the British by William A. Marsano]	—	2	—	2
Ilie [Ilie Nastase: The Side You Never See by Barry Lorge]	—	—	2	2
Van Horn [Overemphasis or Hungry Hill Pride? by Nick Seitz]	2	—	—	2
Mark [Funny and Fantastic: That's Fidrych by Jim Hawkins]	—	1	—	1
Masters [The Whitwams Go to the Masters by Jolee Edmondson]	—	—	1	1
Spring [The Short Season by Jim Brosnan]	1	—	—	1

*Based on 3 points for a first-place vote, 2 for a second, 1 for a third.

JUDGES' COMMENTS

John Chamberlain
News-Coverage Stories

1. Wimbledon [The Hatchetwoman Called Chrissie by Bud Collins]
2. Boxing [The Great Yankee Stadium Holdup by Shirley Povich]
3. Rose [The Reversal Story by Joe Hendrickson]

1. As a rather aged tennis hacker, I've found a way at last to improve my concentration that really seems to work. I simply say "Evert, Evert, Evert" to myself while I am waiting to receive the ball. So I may be prejudiced, out of sheer gratitude, to think that the news story of Chrissie Evert's Wimbledon victory over Evonne Goolagong deserves the Number One palm. It's a good story anyway—far more exciting than the baseball stories, which seemed unable to overcome the dullness of a one-sided World Series.

2. I like the sheer honesty of a story that dares to question the official decision in a match involving Muhammad Ali. Whether Ken Norton was jobbed or not at the Yankee Stadium, the reporter who had the nerve to say that Ali was exposed as a tired old relic exposed himself to a supreme test; he had to back up his point with perceptive observation accurately set down. This he managed to do. A clear Number Two choice.

3. It's always good reading when Ohio State's Woody Hayes is shocked. When the story involves an exciting second-half comeback engineered by a quarterback who gets indifferent marks from the experts as a passer, it makes for something extra.

News-Feature Stories

1. Renée [Tennis Isn't the Only Issue by Jane Gross]
2. Floyd [The Anticlimactic End of the Masters Golf by Edwin Pope]
3. Dorothy ["This Was a Night for Perfection" by Monty Montgomery]

1. The story of the sex-change of a male tennis player, Richard Raskind, into a woman, Dr. Renée Richards, is certainly bizarre. I started reading the feature describing the ordeals of Renée, both on and off the tennis court, with a feeling that it would be a distasteful experience. But the writer carried everything off with amazing delicacy of touch. A fascinating job.

2. How can you turn a runaway Masters golf victory into something exciting? The feature story recounting Raymond Floyd's eight-stroke triumph over Ben Crenshaw manages to be both informative and effective. The flashbacks into Floyd's so-called rakehell past helped a bit.

3. For Number Three in the Features I had trouble. I liked the one about Joe DiMaggio—but for a reader who remembers Gay Talese's *Esquire* story of the "great DiMaggio," written some 10 years ago, there wasn't enough that was different about this year's story on Joe to make it truly memorable. So I'll have to pick "Dorothy," a sympathetic piece about Dorothy Hamill's Olympic figure-skating championship, for the Number Three slot. There are some fascinating glimpses here of the psychological ordeals that any girl has to endure to go to the top in the strange world of figure skating.

Magazine Stories

1. Ronnie [Rebound for Glory by Mark Jacobson]
2. Van Horn [Overemphasis or Hungry Hill Pride? by Nick Seitz]
3. Spring [The Short Season by Jim Brosnan]

1. Growing up black in Brooklyn, in a district that has been primarily Italian turf, can be made endurable by basketball. To bring out all the tensions involved without overdoing it and spilling over into second-rate sociology or third-rate sentimentality takes a deft hand. The author of "Ronnie" has it.

2. I've watched the peewee hockey explosion in southern New England, and have often wondered how a coach could put together a kid team for high-pressure travel and competition without hurting the young players. The story of the Van Horn mites of Springfield, Mass., is vastly reassuring. It rings true in every word it says about "the wonderful resilience of childhood."

3. Although I am generally leery of "in depth" reporting that simply spreads out raw material with no attention to form, I found myself caught up by all the details of a spring training hegira made by an old-time baseball player who has turned writer. There is nothing that is sheerly irrelevant here, and a lot that has flavor.

John Hutchens
News-Coverage Stories

1. Boxing [The Great Yankee Stadium Holdup by Shirley Povich]
2. Connors [Connors Puts It Right on the Line by Ted Green]
3. Rose [The Reversal Story by Joe Hendrickson]

1. By general consensus the larceny perpetrated by the judges and the referee in the Ali-Norton fight was one of the most flagrant in modern boxing annals. It also produced the best story about the heavyweight title bout I have read in a long time, a biting, scornful piece in the fine sports-writing tradition of fearless honesty—and, as well, a terse and vivid account of the action, such as it was.

2. Every sport has its epic encounters, even if that word *epic* is sometimes tossed around a little carelessly. The Jimmy Connors-Bjorn Borg battle for the U.S. Open men's final surely was one of them, with Connors even going so far as to speak well of his opponent. This one is finely captured here—the tension, the relentless pace, the crucial plays that could have gone either way and brought a different result.

3. And speaking of epics, how else would you describe a football game in which a team that was down 3—0 at the half came on to win, 23—10? It took some doing on UCLA's part against Ohio State, and it took some doing to report it as concisely and excitingly, but without breathless heroics, as this writer did.

News-Feature Stories

1. Joe [Where Have you Gone, Joe DiMaggio? by Will Grimsley]
2. Little [Little League Umpire by Leonard Shapiro]
3. Alston [The End of an Era by Wells Twombly]

1. Another piece about Joe DiMaggio, after the countless ones that have gone before? Yes, but this is one with a difference: DiMaggio in the years of retirement, proud and dignified as always, and still the embodiment of class. It is a satisfyingly thorough picture of him—how he spends his time, who his friends are, and so on. Fans of No. 5 will be grateful for this rewarding chance to catch up with an old hero.

2. A warm, entertaining visit with a Little League umpire who obviously has a way with kids. An offbeat sort of sports story, and you may like it the better for that, by a writer who knows how to pass along a winning anecdote.

3. A manager with a record not quite like that of any other — all those seasons of one-year contracts — is saluted with admiration but without sentimentality. A moving look at a quietly great figure who, at the end of his field career, deserved better than he received from the Los Angeles fans for whom he provided so much.

Magazine Stories

1. Money [Baseball's Money Madness by Pete Axthelm]
2. British [How We Blitzed the British by William A. Marsano]
3. Mark [Funny and Fantastic: That's Fidrych by Jim Hawkins]

1. A long overdue study of what money madness, as the author calls it, is doing to the American sports world — to athletes, owners, and the fans who ultimately pay the bill and too often are shortchanged. The key word is *greed,* and this warning is an urgent and valuable one.

2. The author of this one may never write another sports piece, but he should have a little niche of his own in sports-writing lore for his irreverent spoof of the NFL's somewhat silly little essay contest.

3. A sparkling piece this one about the most colorful baseball rookie to come up in many a year. "In all baseball, there is no one quite like him," says the author, and one has to believe it. His hometown fans in Detroit came to know him well during his first season, but others—like this reader—who had wanted to know him better will relish the details they find here.

Jerry Nason
News-Coverage Stories

1. Wimbledon [The Hatchetwoman Called Chrissie by Bud Collins]
2. Boxing [The Great Yankee Stadium Holdup by Shirley Povich]
3. 1st Series [An Easy Victory, If Not an Artistic One by Mike Gonring]

1. For me, "Wimbledon" had all the requisites of top-drawer reporting. The subject (an Evert-Goolagong final in tennis) had vitality, the story a subtle sense of urgency, and the stage had two extraordinary athletes from central casting, so to speak. The writer took you instantly into the heart of the action with a faultless lead paragraph, then proceeded to weave the vitality, urgency, and characters into the tapestry of an extremely skillful report. Once again, as a year ago, it occurs to me that some of the best writing being done today is taking place in the sport of tennis, a sport, alas, that does not turn me on as much as the stories being written about it.

2. "Boxing" was a gutty piece of writing-reporting. Here is a reporter who was adamant in his conviction that the judges defended M. Ali's heavyweight title against Ken Norton far more

convincingly than did Ali himself. The writer never wavered as much as one punctuation mark from that conviction from his "holdup" declarative opening sentence to his final devastating line. An unusual report in that the writer did not let his indignation hinder his mechanics of reporting the bout action.

3. "First Series." Cincinnati's routine sweep of the outclassed Yankees in the World Series didn't figure to be the source of many news-story contenders this time around. It wasn't. The best of them—and almost a prophecy of the games to come—was this candid, baseball-knowing assessment of game No. 1.

News-Feature Stories

1. Nadia [Nadia Is a Perfect Angel by Stan Hochman]
2. Jenner [King of the Decathlon by Dave Kindred]
3. Renée [Tennis Isn't the Only Issue by Jane Gross]

1. "Nadia." That no news-coverage piece from the Olympic Games challenged for the honors in that category was a wonderment to me, but Olympics writing came on strong in the feature division. Two pieces from Montreal were no less than superb. Of the two my vote was captured by "Nadia" because, like the fantastic child-athlete herself, it twinkled in tune with the "Yes Sir, That's My Baby" theme song to which the Romanian super sweetie gave her gold-medal gymnastic performance.

2. "Jenner." This was an outstanding picture in words of the outstanding decathlete at Montreal. Although this particular judge knows Jenner personally, and has since before Munich in 1972, upon reading this story he felt he knows the athlete even more intimately. Thus, it passed about as tough a judging test as can be concocted for a story. All the super athlete's dedication, modesty, and good ol' New England Yankee common sense were woven inobtrusively into this story.

3. "Renée." This was a delicate sports-story subject—transsexualism—handled with understanding and consummate skill. No brazen attempt at stalking a headline with sensationalism here, a temptation to which a lesser writer would surely have succumbed.

Magazine Stories

1. Ronnie [Rebound for Glory by Mark Jacobson]
2. Ilie [Ilie Nastase: The Side You Never See by Barry Lorge]

3. Masters [The Whitwams Go to the Masters by Jolee Edmondson]

1. In the area of magazine pieces, produced more leisurely against more casual deadlines than news copy, subject material is likely to be the distinguishing mark. The writing of them all seems uniformly excellent, one piece as well-executed as the next. Thus "Ronnie," the story of a minority black boy playing tournament basketball at a racially tense high school in Brooklyn, grabbed me from start to finish. The topic is a rare one. The writer told what is essentially a hard-eyed story with sensitivity . . . the way it is. How often has such superb writing been done at the level of high-school sports?—yet there is the incubator, the beginning of it all, the local high school.

2. Right on "Ronnie's" heels in my rating chart came "Ilie"—an informative, beautifully structured and entertaining story of Nastase, the provocative pro tennis player. Again, this was no simple task—explaining the erratic, boorish, and often surly behavior of Nastase while evoking a glimmer of understanding, perhaps even sympathy, from a reader conditioned by sports-page headlines to disdain, if not detest, this controversial athlete.

3. While "Masters" almost qualified as fiction in its presentation, his piece about a touring husband and wife team of golf buffs exploited phenomena of the spectator addicts who journey far to walk and watch the big PGA tournament.

As for the prize-winning photos, the editors were particularly impressed by the drama expressed in the photo of the winner of the action award of $100, "Grandstand Hails Headstand" by Charles R. Pugh, Jr., of the *Atlanta Journal-Constitution.* The feature photo award of $100 went to Mike Andersen of *The Boston Herald American*, a longtime contributor to *Best Sports Stories,* for his amusing "Now Girls, Let's Not have a Row!"

This, then, is *Best Sports Stories–1977,* the thirty-third in our series. May it give you pleasure and bring back memories of a great sports year.

IRVING T. MARSH
EDWARD EHRE

THE PRIZE-WINNING STORIES

Best News-Coverage Story

BOXING

THE GREAT YANKEE STADIUM HOLDUP

By Shirley Povich

From The Washington Post

They staged the great Yankee Stadium holdup Tuesday night when they held up the arm of Muhammad Ali and called him the winner at the end of 15 rounds.

The victim of this violence to simple justice was Ken Norton, the challenger to Ali's heavyweight boxing crown. Norton had just exposed Ali as a tired old relic of the prize ring wars who now talks a better fight than he fights.

But Ali was reendowed with the title he lost in the ring by two judges and a referee intimidated by the old shibboleth that the decision can't go against the champ if the fight is close. Norton was jobbed. The fight wasn't close, and their logic is baseless, anyway. If you've overdrawn at the bank, even by a dollar, you're overdrawn.

Once more it was Ali getting the benefit of some sacred quality attributed to him. Norton licked him in their second fight three years ago, but it was close enough to bring Ali the decision. The vote could have gone against him in that bummer fight with Jimmy Young in Washington a few months back, but it didn't.

Before the bell rang for Round 15 Tuesday night, there was scribbling on this scoreboard. It read: "Ali needs this one big. A KO or we got new champ."

But he blew the fifteenth round, too, to a tireless Norton who managed to catch up with Ali's defensive dance and fetch him a left hook and two rights that were the only telling punches of the round. Ali's title had surely slipped away. On this scorecard, it was 8-6-1 for Norton.

Then came Norton's biggest jolt of the fight. Justice had been kicked in the butt. Norton, who had won the title in the ring, lost it to those little pencils that were marking the official scoring.

Ali was all talk, little fight. Between rounds, he repeatedly went to the ropes, sometimes on all four sides of the ring, to exhort his fans in his own cry, "Norton must fall." But Norton was the most unpsyched opponent Ali has ever faced. With an assurance that stemmed largely from the fact that he had punished Ali in their previous two bouts, Norton was unafraid and more than faintly contemptuous of this cheerleader who was trying to lick him. This guy wasn't George Foreman, who could level a man with one punch.

As a prizefighter, the only thing classic about Norton is his superbly sculptured body that tapers in lines that make Ali look thick-waisted. Norton's fighting style is mostly pursuit, and a bit on the awkward side, with too many roundhouse rights, but unlike Ali, he came to fight.

At thirty-four, Ali had lost the speed that meant everything to him. The fleshiness at 222 pounds is more than baby fat. His performance against Foreman was his own recognition he can't move like he used to. From the opening bell, he was a defensive fighter. Alternately, he went into his dance and his rope-a-dope for long periods, no way to score points except in the glee of his admirers who take almost everything Ali does in the ring.

"Norton will fall in five," Ali had said repeatedly before the fight.

When Round Five commenced, he was warned for holding again. He blew that round, too, with his defensive rope-a-dope, and when, near the bell, he ventured out into the middle of the ring, he got popped with a Norton right.

Ali was winning the delighted shouts of his fans with his new gimmick, a shimmy of the buttocks that he introduced in the third round to taunt Norton, but meanwhile he was losing that round, too. Norton won all five rounds from the fourth to the ninth, and two of the last three, only to be fouled by the ring official at the finish.

Ali miscalculated when he went into his rope-a-dope coverup against Norton for long stretches in the belief that Norton's flailing would bring on the weariness that finally caught up with Foreman in Zaire.

But the thirty-one-year-old Norton was perfectly conditioned for this night, and he didn't weary, and he was slipping in some decent punches in his assaults on Ali's peekaboo defense. When Ali in desperation, tried to break it off, he was clubbed often in the head.

Norton was guilty of only one, unfortunate mistake of no special importance. That was in the thirteenth round when, believing he was completely in command, he mimicked Ali's rope-a-dope retreat into his own corner, and dared Ali to come to him. He didn't bring it off very well, and in fact he lost the round, but that was the last round he lost on this scorecard, despite the official scoring that showed eight of nine markings in the last three rounds in favor of Ali.

Ali's performance was a $6 million fraud on the viewing public. That was his guarantee, and he rarely tried to earn it. The closest he came to having Norton in any serious trouble was in a late round when Norton had to recover from a thumb in his eye. Norton was charging forward in every round with the faith that he was fighting a man who couldn't hurt him, and that was the size of it. Faced with a moving target, Ali had little punch, and his overriding desire was not to get hurt.

The new Ali buttocks wriggle even drew a rebuke from his manager and spiritual leader, Herbert Muhammad, who was at ringside. "Tell him to cut that stuff out."

Ali's corner was a study of depression after they brought Ali in at the final bell. None of the customary joy there, but a terrible fear that Ali had lost this one. Good-bye to that $10 million gate with Foreman. Good-bye title. Ali was awfully tired, and looked merely resigned. Then, Norton got hit, simultaneously by three robbers pulling loaded scorecards on him.

Best News-Feature Story

TENNIS

TENNIS ISN'T THE ONLY ISSUE

By Jane Gross

When Dr. Renée Richards moved to Southern California in February and joined a local tennis club, none of the members knew she was a transsexual. "She was screened like all the members," said Ken Stuart, who manages the club and is married to World Team Tennis player Betty Ann Grubb Stuart. "As far as we knew, she was a female physician with residency in Newport Beach who paid her bills on time."

That is just how Dr. Richards wanted it. The forty-one-year-old ophthalmologist from New York had a sex change operation in August 1975 and moved west to start a new life as a woman. "I moved 3,000 miles," she said yesterday as she drove from a press conference at one tennis club to another club where she would practice on a clay court in anticipation of her Saturday opening match at a tournament in South Orange, N.J. "I left my home, my practice, and my family to assume a new life, alone and anonymously. I didn't know anybody here. There was no reason to tell them. I knew they would find out sooner or later, but I was not going out of my way to let anyone know."

Shortly after her arrival in Newport Beach, Dr. Richards was introduced to a new club member, a cardiologist named Jim Shelburn who had moved to California from Pennsylvania. "I was told we'd have a lot in common," Dr. Richards said, "because we were both doctors who played tennis." When the two doctors were introduced, Dr. Richards realized they had been premed students together at Yale. She recognized him but he did not recognize her. Back then, Dr. Richards had been Richard Raskind—a man.

"We struck up an immediate friendship," Dr. Richards continued, "for the same reasons we had been friends before. When he heard I was an ophthalmologist from New York, he asked If I knew Dick Raskind. I said I knew him very well. Then we played some tennis. He said, "Renée, you have the same damn topspin backhand as Dick." When we were through, he said, "Renée, you're the best tennis player I've ever played with." I wanted to say, "No, you fool, we used to play after chem lab."

Before too long, Dr. Richards's secret was out. In July, she played in a tournament in La Jolla, beating twenty-year-old Robin Harris, the top seed in the tournament. A San Diego television announcer learned of Dr. Richards's sex-change and aired the story. Since then, Dr. Richards has been accepted for entry in the women's division at South Orange and applied as a qualifier at the U.S. Open at Forest Hills. She will play at South Orange, but she has been denied entry in the women's draw of the Open by the United States Tennis Association unless she submits to and passes a chromosome test. She says she will not take the test.

She said she would appeal the ruling requiring such examinations. "I am not against a test of some sort to identify a person's sex, age, or race or other limiting requirement for specific athletic competitions," she said. "In my case, however, I do not agree that the sex chromosome test is an appropriate one at this time and state of medical knowledge. . . . As far as any legal action is concerned, I don't throw that out as a possibility."

Her attempts to compete as a woman have caused an uproar with the USTA and the Women's Tennis Association. In Newport Beach, she is still being received with affection, respect, and graceful equanimity.

When her cardiologist friend heard the reports out of La Jolla, he telephoned her. Dr. Richards laughs as she recalls their conversation. "He said, 'You little bitch, why didn't you tell me all this time?' "

Then there was the reaction of Atilio Rosetti, the teaching pro at her club and a former touring player. "He's a very Latin guy," Dr. Richards said. "Very macho, chauvinistic. He always treated me the way a girl likes to be treated. After La Jolla, I thought, oh my God, how am I going to face Atilio? That day he called me and said, 'Hey, baby, want to hit some?' "

Dr. Richards still had the choice of living her new life quietly. Instead, she has chosen to challenge the tennis establishment and tell her story publicly. "I started getting letters," she said, "poignant letters from other transsexuals who were considering suicide, whose friends and family won't see them. I realized that this was more than just a tennis thing, my hobby; I could easily give that up. But, if I can do anything for those people, I will. I am in a position to try and make people see that such individuals should be allowed to hold up their heads. I realize this is important from a social standpoint. Maybe I can help the public realize that a transsexual is not someone with two heads who minces down the sidewalk."

Dr. Richards is quick and firm in pointing out to the curious that sex-reassignment surgery "is not like going into the dressing room and putting on a skirt." As a small child, she said she dressed up in her mother's clothes, but her sexual confusion lasted longer than playing dress-up. Her mother, who is deceased, was a psychiatrist, and as a teen-age boy Dr. Richards read case histories in her mother's textbooks. "People who felt like me," she said, "were in the back wards of mental hospitals only 50 years ago."

As Dick Raskind, Dr. Richards went through elementary school in Forest Hills and high school at Horace Mann, playing baseball, football, and tennis. After undergraduate work at Yale, she was graduated from medical school at the University of Rochester and began a career as an eye surgeon specializing in children's disorders. In the meantime, she explored the possibility of sex reassignment.

Ten years ago, she went to Casablanca, where such surgery was being done. She was not satisfied with the medical conditions and decided to wait. "Most reputable clinics," Dr. Richards said, "require you to live successfully as a woman in a social context before the surgery." She did that in Europe following her trip to Casablanca.

After returning to New York, in 1970, Dr. Richards married and fathered a son who is now four years old. In 1975, she got a divorce and had a sex-change operation at a private hosital in Queens. "Nobody knew I was doing it," she said. "I rented a cottage in Bridgehampton and was supposed to be writing a book. On August 3, I checked into the hospital. I convalesced at the beach and was back to work after Labor Day."

Those fall months were perhaps the hardest of all. In the hospitals, where she operated, in private practice, and at her teaching job, she was Dick Raskind, wearing a man's wig and a suit. After work, she returned to her apartment, changed her clothes, and entertained those friends who knew. "It was a Clark Kent-Superman life," Dr. Richards said. "It was not easy, not easy."

"It was a tremendous relief to come here," she said, looking out the windows of her apartment onto Newport Bay and nearby Balboa Island. "When I walked into this apartment for the first time, I knew I was Renée Richards and this was Renée Richards's apartment."

The rooms are full of pictures of four-year-old Nicky, and her father, also a doctor, whom she affectionately calls a "crotchety seventy-six-year-old-man." Dr. Richards said she left New York to protect her family. Of her son, she said, "We have a feeling he kind of knows, but not really. He thinks his daddy is the biggest, strongest, and best tennis player and eye doctor in the world. But, he also knows his daddy is different. He has a really strong identification as a little boy and I don't want to shake that. I will never go back to New York because of Nicky. I don't want him confronted with the grief he would suffer." She said she sees her son once a month.

Her father, she says, never calls her Renée, but "he has always been there and always will be as long as he lives. He says he doesn't give a damn what's going on as long as I'm all right. Here's a guy whose son was an extension of everything he wanted to be, medically, academically, athletically. To find out his son was a woman was quite a blow for a man born in 1900."

The same experiences have taken their toll on Dr. Richards, perhaps toughening her for the ordeal she is likely to face in her first major tournament. "It's probably going to be more horrible than I expect," she said, "but it's not going to fracture me. If I can make sure my family doesn't go through unwarranted grief, I can go through it."

Still, she is uneasy about what the reaction will be. "I know," she said, "that I bring the issue of sexuality to the forefront. There has always been a tremendous problem with women athletes fighting the stigma of being lesbians. There has always been that association between muscular women and dykey women. It's really a different issue, but I don't know whether I'll add to it or subtract from it."

Certainly Dr. Richards can clarify certain issues for the ignorant. She was not, she says, a homosexual. "I was very appealing to women," she said, "and women were very appealing to Dick. A transsexual loves women so much he wants to join them. Almost all of us had close relationships with women as sisters and friends."

She can also offer enlightenment on the real or imagined emotional differences between men and women. "I'll have fits of crying and fits of laughing now," she said, "that I didn't have before. Some of it is hormonally related. But, so much of it has to do with the responses of other people and the expectations of society."

Those expectations give Dr. Richards opportunity to enjoy some fits of laughter. "I drive into a parking lot," she said, "and some guy yells that broads don't know how to drive. I could tell him a few things."

But the serious moments seem to come more often. Yesterday, she quoted from a Babylonian stone tablet which she said dated to 1700 B.C. The writing on the tablet said: "When a woman gives birth to an infant that has no well-marked sex, calamity and affliction will seize upon the land. The master of the house will have no happiness."

Best Magazine Story

BASKETBALL

REBOUND FOR GLORY

By Mark Jacobson

From New York

It seemed like a typical spring-fever Friday at Lafayette High in Bensonhurst, Brooklyn. Stillwell Avenue was clogged with punks wheeling the old man's Buick. The schoolyard fence was lined with Italian chicks picking at their Blush-On and smoking Marlboros. Whew! The way they poured themselves into their Wranglers made even the skanky ones look like they had bursting soccer balls for buns. Tempting. But as Ronnie Chisholm, the strongside forward of the basketball team walked by, he didn't check out the action. He even pretended not to notice as the girls' boyfriends, brutal-eyed kids in brown leather, shouted, "Hey, Chisholm, you crazy nigger, win tomorrow or don't come back on Monday." Great school spirit, Ronnie thought. If this had been an ordinary day, The Chiz, being a crazy nigger, would have most likely replied with an obligatory variation on "What kind of crap you talking, guinea mother?" But not today. Today the pressure was too heavy for that kind of risk.

Today it seemed as if everything was coming together. Soon, maybe next week, it would be time to sit down and bust his brains about how to play the college scene and face, if it came to that, the withered prospect of a future without basketball. But today everything seemed to be riding on tommorrow's game with Canarsie. The "City Champs" was at stake.

Tomorrow was for glory—a crucible to test Ronnie's "game." A "game" is what comes from hours of dribbling basketballs on asphalt, shooting for crooked rims attached to reverberating steel backboards. It was on courts like that in South Brooklyn that The Chiz practiced until he had a corner jump shot as rare as radium and twice as deadly. It was also where he learned the deceit of making his eyes go one way and his feet another. It's a quirky, searing, and deceptively stylish way to play, not unlike The Chiz himself. In the playgrounds, everyone's "game" has a personal stamp; there's identity in the way you go to the hoop. And when Ronnie and his friends took the subway to East Flatbush and Fort Greene to challenge kids for courts, the news of The Chiz's "game" spread—just as the reps of other schoolyard stars had. But it would take tomorrow to see if his game would be remembered.

There were other incentives. Last year, when The Chiz was a junior, Lafayette High had been in the City Champs too. Easily the fastest team in the city, they had blitzed through the season undefeated and were ten up on Taft High, bad dudes from the Bronx, with less than a half left in the final. Then came misery. Faced with Taft's impassive consistency, Lafayette broke down. They threw the ball away when they should have held it, kept running when they should have stalled. In the last minutes, egos clashed and fatally wounded their chances. When Taft won 74–70, some said Lafayette had blown the game. But others postulated that they'd never had a chance, that the team was too emotional and schoolyard-bred for its own good, that when the big spotlight came on, their confidence was bound to turn to stage fright. For The Chiz it had been a nightmare; he'd watched his coaches, Gil Fershtman and Ditto Tawil, cry, and he'd sat in front of his locker feeling like death.

Tomorrow would be the payback. For Ronnie it had been another year of moron classes like Applied Physics that he just didn't seem to have any head for, another year of three-hours-a-day practice learning to cram his flowing "game" into structures like "box and ones" and "triangles and twos," and another year of hour-long train rides to Twenty-fifth Avenue, where he'd had to deal with the Italian kids who would love to straighten his hair if they could.

Right now it seemed worth it. Twenty-three games into the PSAL season, Lafayette had won 22. No matter that Canarsie, the team from down the Belt Parkway, had won 23 of 23 and was thought to be the best high-school team in the country. Or that Ronnie would have to pit his skinny body against Curtis Redding, a 6-foot-5 bruiser. After waiting a whole year to get respect, The Chiz wasn't about to be denied. And if the *Post* sports page was calling the game a battle for the Kingdom of Brooklyn, that was all the better. The Chiz didn't give a damn about Brooklyn, but being king of anything sounded good to him.

Time was when the City Champs was the hottest ticket in town. It wasn't long ago (1960) that thousands packed the Garden to watch playground wizard Connie Hawkins of Boys' High go one-on-one with Wingate's fabulous Roger Brown. That was when the PSAL championship was recognized as a glittering celebration for the kids who labored so well at their "games" that New York was considered the basketball capital of the world. Besides Connie and Brown, any number of schoolyard kids went to the pros: Tony Jackson and Leroy Ellis, who played for Jefferson; Billy the Kid Cunningham, who did it all for Erasmus Hall; and Kareem Abdul-Jabbar, then known as Lew Alcindor. Those days you'd check the mug shots of the All-City team in the *News* and know that these cats could burn the Knicks on the half-court.

Later, great players still came, but things had changed. People who remembered Boys' and Jeff as good places to learn trig and get your first kiss began to shudder at the mention of the old alma mater. So many schools they would say "down the drain." Besides, there wasn't much need to watch high-school basketball anymore. Sanitized pro ball was all over the tube. Maybe the Cleveland Cavaliers and the Seattle SuperSonics didn't put their egos on the line every time they handled the ball, but you weren't afraid you'd find one of the players trying to steal your car after the game. The Garden didn't want any part of the high-school crowd either. When wine bottles flew out of the balcony during the 1964 Boys'–Franklin final, that was it. The City Champs was banished to seamy high-school gyms where not more than 500 people could squeeze in to breathe the old sweat.

Some reward for a million head fakes! Out in the sticks like Indiana, kid ball players have starched uniforms from birth and state tournaments are sold out for years in advance. But in the Apple, where the moves really are, no one seems to care. When the money crunch came, the white-socked accountants went straight to the athletic budget. Out of an already tight budget of $2.4 million, they cut $980,000. The entire PSAL program, including the City Champs, could be in danger. Groups like the Save Our Sports Committee have been formed to raise funds, but the future looks shaky. This year the Garden, apparently convinced that the high schools have cleaned up their act, was going to let the City Champs back in. At the last minute, however, scheduling conflicts—in the form of the highly profitable Rutgers–St. John's game, set for some time—came up. The City Champs was shunted off to the St. John's Alumni Hall—not exactly a toilet, but not the Big Top either.

Out at Lafayette, though, The Chiz and the rest of the starting team they call "The Five" don't care about that. They'll play out their drama in a closet if they have to. You don't spend a year on the B train hearing about how you choked on the big one without getting obsessive. Besides, they know they're a special team. They can feel it on the floor. They're all seniors, all veterans of the Taft disaster, and have played together for years and know each other's "game" by heart. On a fast break—with Chiz and smooth Bobby Bishop hitting from the sides, Earl Nesbit and Vinnie Fuller snake-handling the ball up court, and Stretch Graham, one sweet six-foot-seven center, muscling the middle—The Five fly. It could be magic; sometimes during a hot practice on the school's crummy court the ball would move so fast that Chiz would lay one up and then turn to Stretch with amazed exhilaration.

Those nights The Five would hit the subway with burning palms and it seemed that no one could play the schoolyard game as well. They said they were a year older now and not so crazy, but watching them practice you could still see the wages of flying so high. Around Brooklyn the team had a rep for showboating and a cocky streak of meanness. They still screamed at each other in tight situations. Theirs is a schizzy game; and the bettors' line on The Five still said they could collapse as easily as explode.

If the Five play edgy, it makes sense. Lafayette is an edgy school. Walking through the scuffy hallways you may not think high school has changed all that much. The desks still have BOOK YOU carved in them. Kids with wood-block "passes" scurry to the "lav" for a quick smoke. Signs on cork bulletin boards say things like VOTE FOR ANGELA NAPOLITANO—THE GIRL WHO DID THE MOST FOR LAFAYETTE. But this school has its own special tensions. You get a whiff of it when you listen to a "guidance session" that begins with a kid saying he needs a car "so I can get laid more" and ends with the teacher explaining, "You know, Sal, if you spent your energy you use to chase the black kids in the hall on your schoolwork, you'd be a goddamned brain surgeon by now."

Over at the Trieste Salumeria on Bath Avenue, "the white kids' hangout," things are more to the point. Talk to any kid with a blow-dried pompadour and slack mouth, and he'll tell you, "We're gonna fight. For what's ours. We don't want the niggers coming here . . . yeah, call it our turf."

Turf's the trip. At one time Lafayette, a red-brick box built at the tail end of the Depression, was virtually an all-white school, primarily Italians from the Bensonhurst and Bath Beach neighborhoods. Then low-income housing projects attracting black residents were built adjacent to the school. Other blacks came on the subway. The composition of the school shifted to an approximate split of 70 percent white (almost all Italians), 30 percent black.

For the people of Bensonhurst, it was alarming. The old men in front of the Holy Ghost Knights of Columbus hall and in the restaurants under the Eighty-sixth Street El muttered about the invasion of the "melanjohn" (a corruption of the Italian word for eggplant, indicating that their new neighbors were "big, black, and shiny") and how they weren't going to let their neighborhood go down the drain.

Bensonhurst is an old-line neighborhood. If you ride around, you'll see several substantial brick houses that people say belong to "big families." And here the generations still talk. Consequently, the young "bulls" of the nabe have adopted Lafayette as the setting of their vendetta.

The Italian kids see "sociology" in their stand. "Yeah," they say, "the blacks think you're weak if you're white; we're showing them we're not that way. We'll get the respect." And watching the scene, you begin to understand why middle America feels so secure with Italians playing cops on TV. It's probably safe to say that Lafayette is the only New York City high school where the blacks are afraid of the whites. Chiz says it all: "Man, these are the roughest, toughest, craziest white dudes you can run up against. I saw that they were cold-blooded in the Godfather movies, but I didn't expect this."

For The Five, who are all black, it makes things tough. Stretch already has several offers of a new face if he doesn't pull down hundreds of rebounds against Canarsie. But not all the whites dump on the team. Today in Gillie Fershtman's tiny office The Five are hanging out, rapping about how Pumas just might be taking over from Converses and arguing about the merits of Burger King and MacDonald's. A bunch of cheerleaders, all of whom are white, come in, dressed in tight denim. From their necks dangle crucifixes the size of tire irons. They sit down and go through a cheer especially designed for the Canarsie game. It goes: "Canarsie don't be blue, Frankenstein was ugly too." The Chiz cackles, "That's rank. That's the dumbest thing I ever heard." Insulted, a couple of the girls say if Chiz is so smart, why doesn't he teach them "some more of your expressions." "Yeah," coos Diane through her spreading blue eye makeup, "bad means good, right? That's right, isn't it, bad means good?" Stretch says he's not giving away any secrets, but private lessons could be arranged. All of a sudden the room is awash with pungent adolescent glances. Just then two Italian guys burst in looking like boyfriends. "Let's go, girls," they say, "come on out of there." Reluctantly they get up, one saying, "Just don't rush me, Frankie." The Chiz cracks up. Stretch too. They slap hands and there are congratulations all around.

When The Chiz first got here he had a thing about whites. Bensonhurst should have pushed him over the line, but somehow it didn't. The Chiz is still a moody guy; only a couple of weeks ago he was temporarily kicked off the team for merciless bitching. But when he was a sophomore, he was "really crazy. I was out of control then, I think; I ran around and failed everything." Playing ball for Ditto and Gillie hasn't turned The Chiz into a credit to his race, but it has mellowed him out a bit. Ditto told Chiz if he didn't go to classes he'd "kill him." At first Chiz was all resentment, but later he was amazed what a little structure could do for your peace of mind. Later there were incidents that taught him tolerance. The week before the "Champs," the Taft players were calling Chiz, who is very light-skinned, a "white boy." He came back to the bench and told Ditto Tawil. Ditto suggested, "Fix 'em, call 'em nigger." Chiz laughed because for once the whole race thing seemed so stupid.

Now Chiz still snaps, "Do I look like your son?" when Ditto or Gillie calls him that. But he smiles when he says it. And when Stretch moans, "Dad, Dad," to Gillie after someone "murphs" his money, no one makes fun of him. After all, Stretch's parents aren't around—his mother died last year and at seventeen he's trying to bring up the family. Bobby Bishop lives with his grandmother. The Chiz doesn't have the foggiest what his father does for a living.

Ditto knows The Five have it tough; he understands. "I know stuff, bad stuff, about these kids that could break your heart. Maybe Gillie and me don't know exactly what to do for them, but we really try. They bitch, but I think they love us. I know I love them."

Local passions are not lost on Ditto Tawil. Years ago, "when Jewish jump shots were big in Manhattan Beach," Ditto, soon to be captain of the Lafayette varsity, used to go down to the courts looking for a game. That's when the king of the playground was Mark ("Whitey") Reiner, already a star at Lincoln and on his way to NYU. The first time Whitey saw Ditto he told him to beat it and crashed his head into the chain fence. Now Whitey is the coach of Canarsie, and Ditto laughs about the incident. But you can see that Brooklyn boys don't forget.

Whitey Reiner is a winner—probably always will be. And compared with Lafayette, Canarsie High School is a winner, too. The kids have a newer building, a classy white-brick job with a courtyard and fluorescent lighting. They also have much more success with their problems. When Canarsie opened in the early sixties there was heavy racial trouble. The blacks who came from Brownsville and East New York on the LL train took on the neighborhood Jews and Italians. It got dangerous enough to make the front page of the *Times*. Now, however, the "mix" is about 60 percent white–40 percent black and there has not been a major disturbance in years. Currently Canarsie is the kind of place where both blacks and whites come over to tell you that the school is "sixth ranked academically in Brooklyn." There's no razzing of the team in the schoolyard, either. Even the subs are heroes. And today, the day before the City Champs, more than half the school has turned up in blue to show spirit. Even the principal has a blazer on. At Lafayette, no one knows who the principal is; they think he must be a troll who hides behind bulletproof glass.

Whitey, who used to be boys' dean, says the relative tranquillity has come from "organization and discipline," and that's the way he runs his team. The Five's practices are mental battles to weave five roaring "games" together, but at Canarsie it's all Whitey's show. There are no jokes. No back talk. Whitey doesn't have much use for schoolyard ball: He's here to teach basketball, not to feed egos. And throughout Brooklyn, kid players know that Whitey can take your jitterbug doublepump and turn you into a pro. Guard Tyrone Ladson got a "language variance" (a school change to take a course not offered by the school in your district) so he could play for Whitey. Counting up to ten in Italian is strange stuff, but who cares? Whitey is one of the most successful coaches in the city. In his office, where signs like HUSTLE IS ANOTHER WORD FOR SURVIVAL hang, Whitey keeps a detailed file on most local teams. Today he's standing in the corner of Canarsie's spacious gym with his "LAFAYETTE" folder in his hands, making sure his charges know how to drive the middle against Stretch and put pressure on Chiz in the corners. The team is awesome. The backcourt men, Ty Ladson and Tee Waiters, travel with icy assurance. The forward line of Jesse Massey, Charlie Gipson, and Curtis Redding looms like three tight flesh triangles. All biceps and churning feet, the Canarsie five powered through the PSAL schedule, winning games by 30 and 40 points. And as Whitey watches them noiselessly assault the basket, he says, "When Lafayette gets a load of the pressure we'll put on them, they'll fold. They're too crazy. I feel sorry for them—we're going to kill them, you know."

For the Canarsie players, being part of the best team in the city does more than just look good in their yearbooks. Being number one brings the recruiters. All year long people from places like Texas and Missouri have been finding their way out to the ass-end of Brooklyn to watch Canarsie practice. Today, two fair-haired guys in pastel suits and patent leather are here to look at forward Jesse Massey's "perimeter shooting." They are from Centenary College, your average basketball school. Until recently Cententary was an unremarkable liberal-arts school on the Texas-Louisiana border. A couple of years ago it secured the services of Robert Parish, a fantastic basketball player (the kind recruiters call "program turners") and Centenary's became one of the top-twenty-rated teams in the country. Little matter that the NCAA found that Centenary's signing of Parish was in violation of its recruiting rules and placed the school on a six-year probation. Centenary was now on the map and alumni contributions flowed. This year, however, Parish will graduate, so Centenary has its recruiters out, trying to restock the team. "Yep," drawls Riley Wallace, the school's assistant coach and top recruiter, "we've been all over looking for a muscly guard. This Jesse looks nice. I always like New York City boys. They never just stand around like a lot of them others."

Recruiting practices have cleaned up a bit since the days when "free-lance agents" used to roam the schoolyards with a briefcase full of "contracts," but under-the-table money still flows, and shady deals of all types are still conducted. Coaches try to keep on top of the recruiting scene, but sometimes it's difficult. What kind of advice do you give an eighteen-year-old kid like Canarsie guard Ty Ladson, who has offers from more than 200 colleges ranging from Dartmouth to Texas junior colleges?

Over at Lafayette there are offers, too. Stretch has hundreds of them. The funniest one is from Oral Roberts University. Recently Oral Roberts has been coming on strong, basketball-wise, with several top-rated teams. Last month the school sent Stretch a free plane ticket to come down for a chat with Oral himself. Stretch says the good reverend didn't convince him. "Too much praying. My mother used to be very religious, you know. She'd sit in front of the radio listening to those preachers. Nearly drove me insane. Naw, unless he comes up with a blessing for rebounds against Canarsie, I think I'll pass."

Wherever Stretch goes, it'll be outside the city. Taking the subway to St. John's sounds a lot like going to Lafayette—all the hours of working on your "game" should pay off with more than that. Besides, even if you become a star in New York, you go into A & S, and who knows you? Better to go to New Mexico and be a B.M.O.C., play in front of 20,000, and have the governor take you to dinner. Stuff like that blows Ditto's mind: "Here I am telling this big dummy I'll break his nose if he doesn't get to class and he's talking to Oral Roberts—it's crazy."

For some of The Five, the future's not so sure. The Chiz would love to get out of the city, too. "No money here," he says. "No legal money, I mean." But there are problems. He doesn't "predict"—

which means his high-school grades indicate he is incapable of doing four years of college work. He'll have to go to a junior college somewhere and then transfer, which will be a drag—and a shame because everyone knows The Chiz is the sharpest guy on the team. Sharp enough to write a touching and evocative article for the *Post* about what hanging out with The Five has meant to him. And if he makes out in classrooms, maybe it was due more to contempt than to an inability to remember the dates of the Spanish-American War. But try to tell that to a college admissions officer. Gillie and Ditto say they know of a good junior college in Pensacola, Florida, but Chiz isn't into it. Not much chance for glory in Pensacola. Besides, Chiz hears it's cracker territory, one thing he doesn't need after Lafayette.

But that crap's for later. Business now. The Five are in the locker room at St. John's Alumni Hall getting into their red-and-white uniforms for what will be, no matter what, their last game together. The seasick-green room alternately resounds with rowdy screaming and dead silence, as if The Five are all manic-depressives with extremely tight sine curves. Still, you can feel the arrogance. People ask Chiz if he's nervous. He crosses his eyes, shakes like an old man, and shouts, "I'm tense, I'm tense." When Whitey comes in to wish The Five luck with some hokum about "It's for Brooklyn, boys, remember that," Chiz can barely suppress a smirk.

Outside, the frenzy whips. The Lafayette cheerleaders, their thighs flashing beneath pleated maroon skirts, lurch into their "Lafayette . . . boom, boom . . ." cheer. Across the way Canarsie counters with "Canarsie . . . boom, boom . . ." The wooden benches are filled with young blacks with stainless-steel combs sticking out of their Afros and white kids in marshmallow-heel clogs. Even on the Lafayette side they're talking to each other. Everyone stomps his feet as the teams run onto the court.

Going through their warm-up drills, The Five look woefully thin standing next to the Canarsie squad. Ditto, although acknowledging that once again Whitey has the power on his side, tries not to notice. "We'll fly over and around 'em," he says. Up in the stands, the recruiters are not so charitable. "Speed and size," says a chubby who brags that he was assistant at a Louisiana college at the time the school was hit with "228 violations, a record." Money comes out of pockets. Immediately Canarsie is installed as a ten-point favorite.

From the opening tap, things look inevitable. Everyone expected The Five to have trouble off the boards, but this is ridiculous. Jesse Massey and center Charlie Gipson crush Stretch away from the ball. When Chiz comes over to help, Curtis Redding blasts him with an elbow to the eye. Canarsie's all over the place. They hover like air pollution, grasping until The Five cough up the ball. It's a first half of horrors. For Chiz, there's no room to crank up the feather touch; Curtis's hands are so close he can read his palms. Lafayette's only bright spot comes when the PSAL officials order the Canarsie cheerleaders to sit down, sparking a tearful protest. And after playing like sludge for two quarters, The Five are lucky to be behind only 38–27.

In their locker room, the raucousness is gone and panic is setting in. Gillie is trying to tell them how to keep the ball away from Curtis, but he is drowned out by recrimination about who's to blame. For the first time The Five's natural edge is melting into nerves. It's as if all the near-death scenes in the playgrounds and the kids in the Buicks promising "five white-knukle sandwiches" have taken their toll. But two years in a row? This couldn't really be happening. Maybe everyone was right in saying The Five were too crazy to win. The Chiz begins to feel the desperation as he slams his fist into the locker.

It is time to collapse, but The Five, sons of entropy, choose to explode instead. As soon as the second half begins, you can feel the heat. Earl and Vinnie touch the pulse first and begin to force Ladson and Waiters into mistakes. Stretch rips the ball from Charlie Gipson and the charge is on. Chiz and Bobby, their eyes flashing like tops of police cars, find their "games" and fill the hoop. The schoolyard magic was pumping now, dizzying methodical Canarsie with its recklessness. The Five close in. The Lafayette cheerleaders, near suicide at half time, call for "AC-tion, AC-tion, BOYS!" Italian kids with megaphones scream, "Tonight we own Brooklyn."

At the end of the third quarter, The Five have moved within two points, 48–46. As Ditto says, they are flying, and across the court Whitey is sweating. In the huddle, the Chiz, his blood pressure doing double time, can't sit down. He sneers out at the crowd, as if to give a big stiff one to everyone who said he'd choke. But when Waiters steals the opening tap for the fourth quarter, bad things begin again. The mad spasm has been just that, and it has fallen short. Three times The Five come down the court with a chance to tie. They never do. As the recruiters said, you got to go with size and speed—even against magic. Canarsie has opened the score to 57–52 by the time Vinnie fouls out. There are four more minutes to go then, but essentially the game is over—once you break up The Five, forget it. By that final buzzer the Canarsie cheerleaders have returned from the grave and are pointing at The Five, screaming, "U can't beat the blue, U can't beat the blue." The Canarsie players hoist Whitey on their shoulders and hold up their index fingers to show that they are "number one." PSAL people search desperately for Brooklyn

Borough President Sebastian Leone and Comptroller Harrison Goldin, who are supposed to give out awards. It is quite a parade. And The Chiz, staring at the ceiling and feeling like death still another time, almost gets trampled.

A few days later, back in Bensonhurst, things are only a little better. Yesterday the Converse Rubber Corporation gave a dinner and The Five had to sit around and watch Canarsie get trophies twice as large as theirs. The Chiz is happy to report that The Five didn't wind up with cement shoes after losing. But as they walk down the halls they are continually followed by people who make gagging, choking sounds. No doubt it will go on until June.

But The Five will try to ignore it. They're too busy dealing with the mundanities of American history and study hall to fight anyway. Stretch has it easier than most; today he got another plane ticket, this one to Southern Methodist University. "Those religious boys are really after me," he says. He might even go to Oral Roberts after all. But for The Chiz, it's eight straight classes. With Ditto watching over you it's crazy to cut. Maybe he'll "predict" yet and avoid Pensacola. But as Chiz sits in Lafayette's dump auditorium, where there is no curtain, only a backdrop that says "asbestos," he's thinking of alternatives. The *Post* guy loves his story and wants him to write again, perhaps the story of his life this time. That's something. He will think about it a little more tonight; he's got a date to meet the rest of The Five to shoot some hoops.

Other Stories

OLYMPIC GAMES

NADIA IS A PERFECT ANGEL

By Stan Hochman

From the Philadelphia Daily News

The pianist tinkled into the middle portion of the music for Nadia Comaneci's floor exercises. The Forum crowd giggled. They recognized "Yes, Sir, That's My Baby" right away.

No, sir, I don't mean maybe. Nadia Comaneci was out there dancing, prancing, romancing and the crowd was loving every graceful moment of it. Floor exercises. What an incredibly drab name for what Nadia Comaneci was doing out there in the middle of the Forum, glinting like one of those old Roseland ballroom fixtures with 1,000 tiny mirrors.

Yes, sir, that's some baby. The Queen of the Olympics won't be fifteen till November. She wears her hair in a ponytail, ties it with twists of yarn, has a beauty mark on her left cheek, the teeny-tiniest of voices, and nerves like barbed wire.

She displaced Olga Korbut as Queen of the Olympics yesterday, winning the all-around gold medal. She's got Olga's number. She's also got a number of her own. It's 10. That's perfection in gymnastic scoring. Had two 10s yesterday.

The computer wasn't ready to handle a 10 because no one had ever received a 10 in Olympic competition before. The world wasn't ready for a fourteen-year-old Romanian kid and the gutsy things she does on the balance beam or the scary choreography she brings to the uneven parallel bars.

Bela Karolyi is her coach. Handsome bloke. Flung the discus, threw the hammer. Thinks there's nothing puzzling about a discus thrower coaching a gymnast.

Spotted her in a schoolyard in Gheorghi Gheorghin-Dej, her hometown, which looks like the Romanian equivalent of Walla Walla. He was out recruiting gymnasts.

Saw these two kids prolonging recess, pretending to be gymnasts.

Then they vanished inside the school and he prowled the classrooms looking for them.

Finally, he asked each class, who wants to be a gymnast? All the kids raised their hands. But these two kids raised their hands and yelled at the same time so he knew he had found them.

The other one is a ballet dancer. Nadia Comaneci is Queen of the Olympics. Well, not overnight. There were some tumbles, some bruises along the way. Not many. But Karolyi remembers one.

"She entered her first meet at age seven," he recalled the other day. "The World Juniors. She finished thirteenth. I gave her a Canadian doll, an Eskimo, made of sealskin. She still carries it around.

"I didn't want her to be aware of superstition, but I told her, 'You must never finish thirteenth again.' "

She never has. Proably never will. She is 5-feet tall, weighs 83 pounds, has muscles like a hard rubber hose, supple yet strong.

Karolyi didn't look at that schoolyard gamin and see Olympic greatness. He's good, but he's not that good. "You don't look for a physique," he explained. "You look for enthusiasm, energy, style. It's natural with her. She could always do things other people couldn't do."

She does things other girls wouldn't dare. Does them without a flicker of fear. Yet she seemed squeakily ill-at-ease at the mass press conference yesterday. Was she more nervous in back of the microphone than doing a backward flip on the beam?

"I'm not nervous now," she squeaked.

Has she never been, in her whole sweet life, nervous?

"Yes," she piped, "when I was fighting with my brother." It was the sweetest, warmest peek inside that cool facade she has managed to build.

People kept hammering at her about worlds to conquer because she has five 10s in competition so far and there is no such thing as 10.5 in the rules.

"I will keep trying to get better," she promised. "I will add new elements, work on different things. I will try to perfect myself."

That part of the world still competing in the XXI Olympiad knows about her now. It is not a concept she can grasp. Or, grasping it, she is content to let it slither through her long, lean fingers like soapsuds.

"I feel just the same as I did before," she said, and the questioning turned to other things. Perhaps she feels differently, but will not yield to it because she's had a week-long look at Olga Korbut, who was Queen of the last Olympics.

Olga is twenty-one now and looks forty-one, gray half-circles under her eyes, lips lemon-sucking tight. She toppled during a simple floor exercise early in the week, she bobbled a couple of vaults.

Yesterday, the Forum crowd rallied in her corner, hooting at some harsh scores for the old Queen. At the end, Nadia won easily, with youthful Nellie Kim of Russia second, and the lovely Ludmilla Turescheva third.

Nadia keeps telling people she was not inspired by Olga to become a gymnast. Says she was splashing in the Black Sea surf in October 1972 when Olga was getting her Olympic crown. Wasn't even watching on television. She was 10 and maybe she had to go to bed early?

And maybe there's a ten-year-old in Paris, France, or Paris, Kentucky, who's been watching Nadia Comaneci do those incredible twists and leaps and cartwheels and might come gunning for her in 1980. Will she have gray half-circles under her eyes or will she still be glinting like those 1,000-mirror globes?

Karolyi snatched the microphone to answer. "Nadia is very young still," the interpreter said. "She has fourteen years. At the next Olympics she will have eighteen years. And I consider that the perfect age.

"She will give the most she can give at eighteen."

Karolyi waited for the interpreter to finish, then he glanced over at Nadia lovingly, like a father. Yes, sir, that's some baby. No, sir, he don't mean maybe.

OLYMPIC GAMES

KING OF THE DECATHLON

By Dave Kindred

From The Louisville Courier-Journal

By his wife's testimony Bruce Jenner has been charged with eccentricity. "At the grocery store or the bank, he's always going through the motions of throwing the discus," she said. Jenner confesses. "I set up a hurdle in our living room and go over it 20, 30 times a day," he said. At last the cabbage and cashiers are safe, to say nothing of Mrs. Jenner's vases, for the dear boy has done it.

Six years in the doing, first a thought so bold as to be dismissed for fear it would never be realized, later a dream so real it consumed him, the Olympic championship in the decathlon today belongs to Bruce Jenner, twenty-six years old, 6-feet-2, 195 pounds, a classic athlete who set a world record in the Games' most demanding event.

The Olympic motto is "Swifter, Higher, Stronger." Of all the Olympic sports, none is the match of track and field when it comes to demanding all of that. And only the very best men dare try the decathlon. It is 10 events in two days, asking of a pretender proof that he can run very fast, jump very high, and throw heavy objects a long way.

By a fellow's contours you likely can name his event. Hammer throwers come with bartenders' bellies. Sprinters are stick men. You couldn't knock over a shot putter with a wrecking ball. The decathlon men, they are the stuff of statues, perfectly done by The Great Track Coach in the Sky.

When Mark Spitz fell in the water a lot at Munich and came out with seven gold medals, Madison Avenue was right there with greenbacks, fanning him dry. America, for the next year, was tortured by the omnipresence of the finned one. If not selling watches, he sold milk. To get even, some people bought sundials and goats. Somebody said Spitz made $5 million on the deals.

Then Bruce Jenner's next move should be the rental of a Brinks truck. Prince Valiant with muscles, he's also smart enough to know that a gold medal in the decathlon, while worth some money, isn't worth making a fool of himself.

"I really don't know what I'll do next," he said after telling reporters the Olympics was his last track meet. "People have told me I should go into television. But I don't know if I could do it. Whatever I do, I want to be comfortable in it and do a good job. I've built some credibility as an athlete and I don't want to do anything to tarnish it."

Long before the Olympics, Bruce Jenner thought of money. "When I first started, I wasn't in it for the money," he said a year ago. "But now . . . I can see the financial rewards if I win the gold. If I do, I'd be set for the rest of my life. It's on my mind more than ever before. When they hand you the gold medal, it doesn't give you a blasted thing, but it makes you a marketable item. You take the medal and see what you can do."

Whatever Jenner makes with the gold, whether he hurdles refrigerators in his living room or throws a discus into the grocery's breakfast of champions, it won't be too much. In another Olympiad marked by the United States' diminishing dominance in track and field—from 12 golds in Mexico City to six in Munich and four here so far—Jenner's performance lifted hearts.

Imagine. A movie. Our hero is handsome beyond right. His wife is a beautiful blonde who wears a yellow T-shirt with the words "Go Jenner Go" on the back. The front needs no help. Our hero is winning the decathlon, the event that from Jim Thorpe's day has been the measure of the world's greatest athlete.

If our hero runs well in the last event, the 1,500 meters, he wins the gold medal with a world-record point total. And while he's running, his wife is in the stands, surrounded by photographers and reporters, and—yes! yes!—she is waving an American flag. Boffo stuff.

And when our hero wins, a scuffy kid leaps out of the bleachers, one of 70,000 people who have been cheering for him for 10 hours that day, and—yes! he hands our hero an American flag that he holds aloft to thunderous recognition.

Around the track he goes. And near the end of his victory lap, our hero trots off the track and lifts his wife out of the stands, and right there in front of the world they kiss and share whispered words.

That's exactly what happened yesteday. "I've felt in my whole career—well, I don't know what is guiding me—but today I felt like my whole life pointed to winning this track meet," Jenner said. "I felt it was fine."

Preordained victory. "I told Chrystie," he said, revealing his side of the whispered conversation, "that at last it was all over, I've done all the running, she's been working to support us. She has as much invested in this as I do."

Love. "I'm pleased I won," he said. "I have to say our system wins. [Of 14 decathlons, the U.S. has had 10 winners]. I did all the work, sure. But I grew up in a country that allows you to do what you want to do."

Patriotism. "Am I the world's greatest athlete?" he said, repeating a question. "Well, when I stand over that little white ball and make contact it always seems to go to the right."

Modesty. Whatever Bruce Jenner is selling this year, buy.

OLYMPIC GAMES

"THIS WAS A NIGHT FOR PERFECTION"

By Monty Montgomery

The night ended as it should, the pretty American girl in tears on the victory stand, a half-empty hall of well-wishers and event-watchers applauding. And yet it was a night without drama.

Because after 10 years of skating lessons, a seventh of the allotted span, after placing second twice in the world championships, the outcome was known days before the crowd assembled to watch Dorothy Hamill don the Olympic gold medal. As a celebration, it more resembled a coronation than the birth of a new princess in the royal family of skaters. All the work had been done, the hypnotic Carlo Fassi had produced his second gold medalist, and John Curry, the first one, sat in the stands and never took his eyes off Hamill from the moment she came on the ice to warm up. The cycle was complete.

Miss Hamill had only to skate well, which she did, and the crowd would see what it came to see, a nearly inevitable victory.

For this spectator, waiting two hours for Dorothy, watching 19 other skaters, only one other four-minute span came alive with the magic of youth this sport is intended to convey. I had heard there was a twelve-year-old in the competition, a Russian girl, but Elena Vodorezova was, from the moment she stepped on the ice, a wonderment.

It is one thing to be in the Olympics, it is another thing entirely to be twelve years old and in the Olympics, but that is what happened in this city last night, and it brought tears to more eyes than mine. There was a curious movement to Elena's body when she executed her flying double and triple spins. I think it is a reasonable explanation to say that her skates are just too heavy for her.

I spoke with a Canadian television commentator just before the night began, and she said there "are too many girls in this competition. Their bodies are so undeveloped, they are so ungraceful, just like ponies."

Elena Vodorezova, you finished fifth in this competition. But that is not the important thing. Some of us, not the judges who gave you such low marks, but some of us, well, there is nothing we would rather see than ponies running, leaping, the way they do when they are young—lively and learning how to do things.

But this was a night for perfection. After Dorothy Hamill's performance, I asked John Curry to write down the words he thought appropriate. The note he handed back said all you could say about Dorothy Hamill's ascension. It was "flawless," she was under "perfect control." She was "smashing." Most of all it was "clean." And she is "THE BEST."

So, Dorothy Hamill had done what she was expected to do, Carlo Fassi had done what no coach in the history of figure skating had ever done in a lifetime, created both Olympic gold medalists in individual figure skating.

Fassi took Dorothy and John to Garmisch, West Germany, for two weeks of practice before checking them into Olympic Village February 1. At Garmisch, they practiced seven or eight hours a day, beginning at 7 in the morning.

It was lovely for the skaters except for their tiny rooms in the Zugspitz Hotel. Dorothy, with four pairs of skates, a dozen skating outfits, and her everyday clothes, began to worry about her housekeeping ability. "It was such a dump, my room. I tried, but with all my stuff, I couldn't keep it clean." Still, last Thursday, when the pressure in Innsbruck and fear of the flu began to haunt her, Dorothy went back to Garmisch to practice and relax.

Curry did not go with her. They had been almost inseparable, the beautiful American girl who says she has no boyfriend now, and the transplanted Britisher who lives in Colorado Springs. Curry went to see Dorothy that night and they talked about her skating. He would tell her what he told anyone who asked him: "Dorothy is ready to win."

In the athletes' discotheque at Olympic Village, a soft drink and slow music scene out of the late fifties, the mood changed when Dorothy and John arrived to dance. On the night before the opening ceremonies she went to the disc jockey and asked for fast music and then she and John went on the floor and in minutes the dawdling couples left their Cokes and apple cider and the whole atmosphere moved from sobriety to gaiety. The way they moved together was an unrefusable invitation to dance.

All last week Dorothy had been almost totally isolated from reporters. The explanation given by Fassi was mixed, one part her fear of crowds and the flu, one part Fassi's fear of making her even more nervous. While most athletes were hounded whenever they appeared, the warning from Fassi worked miracles. Hamill was seen most days wandering by herself through the sports shop at Olympic Village. No one approached her.

Off the ice, she moves with a certain helplessness, like the Dorothy in *The Wizard of Oz*. It is partly her size, 5-feet-3, but mostly her eyes. Not even the contacts she wears keep her from wandering, bumping into things, and squinting. Two nights before the final program, she came into the Golden Adler restaurant looking for a table. She stared a bit, eyes glistening in the light from the chandelier, and realizing the restaurant was full, stepped back into the night. The few reporters who recognized her sat and watched without reaching for their notebooks and pens.

In the competitiveness here, she became the center of a circle of decency.

Her position in the field after the compulsory figures, those excruciatingly perfect little carvings on the ice, was the best of her career. Then her short performance Wednesday meant that nothing but an act of God could keep her from winning the gold last night.

The short program began with one of those classic Hamill brushes with disaster—or so the audience would believe. A full crowd had gathered in the ice stadium before the performance to watch the girls warm up. The stadium had that healthy buzz you hear in Boston during Stanley Cup games. The house is full, but the tension has just begun to build.

The public address announcer asked the twirling girls to leave the ice. Dorothy skated a bit more, making little jumps and turns, moving obliquely toward the exit. As she approached the open door, skating more and more swiftly, she suddenly launched herself into the air and attempted a flying sitspin. All she got of it was the sitz, sliding across the ice on her sitzer. No one laughed. Between the fall and her performance, the audience watched 19 other skaters and waited to see if Hamill's legendary lack of composure would destroy her chances.

Of the 20 girls on the ice that night, only Dorothy would go out and skate the mandatory figures of the short performance as though it should be a beautiful moment, the piece of art that John Curry had talked about.

So what will come of this moment of art, this four minutes of gaiety, charisma, and the perfection seen by hundreds of millions on television? Is Dorothy Hamill the same girl today as the one a few days ago who was talking about going to a trade school and becoming an interior decorator?

Last night's gold medal is worth, when the banks open Tuesday, something like $2 million for a three-year contract with the Ice Capades or Follies.

OLYMPIC GAMES

THE BARBIE DOLL SOAP OPERA

By Dick Young

From the New York Daily News
Courtesy of the New York News

I have it on the strongest authority that Princess Anne did not have to submit to a sex test to compete in the Olympic Equestrian events. There are three sports for which the sex test is not required, there being no distinction between men and women in the competition. These are the equestrians, the gun-shooters, and the yachtspersons. It matters not whether you are male or female, but how you play the game.

This must be a warming thought to Bella and the rest of the egalitarians who might also be wondering about woman's menial role in these Olympics. Have you noticed who serves up the medals—gold, silver, and bronze—to the victors? Girls do. Like waitresses, they carry trays to the victory platform and stand there, rigid, with a medal on each tray. They are not required to remove the dirty dishes.

I am not as exercised about Olympic sex as I am about age. Of recent Games, the whole schmeer has been made into a Children's Crusade. This is the work of the TV people, who care little or nothing about sport, only sport for ratings. Thus, if it serves their purpose to turn a major sports event into the Bolshoi Ballet, they will do so.

TV producers are, in this way, following closely the historic trail of Hollywood producers. Many years ago, in the days of the early talkies, it was learned that the American public would eat up the child star. Thus was born the Shirley Temple syndrome, with six-year-old girls singing (singing?), tap-dancing, and dimpling their way into the hearts of millions. Audiences laughed and cried with Jackie Cooper and Judy Garland, with Margaret O'Brien, with Mickey Rooney. The audiences also spent a fortune on movie tickets.

Suddenly, there was a small problem. Mickey Rooney began to shave and Margaret O'Brien began to give visual evidence of not being nine years old. No matter. Just tie her hair in pigtails, dress her in fluffy pinafore, and she will look eight when she's fifteen. (Mickey Rooney, a blessed runt, played kids parts while he was playing with Ava Gardner.)

Enter now, Roone Arledge, the Sam Goldwyn of TV sports. TV, being in its early-talkie stage is ready for the child star, he decided in Munich. Olga Korbut was born—seventeen years old, going on twelve. Focus in on her pigtails, her girlish grin, her public dynamism. Gimme that close-up. Zoom in on her. That's it. Follow her. Cutesy-cutesy.

Back in America, the people gulped it down. How sweet. How lovable. Just like a Barbie Doll.

Do you know who won the gold medal for women's gymnastics in Munich?

Ludmilla Turescheva. The other day, Sally Quinn wrote Olga Korbut won it. Who could blame her? On TV, Olga Korbut did win it. Everybody thought she was champ. Nobody paid attention to Ludmilla Turescheva, the brooding, grown woman of twenty. Too old, too tall. Not cutesy-cutesy enough.

TV made Olga Korbut the way it made Richard Nixon, and the American public went for both. It's the great TV brainwash job.

Four years later, TV decided Olga was a has-been. She was twenty, and there is a new cutesy-cutesy. Zoom in on her. Close-up. Follow her. Get that smile. Catch those pigtails flapping. Nadia. Nadia Comaneci. Cohmah-neech! The Romanian Barbie Doll with the melodious, Italian-sounding name. Fourteen years old. Eighty-eight pounds. Five-feet-nothing. Cutesy-cutesy, plus a ton of talent.

The judges are swept up in the hysteria. They adopt Nadia Comaneci. Never before, in the history of Olympics, had they awarded perfect 10-point judgments. Now, they were handing them out like massage-parlor leaflets on Eighth Avenue. Five 10s for Koh-mah-neech. TV has done it again.

Olga? When the TV camera closed in on her, it tore your heart out. There she is, yesterday's Barbie Doll, black circles of pressure under both eyes. A worn-out, broken doll. Twenty-one years old, looking like forty. Even the judges have abandoned her, charging her with phantom mistakes, subtracting points from her efforts.

"I feel so bad for her," said Ronnie Young over the phone today, "I never liked her because of hamming it up, but I really feel sorry. Olga deserved a 10 on her compulsory. She had an even layout mount and added extra to it. She stayed in her handstand longer than required, and did a beautiful job of it, but they gave her a 9.9. The 9.5 they gave her in the beam was just awful."

Veronica Young, sixteen, is a gymnast, the resident expert in my home. The trouble is, she is much heavier than 88 pounds, and in gymnastics, the smaller you are the better. It is much easier to control a tiny body. The minnow swims with more grace than the whale.

I have a grave suspicion that somewhere near Pinsk, the Communist bloc have built a laboratory that specializes in turning out 7-foot basketball players and 4-foot gymnasts. One day, they will develop a cutsey-cutesy that is all pigtails, dimples, and arms raised overhead, nothing more, weighing 8½ pounds, and the Olympic judges will award her straight 11s.

OLYMPIC GAMES

GOOD AS GOLD AGAIN

By Cooper Rollow

From the Chicago Tribune
Courtesy of the Chicago Tribune

Lo, ye of so little faith!

The United States basketball team, scorned and ridiculed from its inception, burned Yugoslavia with speed and buried the Slavs with youth Tuesday night to win the Olympic Gold medal and atone for the mockery of Munich.

The final score was 95–74, and it was hardly a struggle at all. Before a capacity flag-waving throng in the Forum and a huge television audience, the boys in red, white, and blue showed the world how our native game is played.

It is played with players like Adrian Dantley, who scored 30 points and was an offensive dynamo. It is played with men like Quinn Buckner and Phil Ford, the slickest pair of thieves since the great Brinks robbery. And it is played by people like Phil Hubbard and Scott May, who totaled 12 rebounds.

The United States came out running, and it was no contest from the start, as the blistering Yankee pace bewildered the slower, aging Slavs, two of whom were competing in their third Olympics. Coach Dean Smith threw everything in the basketball book into this championship game, including a full-court press and a devastating fast break.

The only ingredient missing in the climactic seventh United States victory was head-to-head revenge over the Soviet Union, which inflicted America's only Olympic basketball defeat in history when Uncle Sam's team was jobbed by officials in the final seconds four years ago in Munich.

An American-USSR final became impossible when the Soviets were beaten Monday by this same Yugoslavian team, which last week had lost to the U.S. 112–93 en route to the finals.

For Smith, the victory was sweet vindication for charges that he loaded the 1976 American squad with players from his own North Carolina team and the Atlantic Coast Conference.

Load it up he may have, but it would be impossible to measure the contributions of two of Smith's good ol' North Carolina boys to the undefeated Yankee team which took the victory stand Tuesday night.

Mitch Kupchak scored 14 points and played a smart game at center, even though he required occasional help on defense against the muscular Slavs. Ford was a ball hawk extraordinaire. His frequent steals in tandem with Buckner in the early going showed the world what a fast break, American-style, looks like.

The United States built an 8–0 lead before Yugoslavia got on the scoreboard and took a 50–38 edge into the half time. Smith made certain all 12 of his players got into the game, enabling the Slavs to close the gap to 13 points at 77–64 with nine minutes remaining.

But Ford stole the ball and dribbled the length of the court for a lay-up which sent the Yanks spurting. As the final second ticked off, Buckner, the pride of Thornridge High School, was standing at midcourt just past the 10-second line, the basketball cradled lovingly in his left hand, and his clenched right fist upraised in celebration of the return of the Gold standard to America.

When the final horn sounded, Buckner, joined by Ford, leaped into the air and immediately were surrounded by American teammates in a midcourt celebration which long will be remembered.

Ten minutes later, the hugely partisan American crowd throbbed with emotion as the U.S. squad which had been so often berated because of a lack of "super-stars," particularly at center, took the stand, front and center, for the medal ceremony and playing of the National Anthem.

About the only thing the Slavs won on this night of American triumph was the opening tip, and they didn't do anything with that. Kupchak chalked up the first United States points with a jumper from the side.

The U.S. immediately went into its full-court press, Ford committed his first of many larcenies to feed Dantley a lay-up, and Dantley had pumped in four straight shots before the Yugoslavians knew what hit them.

Dantley, the Notre Dame product, left the game after four minutes of the second half when he caught a fingernail above his right eye. He returned later with the wound taped.

May, who with Buckner represented the Indiana Hoosiers, wound up with 14 points in addition to his five rebounds. Buckner also contributed five rebounds to the United States team which demonstrated conclusively that there still is no basketball like American basketball.

OLYMPIC GAMES

PARADE OF THE ELEPHANTS

By Doug Clarke

From the Cleveland Press

Just as one goes to the zoo and is drawn—as if by a magnet—to the cages housing the boas, the pythons, and the gorillas, so too was I pulled in the direction of St. Michel Arena last night.

Young men in fancy T-shirts, their muscles flexed and poised for a quick comparison in macho, pretty girls with wonder in their eyes, and kids who have seen the Charles Atlas ads in the back of comic books are lined up outside the arena waiting to be both fascinated and repelled at the same time.

For on this night of the Olympics the *poids super lourds*—and the French name for them instills far more awe and distinction than does "super heavyweights"—would compete for medals in weightlifting.

That no one could compete with Russia's Vassili Alexeiev, a 344-pound behemoth who became the Eighth Wonder of the World by grunting 562 pounds of iron above his head to set a new world record—did not matter.

It was Alexeiev—and a show—they came to see. Both were grand and grotesque, titillating and traumatic, all at once.

They marched out on stage to music, the audience giving a staccato clap to the tune—and it strikes you that this can only be the parade of elephants.

Of the 10 strongmen, there is one who sticks out from the others—Alexeiev. He has a 58-inch chest and a 48-inch stomach, although the bulbous, quivering stomach protrudes far more than the chest. He is Jackie Gleason in bikini underwear and a 1900 bathing suit top.

Marching in line across the stage, he looks The Poor Soul. It isn't until later, when he is stalking and concentrating on the bar in front of him, that you realize this is really a Reginald Van Gleason—a showman and a ham who enjoys strutting his stuff.

It is both comic and tragic theater, the two masks constantly changing place with each competitor. Back stage, you can hear barbells dropping and feel the building shake as the men toss around their playthings to warm up.

The men walk through a door, sniff smelling salts and grimace, put chalk on their hands and then ascend the stairs. As they make their studied approach to the weight, the audience goes "ssshhh," and the house falls quiet waiting for these hippo-like Lorin Maazels to take up their batons.

Fernandez, the Cuban, looks aghast at what he is undertaking as his mouth falls open; Wilhelm, the Arizona school teacher, jerks more than he can handle and roars "aaa-r-g-hh;" Losch, the German, stalks the weight like he hates it and gives the bar a dirty look as he drops it; Pavlasek, the Czech, is The Great Actor, running to the bar, then stopping to lift his eyes and mumble.

When Gord Bonk, a German who recently broke the Russians' record by hoisting 555 pounds, cleans and jerks 517, Alexeiev immediately opts for 562 pounds and gets the house buzzing. He is not about to toy with dainty and lesser weights.

He struts around, hitches up his belt brace, eyes the bar, approaches . . . then backs off for dramatic effect. He gets it and starts his routine all over again. When he stoops over, his giant stomach is quivering beneath him.

As he jerks it above his head, he emits his first grunt of the night. He wobbles, arms trembling, then holds the bar aloft. When he throws the weight down, it bounces and he dribbles it once. The audience erupts.

"Bravo . . . bravo," they are yelling. Alexeiev waves to the crowd and bows. The crowd eats it up and he is gobbling back.

Later, he says, "A medal is a medal, but a world record is something else." A hostess sits down next to him and he hugs her. She giggles.

I ask him how and why he began weightlifting and if he was ever a 95-pound weakling. A frown passes over his forehead as the interpreter relays the question and he answers, "It is a long story. I would rather not say."

They ask him if he rehearsed that grunt and he says that he did not. A TV man asks him if his two sons will be weightlifters and he answers, "I will be training with the children of my children."

He says that he works as a "mine engineer" and that his heroes as a teen-ager were Russian legends. "And now I am eager to join my wife, my children. I also like music and literature," he adds.

Alexeiev then walks around the stage like a great overgrown boy, shaking hands with people who want to touch the strongest man in the world.

"I just like him because he is the strongest and so big. I think it's neat to be able to do that," says a girl from Toronto.

"I guess I came because you're curious about feats of strength. I don't know why, but I feel a little sorry for him. It must be a lonely life," adds a Montreal man.

"I sure would like to have my picture taken with him," another girl says.

Alexeiev would have been pleased.

TENNIS

THAT HATCHETWOMAN CALLED CHRISSIE

By Bud Collins

In swept the zephyr from the plains of New South Wales, charging to the net for one last volley. It was Evonne Goolagong's final shot at holding off a grim reaper in white dress, that hatchetwoman called Chrissie.

Goolagong plunked her volley to midcourt rather than sharply hitting it away, and all she could do was shrug at the concluding stroke: a two-fisted Evertian lob that sailed over the Aussie and landed in the dust just short of the baseline.

Not until then, the match point two hours distant from the beginning of this crackling battle for female supremacy in a game called tennis, could you be sure who would win. Christine Marie Evert, once and now again champion of Wimbledon (6–3, 4–6, 8–6), and the Aussie, Goolagong, both had innumerable moments of brilliance. But Evonne's athletic ability couldn't carry her to a second title, even though she was ahead, 2–0, in the third set, and had break points for 3–1.

Ultimately the Big W went to the woman with the iron innards, the young labor leader who was made for this kind of test. It was one of the ironies of the hot and gusty afternoon in Center Court that the twenty-one-year-old Evert who wanted this title above all, will lead her flock—the Women's Tennis Association, of which she is president—in a snub of Wimbledon in 1977, "unless we get equal parity with the men in prize money." Evert insisting the cash "means nothing," but that the women merit just as much of that nothing as the guys, earned $18,000.

When Ilie Nastase and Bjorn Borg collided for the men's championship first prize was $22,500.

Another irony was that despite Evert's incredible strokemaking, her clever forays to the net, and crunching volleys—frequently taking the attack away from the customary attacker, Goolagong—she couldn't win the full-house crowd of 14,000. London has adored Sunshine Supergirl Goolagong since 1971 when, as a nineteen-year-old, she danced and glided to the championship, dethroning Margaret Court.

"I got mad because they were so one-sided," Evert said, "and I think that helped me." The audience lamented each loss of a point by Goolagong and applauded madly when she scored, even for Evert's mistakes.

Evert, however, isn't looking for warmth when she goes to work. She supplies her own with barrages from the baseline, and is always a cool hand. "When Evonne won the second set, I really lost heart. I didn't feel like a winner," she said, although her appearance and performance belied the feeling.

She seems to need only herself. "Last year my dad [teaching pro Jimmy Evert of Fort Lauderdale] was here, and I think I tried too hard to win it for him. He stayed home this time, and I gave him a nice surprise. I think that down in his heart he believed I could never beat Evonne on grass—but he wouldn't let that on to me. He cried when I called him right after the match."

Nevertheless, there was support and help for Evert, who won her first Wimbledon two years ago over Olga Morozova. As Princess America became the queen, the old queen in abdication, Billie Jean King, cheered her successor on from the friends' box. "Billie Jean and Rosie Casals kept motioning me to get into the net and it made the difference at the end," said a smiling Evert, who has conquered her fear of frying at the net.

She raced forward on strong forehands, and finished the points with bludgeoning forehand volleys to rise from 15–40 at 1–2 in the last set, and canceled the third break point in that critical four deuce game with a ringing forehand winner.

"Chris put me off by volleying so well—she's never done that against me before," said Goolagong, who probably had sailed through to the final too easily, losing no sets. She wasn't aggressive enough, letting herself get caught up in too many backcourt rallies, during which both mastered the dry, crumbling court and the bad bounces better than any of the men.

"It came down to a battle of the minds—who would hang in there longer," said that death-grip hanger, Evert. "I was a little smarter, a little tighter on the big points. I played them better."

Goolagong agreed. "I didn't do my best volleying when I had to."

From 0–2, Evert streaked to 3–2. Thereafter it was all marvelously hectic, the most exciting and best played final since Court tipped King six years ago, 14–12, 11–9. Goolagong took Chris's serve and it was 3–3. She kept going to 4–3 on her own, riding out two break points.

Evert crashed her groundies to 4–4, and leaped for a serve-breaking volley. There she was at 5–4, and it was time for Goolagong's toughest stand.

"For some reason I didn't have the adrenaline flowing in that game. I wasn't excited," Evert said. "Evonne was." The Aussie banged out a break in four points, and stepped ahead again, 6–5.

The rest was Evert. Goolagong had 40–30 in the thirteenth game, but Evert bashed an overhead, and Goolagong played two loose points. "I knew I'd think about this for a year if I didn't beat her," said Chris, who served it out from 7–6. Evonne fought to 30—all, shocked her following by socking a simple forehand return over the baseline, and was interred by that closing lob.

"It wasn't the same Evonne who beat me in the Virginia Slims final," said Evert after snapping Goolagong's 26-match streak, including two involving herself.

"There wasn't quite the look I see in her eyes when she's super-tough."

Evert's eyes were blazing combatively, especially down the stretch, as she increased her own winning streak to 17, recapturing her No. 1 status and made Goolagong one of a handful to lose three Wimbledon finals.

It has been four years since these two launched The Rivalry of the Seventies as kids in the same playpen. Goolagong won then, also a gripping three-setter, establishing the tone for their planetary feud, and she won their three subsequent meetings on grass.

Evert, however, leads, 17–11, and says, "It's easier without Billie Jean here in the singles. Just her presence made us all tense."

The men's doubles went to the Mexican-American alliance of Raul Ramirez and Brian Gottfried, 3–6, 6–3, 8–6, 2–6, 7–5, over Aussies Geoff Masters and Snake Case, but that was anticlimactic to Evert.

The hatchetwoman is in charge, and—look out, ladies—her blade can only get sharper.

BASEBALL

WHERE HAVE YOU GONE, JOE DIMAGGIO?

By Will Grimsley

From The Associated Press

The tall, straight-backed man with silver hair had managed to penetrate only a small portion of the hotel lobby when he was besieged by a cluster of middle-aged women.

"Oh, Mr. DiMaggio, may I have your autograph?" a motherly type with thick-lensed spectacles gushed. "I drink your coffee all the time."

"Thank you, ma'am," Joe DiMaggio responded politely. "Where are you ladies from?"

"Vancouver."

"That's a very nice city," DiMaggio said in a low voice.

"Please put a name on the autograph," the woman said. "Make it to Andrew."

DiMaggio blanched a bit and obliged.

A moment later DiMaggio and a couple of friends were wending their way toward the coffee shop when they encountered another barrier: a cordon of conventioneers wearing name tags on their coat lapels.

"Hey, Joe," barked one of the men. "My brother and I followed your career all the way. We saw every game we could. Will you sign one for my brother? He'll go out of his mind."

DiMaggio smiled graciously. "What's his name?" he asked.

"Tommy."

With broad, bold strikes, Joe etched: "Best regards, Tommy, Joe DiMaggio," and returned the pad.

"You're the greatest, Clipper," the man said, giving DiMaggio a slap on the back. Then he reached up to squeeze Joe's left arm. "All muscle, you oughta still be hitting 'em, Clipper."

DiMaggio winced but said nothing.

"How do you stand this all the time, Joe?" a friend asked. "People stopping you, interrupting you at dinner, banging you on the back?"

"The airports are the worst, when you have a lot of things to attend to," DiMaggio replied. "It takes the kick out of traveling. But you can't slough anybody off. After all, you have to be glad they remember you."

They still remember Joe DiMaggio, a quarter of a century after he took his last classic swing of the bat for the New York Yankees. He is one of the last of America's classic sports folk heroes, an impeccable, dignified contrast to the antiheroes, with their agents, presidential salaries and controversies, now populating the world of sports.

Older generations recall the rhythm and effortless grace that made him perhaps the greatest baseball center fielder of all time and the booming bat that helped propel the Yankees to 10 American League titles and nine World Series championships between 1936 and 1951.

In living rooms around the country, housewives see him on their television screens as a pleasant and persuasive middle-aged man in a conservative business suit extolling the merits of an electric coffee maker called Mr. Coffee.

In the New York area families also catch him on the tube, either surrounded by a flock of kids at Yankee Stadium or sitting down with an Italian family in the Bronx, talking about how nice it is to save at the Bowery—the Bowery being the Bowery Savings Bank.

"See that guy?" the man of the house is almost sure to say when a DiMaggio commercial comes on, "That's the Yankee Clipper. Never been another like him. I remember one day at the Stadium, with Bobby Feller pitching for the Indiana . . . ."

"He seems like such a nice fellow," the wife remarks.

That's how it goes; at least, so say the advertising agencies.

If DiMaggio was impressive in Yankee pinstripes—6-feet-1½, a lean 190 pounds who moved like flowing water—he is much more handsome and striking as a man approaching his sixty-second birthday.

He has retained his athletic figure, paying close attention to diet and exercise. He is flat-bellied, straight as a poker, less than 10 pounds over his playing weight.

Silver-gray hair, which he is too proud to dye, has softened his strong Italian features. Dark eyebrows frame dark-brown, expressive eyes. His face is deeply tanned, reflecting hours on the golf course, and is virtually unlined.

Off the screen as well as on it, he exudes a warmth and open friendliness that was foreign to him as a player. He has come to like people. He enjoys being around them.

His closest friends are not members of the jet set, the Hollywood community, or the smart sports whirl. Rather, they are people he met over the years—a businessman who flies him around in a private plane, a shirt-maker, a pub keeper, a publicist. He has fierce loyalties.

In his playing days, DiMaggio was timid and retiring. He was known as a loner even among his teammates. He was not a party guy. He avoided controversy and fanfare. He guarded his private life studiously.

Today he is an attractive bachelor, twice wed to movie actresses in marriages that didn't work out, a restless man apparently torn between conflicting desires.

On the one hand, as a heritage from his baseball days, he has an urge to travel, see new things, and meet new people. On the other, there is the temptation to pack it up and retire to a life of ease on San Francisco's Fisherman's Wharf, where he grew up as one of the nine offspring of an immigrant Italian fisherman.

"I find it always good to get home and rest," he said. "But after a while, I get edgy and am off again."

Within the past few weeks, DiMaggio's odyssey has taken him from San Francisco to New York, Boston, Los Angeles, Las Vegas, Toronto, and a trio of cities in Pennsylvania—Erie, Harrisburg, and Williamsport.

He attended the Little League baseball finals at Williamsport. He emceed a Scout-O-Rama as a favor to a banker friend. He attended a sports carnival in Toronto. He even served as celebrity host of a bocci tournament in Las Vegas and took down third prize. Most of his appearances are made in the interest of good will.

"I am cutting down on old-timers games," DiMaggio said. "This year, I went to the two in New York and also the Angels' game in Los Angeles. I went to Los Angeles as a favor to my old friend, Red Patterson (Angels' president), but there was another reason, too. I got a chance to take my granddaughters to Disneyland."

Joe's granddaughters—Kathy, fourteen, and Paula, twelve—have brought fresh enthusiasm to the ex-ball player's life. They are the daughters of his son, Joe Jr., by the Clipper's first wife, Dorothy Arnold. Joe Jr. is a successful trucking executive in Northern California.

"Kathy is going to be a fine athlete," Joe says proudly. "She is a big girl already active in swimming and track. Paula clings to her grandfather. Both like fishing. Every chance we get, we are out on our boat, *The Yankee Clipper.*"

Home for DiMaggio is a brownstone house in the Marina section of San Francisco which he purchased for his parents nearly 40 years ago and, after their death, shared for a brief time with his second wife, the late Marilyn Monroe.

Now the house is cared for by Joe's sister, Marie, who also handles a big part of Joe's correspondence and appointments. Joe's mail is voluminous, having mushroomed with his television commercials. He doesn't have an agent or a secretary.

"Sometimes I am pretty hard to catch up with," Joe said with an amused smile. "All my mail and telephone calls go to the restaurant. I pick it up when I return to the Coast."

The restaurant is DiMaggio's Restaurant, a familiar eaterie on Fisherman's Wharf, built in 1937, formerly jointly owned by Joe and brother Dom but now run by Joe's older brothers, Tom and Vincent.

It is a regular hangout for the former Yankee star when he is home. There he hobnobs with old cronies and fishermen, who refer to him as "The Clipper" and treat him as one of the home folks, not as a hero. DiMaggio likes that.

Joe's father, Giuseppe, called "Zio Pepe," immigrated from Isola delle Femmine, an island off Palermo, and first settled in the small fishing village of Martinez, a few miles to the north of the Golden Gate Bridge.

Joe was a year old when the family moved to San Francisco. Giuseppe wanted all his sons to follow in his footsteps but instead they became fascinated with the great American pastime. Joe, Vince, and Dom all had successful major-league careers. Another brother, Michael, fell from a boat and drowned in 1953. Tom, the oldest, remained a fisherman and became the family breadwinner.

"Tom would have been the best ball player of all," Joe says.

When DiMaggio attends old-timers games, he usually shows up not in his familiar Yankee uniform with big 5 on the back but in a dark suit, white shirt, and tie. An exception this year was the Yankee show at which Joe agreed to don the uniform but refused to play in the two-inning game.

He talked about this recently during a moment of relaxation in Las Vegas, where he was attending the celebrity bocci tournament.

"Let's go into the bar and have a drink," a friend said.

"You know I don't drink," DiMaggio said. "I am going to the coffee shop."

In the coffee shop, he ordered peaches and cottage cheese.

"Is that all?" the waitress asked.

"That's all," replied DiMaggio.

"It's my ulcers," he said. "They give me fits. I haven't smoked in 10 years—used to smoke three packs a day. I seldom drink—not that I am a prude or hypocritical, understand. I never particularly cared for it."

DiMaggio then said the reason he did not suit up and take swings at bat in the old-timers games was largely the same one that brought about his retirement in 1951.

"I don't want to get out there and embarrass myself," he said. "I had a lot of injuries when I played, aches and pains that are still around. My back kills me most of the time. I had operations on both my heels for bone spurs. I have arthritis and tendonitis.

"If I took a cut at a ball it would be a swing like an old woman. I don't want people to remember me that way. Right now, I couldn't throw a baseball from here to that table over there, unless I did it underhand."

The waitress served the peaches and cottage cheese and then asked DiMaggio: "Do you remember Lee Prewitt? He's our cook. He said he was inducted into the service with you."

"Monterrey, California, 1942," Joe recollected. "It's been a long time and there were a lot of guys. I don't remember, but tell him to come out and say hello, maybe I'll know him."

Later a lady brought one of the hotel's cloth napkins over to be signed.

"The hotel's not going to appreciate this," Joe said, putting a felt pen scrawl over the orange piece of cloth.

Turning back to the subject of old-timers games, DiMaggio said they can be dangerous even for healthy players.

"I remember Earl Coombs got badly hurt in one of them," he said. "Charlie Gehringer broke an Achilles heel and was laid up a long time. Home Run Baker skinned his nose in a slide, and Dizzy Dean hurt his nose trying to scoop up a ball. You take chances."

DiMaggio's venture into TV commercials has given his life a new dimension, although he sometimes appears to feel slighted by the sport on which he left such a powerful imprint.

He was one of the giants of the game, succeeding Babe Ruth as the great performer and gate attraction of the country's most successful ball club. He was the first $100,000-a-year player. He made the American League All-Star team in each of his 13 seasons and three times was voted the Most Valuable Player. His 56-game hitting streak in 1941 is a record that may never be broken.

After retiring, DiMaggio did a stint as Yankee broadcaster and batting coach, then spent two years as vice-president and batting coach with the Oakland A's. He has been out of baseball 10 years.

A few years ago, Commissioner Bowie Kuhn offered DiMaggio a role as a baseball ambassador-at-large. Then came the matter of salary. "Ten thousand dollars," the commissioner said. Insulted, Joe walked out.

Later, when George Steinbrenner became owner of the Yankees, friends suggested the Yanks could use Joe's public relations attributes. Steinbrenner discussed it with Joe. Joe asked for details. He never heard another word.

"A friend asked me about making a commercial for the Bowery Savings Bank about five years ago," Joe said. "I was hesitant at first. I was afraid I would freeze on camera. But it turned out well.

"Then the Mr. Coffee people approached me. The agency said it had screened 200 personalities and I had been picked. But my contract runs out this year."

Trade journals say that, largely from DiMaggio's exposure, the once small and struggling firm grew into a multimillion-dollar business with a major share of the electric coffee-maker market.

DiMaggio disdains all other types of TV appearances, particularly talk show. Talk hosts such as Mike Douglas, Merv Griffin, Johnny Carson, and Dinah Shore have tried in vain to get him before camera.

"They don't want me to talk baseball; they just want to pry into my private life," Joe said.

DiMaggio is still keenly sensitive about details of his marriage with Marilyn Monroe. They were married in January 1954 and the marriage dissolved in 1955, victim of a clash of temperaments. Joe was quiet and averse to publicity; Marilyn was ebullient and obsessed with a screen career.

After the divorce, DiMaggio grew cool toward one-time show business friends such as Frank Sinatra, Peter Lawford, and other members of the so-called Rat Pack. He never forgave the tinsel and fakery of Hollywood for "destroying a beautiful life." He once said he hadn't seen a movie in eight years.

"I was never a member of the [Sinatra] Rat Pack," Joe said vehemently. "I don't even like the name 'Rat Pack.' "

When Marilyn died in 1962 it was DiMaggio who made the funeral arrangements and dictated who could and could not attend the services.

A deep devotion for the actress lingers, friends say, and no one dares raise her name in Joe's presence.

The Yankee Clipper still has fresh flowers placed on her grave twice a week.

BASEBALL

BASEBALL'S MONEY MADNESS

By Pete Axthelm

Charles O. Finley, Oakland's connoisseur of the outrageous, outdid himself last week—and triggered the most convulsive big-money crisis in recent sports history. Just hours before a midseason deadline would have made trading impossible, Finley held an unprecedented $3.5 million clearance sale of three star players. Within 48 hours, the normally accommodating commissioner Bowie Kuhn provided an even bigger jolt: He slapped down Finley and vetoed the sales. Before the bizarre week ended, the shock waves touched every level of the game.

Outfielder Joe Rudi and relief pitcher Rollie Fingers reported to the Boston Red Sox, which had paid $1 million each for them, slipped into new uniforms—and then found that they couldn't play at any price. Southpaw Vida Blue, the New York Yankees' $1.5 million purchase from Finley, prudently stayed in California. But Yankee manager Billy Martin penciled Blue into the rotation and howled when Kuhn prevented Vida's arrival. "I'm pitching Bowie tomorrow," snapped Martin. "Is he right- or left-handed? Or does he know?" Everyone from Kuhn to the most casual fan knew one thing: Baseball had been thrust into a new era of wildly spiraling prices, unpredictable player movements—and angry recriminations and lawsuits.

"Kuhn sounds like the village idiot," blustered Finley. Players Association leader Marvin Miller accused the commissioner of "plunging baseball into the biggest mess it has ever seen." And Martin, with the wisdom of the dugout, added, "'I can believe Watergate. I can believe those guys fooling around in Washington. But I can't believe we in baseball could do something like this."

The Finley-Kuhn clash also raised some larger questions about the balance of power in modern baseball. With new court-ordered freedom to play out their contracts and offer themselves on the open market, players are wielding exhilarating new clout. Finley was only the boldest of owners who have beaten players to the punch by shipping them out before they can walk away. And now even the commissioner had taken a stand.

The Finley caper was the most dramatic sign yet of the money madness that has gripped sports. Even as Kuhn was deliberating, the near-bankrupt American Basketball Association coughed up $13 million to buy the admission of four teams into the National Basketball Association. Framed against a flurry of million-dollar deals that have recently enriched an attention-starved fullback, a weak-kneed hockey player, and assorted other jocks and their omnipresent agents, the week's "sports events" seemed a major step in the evolution of fun and games into an even more hardheaded money scramble. Certainly, the battle for the sports dollar has never been hotter. As Finley himself declared, "The day of reckoning is now."

For Finley, the reckoning began when almost all of his traditionally rebellious stars refused to sign contracts. Plagued by business setbacks and facing a pending divorce settlement that could be ruinous, Finley was unable or unwilling to increase his offers; sometimes he seemed demoralized enough to simply watch his players leave him.

But last week Charlie moved suddenly to bail himself out. Rudi, twenty-nine, the player without a weakness, was offered to Boston along with reliever Fingers, twenty-nine. Red Sox owner Tom Yawkey, with money to spare but the years running out at age seventy-three, jumped at the chance to buy a possible pennant for a mere $2 million.

Blue was a trickier matter. Gabe Paul, president of George Steinbrenner's Yankees, flew to Finley's Chicago headquarters to express the Yanks' interest—but Paul wanted Blue, twenty-six, already signed.

The Yankees didn't want to have to talk salary with a man they had just valued publicly at $1.5 million. So Finley telephoned Blue, dangled the prospect of playing for New York, and prevailed on him to sign a three-year, $600,000 contract. The Yankees purchased Vida, then negotiated a nine-player deal with Baltimore to get Ken Holtzman. With fast dealing and Steinbrenner's wallet, the Yankees had reassembled Blue, Holtzman, and last year's $3.8 million free agent Catfish Hunter in a premium-priced replica of a staff that once won three straight World Series for Finley.

Amid the local pennant speculation, Kuhn the next day summoned Finley and the other parties in the sales to his New York office—but no one expected the bombshell that was to follow: "The meeting was quiet," said one participant. "No violations were alleged and the commissioner didn't express any opinion." Finley, resplendent in bright green and gold, emerged from the session in a cocky mood. "I'm always glad to come here," he said, "and teach Mr. Kuhn the facts of life as regards baseball."

But this time Kuhn did the teaching. In ordering the players back to Oakland, Kuhn cited a 1921 rule giving the commissioner the power to "pursue appropriate legal remedies" to preserve "the honor of the game." Critics wondered if his move was either appropriate or legal. In effect: He seemed to be saying that while selling players is allowed, selling them in million-dollar lots is not. There was also speculation that Kuhn acted under the powerful influence of Walter O'Malley of Los Angeles and other old-guard owners whose affection for the cantankerous Finley is exceeded only slightly by their love for the arriviste Steinbrenner. In any case, after seven dormant years in office, Kuhn had risen up to claim an authority rarely invoked since Kenesaw Mountain Landis became baseball's first commissioner in the wake of the 1919 Black Sox scandal.

Back in Oakland, Blue, Rudi, and Fingers were as puzzled as anyone; the million-dollar players didn't even know who was going to sign their next paychecks. But wherever they wind up playing, they are the most publicized hostages of big-money sports.

The war is not one in which it is easy to take sides. In one camp—or tax shelter—are the team owners, crying poverty from the choice tables in the best restaurants, issuing commands like petty dictators, and bartering athletes for fabulous sums made almost meaningless by depreciation write-offs. On the other side are the players, many of them intoxicated with self-importance and seemingly determined to use their freedom from lifetime "servitude" to alienate those same customers who make their salaries possible. In the new major sports of arbitration, collective bargaining, and holding out for more money, both owners and players leave the fan wondering how he can possibly root.

Among baseball owners, for example, one can pick from characters with the public-be-damned attitude of Finley or the self-styled Yankee pride of Steinbrenner, who was convicted of making an illegal Nixon campaign contribution and now enjoys enforcing strict grooming rules on grown men. Basketball followers can point to the arrogance of the Buffalo Braves' Paul Snyder, who paid huge sums to mediocre players, and then promptly shifted the blame to his coach and even to the city of Buffalo itself—and next tried to bail out by peddling the plundered franchise to Florida. And no one in hockey can forget the crafty Toronto Maple Leaf entrepreneurs, who once skimmed so much so carelessly that they wound up in jail.

Then there are the players, who sometimes outdo the owners in driving away any possible public sympathy. When former Oakland slugger Reggie Jackson refused to report to Baltimore for several weeks after he was traded this spring, his demand to earn his $200,000 salary in the city of his choice gained little applause from most of his wage-earning fans. And when self-proclaimed intellectual pitcher Mike Marshall of the Los Angeles Dodgers isn't sneering at the people who buy the tickets, he finds time to ridicule his own team's infielders as "cigar-store Indians."

Modern athletes didn't invent disloyalty, any more than Charlie Finley originated the idea of breaking up a team in return for cash. Connie Mack, a grand old patriarch of the national pastime, disbanded his Philadelphia A's and sold immortals like Lefty Grove in two separate celebrations of greed. And no single star has ever pursued big-league bucks with less regard for local loyalty than Walter O'Malley's Dodgers, who abandoned Brooklyn back in 1957. But the modern stars get high marks for trying.

No sports heroes ever meant more to franchises than Kareem Abdul-Jabbar of the NBA's Milwaukee Bucks or Bobby Orr, the "messiah" of hockey's Boston Bruins. Both stars led their teams from the depths to the heights and became inextricably connected with the clubs in the minds of the fans. Last year, however, Abdul-Jabbar announced that the cultural facilities of Milwaukee no longer met his standards; he demanded and got a trade to Los Angeles. And this year Boston's beloved Orr became a free agent and sold his surgical knees to Chicago for $3 million. Both players had legitimate grievances and sound business reasons for their defections, but their decisions still had an unavoidable impact on fans.

Finley's present A's are the most obvious casualties of the money war. But last week's explosion was only a climax to a test of nerves that began six months ago when arbitrator Peter Seitz rocked baseball by declaring former Dodger pitcher Andy Messersmith a free agent.

Unlike Catfish Hunter, who became a free agent and then a Yankee millionaire a year earlier because Finley had reneged on a contract provision, Messersmith was freed because of a principle. The issue was the reserve clause. Standard contracts in most sports include such an item: When a player doesn't want to continue with his club, he may play out one season at a stipulated pay cut and then free of his obligation. In football, this provision was modified with the Rozelle rule, which allowed commissioner Pete Rozelle to dictate that a team signing a free agent had to give compensation to the player's former team. Baseball, on the other hand, employed a simpler method and insisted that the reserve clause was perpetually self-renewing.

In other words, under a unique legal interpretation that might have been passed down from Caligula, the owners claimed that no matter how often he tried to play out his contract, an athlete was a lifetime possession. Players like Messersmith argued that after playing one year unsigned, an athlete could seek employment on other clubs. And Messersmith won.

So did athletes in other sports. Through various judicial rulings, out-of-court settlements, and arbitrations, all pro team members now have varying degrees of freedom to play out options. Details are still being worked out, and negotiators on both sides are aware of the need for a system that maintains order and competitive balance. But the players won a huge victory when Messersmith asserted the principle of freedom—and Seitz agreed.

The owners' first response was characteristic. They fired Seitz. Then the wealthier members of the owners' club got in line to offer money to Messersmith. When Ted Turner, the aggressive new owner of the Atlanta Braves, won the bidding war, it only added to the owners' discomfort. "We had tried to be open-minded about the payroll problems of franchises that were in trouble," says Jerry Kapstein, thirty-two, the low-keyed agent. "Then we saw a team that didn't draw one million fans last year come up with $2 million for Andy. Obviously, some clubs weren't in as much trouble as they had pretended. It was time to take another look."

"There's no way we can operate with astronomical, unjustified salaries," retorts Finley. Kapstein also claims that Finley, who made his fortune in the insurance business, snorted at one point, "All you players want is security. That what's wrong with America today."

No one understands the money revolution in sports better than George Allen, who may be the fastest man in football with somebody else's checkbook. As coach and general manager of the Washington Redskins, Allen recently increased the biggest payroll in pro football by signing free agent John Riggins, formerly the only quality offensive player on the New York Jets. Tired of carrying the Jet burden almost unnoticed while faded quarterback Joe Namath earned about seven times as much money, Riggins offered to stay with New York only if the Jets matched the $450,000 they pay Namath annually. "It was my way of saying, 'It's been nice,' " Riggins said of the impossible demand. Then Allen called him—with a contract giving Riggins $100,000 a year for the next 15 years, in return for five years of playing. "Now we've more or less sold our bin for the year," said Redskins president Edward Bennett Williams. "But we can still do okay financially—if we go to the Super Bowl."

Out of a total of 1,000 players in pro football, only 41 have played out their options. Because the courts have overturned the Rozelle rule, more players may seize the opportunity to switch teams. But except for a handful of genuine gate attractions like Buffalo's O. J. Simpson—who may soon be traded to a West Coast team at his request—football players may find the promise of wealth somewhat illusory. To hear owners tell it, pro football may be the sport with the least room for economic growth. Stadiums are nearly full, ticket prices about as high as the market will bear and, as Williams says, "In terms of television revenue, our head is on the ceiling."

"Because football grew so much during the 1960s, there's not much more room," agrees CBS network president Robert Wussler. "Inflation may increase their numbers slightly but that's about it. Baseball may be in a better television position because of very strong local ratings. But basketball has the biggest room for growth, especially now with the merger bringing Julius Erving into the NBA—and bringing who knows what to strengthen the Knicks in our most important market. That kind of surge is already behind football. But don't forget, these owners cry a lot of crocodile tears. One man's loss of $1 million may be another accountant's profit. When some owners moan about their overhead their, vanishing profit margins, I always think of the old advice—'If you have to ask how much it costs, you can't afford to own it.' "

The American Basketball Association couldn't afford it. But the fiscal and egotistical spoils of pro sports were so tempting that most ABA teams endured disastrous losses this year in the mere hope of surviving long enough to be invited into the NBA. Last week, the NBA opened the way for the four strongest ABA franchises, in return for $3.2 million per team—in cash up front. For the fans, the best thing about the merger is the exposure of Erving, the incomparable Doctor J, to greater competition and TV audiences. For owners, the new arrangement means the end of a near-suicidal bidding war for talent. "But the merger will be good for players too," says agent Irwin Weiner. "With teams being more stable, good players stand a chance of getting even more money. A price has been set, and you can't expect a superstar to come down from his level."

Weiner and his fellow agents have themselves reached a kind of superstar level—or depth, depending upon one's point of view. In style, the men who represent the athletes range from the likes of respected Boston attorney Bob Woolf and brilliant media manipulator Mark McCormack of Cleveland, down to the mere fly-by-night backroom hustlers. But the top agents are indisputably among the most powerful figures in sports.

Kapstein, for example, represents dozens of baseball players, many presently unsigned; his decision conceivably could affect the very survival of franchises in trouble spots like Baltimore and Minnesota. Agent Ed Keating certainly altered both the economics and standings of pro football as he guided former Miami stars Larry Csonka and Paul Warfield into the now defunct World Football League and then back into the NFL with new teams.

In basketball, Weiner and Players Association lawyer Larry Fleisher wield similar potential power. Under the umbrella of his Walt Frazier Enterprises, Weiner represents not only Frazier of the Knicks but many of Walt's top rivals, including Doctor J and George McGinnis of Philadelphia. "Powerful? I don't know what that means," says Weiner. "In any business, when you go into a man's pocket, he won't like you. So some owners make us sound like greedy guys. But we didn't create the market. We've just pushed the market to capacity."

Shrewd hockey lawyer Alan Eagleson of Toronto has probably pushed farther than anyone. His critics even claim that he has helped ruin the sport by creating an entire generation of overpaid, modestly talented skaters who extend themselves only when it doesn't interfere with their countless outside enterprises. By playing off the upstart World Hockey Association against the established National Hockey League, Eagleson has shifted that sport's balance of power drastically in favor of the athletes. And despite charges of conflict of interest, he'll continue to rule as head of the Players Association combined with his position as representative of hundreds of individual players—including millionaire Orr.

In the aftermath of last week's upheavals, confused fans and irate traditionalists are entertaining some apocalyptic visions. With judges drawing up the ground rules and agents directing players more effectively than many coaches, pro sports may never inspire the innocent fantasies they once did. But while the sports business will never be quite the same, it is not necessarily plunging into a dark age.

"In the long run," predicts the levelheaded economist Roger Noll, who has edited a long Brookings Institution study of sports, "pro games will appear much as they always have, except that players will be making much of the money that once went to owners."

For all their problems, the owners can probably afford the change. A businessman in search of maximum profits would never choose the sports field. Even in the boom years of sports, most owners have accepted relatively low-percentage returns on their investments in exchange for fringe benefits in their tax returns and ego-building social situations. Because of generous depreciation allowances, an owner can often write off several million dollars a year as paper losses, cutting taxable profits or even producing net losses that can be written off against the income from his other businesses. If the Yankees eventually do get Vida Blue for $1.5 million, for instance, owner Steinbrenner will be able to depreciate the entire purchase price in five years. Owners of strong franchises seem to have considerable margins for adjustment. Weaker owners are already moving toward common-sense safeguards such as last week's basketball merger.

Noll also envisions a series of less-than-traumatic changes that will avoid the specter raised by the Yankees and Red Sox in their abortive purchases from Finley. Most important, he calls for sharing of all broadcast and gate revenues throughout a league; if income were evenly divided, it would be unlikely that a few big-city teams could earn enough to buy up all the free agents and ruin competition. As an additional safeguard, Noll might impose a ceiling on total salaries—but he doesn't believe that would be necessary in the long run.

Smart players seem to have a stake in fair competition, and Miller, of baseball's Players Association, says that they are negotiating for a system that would keep a check on frantic migrations by free agents. At present, players are willing to play perhaps six years of their careers before exercising their rights to become free agents. The owners are holding out for an eight-year limit, but the difference hardly seems to be a major stumbling block.

In addition, owners and players are reportedly moving toward agreement on a quota system that would prevent stockpiling by certain teams. Under one proposed plan, if there are fewer than 12 free agents at the end of a season, no single club will be allowed to sign more than one. If the total is between 13 and 36, each club will be limited to two. The progression beyond that figure has not been settled upon, but Miller insists that there will seldom be more than 30 free agents in a given year.

Shifts in attitudes and economic structures will not proceed smoothly, of course. A few weak franchises in big-league sports may not survive the new era, and some diehard executives may simply give up. The owners may also have to face the fact that instead of paying each other huge sums in order to possess new players, they will have to allocate more money directly to those players. In light of these prospects, Noll is probably correct when he foresees a few years of relative flux before any real stability is achieved. But every-man-for-himself chaos has become the American way of sport, and last week's events only fortified the rich sporting tradition as expressed by Billy Martin. "It's our money," Billy growled at one point, "and we'll spend it any way we want."

TENNIS

CONNORS PUTS IT RIGHT ON THE LINE

By Ted Green

From the Los Angeles Times

Years from now, when Jimmy Connors owns most of Las Vegas and Bjorn Borg is back in Sweden teaching his 10 blonde children how to hit one tennis ball after another and never, ever lose their cool, they may still talk about the 1976 U.S. Open men's final.

They'll remember how Connors and Borg slugged it out for more than three hours like a couple of street fighters. How both played sensational tennis early—and got better as the match wore on. How Connors won a dramatic tie breaker in the third set—the crucial third set—by hitting shots in do-or-die situations that most players merely dream about.

And they'll ultimately recall how Connors, in a confrontation between the world's two best players which may or may not have decided who is *the* best, finally won.

The scores Sunday were 6–4, 3–6, 7–6, and 6–4. They go into a record book, soon to be forgotten. But the match itself probably won't be, not by the sellout crowd of about 15,000 at the West Side Tennis Club and the national television audience which saw it.

Great is an overused word in sports journalism. So call this one very, very good.

"I had to play my absolute best to beat him," Connors said afterward. "It's like this every time we play—we kill each other. He hits those big topspin shots that I have to whack away at up by my shoulders, and he has to return balls coming to him at a million miles an hour.

"He has a lot of guts and a lot of heart. I knew there was no way to take him out of the match until the last ball. That's why it took me about five seconds to realize I'd actually won. I gave the full amount of what I had to give. I'm just glad I don't have a match tomorrow."

This was high praise coming from Jimmy Connors, who usually doesn't have too much of it for anyone.

Borg reciprocated and then mostly went back to the positively scintillating finish of the third set, when Connors fought off four set points to win the tie breaker, 11–9, and the set, 7–6.

If Borg had won it instead, if Connors hadn't reached back for something extra and hit what Borg time and again called unbelievable shots, Borg, not Connors, might be U.S. Open champion this morning.

"On two of those four set points," Borg said, "he hit unbelievable approach shots. He hit the lines. You want to win that tie breaker so badly, and you have to be very, very lucky. Luck wasn't on my side but he also hit unbelievable shots."

And when Connors finally put away Borg, who never quit, he also finally ended talk that he'd gone two years without winning a major title—talk that, by this time, had clearly gotten under his skin.

The other day Connors lost his temper when a reporter reminded him of his 1975 losses in the finals of the Australian Open, Wimbledon, and Forest Hills. Sunday he was more composed but just as sarcastic.

"Most of all I wanted to win here so you people wouldn't keep bringing up '75," he said. "I'll be back here next year so you guys can say, 'He hasn't won anything since '76.' "

In fact, it was Connors' eleventh tournament victory of the year. But it was the one even he, in a quieter moment last week, admitted he needed most. Because it was the U.S. Open. And because, as it turned out, his last obstacle was Borg, who most people in tennis ranked No. 1 on the basis of his winning Wimbledon and the World Championship of Tennis.

Connors wouldn't say it was his biggest win ever—at twenty-four, he has already had plenty of those—but he did say it was "very satisfying," and for him that was saying a lot.

Connors, who didn't lose a set in seven matches here until Borg broke through in the second on Sunday, won $30,000 to add to the almost $500,000 he'd already made this year and the 500 zillion he's made since the advent of challenge matches . . . which, by the way, someone brought up as a possibility now that Connors-Borg seems to have emerged as the fiercest and most exciting rivalry in tennis.

"Challenge match," Borg said. "Yes, I would like that."

This year the question of who's No. 1 apparently is still open, especially because Sunday's final which wrapped up the 12-day, $416,000 tournament was so close and could have gone in Borg's favor with one swing of the racquet in that third-set tie breaker.

Connors himself said he didn't know if he was No. 1. He said whoever wins the Masters tournament in December can claim that distinction. But Borg, because he took seven weeks off after Wimbledon, may not qualify because he didn't play enough over the summer.

Connors has now beaten Borg three times this year and is 6 and 1 lifetime. Most of the matches weren't close.

But close only begins to describe what happened Sunday. Borg, for example, actually won more total points than Connors, 123–121.

The two went at it nonstop . . . Connors uninhibitedly flailing away and nailing the ball so hard he was grunting . . . Borg sending so many of those shots back with those funny but oh-so-effective topspin forehands and two-hand backhands—at all kinds of angles and speeds.

And, really, this Open turned on the outcome of the tie breaker.

On Borg's first set point (at 6–4), Connors crunched an approach shot and hit an easy putaway at the net. On the second (6–5) Connors, as he did so often, gambled by going for a big forehand down the line—and won. On the third (8–7), Borg hit a terrific topspin, cross-court forehand only to have Connors lunge and hit a backhand volley winner. And on the fourth (9–8), Connors hit still another approach within inches of the baseline and finished the point with a putaway.

Having tied the tie breaker at 9–9, Connors, gambling again, went cross-court with a two-handed backhand, then hit an overhead for the point. When it flew past Borg he clenched his fist and slapped his side, imploring himself to do it just one more time. He didn't have to, though, because Borg made an unforced error, hitting a backhand wide from the baseline.

Game to Connors. Set to Connors. Momentum to Connors.

"That gave me a big lift," he said.

Borg? "I was a little disappointed," he said.

"As we walked to the sideline," Connors said, "Bjorn did look a little disgusted. He kind of threw his racquet down."

That was about as much emotion as Borg showed in 12 days and seven matches, except for the small wave to the crowd which cheered him for more than a minute when he mounted a podium to accept the runner up check for $15,000 in postmatch ceremonies.

But as Borg likes to say, he let his magic wands do the talking. Connors, of course, had one of his own, and together, they may make their own kind of magic for quite some time.

BASEBALL

LITTLE LEAGUE UMPIRE

By Leonard Shapiro

From The Washington Post

He has been berated by belligerent parents, cursed by angry managers, and nearly killed by a heart attack brought on mostly by the pressures of scheduling his umpires for a season of games.

But most of what Tom Hunter remembers about his dozen years as a volunteer Little League umpire involves the good times, and especially all those screwball situations that only a bunch of twelve-year-olds could possibly create.

There was the time, for example, when a youngster found himself about to be tagged out in a rundown between third base and home plate. "The boy just stopped dead in his tracks and screamed 'TIME OUT' at the top of his lungs." Hunter said, "What could I do? I called him out."

Another day, a boy was standing on second base. "All of a sudden, he just took off running backward. 'What's the matter, son?' I asked him. 'Got to go to the bathroom,' he says. So I called time out and let him go."

There are other zany tales. A manager screams at his left fielder to "come on in" against a weak hitter. The manager turns around, and suddenly there is no left fielder. The manager looks down the bench, and there is his left fielder. "You said come on in," says the little boy, "so I did."

"I've umpired everything," Hunter said the other day, "and Little League is the toughest. First of all, the bases are shorter, so everything happens so quick. The big problem, though, is that the boys are so unpredictable. There's no telling where these kids will run, where they'll throw it, what they'll do. That's what makes it fun."

Hunter is thirty-six, the father of three sons and a Little League parent for 12 years. He works the Fairfax Little League now and does at least three games a week. He gets no pay and wouldn't take it if it was offered.

"He'd be out there every night if he could," said his wife, Mary. "The place is like a magnet to him."

Last year, Hunter was the chief umpire for the league, and that involved scheduling 75 men for games from April to mid-July, in addition to handling games every night of the week and all day Saturday.

One day, Hunter went over to a local high school to watch his son play, and felt "the most horrible pain in my chest you could ever imagine." Somehow, he managed to drive himself to the hospital and spent 19 days there recovering from a severe heart attack.

He has since changed jobs, from construction work to selling sporting goods, and he has given up the administrative work or the league. "But I couldn't give up umpiring," he said. "The doctors said fine, in moderation, so here I am."

The Fairfax Little League seems to be a first-class and—you'll pardon the expression—professional operation. A lot of people say that is precisely what is wrong with Little League baseball, but there are enough believers in the program in Fairfax to keep 800 kids in cleats and double knits for four months.

The field is immaculate, the base paths are raked before and after every game, and the snack bar serves up the best "Little League steaks" this side of Memorial Stadium. For the uninitiated, a Little League steak is a hot dog.

The kids are well-behaved, and so, for the most part, are the parents and managers. There was one leather-lunged father who stood proudly behind home plate watching his son "hum it in there, big fella" until the boy's manager asked him to take a walk. "You're making him nervous," he said. So the father watched from center field.

But no one bothered Hunter or his colleague, Bob Logan, as they called them as they saw them.

"Nah, these people are real good," said Hunter. But not always.

Once there was a manager who kept complaining about balls and strikes. "I walked over to the dugout," Hunter recalled, "and he said to me, 'You can see 'em better from here than behind the plate.' 'Fine, I'll stay here and call 'em.' I told the pitcher to go ahead and throw and he did. I called 'strike' and the manager shut right up. He got the message.

"The worst place is out at Manassas Park. Man, I hate to go out there. Those people are kinda crazy. There was a playoff game a couple of years ago and I was doing the bases.

"There was this red-headed lady in the stands, and there was a close play. I called the guy safe, and she went crazy. Then there's another close one, and she's really going nuts now.

"I think she had a six-pack right next to her. Well, anyway, the team she's pulling for has a boy who must be 6-feet tall and weighs 200 pounds. He comes up and hits a ball way the heck over the fence.

"The other manager comes out and says, 'Would you mind checking his bat?' Well, it's a Louisville Slugger, must be 38 inches long and weighs 40 ounces. I couldn't even swing it. So we disallowed the home run.

"That's the last straw for old redhead. She rushes the fence, and they hold her back. She stays on us the whole game, follows us into the parking lot after it's over, and cusses us out again. I think the only thing that saved us from getting beat up was the fact that her boy's team won."

But there are other times when Hunter is not such a stickler for the rules. The other night, he called a third strike on a player and the little boy flung his bat toward the dugout, grounds for automatic ejection.

"Didn't you see him?" someone asked Hunter.

"Nah," he smiled. "I knew he was gonna do it, so I just turned my back."

GOLF

THE ANTICLIMACTIC END OF THE MASTERS GOLF

By Edwin Pope

From the Miami Herald

Raymond Floyd's golden golf-sticks were quicker than TV's eye Sunday. The fortieth Masters Tournament was over before it even started for millions tuning up tubes around the world.

The hammer fell on five-time champion Jack Nicklaus when he bogeyed the fifty-seventh hole—Sunday's third—more than an hour before television picked up the action at 4 P.M.

That dropped Nicklaus out of the chase, nine strokes behind Miami's unfaltering Floyd. Thus, except for a desperate 67 by Ben Crenshaw, which would bring him no closer than eight strokes to Floyd, CBS-TV was left with all the living-room impact of a falling sofa pillow.

Even large numbers of some 60,000 paying customers wading through the wisteria and azalea of Augusta National began drifting away then. All that remained for TV was to plod dutifully after Floyd in a finish as soul-stirring as Lawrence Welk.

"I honestly believed the tournament was over before I even teed off," said Floyd, who led Nicklaus by eight going in. "I just didn't want to win it sloppily."

He didn't, whisking in with a 70 that Crenshaw called "absolutely remarkable under the circumstances."

In the anticlimactic end, this Masters did two things.

Floyd's total 65-66-70-70—271—tying Nicklaus's record set in 1965—established him at age thirty-three as a golfer whose full potential equals that of anyone now active. That concedes, at the same time, that Floyd has no earthly chance of equaling Nicklaus's 16 major victories.

Second, finally fulfilling his potential for the first time since his 1969 PGA tital, Floyd staked himself as sport's best advertisement for total reformation since baseball's Billy Sunday turned from carousing to evangelicizing nearly a century ago.

"He was Good Time Ray in the old days," said Larry Ziegler, who tied Nicklaus for third 11 long strokes back. "He got all the run out . . . just like I've heard Billy Sunday did . . . and nobody knows how hard Ray has worked since then."

Appropriately, Billy Sunday played the outfield in the late 1880s for National League Chicago, which happens to be Floyd's current fourth passion behind wife, Maria, and two little ones.

Mrs. Floyd didn't catch all of the mister's final act. The former Miami fashion instructor had to nurse their two-month-old, Robert, part of the day.

She got there in plenty of time to yell on the fourteenth hole, "Air mail it, Ray, before the wind comes up!"

She missed very little. If this had been a prizefight, they'd have called it a TKO early in the fourth round.

Floyd just danced, pecking, and jabbing to 14 pars with his three birdies and a bogey—"just keeping in control."

But for Crenshaw, the rest of the field simply beat itself to death. Only nine players did the last 18 under par. This roguish old course turned the others off every time they tried to turn on.

"I feel about like I won my 'own' tournament," Crenshaw said. "I'm tickled to death just to be second to a guy playing like Raymond. He has to be as good as anybody right now. When he's hot, he's unbeatable."

Floyd added: "I'm tired of being a mediocre player. From now on, my goal is to win everything. With this kind of control, I've got a shot to do well."

Best indication of Floyd's "control"—only six holes over par among 72—is that Crenshaw's 279 would have won an astounding 28 of the 39 previous Masters and gotten him in a championship playoff in five others.

Many of us may be indictable for overstressing Floyd's old rakehell side and understressing his postivisms.

But he did not come by the "playboy" label accidentally. "I've never been drunk on a golf course," the older and wiser Floyd said Sunday night, "but I've started a few rounds with hangovers."

Surely he began Sunday's finish free of any hangovers save perhaps a faint spectral image of last year's gripping Masters. Johnny Miller and Tom Weiskopf could have forced a playoff with Nicklaus by dropping birdie putts on the seventy-second hole in 1975. Their misses still left that audience in an exhilaration all but unique among viewers both "live" and the television variety.

That 1975 Masters may have been the most suspenseful since the first of all "majors," the British Open of 1860. Maybe TV should have replayed the thirty-ninth Masters this Sunday. There was nothing here for anyone but Floyd fans and sadists.

"The last time I had this much fun," said Ziegler after his hopeless struggle, "was a root-canal operation."

Yet the 1976 Masters carried a certain appeal.

Here was baby-faced Floyd—more like a Baby Face Nelson using golf clubs instead of submachine guns—bending his back to a wire-to-wire victory to blow the minds of six superstars who have won 19 of the 39 Masters. These have been Nicklaus and Arnold Palmer and Gary Player and Ben Hogan and Sam Snead and Jimmy Demaret.

Of that group, only Nicklaus in 1965 shot as well as Floyd. And Floyd's birdie at Sunday's fifteenth, the sixty-ninth hole of the Masters, smashed Demaret's 1950 record of playing the 16 par fives in 13 under par. Floyd was 14 under for the par fives.

"After that, I figured I'd just try to walk the last three holes without getting hurt," Floyd said. "That's the first time it even occurred to me that I had a shot at Nicklaus's 271 record."

It also was there that a spectator shouted, "Hey, Raymond, play all the rest of the way with your putter, so we can have a little suspense!"

Not even that would have done it.

Possibly, right there, both hands on the doorknob to his shining hour in 13 years of professional golf, Floyd's mind flashed back a dozen years to starkest contrast.

He was Ken Venturi's partner the day of Venturi's anguished triumph in the 1964 U.S. Open in Washington, D.C. That final round was 36 holes, and it was played in heat that only a hung-over human can fully understand. Yet Venturi, not Floyd, was prostrated by it for a time.

Floyd was only twenty-one then. He was awed by Venturi's courage, "playing the twenty-fourth through the thirty-sixth holes without even knowing where he was," Floyd said.

When Venturi flicked in the final putt, Floyd raced across the Congressional Country Club green. He snatched Venturi's ball from the cup. Then Floyd burst into tears.

Here Sunday, Floyd hid any tears he might have had for winning the crown most golfers cherish only slightly less than the U.S. Open. "I just never dreamed of tying Nicklaus's record," he said easily. "It's still sort of unbelievable to me."

Floyd's caddy was not ashamed to weep. His name is Fred (Hop) Harris and he had only a cameo part in the folderol connected with every Masters windup.

Coronations belong, or should, to another time and another country. The post-Masters ceremonies can be the essence of pomposity and dullness.

However, being neither so jaded nor wealthy that he can shrug off a check for more than $1,000, caddy Harris found the official presentation just as intriguing as Floyd did for his $40,000 prize.

"I only got Raymond three years ago, and that was because the other caddies thought he was so cheap," Harris said. "In fact, Raymond once fired a caddy here, and all the caddies back in the yard were praying against him that year. But he ain't cheap, and he's my man, and he's the best."

Those also were the sentiments of Maria Floyd. "I know Raymond's reputation from top to bottom," she said. "They called him a swinger and he was. Somebody had to land him, though, and I was the lucky one."

She paused, and said, "I'd never seen a golf tournament until I met Raymond at the Palm Bay Club in Miami. Until then, I thought a country club was just a place where you go to have dinner."

Now she knows.

GENERAL

HOW WE BLITZED THE BRITISH

By William A. Marsano

From TV Guide

[At the beginning of this season, the NFL held a Bicentennial essay contest. Youngsters fourteen to eighteen were asked to write about "The NFL's Role in American History." This entry arrived too late for the contest deadline. It is by Billy Marsano, age 28-36. Even though he is slightly overage—and unable to get his tongue out of his cheek—we print it here because of its enduring qualities.—Ed.]

Some people think the NFL's role in American history is very small. They point out that our nation was founded in 1776, and the NFL in 1920. This is only a technicality. The fact is that team spirit, drive, desire, and giving 110 percent—the NFL's favorite qualities—were the guiding forces of the men who won our independence. No NFL spirit, no USA—it's as simple as that.

I would like to cite a few examples to prove my point.

Spring 1774: The first team, the Minutemen, is formed, laying the foundation of the two-minute drill.

April 18, 1775: In a wood opposite Old North Church, Paul "Too Tall" Revere thinks the thoughts that made men free: "One if by land, two if by sea. Or is it two if by land . . .?" This paves the way for Frank Gifford.

April 19, 1775: The Revolution kicks off with the battles of Lexington and Concord, which pit the Colonial Minutemen against the British Redcoats, or "Monsters of the Midway."

May 12, 1775: Ethan Allen's green but well-coached Green Mountain Boys hit pay dirt at Fort Ticonderoga. "The British were in a prevent defense." Coach Allen says, "So we just worked the seams of the zone and took what they gave us." An important victory for the young expansion army.

July 4, 1776: Thomas "Bubba" Jefferson's Declaration of Independence is approved by all 13 colonies, or franchises. John "Papa Bear" Hancock is the first to sign.

August 27, 1776: The Colonials are edged by the British in the Championship of Long Island, but learn an important lesson: They have to play the war one battle at a time. "They really put the wood to us," Gen. Israel "Izzy" Putnam concedes in the postbattle press conference. "They ran traps and counters at us all day, and our offense couldn't get untracked."

August 30, 1776: Alex "Pete" Hamilton creates the Continental Code, which consists entirely of *X*s and *O*s. There are technical difficulties (couriers, for example, object to carrying the heavy and cumbersome blackboards), but in 1780 the code leads to the unmasking of Benedict Arnold and Major André. Arnold makes good his jump to the other league, but André is captured and "put on irrevocable waivers."

Fall 1776: "Dr." Benjamin Franklin goes to Paris to deal for veterans to shore up the Colonials' sagging offensive line. Franklin was famous for his "Poor Richard" sayings, which included "The future is now," "There's no tomorrow," and "On any given Sunday. . . ." Now he charms the French court with witty remarks on draft choices and Hungarian place-kickers, and soon makes a deal that is "good for both clubs."

December 26, 1776: While the Hessians hold a Christmas drinking party in Trenton, Gen. "Broadway" George Washington leads his squad across the Delaware—and wins big! "This proves the importance of team discipline," Washington tells the press. "The Hessians had broken training, and all they had was a bunch of tight ends." With the Hessians out of contention, the Colonials now have "momentum going for them."

January 3–October 7, 1777: An aroused Colonial squad sticks it to the British, who can't put it together. The Colonials win a six-battle series, 3 victories, 2 losses, and 1 tie. Biggest break: On October 17, England's great competitor, Gen. Johnny "White Shoes" Burgoyne decides to "hang 'em up."

Winter 1777: There's a break in the action at Valley Forge. This is a hard time for the surprising young Colonials. Their starters are weary, their reserves are thin, their backs are to the wall. Morale is low because of short rations at the training table and tattered uniforms—even though the Continental Congress (chanting "Deefense!") sends rush shipments of slogans for the locker-room walls. Washington stands by his men, proudly saying, "They can play both ways" (with shoes or without). And when sunshine patriots seek to oust Washington (they sing "Good-bye, Georgie" in the stands), the

Colonials support him, saying, "He'll play with pain." All winter long, everyone hangs in there.

June 28, 1778: The Colonials are really up for the Battle of Monmouth, and they come storming back to win. In a standout performance Molly Pitcher shows great second effort when she replaces her fallen husband. "She's some kind of patriot," Washington says. Momentum shifts again.

September 30, 1781: The Playoff at Yorktown begins, and an optimistic Washington notes prophetically in his diary, "Suddenly it's a whole new ball game."

October 19, 1781: Gen. Charles Cornwallis ("from the University of Mars") quits on his team and surrenders. The clock runs out, and the gun sounds.

NFL-style drive and desire was important off the field, too.

Tom "Rights of Man" Paine stirred Colonial youngsters with the saga of General Lafayette, who became an American hero even though, as Curt Gowdy has so often pointed out, "he had to overcome a double handicap: He was born French, and he suffered from scarlet fever as a youth." Patriots studied detailed analyses of Gen. Horatio "Big Bird" Gates's "hurry-up offense" and Gen. Anthony "Spider" Wayne's innovative zone defense (since expanded to 10 volumes by Al DeRogatis). Children spiked the ball in the streets of Philadelphia, and even a nameless tailor aided the cause by inventing the eight-button tunic, so similar to what Hank Straum would wear two centuries later.

When it was all over, the new United States of America had gained freedom—and parity with other nations. The nation's character had been formed—that of a society that would one day produce the National Football League as its highest expression of achievement.

And it didn't stop there. Only a few years later, in 1812, the British attacked again. In Baltimore, Francis Scott Key was watching the bombardment of Fort McHenry when he conceived the theory of the long bomb. Key had a keen mind and a gift for poetry that sprang from his training as a lawyer. (He had already written the tender lyric "Winning Isn't Everything—It's the Only Thing.") During the attack, he made extensive notes on the "bombs bursting in air." The next day, he put them into a poem, which later became a song. Today this song is played before every NFL game and is used on other patriotic occasions as well.

HOCKEY

OVEREMPHASIS OR HUNGRY HILL PRIDE?

By Nick Seitz

From Hockey Magazine

The Van Horn mites of Springfield, Mass., will play 100 hockey games this season. If you're keeping score at home, that's 20 more than the National Hockey League teams will play during the regular season.

Van Horn plays all over New England, in the New York City area, and in Canada, often traveling in big, comfortable chartered buses.

Most of the 100 games are against top squirt squads, because there aren't many mite teams that can stand up to Van Horn (mites are seven and eight years old, squirts nine and ten). If Van Horn loses a half-dozen games, it will be a bad year.

The people behind the Van Horn program flatly want this to be the best mite team anywhere, and it probably is. If a national tournament were conducted for mites, Van Horn would be a lopsided favorite to win it.

The question is whether such a high-pressure approach is healthy for such young players. At the mite level, after all, substitutions have to be made so a winger can go to the bathroom. A coach's toughest job can be lifting his little tigers over the boards for a line change in a rink with no doors.

Even the Russians, with their assembly-line hockey factories, do not believe in formal competition before the age of twelve. Can a program like Van Horn's be justified?

The first time I was exposed to it, I didn't think so. But my judgment may have been colored because I was cheering for the other team.

I have a seven-year-old son who plays for the Mid-Fairfield mite travel team in Connecticut, and Van Horn came down for a game early this season, preceded by an all-conquering reputation. The Van Horn coach had warned our coach not to suit up any fringe players. Van Horn carried only two lines, he said, and they could skate and shoot and hit better than the opposition we were used to.

What sounded boastful turned out to be good advice. I made it to the Van Horn game during the third period and was greeted by my wife, who looked as though she had just seen Frankenstein's monster. "Greggy's playing goal!" she almost shrieked. "I'm petrified!"

Our seven-year-old, in his first year of organized hockey, is not a goalie but has been exposed to the position a few times in house-league games. When the regular goalie left town for the weekend, which may have been the better part of valor, Greg replaced him.

Greg looked over and waved his stick. That was about the last free second he had. The Van Horn Blasters, wearing handsome new red, white, and blue road uniforms, assaulted the net in tidal waves—2 on 1, 3 on 1, 3 on none—and let go hard, rising shots. By the end of the game, the score was 8–0. It seemed more like 80.

I tried to console Greg as he climbed out of the bulky goalie pads afterward. With the wonderful resilience of childhood, he piped, "It's OK, Dad. Bernie Parent couldn't have stopped those guys."

It is the relaxed custom with our mites for parents and friends to join the players in the locker room, helping them out of their equipment and talking over the game. This night both teams were sharing a large, open dressing area, and our amiable conversations were cut off by the bellowing of the Van Horn coach.

He ordered his players to sit together on a bench. Then he roared at them about careless checking and passing. He is a hulking man, with the jaw of a steam shovel and the voice of a concrete mixer, and he went on for fully 10 minutes, occasionally breaking into light profanity. His players barely breathed.

When the tirade was over, one of our parents said emphatically, "I wouldn't let my kid play on a team like that in a million years." We all agreed. If ever there was a case of overemphasis in youth sports, this was it.

While that may be true, it is, I was to learn, too easy a conclusion if you haven't heard the other side of the story.

For one thing, the Van Horn mites learn through experience to play the game correctly from the start, without forming bad habits that will have to be undone later. I wish I had learned to play golf and tennis that way.

We played Van Horn in Springfield a couple of weeks after the first game. Before the afternoon game, our coach, Fran Guiliano, stressed repeatedly to his players that they would have to play their positions and work together to have any chance.

They didn't listen to him well enough and lost, 0–12, worse than the first time, as Van Horn played textbook hockey.

That night, we met another Massachusetts team, Westfield, and won, 3–0. Our team played 100-percent better position hockey than it had against Van Horn.

"Playing Van Horn was an education for our kids," said our coach. "I can talk to them about position hockey all day, but Van Horn made them appreciate it. We did to Westfield what Van Horn did to us."

In learning to play position hockey, the Van Horn mites, whom I saw play again the following day, do not appear to suffer physically or emotionally from their coach's stern treatment. He will jerk a player out of a game for making a mistake, but the player takes it well.

"I think they realize that behind that gruff talk is a man who cares about them," says Bob Stearns, who works with a good mite team in Ridgefield, Conn., that lost to Van Horn, 0–19, this year and then improved rapidly. "I don't see any bad effect on them. I don't buy profanity with kids myself, but I get the impression they'd lie down in the highway for him after a game."

The Van Horn coach is Andy Quirk, and stories about his toughness are becoming legend in Massachusetts hockey. In practice, he will tie a rope on a boy who has been wandering out of position—and reel him in when he starts to stray.

This season he got a new goalie—a boy who had a bad habit of turning his head on high shots. It is a habit that can result in serious injury.

Quirk brought his twelve-year-old son to practice and gave him a sack of pucks. He ordered the goalie to lie on his back in the crease. For an hour Quirk's son stood over the goalie and dropped pucks on his masked face. The goalie, cured of his shyness, hasn't turned his head since.

Quirk, a fiftyish auditor with the Travelers Insurace Companies in Hartford, Conn., a 30-minute commute from Springfield, welcomes questions about overemphasis in his coaching. "I'm not concerned that it's too much hockey too soon," he says. "Hockey is different from other sports. Springfield is the birthplace of basketball. Kids shoot baskets three hours a day. In hockey we don't have the ice to play like that.

"If we had natural ice, we wouldn't have a program this extensive. If we could get competition close to home, we wouldn't travel. But if you're going to be good, you have to skate and you have to play the best.

"People see us reprimand the kids during the games, but they don't see us kiss 'em and compliment 'em in practice. I treat them all equally, including my son who's on the team. All the Van Horn coaches get on the kids."

All the coaches and players in the program, which carries through the bantam age division, are from the Hungry Hill section of southwest Springfield, an old Irish enclave like South Boston. Van Horn is the name of a park in the area. Youngsters in the neighborhood are expected to compete in sports as their fathers and older brothers did before them.

Andy Quirk played his hockey in nearby Holyoke and is a longtime resident of Hungry Hill. "The parents know me—I get no resistance," he says.

Before the season, Quirk calls a meeting of parents whose sons have been selected for his A team. He tells them it is going to cost them a lot of money—$500 for ice time, plus more for equipment and travel. He tells them he will accept invitations to any tournaments within reason—he won't travel on Christmas Day, but he probably will on Easter.

"I make it clear that it's going to be plenty of hockey, that we're out to win and that there'll be no concessions to other family activities," says Quirk. "I tell them that if it's not for them, let me know in the next couple of weeks. I haen't had anybody drop out in my two years."

The mites come to Quirk having learned basic skating skills, including crossovers and skating backward, in weekly intramural sessions for four-, five-, and six-year-olds. They have worked together once a week the preceding summer.

Then, for the first six weeks of the season, until mid-October, Quirk practices them heavily—nearly every day for an hour—but schedules no games. He practices full-ice only, refusing to share the rink with another team because, he contends, it leads to lazy skating.

"Other teams play games before we do, but we learn what we're supposed to do," he says. "We walk the kids through plays until they know them by heart. A blackboard doesn't work at this stage—the kids don't have the attention span.

"We let them know we expect a lot from them, and we show them what we mean by position hockey. We don't give them too much. We have a basic breakout play, using our wings for long passes. In the offensive zone we use a triangle attack, moving the puck from wing to wing behind the cage and then to the slot. We also utilize our point men more than other young teams.

"Defensively, we teach them to cross coming back. One man goes for the puck-carrier and the other man goes in front of the net.

"Once we start playing games, we play four and five times a week and don't practice much."

What will happen to these seven- and eight-year-olds in the next few years? Will they tire of hockey by the time they're teen-agers?

"The program is 15 years old and I see no evidence of that," says Quirk. "Look at the all-Western Massachusetts high-school team and you'll find three or four Van Horn kids every year. We have several fellows playing major-college hockey. Another's in the North American Hockey League. These players didn't burn out. They got started right."

Would you want your young son to play for the mighty Van Horn mites?

WORLD SERIES

AN EASY VICTORY, IF NOT AN ARTISTIC ONE
(World Series Game I)

By Mike Gonring

From The Milwaukee Journal

This is the Fall Classic? Come on.

Baseball's biggest show, the World Series, opened in Cincinnati Saturday with a deadly dull game at Riverfront Stadium, a game that left Cincinnati Manager Sparky Anderson apologizing for his team, even though it had beaten the New York Yankees with ease, 5–1.

Somebody had to apologize, because it was not a gala opening. For most of the game, the Reds looked like the Big Red Tonka Truck, not the Big Red Machine.

The "best outfield ever" booted a couple of balls; Anderson asked his slowest runner to steal second base with two out with predictable results; a runner was hit by a ground ball; and the Reds' star left hander, Don Gullet, looked about as sharp as white socks with a black suit.

Were the Reds still awesome, someone asked New York Manager Billy Martin. "Hardly," said the manager, with disdain.

But they still handled the Yankees as if they were the Chicago Cubs, and that led many to wonder if they'd be home after the fourth game. The Yankees, starting right-hander Doyle Alexander, who for some reason has yet to sign a contract, were mismatched. Despite their rough spots, the Reds had no trouble. "A lot of people expect us to run over everyone," said catcher Johnny Bench. "But machines just grind things out. They run over some people, but they just grind things out and continue to make steady progress."

Said second baseman Joe Morgan: "We do what we have to do to win. We played very good baseball. I thought we played fine baseball today."

But Anderson didn't. "I did not think we were very aggressive today," he said. "And I didn't think that Gullett had his sharpest day. He threw nothing like he threw against Philadelphia.

"We're better than that. I think that as the series progresses, you'll see us better than you saw us today."

The Yankees probably would not welcome that sight. Before he left with a severe ankle sprain in the eighth inning, Gullett had given up only five hits and one run, even though he had pitched behind the hitters much of the game, had hit a batter, and had walked three.

"Actually," said Martin, "we hit more line drives for outs than they got hits."

But despite that, and despite the fact that Anderson, Bench, and Gullett himself agreed that he was not sharp, Gullett was tough enough for the Yankees. In one inning, the seventh, he hit one batter and walked two, but the Yankees still couldn't score.

Everyone assumed that Gullett would be the superior pitcher in this game, a battle between two unsigned pitchers, both represented by Superagent Jerry Kapstein. Gullett had been strong in the playoffs. Alexander, a marginal starter, had not pitched in three weeks but was called into action because of the toll that the playoffs took on the Yankee pitching staff.

And Alexander fell behind early. Morgan, batting with two out in the first, hit a home run over the right-field fence. When he crossed home plate, he turned to the stands, waved his hand, and tipped his cap.

"My wife was sitting there," he said. "She was worried because I didn't get any base hits in the playoffs."

Then Tony Perez singled, the first of three hits for him. And Anderson had him try to steal second. Despite a bad throw by Thurman Munson, the slow Perez was out. "One of my seldom mistakes," Anderson said.

The Yankees tied it in the second when Lou Piniella doubled, Chris Chambliss moved him to third with a ground ball to the right side, and Graig Nettles hit a sacrifice fly. But the tie was short-lived.

With one out in the third, Dave Concepcion tripled to left center, and Pete Rose drove him home with a fly ball, and the Reds were ahead for good.

The Reds bungled in the fourth when Perez, who had doubled, was hit by George Foster's slow ground ball to third, but they added a run in the sixth with their only stolen base of the day a factor. Ken Griffey, on first with one out, stole second when Morgan struck out, then scored on Perez's single.

They got their last two runs in the seventh. Foster singled and

Bench tripled, with Elliott Maddox misplaying the ball in right. Exit Alexander, who ought to sign soon, enter Sparky Lyle. A wild pitch scored Bench, and Cesar Geronimo tripled before Lyle retired the next three hitters.

The Yankees made little runs at Gullett, but little they were. In the fifth, Chambliss singled but Nettles hit into a double play. Then, when Maddox tripled Foster misplayed the ball off the wall, but Willie Randolph flied out.

In the sixth, Stanley walked and Mickey Rivers, trying to bunt for a base hit, bunted into a force play instead. Then Rivers, king of speed in the American League, tried the arm of Bench, king of arms everywhere. Bench won, and Rivers was out stealing.

"He didn't have a jump," Bench said. "As easily as I threw him out this time, he might steal the next time."

Roy White hit a fly ball to left center that looked as if it would be the third out of the inning, but Geronimo one-handed it and dropped it for a two-base error. Thurman Munson singled to right, moving White to third, but Piniella lined out.

In the seventh, Gullett hit Chambliss with an 0–2 pitch, but Nettles hit into another double play. Then Gullett, struggling badly, walked Maddox and Randolph. But when Martin sent up Otto Velez to pinch-hit for Stanley, Anderson didn't even flinch. Gullett stayed in and Velez struck out.

Gullett's day finally ended in the eighth when he hurt his ankle stepping off the mound. Pedro Borbon finished up.

The game was historic for one reason. The Reds were forced to use the designated hiter, and the chosen one, Dan Driessen, went 0 for 4. But Anderson, although admitting that he would rather send up Driessen than Gullett, still hates the rule.

"I've changed my mind about it," he said. "Instead of being bad, it stinks."

WORLD SERIES

THE DEADLY COMBINATION
(World Series Game II)

By Thomas Boswell

From The Washington Post

They should be in extra innings now, the New York Yankees and Cincinnati Reds, still locked up 3–3 in what will probably be looked back on as the pivotal game of this World Series.

The Yanks' Catfish Hunter should still be on the mound, pitching his heart out, showing the mighty world champions that they should have knocked him out in the third and fourth innings when they had the chance.

Manager Billy Martin should still be on the top stop of the frigid Yankees dugout, pleading with his hitters to get to Reds hurler Jack Billingham and win this second game of the Series and send the whole shebang back to New York tied one game apiece. "They're in the tough spot, not us," Martin was ready to say.

Instead, the Reds were 4–3 winner and lead the Series, two games to none. The Reds know too many ways to win and have planted the idea of defeat too deeply in their enemies' minds. Tonight it came with two out in the bottom of the ninth and no one on base. The Yankee ace, Hunter, had retired 15 of 16 hitters. He was winging, pitching the Reds high and away and then in on the fists. He dared them to hit his fastballs over the distant fences on this 39-degree night. He smirked at their long fly outs.

Then, instead of these towering drives that meant nothing, Ken Griffey hit the sickest of little choppers straight at Yankee shortstop Fred Stanley. For any other batter in the majors it would have been the simplest of outs, no reason to hurry. Extra innings, here we come. But Griffey, like all the Reds, is preceded by his reputation, a reputation as the fastest man to first base in baseball.

And Stanley rushed the play, knowing about Griffey's 38 infield hits this year.

First baseman Chris Chambliss had to stretch a bit more quickly to get the ball a few inches sooner.

Stanley's throw was not too bad, just a bit high and off the mark. Chambliss' stretch was not that premature. But the combination was deadly. Griffey, who should have been out to end the inning, ended up on second base as the throw whizzed past the tip of Chambliss' glove into the Reds' dugout. Two-base error, it was ruled. Why not score it one more for the Red terror?

Somehow, the game ended then. The 54,816 Reds' fans stood in their red parkas, their orange-and-black Cincinnati Bengals football stocking caps—for this, as Martin said, "wasn't no baseball weather. Playing tonight was ridiculous."

Martin ordered Joe Morgan walked, but it was just a matter of picking the gallows or the electric chair.

It didn't seem to matter. The Yankees were going back to their new $100 million Yankee Stadium in a box with "Reds 2, Yanks 0," on the top. It was just a matter of picking the executioner.

Tony Perez was next. The first pitch was a fastball down the middle. Every pitcher knows he cannot fall behind the Reds sluggers. He must come in. So Hunter came in. And out the ball went, on a darting line into left field for a clean single.

The crowd roared as Griffey sped home with the 4–3 victory.

The Yanks walked off with blank expressions. Perez, who has driven in 90 or more runs each of the last 10 years, who has knocked in eight runs in his last five World Series games, who has gone from the Reds' perennial postseason goat to perhaps its steadiest pressure hitter, jumped into the arms of his teammates and they carried him off.

"Oh, yes. We are very pleased," said Perez. "Now we go to New York and maybe we only have to play two games."

This is what the Reds want. They have never said it publicly, but they were annoyed that the Boston Red Sox extended them to seven games last October. They all say the Yankees are a better team. They say it because they want to spank the New Yorkers in four straight. They want a perfect 7–0 sweep of the postseason.

The Reds could have made tonight's victory quicker, more one-sided and less exciting if they had just knocked out Hunter when he asked them to.

His fast, almost-awkward pitches over the middle of the plate in the early innings were an invitation to send this man with an impeccable 4–0 World Series record and a 2.18 ERA to an early shower.

But Hunter's catcher, Thurman Munson, saved him with a throw and a catch in the second inning, two plays that kept Hunter around for one of his finest hours.

The Reds opened the second with a double, a single, a double, a walk, a single, a walk, and a sacrifice fly. But Hunter survived.

After Dan Driessen's opening double and George Foster's run-scoring single, Munson threw out Foster on a steal attempt.

Perhaps Foster should not have run so disdainfully on the very first pitch. That is Morgan style, as he had already shown in the first inning. Munson's perfect peg was his rebuttal: "Morgan, maybe, Foster, no."

So when Bench doubled, Geronimo walked, and Concepcion singled home Bench, Martin could still stay with his right hander. With one out (thanks to Munson), rather than none, Hunter was still just one double-play pitch from escape.

When Concepcion stole second and Rose walked to load the bases, Hunter was given one more chance. He got Griffey to hit an inoffensive fly to short center.

But Geronimo challenged his opposing center fielder to a test—his feet against Rivers's arm. Had Geronimo been doing the throwing, he probably would have pegged himself out by 10 feet. But Rivers's arm is a well-known rag. His sad two-hop throw to home was late and the Reds had their third run of the inning.

Munson dispensed with Morgan to end the inning, making an excellent running catch of his foul pop before pounding into the box-seat railing.

Hunter, given a reprieve, showed why he is one of only four pitchers in history to win 200 games (201) before his thirty-first birthday. That the others are Walter Johnson, Christy Mathewson, and Cy Young gives some idea of Hunter's feat.

The Reds loaded the bases in the third, but Concepcion and Foster were struck out when they had to be. In the fourth, Rose and Griffey drove the outfielders that the Yanks were frantically moving around by means of walkie-talkies onto the warning track for long drives. Morgan slammed a triple. But Hunter got Perez to pop up to center to end the inning.

"I said to myself, 'The darn Catfish is off the hook again,' when we let him off in the fourth," said Reds' manager Sparky Anderson. "To tell the truth, I never thought we'd get him once he got rolling."

And while his teammates gradually wiped out their deficit, Hunter did roll. After Perez, he retired a dozen in a row before a Bench single, then mowed down three more before Griffey's fatal hopper. Pointing his spikes toward Rivers in center, then challenging the best lineup in baseball with fastballs and quick little sliders, Hunter was the master of audacity, daring the Reds to hit him again though they had already proved they could.

The Yanks' conquest of little Freddy Norman took time. The cute lefty lasted into the seventh with his pitching. When the Yanks needed a big hit they could be counted on not to get it. They have mastered the art of minimizing rallies in this Series.

In the fourth, Munson, Chris Chambliss, and Graig Nettles all singled for one run; but Elliott Maddox—when any grounder or fly would have scored a man—fanned with Chambliss at third and one out. Norman only struck out one other man.

In the sixth Piniella singled and Chambliss (now 14 for 28 in the seven-game postseason) singled to the opposite field. But Nettles popped up and Maddox (again) grounded into a double play.

The least likely source of combustion in the frozen-fingered New York lineup caught fire in the seventh. Willie Randolph singled and scored on Stanley's hit-and-run double into the left-field corner. When Roy White singled Stanley to third, Jack Billingham came on.

Munson greeted him with a run-scoring groundout to tie the game, but that was Billingham's only imperfection. He retired the last eight men for the victory.

The Yankees were hardly gracious in defeat. They fumed that the first Sunday Series game ever played at night (to accommodate TV) had forced them to play in 39 degree weather. Martin groused that: "Every time they hit a blooper it fell in. Do you know what a blooper is? We're hitting line drives and they're caught. The luck isn't with us."

WORLD SERIES

THE REDS ARE MAKING A JOKE OF THE SERIES
(World Series Game III)

By Lou Chapman

From the Milwaukee Sentinel

If they put the World Series on Broadway, it would be the biggest comedy hit of the year. They could steal the title from an old television show, "Laugh In."

It's so funny it's tragic the way the Cincinnati Reds reduced the New York Yankees to a comical version of a baseball team Tuesday night. This time Billy Martin's American League champions succumbed, 6–2, before 56,667 disappointed followers.

The only real violence came from the right-field stands when Cincinnati right-fielder Ken Griffey was hit by a flying object. Reds Manager Sparky Anderson said later he believed it was an orange. Otherwise, the Reds supplied most of the flying objects. They had 13 hits and Dan Driessen, the Cincinnati designated hitter, had a perfect night with a homer, double, and a single.

Anderson, however, insisted later that despite this bombardment, the DH has no place in the game of baseball.

"It's not right to send up one of your biggest bombers to hit for a pitcher," he said.

Martin continued to insist later that the Reds are dazzling the Yankees with bloopers, saying the Reds had only three legitimate hits.

Two of those, of course, were Driessen's homer in the fourth and Joe Morgan's double down the right-field line in the eighth.

But Martin had to admit the Yankees are in a precarious position, down 3–0 in the Series. It will be over on Wednesday night unless Ed Figueroa, the Yankee starting pitcher, can stifle the Reds.

But as the broadcasters say, there's no tomorrow after Wednesday for the Yankees, who will face Gary Nolan in what might be the Series finale.

So far the Yankees have made this Series the biggest fiasco in history. The Orioles swept the Dodgers once, but it took brilliant pitching to turn the trick.

The Yankees, however, had made a joke of what should be baseball's proudest moments. They have fouled up in the field, with the bat, and on the bases.

Everyone said the best way to beat the Yankees was to keep Mickey Rivers off base. Well, he was on base four times Tuesday night on a walk, two singles, and a throwing error on his first inning bunt.

Still, the Yankees managed only two runs to make it a measly total of six in the three games. And even with Rivers on base, they suffered the humiliation of seeing him picked off at first.

Ironically, the Reds' right-handed starter Pat Zachry, who beat the Yankees, is a former worshiper of the New York Club.

The Reds' winner, with relief help from left-hander Will McEnaney, once played games in his backyard home back in Waco, Texas, pretending he was a Yankee.

This time, he didn't have to pretend he was a pitcher. Before leaving the game in the seventh Zachry earned the grudging admiration of Martin with his changeup, control, and an excellent slider against the Yankees' right-handed hitters.

The only Yankee batter to get an extra base hit off Zachry was the last person you'd expect to get one. Certainly, he was the last one expected to hit a home run. You can take Jimmy the Greek's word on that.

Mason, who hit .180 all year and had only one homer in the 1976 season, hit one into the right-field stands in the seventh. Mason's last homer came on May 8 at Oakland, off Glenn Abbott.

The Reds, meanwhile, went about their business of decimating Yankee starter Dock Ellis, whom they touched for three runs in the second and another on the twenty-five-year-old Driessen's homer in the fourth. Ellis's successor, Grant Jackson, was charged with the Reds' final two runs in the eighth, when the National League champions were ignited once more after the Yanks' flare-up in the seventh.

It was 49 degrees at game time, good Brewer weather in Milwaukee's County Stadium. And if the truth be told, the Yankees Tuesday resembled the Brewers performing against the Yankees.

Before the game, the Reds' catalyst Pete Rose exclaimed, "Happiness is winning." When asked about the weather, he exulted, "It's 75 and sunny."

Ellis, who started for Pittsburgh in the 1971 Series against Baltimore, and lasted only two and two-thirds innings, went a little longer this time. Dock was docked—or, rather, decked—in the fourth.

Before that the Reds got to him for three runs after Driessen's infield single, which was deflected off Ellis's glove. Driessen would have been out but for a bad throw to first by second baseman Willie Randolph. It was ruled as a hit by a generous scorer and gave weight to Martin's argument about Cincinnati's bloop hits. Driessen then moved to third on George Foster's ground double to right center and scored on Johnny Bench's line drive deflected off Chris Chambliss' glove.

Foster, who took third on the hit, also scored on Cesar Geronimo's force of Bench at second. The Reds had still another run on the board when Dave Concepcion blooped a hit—there's that word bloop again—to left, scoring Geronimo, who had stolen second.

Driessen then made it 4–0, Reds, and for trivia buffs it was the first homer by a National League designated hitter in Series history.

The Yankees came to life briefly in their half of the inning by touching Zachry for their first run. He had given up just one hit. This time Chambliss led off with a single and Graig Nettles walked with one out. Oscar Gamble then singled to center scoring Chambliss.

But Zachry, whose best friend is a dog named Bronc, put his teeth into his work and suppressed the Yanks until the seventh when Mason homered, Rivers walked, and Thurman Munson singled after Roy White's forceout.

Left-hander Will McEnaney promptly disposed of Chambliss on a bouncer to the mound and whipped through the next two innings, although getting into a minor jam in the ninth.

The Reds, meanwhile, ignited by Mason's homer, blasted for another two runs in the eighth.

Rose singled and moved to third on Griffey's single. Morgan doubled down the right-field line to score Rose, Griffey moving to third.

Dick Tidrow replaced Jackson and got Tony Perez to bounce to short. Griffey was tagged out in a rundown between third and home, but Morgan slid in safely at third and Perez, safe on the fielder's choice, took second.

Foster singled to left scoring Morgan after Driessen drew a intentional walk to load the bases. Foster's single to left scored Morgan.

The Yankees made their last gasp in the ninth on singles, by Rivers and Munson. But ironically, Chambliss, the hero of the final American League playoff game with a homer, this time flied to Foster in left for the game ender.

So now, the Series might end on Wednesday night, although Martin, always the optimist, has named Ken Holtzman his starter in the fifth game.

Billy is a desperate man, grasping at straws—even at Holtzman, whom he has ignored throughout the Series.

WORLD SERIES

A HISTORICAL PRECEDENT
(World Series Game IV)

By Murray Chass

From The New York Times

History and the Cincinnati Reds proved too strong a combination for the New York Yankees to overcome last night as the Reds won the World Series by completing a four-game sweep.

With Johnny Bench hitting two home runs and driving in five runs, the defending champion Reds captured the fourth game, 7–2, at Yankee Stadium and became the first National League team in 54 years to win two consecutive World Series. They also became the first team in baseball to march through the pennant playoffs and Series undefeated, a total of seven games.

"I told one of our coaches," Sparky Anderson, the Reds' silver-haired manager, said minutes after the final out, "that if we beat Steve Carlton of Philadelphia in the first game of the playoffs, we were gonna win seven straight games."

Indeed the Reds won three straight from the Phillies for the National League pennant and then ripped through the Yankees for four straight victories in the first Series sweep since the Baltimore Orioles unloaded on the Los Angeles Dodgers in 1966. Six of the intervening nine Series lasted the full seven games.

The Yankees, who have been waiting since October 14, 1964, to win their one hundredth Series game, succumbed to historical precedent as well as to the mighty Reds. Fifteen times in the previous 72 Series one team had won the first three games. Twelve times that team also won the fourth game. In the other three instances, that team lost the fourth game, but won the fifth. In other words, no team ever had come back to win the Series after losing the first three games.

The Yankee season that began with optimism April 8 and peaked with Chris Chambliss' pennant-winning home run last Thursday night, ended at 11:11 P.M. when Roy White's routine fly ball descended into George Foster's glove in left field.

Even before the ball reached Foster, the other Reds were running off the field, trying to avoid the crush of humanity they expected to storm out from the stands that had held 56,700 fans.

Some fans did race onto the field and tear up chunks of grass, but nowhere nearly as many as the number that attacked the turf of the $100 million stadium seconds after Chambliss hit his homer last week and gave the Yankees their first pennant since 1964.

Most of the fans filed quietly out of the stadium after the Yankees had suffered their third four-game sweep in 30 Series appearances.

Billy Martin, the fiery Yankee manager, wasn't around to see the final out of his first Series as a manager. Bruce Froemming, the first-base umpire, ejected Martin in the top of the ninth inning, just before Bench hit his second homer, a three-run belt off Dick Tidrow that sealed the Reds' triumph.

Bench's first home run, a two-run shot off Ed Figueroa in the fourth inning, vaulted the Reds into a 3–1 lead, and they never trailed again. For his total Series efforts—eight hits in 15 times at bat and six runs batted in—the twenty-eight-year-old catcher was named the most valuable player.

"What a relief it is for me to do something for the team after I didn't do much all year," said Bench, who batted only .234, hit 16 homers, and drove in 74 runs in the weakest offensive year of his major-league career.

Bench wound up with a .533 average for the four games, the fourth best average in the Series' 73-year history. He overshadowed the performance of the Yankee catcher, Thurman Munson, who rapped four straight hits last night, tied a Series mark with six straight hits, and finished with a .529 average on nine hits in 17 times at bat.

Munson, a leading candidate for the American League's Most Valuable Player Award, was in the on-deck circle when White, the team's elder statesman, made the last out. By that time, though, it was obvious that the Reds were the best team in baseball.

Despite taking a lead for the first time in the Series—1–0 in the first inning on Munson's single and Chambliss' double—the Yankees, in the entire Series, never really challenged the Reds, who had breezed through National League competition with 102 victories. The Yankees scored only eight runs in the four games.

After Bench hit his first home run, Gary Nolan, who was starting his seventh Series game, held the lead and then Will McEnaney relieved him in the seventh and picked up a save. The left hander also gained a save in the Reds' seventh-game triumph over the Boston Red Sox last season.

McEnaney replaced Nolan, a twenty-eight-year-old right hander who nearly had his career ended two years ago by a shoulder ailment, after Munson had stroked his fourth single. The Yankees trailed by only 3–2 at the time—Munson had singled across the other run in the fifth—but McEnaney quickly retired Chambliss on a checked-swing grounder for the third out.

The Reds, who won only one game in losing the 1939 and 1961 Series to the Yankees, secured their victory in the ninth.

Figueroa, the Yankee starter, opened the inning by walking Tony Perez, then tossed a wild pitch that enabled Perez to go to second with Dan Driessen at bat.

With Perez at second and Driessen still at bat, Martin tossed a ball out of the dugout.

The ball, which had just been tossed out of the game, wandered in the direction of Bill Deegan, the home plate umpire. Froemming, from his first-base spot, spun toward the dugout, pointed at Martin, and motioned that he was gone.

"He [Deegan] threw three balls at me and the last one almost hit me in the throat, that's why I threw it back," said Martin, the first manager to be ejected from a World Series game since Shag Crawford threw out Earl Weaver of Baltimore in the fourth game of the 1969 Series between the Orioles and the New York Mets.

Martin raced out of the dugout and immediately began jumping and screaming and hollering. The umpires restrained him and finally he departed quietly.

"We have a riot situation here and Martin knew it," Froemming explained afterward. "It's a touchy situation and to have Martin start something at this point is something we can't tolerate. I told him if he stayed any longer he could cause a riot, and when I said that, he left."

With Martin gone, Yogi Berra assumed command of the Yankees. Yogi was the manager when the Yankees last were in a Series in 1964.

Berra made his first and only appearance on the field during a game in this Series after Figueroa walked Driessen. Yogi went out to change pitchers and received a lusty ovation.

Tidrow, a strong reliever for the Yankees over the second half of the season, retired the first batter he faced, Foster on a fly to center. But then came Bench and, on the first pitch, there went a Bench fly ball toward the left-field stands.

White raced back to the wall and, throwing his right foot halfway up the blue padding, leaped as high as he could. But the ball soared softly above his glove and landed in the first row.

That gave the Reds a 6–2 lead, and consecutive doubles by Cesar Geronimo and Dave Concepcion followed to make it 7–2.

All that stood between the Reds and their goal now were three outs in the Yankee half of the ninth inning.

Otto Velez batted for Jim Mason and McEnaney struck him out. Mickey Rivers, almost a forlorn figure in this Series, after being so instrumental in the Yankees' pennant drive, was the next batter and he socked a line drive toward third that Pete Rose intercepted.

In the fifth inning, Rivers had blooped a single to right and had stolen second base, something no one had done on Bench in the Reds' previous 26 postseason games, not since Matty Alou of Oakland stole in the second game of the 1972 Series. But Rivers's steal was a belated effort for the Yankees, who ran so effectively during the regular season but who tried only two steals against the Reds.

White was the batter with two out in the ninth inning and he could not stir things. He lofted a fly to left; Rose and the rest of the Reds started running toward the dugout and the ball nestled into Foster's glove.

It was 11:11 P.M. and there would be no need for a 6 P.M. game today. Chunks of white paper swirled in the wind and eventually floated to rest on the grass that was part of the $100 million the city had spent refurbishing Yankee Stadium.

Martin and George Steinbrenner and Gabe Paul brought—or bought, as some people charge—the Yankees a pennant. But they didn't have enough weapons in their drastically revamped arsenal to overpower the Reds.

The one hundredth World Series victory will have to wait at least until next year.

TENNIS

ILIE NASTASE: THE SIDE YOU NEVER SEE

By Barry Lorge

From Tennis Magazine

"Life is a game, boy. Life is a game that one plays according to the rules."

"Yes, sir. I know it is, I know it."

—J. D. Salinger
The Catcher in the Rye

Ilie Nastase and Arthur Ashe were sitting at a table, beside each other and far apart, like bookends on an empty shelf a million miles long.

Nastase fidgeted uncomfortably. Ashe—stone-faced and, by his own description, "incredibly hacked off"—refused to look at him. Nastase knew it was no small feat to have made Ashe lose his celebrated cool, but he wasn't proud of what he'd done. He was genuinely contrite, squirming like a kid who has ruined a birthday party, feels terrible about it, and would like to hide out for awhile in the hope that all will be forgiven. His gloomy contenance said, in a Holden Caulfield kind of way, "I feel awful, if you want to know the truth."

"I just decided I wasn't going to put up with his crap a second longer," Ashe seethed, explaining why he had rashly fumed off the court at Stockholm's Kungliga Tennishallen a few minutes earlier while leading Nastase in the final set of their match in the Commercial Union Masters playoff last December. Ashe had been infuriated by what has become Nastase's standard modus operandi—stalling, cursing, disputing calls, creating his own special brand of disorder in the court.

Ultimately, Ashe's act of vigilante justice was given official blessing. Even though he left the playing area and technically should have been defaulted, the match was awarded to him the following day by officials of the International Lawn Tennis Federation, on the basis that his actions had been prompted by Nastase's blatant abuse of the rules. In effect, they were agreeing with Ashe's stated opinion that "Nastase is a detriment to the game because he is a source of anarchy."

Nastase, for his part, accepted the verdict stoically. Sitting in the press interview room, next to Ashe at that six-foot table that seemed infinitely longer, he mumbled a few words but didn't really say anything. He knew he had, once again, pushed a patient man too far and he regretted it. He would suffer the consequences as cheerfully as possible and hope that doing so would erase the episode from memory—like a child who fervently yearns that a spanking will wipe out whatever misdeed brought it about.

Nastase, is, in many ways, a twenty-nine-year-old Romanian Holden Caulfield—a pathological but fundamentally nonmalicious breaker of the rules, misunderstood and inwardly pained more than anyone imagines by his own compulsive iconoclasm and lack of self-control. He means well and intends to keep his word every time he promises he's going to shape up, but it never seems to work out that way.

The brush with Ashe in Stockholm was just one episode in a dizzying and by now monotonous series of disqualifications, controversies, chaotic and distasteful scenes. His conduct, never recommended as a model for Boy Scouts, has grown more offensive. His language and gestures, which once merited only an *R,* are now rated *X.*

His outlandish conduct is indefensible, and even some of his best friends and staunchest defenders have found their endurance wearing thin. When referee Charles Hare finally lost patience after three days of reprehensible conduct and tossed Nastase out of the American Airlines Tennis Games at Palm Springs, Calif., in March, he was loudly applauded. A tangible kind of mob psychology surfaced; throughout the land the cry was heard, "The guy certainly had it coming to him . . . give 'im hell, Charlie."

Much of the public has come to regard Nastase merely as an incorrigible delinquent, but he is a much more complicated personality than that.

"One thing few people realize or appreciate is that the guy is extremely sensitive," says his agent, Bud Stanner. "He gets hurt easily, and the hurt stays with him a long time. His gut grinds more than most people think. He probably is the best tennis player in the world today, when he wants to be, but I'm not sure he really knows that. I think he has a deep-seated sense of insecurity."

Ion Tiriac, the hulking patriarch of Romanian tennis, who was Nastase's mentor before losing control of him, puts it more bluntly: "He is scared to lose, he is scared to win, he is scared of everything. Nastase does not have a brain; he has a bird fluttering around in his head."

Nastase has never made claims on his own behalf to any great mental ability. "I have temper. Who is perfect?" he says. "If I cannot do these things on the court, I cannot play, I just get ulcers. This is Nastase. I cannot change. I am a little bit crazy." He is reminiscent of Holden Caulfield confiding, "I'm a madman sometimes. I swear I am."

One suspects that if the jumbled thoughts and feelings in Nastase's psyche could ever be verbalized, the narrative that would emerge might be something like Caulfield's. There is a side to Nastase that the public seldom sees—an unarticulated but deeply felt succession of private demons and insecurities, wild highs and depressions, unvoiced emotions and perpetual restlessness.

"He's interesting, because as soon as he gets to a tournament he starts setting up his plans to leave," notes Stanner. "He says, 'Well, if I lose today, I'll go here.' I kid him about it becaue he's always planning where to go next before he plays the first match at the place he's at."

With the possible exception of Evonne Goolagong, there is no more naturally gifted player in the game. When he keeps his fragile psyche together, Nastase is an incomparably graceful and breathtaking artist. He has been called "a zephyr, a wizard." But all too often his flighty behavior obscures both his genius as a player and his basic goodness as a human being.

Nastase is not a dishonest person. "I think if he played a tournament without officials, he'd have no problems," ventures Stanner. "If he relied on his opponent and himself to make the calls, there wouldn't be a problem." Lines-persons and umpires are his own personal tormentors.

If it was up to his honor, most of his colleagues agree, Nasty wouldn't cheat. But in his convoluted code of ethics, the presence of authority figures means anything he can get away with is fair. He is, unquestionably, a shameless gamesman, a con artist who tries to rattle and psyche opponents and steal whatever advantage he can.

Off the court, however—away from the pressures that feed his neuroses and stretch his high-strung personality until it snaps—Nastase is a delight, a joyous if somewhat mercurial character. Despite his dark moments he is by nature wonderfully ebullient, energetic, bursting with life. Beneath what many consider his cheating heart lies a kind, generous, gentle soul. His life is nonstop banter, noise, color, action . . . he relishes good food, stylish clothes, fast cars, a jet-set life-style. He goes a mile-a-minute, and likes to take friends along for the whirl at his pace.

He is probably the most photogenic man in tennis, his countenance a playground for expressions. Ecstasy, anger, futility, disappointment—moods march easily across his delicate Latin features. He can look angelic or mischievous. His pout is definitive. His persecuted look makes King Lear seem chipper. When he smiles, the sun glistens in his eyes and they are full of a kind of youthful merriment.

Nastase is decidedly human. He has more than his quota of foibles, frailties, and hangups, but a rare ability to soar as well. He is one of those engaging individuals who gets excited about things; and therefore gets us excited too, reminding us that life is there for the living. Nastase is hardly profound, deep-thinking, or philosophical, but he is vital and alive. He has an innate understanding of what Murray Burns, the hero of Herb Gardner's *A Thousand Clowns,* called "the subtle, sneaky, important reason why he was born a human being, and not a chair."

Nastase is at heart a clown, in the best sense of the word. He is fun-loving, spontaneous, and has a natural gift for comedy as well as burlesque. He can be a splendidly good-natured vaudevillian on court, sticking his head into TV cameras, playing soccer with tennis balls, bringing down the house with improvisational slapstick or hilarious asides.

It is only when he gets upset and becomes surly, starting his tirade against opponents, officials, and spectators, that the wrath of authority descends on him. Sadly, his petulant side has become exaggerated, overshadowing the fact that he is still the sport's most entertaining character.

His off-court personality is playful as well. He thrives on being the center of attention and fun. Given his druthers, Nasty would undoubtedly love to be Bill Veeck, or Santa Claus.

One year during Wimbledon, he kept coming out to the All-England Club in disguises—a fake walrus moustache and gigantic shades one day, a vendor's uniform the next. (He sold half a dozen ice lollies before his identity was discovered.) When the Masters was played in Australia, he spent two hours on a sidewalk passing out leaflets and chatting with passersby.

Dismayed one time that an opponent was allowed to wear a tie-dyed T-shirt in a tournament, Nastase appeared for his next match in polka-dot pajamas. And after he and Ashe, playing doubles together at Louisville last summer, had been scolded for wearing different color outfits, Nasty came back the next day with his face blackened, looking like a refugee from a minstrel show. "Now we are the same color—no problems," he beamed to his partner, who dissolved in uncontrollable laughter.

Nastase is an incurable practical joker and incessant needler. The evening before his altercation with Ashe in Stockholm, he was in a relaxed, expansive, jocular mood, holding court in the lounge of the opulent Grand Hotel. He was looking forward to the match against the man he calls, with his inimitable flair for nicknames no one else could possibly get away with in good grace, "Negroni."

"Tomorrow I just drive Negroni crazy," he told a group of journalists, who were thoroughly charmed. "I do everything, I tell you. I use old tricks, all new tricks, everything. I have some new songs. I make Negroni so mad he will turn red. But of course, first he must turn white."

As if on cue, Ashe appeared at the door. Nastase beckoned him over: "Hey, Negroni, we are just talking about you. I say tomorrow I make you so mad you turn white, then red. Is good trick, huh?"

Ashe walked over to him, grinning like a Cheshire cat. He finds Nastase as irresistible, off court, as nearly everyone else does. Nasty patted him affectionately on his Afro. "Hey, Brown Sugar," he cooed, "tomorrow I make you white."

Nastase returned his attention to his spellbound audience. "I do this because the last time we play, in Paris, semifinals, Negroni does everything like I do—all bad things," he said, rewriting history to fit his own slant. "He is two sets to love behind, and he is like this"—he bowed his head in a hangdog expression worthy of the most accomplished thespian—"and then for the rest of the match Negroni is behaving like me: stall, talk, all naughty things. On match point, he is talking for five minutes.

"After I lose, in dressing room, I am so mad, I say, 'I don't forget this, Negroni. Next time I get you, I promise.' So now we play here and I drive you crazy for sure." With that, he patted Ashe on the head again and exited, stage left, as the assembled group marveled at his exuberance. When Ashe and the journalists went to pay their checks shortly thereafter, the bartender informed them that Mr. Nastase had picked up everyone's tab for the whole evening.

Ashe, who condemns Nastase's on-court histrionics but insists "he's the kind of guy you can't stay mad at very long," wouldn't find even the slightest trace of racial insult in Nastase's monologue.

Nastase has given biting nicknames to most players. Bob Hewitt, or any other South African, is "Racist" . . . Jan Kodes is "Russian," which is about the worst thing you could call a Czech . . . other East Europeans are "Commo," to cite just a few. None of them are offended.

"He's got a name for everybody," says Cliff Richey, who answers to The Animal. "We all know he doesn't mean anything by it. On the court he's done things to me that no one should have to take—I think he's an insult to everybody in tennis that way—but he's not really a malicious guy at all."

Nastase's needling may well be a shield he puts forward to protect an essentially vulnerable personality. "He bruises much more easily than people realize," says Stanner.

Nastase needs desperately to be loved, and he reacts desperately when he isn't. The recent deterioration in his behavior is doubtless attributable, at least in part, to frictions in his private life; distressing marital problems, the pressures of more business and tournament commitments than he can handle, the frightening and frustrating realization that he is alienating friends but unable to control himself.

Nastase reportedly has been deeply hurt by a falling out with his Belgian-born wife, Dominique—who was once perfectly described by columnist Wells Twombly as a "lady of shimmering beauty, a brunette who doth teach the torches to burn bright." Long disturbed by her husband's churlish conduct on court, "Nicki" stopped coming to watch him. Since the birth of their first child, daughter Nathalie, in March 1975, she has also been reluctant to travel, preferring to stay at her parents' home in Brussels. This rift, those closest to Nastase concur, has troubled him enormously because he still loves his wife deeply and finds it difficult to cope with her disapproval.

When he first became a figure of international prominence in tennis, Nastase was looked upon with benevolent amusement and hailed as "a charming aberration," the sport's dashing contribution to the antiheroic culture. But eventually, over a period of several years, he severely taxed the public's affection. People tired of his act, at least the vulgarity. Psychologically, he was not well equipped to meet the pressures of being No. 1, which he was in 1973, and as expectations mounted, he acted up more and more.

Nastase could never make it as a loner, the way Jimmy Connors did in 1974. He needs people to cling to. When the compassion and forgiveness that he had come to take for granted disappeared, and he found himself sometimes ostracized, he was hurt and confused.

"There came a point when guys just started cold-shouldering him," explains Tom Gorman. "No matter how much you liked the guy, there was a limit to how much garbage you were willing to take on the court. It wasn't a conspiracy—everybody just sort of got tired of having their faces rubbed in it and started ignoring Nasty. That really got to him. When Nasty thinks people don't like him, he's a basket case."

Now Nastase, the colorful enigma, is at a crossroads. He has lived the life of a character you see in the movies. He has driven fast cars on two wheels and managed to get the fenders out of the way of obstacles just in time. He has enjoyed a go-go life-style, grabbing gusto like the man who only goes around once in a Schlitz commercial. He has survived ruckuses and tight squeezes relatively intact.

But he has come to the part in the film where the music turns slow and melancholy, and the beat hangs heavy on the heart. The hero has pressed his luck a little too far. The world he has tweaked is goosing him back. The authority he so blithely flaunted is out to get him. His playworld—even his fairy-tale romance—is unraveling around him. He's starting to realize that he might have irretrievably blown a good thing, and that awareness is eating away at him savagely.

The film is still shooting, the ending undecided. It depends most of all on Nastase himself, and how he comes to grips with his perplexing troubles. And because he is basically a very decent and feeling human being, those who know him hope he gets his act together in time to live happily ever after.

BASEBALL

THE END OF AN ERA

By Wells Twombly

From the San Francisco Examiner

In the late afternoon, as the smothered sun turns the smog a grotesque and eerie shade of pearl, cars are peeling off the freeway tentacles heading for the nation's most expensive box canyon. The freeways are clogged. Years after the Dodgers shattered one of the nation's most endearing myths by leaving Brooklyn and moving into the place where Don Julian Chavez, an early grandee, kept his goats, the city of Los Angeles still considers major-league baseball to be the epitome of chic.

It is the only city that has never experienced the trauma of having the manager fired. Few franchises can make that claim, because Walter Alston came with the territory. Now he is only another retired manager, an almost unthinkable statement. Down in the bowels of the stadium, below the flowered terraces and polished walks, the most durable of modern managers removes a pair of red-and-white checkered slacks with flared bottoms. He places a white double-knit sports shirt on a chair. On the floor are his white shoes, the type that tourists wear when they visit Los Angeles. It is his concession to modish. He speaks slowly, acting like a man who still feels mildly out of place.

This is a child of the Midwest with no prodding urge to be anything but a product of the prairies and the dark earth. Shooting pool, gunning for pheasants, and making cabinets in the basement are his only true passions. His home is Darrtown, Ohio (a hamlet of 279), and he has always felt uncomfortable in a city that worships such plastic temples as Disneyland, Knott's Berry Farm, and Grauman's Chinese Theatre.

As the only manager the Dodgers have known since they arrived in 1958, he was not, until this season, either idolized or largely criticized. He was simply there, a presence not to be examined, either for faults or great virtue. This was a stern father figure by the time he reached Los Angeles, although he had been badly criticized for being too weak with the old Brooklyn team.

He retired just the other day, after a mere 23 seasons in the sun, after only seven pennants and four world championships. As a player he was an utter failure, handling two chances for the St. Louis Cardinals at first base and making one error. In his only time at bat, he struck out against the great Lon Warneke of the Chicago Cubs. But he outlasted so many managers it was almost laughable. Every year he would sign a one-year contract, tempting fate as no other man had. They came and they went, but Walter Emmons Alston was indestructible.

This summer has been something different. They mocked him at Chavez Ravine, they hissed and they booed. They expected him to catch the super team of the decade, the Cincinnati Reds, and it didn't work out. Alston began to change, at age sixty-four, a time when most men start growing weary of the mundane world. When the press climbed on him, he told the sports editor of one newspaper that he was "an overstuffed pig." And that wasn't like the Alston the world had come to think it understood.

"There just comes a time when whatever you have been doing seems to be enough," he said, like the college graduate and former teacher that he is. "I've had a great 23 years and now Pete O'Malley is entitled to appoint the manager he wants. It's a new generation and I'm going to have a full-time job upstairs and be part of it."

Walter Emmons Alston has always been a symbol of the good earth, of middle America, of gently aging men who carry pictures of their grandchildren in their wallets. He was an uncomplicated soul who relaxed by playing billiards, shooting trap, or handcrafting furniture in his basement workshop.

There was a Hollywood-style story going around about him a couple of years ago, which made him laugh out loud. Go ahead and tell Lela (his wife), he said. If she believes that, then, he'd confess to anything. It simply wasn't true and the gossip columnists could all take a free-lance swim to Catalina Island during a riptide. If you stay in that town long enough, they'd link you up romantically to Lassie. Alston was the absolute last resort. Whoopeee!

This was baseball's championship square and Billy Graham would sin before he did. To most of his players, he was a reasonable man who did not show emotion to the troops unless it was absolutely necessary. Even at his age he is impressively strong, quite capable of intimidating a younger man. If you didn't play well for Walter Emmons Alston you were quickly out of the lineup. He had no regard for a player who didn't work hard and pay attention to his trade.

"The best part of the man," said Maury Wills, "is that he didn't know what racial prejudice is. He almost had to be told. I honestly believe that if you asked Walter Alston whether a man was a black or a white, he would have trouble trying to recall. He and Jackie Robinson clashed, but it was a meeting between strong-minded men. Jackie was just another tough guy. If you walked up to him today and asked if Jackie were black or white, he'd be stuck for an answer. Prejudice is foreign to the man because he doesn't think that way or see that way."

They sort of hoped that the Los Angeles Dodgers would make a serious run at the Cincinnati Reds this year and it didn't happen. Trades were made and nothing occurred. The customers no longer tolerated this most tolerable of men, this man whose mind saw no color line, who never deviated from the path of decency, who simply believed that managing well and playing well was the best answer. Someday they will commission a sculptor to put his strong, simple features onto a plaque and they will bolt that chunk of bronze to the wall at Cooperstown, where baseball stores all its holy relics. He couldn't possibly miss.

BASEBALL

FUNNY AND FANTASTIC: THAT'S FIDRYCH

By Jim Hawkins

From The Sporting News

Look, strutting around out there on the pitcher's mound. . . . It's a bird. . . . It's a plane. . . . No, it's a bird, after all. But not just any bird. No, indeed.

That, my friends, happens to to be The Bird—the one and only Mark Fidrych.

In all of baseball, there is no one quite like him. As a matter of fact, in this bicentennial season, he may be a historical first.

He is fresh. He is funny. He is fantastic. He has also been uncommonly successful.

You can count on the fingers of a single hand the pitchers who have enjoyed a rookie season comparable with Fidrych's.

It has been incredible.

Not since Denny McLain won 31 times in 1968 has any athlete so captivated the attention—and affection—of Detroit.

Fidrych has this town turned on. Everywhere you go, all any one wants to talk about is The Bird. He has already had at least one baby named after him and been the subject of a debate in the Michigan legislature.

He personally packed the park twice in six days, as 98,887 flocked to Tiger Stadium to see The Bird perform in those two games.

And Fidrych didn't let them down.

In fact, the Tigers' flaky, frizzy-haired phenom had the fans in a frenzy. When was the last time you saw 50,000 people refuse to leave their seats or stop clapping until a gangling twenty-one-year-old came back out on the field for a curtain call?

Tiger Manager Ralph Houk, who has been around a bit, readily admitted, "In all my years in baseball, I've never seen anything like it. I don't think even Walter Johnson started this fast."

But then there never has been anybody quite like The Bird before.

He talks to the ball, pointing it toward the plate like a dart, telling it where to go. . . . He gets down on his knees before every inning and pats the dirt on the mound into place with his left hand. . . . He sprints on and off the field and struts around the mound like a mad stork after every out, applauding his teammates and calling for the ball back.

He also wins.

Call it color. Call it charisma. Call it leadership. Call it inspiration. Call it magic. Call it what you will.

The Tigers win when Fidrych is on the mound—and that's what counts.

He's almost too good to be true.

This spring, the skinny, curly-haired rookie wasn't even on the major-league roster. For the first month of the season, he sat idle while Houk patiently waited for the right moment.

But once Fidrych got started, there was no stopping him. By early August, he owned 11 victories and had lost only 3. He had completed all but two of his 15 starts and compiled a gaudy earned-run average of 1.80, best in the majors.

Of course, he was named to the American League All-Star team and was accorded the unusual honor of starting for the AL as a rookie. He turned out to be the loser, granting the first two National League runs and four hits in his two-inning stint.

That performance brought forth no alibis from The Bird. "I was up for the game, felt good, wanted to throw good," he said.

Anyhow, his legion of fans quickly forgave him for that episode. For some time now, he's been touted as a leading candidate for Rookie of the Year.

The Bird's record remained flashy despite a couple of tough-luck defeats by 1–0 scores in July. Loss No. 3 was by 1–0 to the Orioles in Detroit on July 29. A crowd of 44,068 was on hand for that one, in which The Bird fanned eight, walked one, and yielded six hits while losing on an error.

Attesting to Fidrych's gate appeal is the attendance figure of 334,123 for his last eight starts through July 29. That's better than 41,000 per game.

But there's much more to the story of Mark Fidrych than mere statistics, impressive as those numbers may be.

Although he naturally prefers to think of himself as normal, Fidrych is a full-fledged flake.

He amused his teammates this spring by poking his finger into the coin return slot every time he passed the pay phone in the Tiger clubhouse—just in case someone had forgotten to reclaim his dime.

And he purposely spit tobacco juice all over the front of his own shirt. "I want the guys to know I chew," he exclaimed.

When the Tigers were in Anaheim in April, Fidrych discovered he couldn't buy a drink because the bartender didn't believe he was twenty-one, and Mark had left all his identification back in Detroit.

So Fidrych sought out Tom Veryzer and borrowed the Tiger shortstop's ID cards.

Now, Fidrych and Veryzer are not exactly identical twins. Fidrych is 6-feet-3 and skinny; Veryzer is 6-feet-1 with a stomach that tends to stick out above his belt.

And the bartender, who had seen that particular trick tried once or twice before, immediately noticed the discrepancies.

"What did you say your name is, young man?" he inquired as he carefully studied the documents bearing Veryzer's name spread out on the bar before him.

"I'm Mark Fidrych," The Bird replied proudly. "I pitch for the Detroit Tigers."

Or how about the night last winter when Fidrych went out on the town with one of his buddies back home in Massachusetts?

But let Mark tell it.

"We went to this discotheque," Fidrych recalled, "and we laid down on our backs and rolled around. The lady even introduced us and everything. She said, 'Ladies and gentlemen, you're now going to see a new dance step: The Fried Egg.'

"My friend invented it. We laid down on our backs and rolled around, bumping into each other. It was really neat to do. The people loved it. They clapped and thought it was great. But the bouncer asked us to leave. I guess he didn't think it was so funny.

"I don't care what people think about me," continued Fidrych. "Let them think what they want. I know I'm not a flake. I'm calmer now than I used to be. As you get your feet wetter and wetter, you tend to settle down. I fooled around more in the minors than I do now because everyone else down there was doing it, too. Here, a lot of guys are married."

When it was decided that Fidrych was definitely going to make the club, General Manager Jim Campbell took him shopping for a new wardrobe in downtown Lakeland.

After all, the Tigers don't travel in T-shirts and blue jeans—and that was the only thing Campbell had ever seen Fidrych wear.

When they arrived at the store, the Tiger GM told the high-strung young pitcher to pick out a couple of leisure suits. Fidrych first inspected a few of the cheaper models, and even then appeared to be awed by the price.

"Don't worry," said Campbell. "Pick out something you like. These are on the Detroit club."

Fidrych immediately sprinted to the high-priced end of the rack.

Fidrych drives a new green subcompact car, which he admits is totally out of character with his image.

"It fits my salary, not my personality," he explained.

"I'd like a motorcycle, but I'd really like to drive a truck. An old beat-up one. That's me. I'm a truck man."

If Fidrych wasn't playing big-league baseball, the hottest hero Detroit has had in years would probably be home in Northboro, Mass., outside Boston, pumping gas in a service station.

Even now, Fidrych prefers to pump his own gas and check the oil when he stops for a fill-up.

His suburban Detroit apartment is austere by big-league standards. He doesn't even have a telephone. "Sometimes I get lazy and let the dishes stack up," he confessed. "But they don't stack too high. I've only got four dishes."

Although he has been doubling the usual Tiger attendance every time he pitches at home, Fidrych is still making the minimum major-league salary of $16,500. And Campbell says he has no intention of tearing up The Bird's contract and giving him a big raise.

However, Campbell did admit the club might take good care of The Bird after the season ends.

But Fidrych seems satisfied.

"I don't need a raise," he insisted. "I'm still in the game. That's what counts."

In that one week when he filled Tiger Stadium twice and beat New York and Baltimore, Fidrych turned away five would-be agents. He explained, "Only I know my real value and can negotiate it."

But at the same time, he worries aloud about answering his daily deluge of fan mail because "10 letters times 13 cents is a lot of money."

It seems everyone loves The Bird.

That has been Fidrych's nickname ever since he first signed with the Tigers in 1974 and was sent to Bristol (Appalachian), where one of his teammates noticed that Fidrych bears a distinct resemblance to Big Bird on "Sesame Street."

But there's obviously a lot more to The Bird than his antics on the mound and his peculiar conversations with the baseball.

He's also one helluva pitcher.

"He's not quite as flaky as they say," insisted Houk. "When he's on the mound, he doesn't know there's anyone else around. He talks to himself to help his concentration. And as a rule, we play good in the field behind him. Players like to play behind a guy who throws strikes."

"At first, some opposing players didn't like it when he was out there talking," said rookie catcher Bruce Kimm, who has been behind the plate for each of Fidrych's efforts. "It really bothered Rico Carty of the Indians. But he pitches fast to them, so they know he's not playing games.

"He's got fantastic poise and great confidence," continued Kimm. "He's like a guy who's been around for 15 years."

"It's exhilarating being out there with him on the mound," said Tiger right-fielder Rusty Staub. "It's hard not to be up when he pitches. There's an electricity he brings out in everybody. Everyone can see the enthusiasm in Mark. He brings out the exuberance and youth in everybody.

"He's the most exciting thing I've seen," continued Staub, who has created a little excitement himself. "I've never seen a city turn on like this. I've seen Tommy Seaver go out and mow 'em down. But I've never seen anybody electrify the fans like this."

"The Bird has better concentration than Denny McLain," commented Mickey Stanley. "And concentration was McLain's strong suit."

The secret of Fidrych's sudden success is simple: Basically, he throws two pitches, a fastball and a slider. He keeps the ball down around the batter's knees and he consistently throws it over the plate.

Each team he has encountered has come away impressed. "The kid's not crazy," remarked Baltimore's Reggie Jackson, after Fidrych had blanked the Birds for his first big-league shutout. "He knows what he's doing. He gave me a couple balls to hit, but I wound up hitting 320-foot fly balls."

"He's good for baseball," added Brooks Robinson. "I hope he wins 30—but not against us."

Informed that Yankee catcher Thurman Munson had called him "Bush," Fidrych replied, "They can call me Turkey, they can call me Bush, they can call me anything they want. But my teammates don't call me Bush, and they're the ones who count.

"They're the ones who are making me. I don't make them. If I was making myself, I'd be striking out everybody. If they don't play well behind me, I'm not even here. I can't believe what these guys are doing for me. I feel so good. I don't know how to say thanks."

Before leaving the field after each victory, Fidrych darts from player to player, shaking hands with each of his teammates who took part in his latest success.

And when the fans refused to leave until he emerged from the dugout to take a bow after beating Baltimore, Fidrych tried to coax the rest of the team to come out on the field with him.

Finally, two security guards literally had to grab him and pull him out into full view of the capacity crowd, which immediaely responded with a standing ovation.

"I'm just loving it, I'm just loving it," said Fidrych as he sat on the floor in front of his locker, sorting through several boxes of fan mail. One of his teammates had placed a telephone on a stool beside him—just in case President Ford decided to call.

But what if this has all been just a dream? What if he wakes up some morning and finds he's really still in Evansville?

"What a dream!" The Bird exclaimed. "What a dream!"

GENERAL

THE WHITWAMS GO TO THE MASTERS

By Jolee Edmondson

From Golf Magazine

Fred Whitwam leered at the broken yellow line—stitches in the asphalt being consumed by the Winnebago at a law-abiding 55 miles an hour. It was four in the afternoon, and he had driven a grueling stretch since pulling out of the KOA at dawn. An abrupt transition from the clean sweep of freeway to a two-lane blacktop with roller-coaster curves made his fifty-four-year-old heart thump with apprehension. He was tired. He wanted nothing more than to steer the big domicile on wheels off the road and nap for 30 to 40 minutes.

But he resolutely stiffened his posture and stifled a yawn. A hundred more miles to the next campground. He rubbed the back of his neck and sternly told himself that he could make it, because floating at the back of his mind, always, was the vision of his destination: a lush plot of earth where the coloring book pink of azalea explodes against a blue sky. Where the scent of magnolia mingles with cool spring air to concoct an intoxicating whiff for smog-sore-nostrils. Where stately white homes stand out like Tiffany diamonds on green velvet. Augusta National.

Fred looked over at his wife, Ellen, a rather fleshy woman with tightly curled brown hair and tiny eyes that were always merry, laughing, as if she had just heard an acceptably risqué joke. She was in the passenger seat sipping gingerale through a straw and gleaning instructional information from the pages of *Golf Magazine*, conjuring up the image of a research scientist peering through a microscope. "Pa," she announced without glancing up, I think "I've found a cure for my duck hook. . . ."

Fred, stretching his increasingly flabby frame while one hand gripped the wheel, interrupted her, "Well, Mama, by my calculations we should be rolling into Augusta by eight tomorrow morning if we leave the campsite at 3 A.M. Just in time to watch the boys hit a few practice shots before the first round. I figure if we hit it right, when he's walking from the driving range to the putting green, we just might be able to angle a few tips from Arnie. He's that kind of guy, you know. Down to earth. He'd be real congenial about something like that."

The thought of standing face to face with Arnold Palmer made Ellen dizzy. Her mind was a collage of the legend in varying phases of body language—photos she had glimpsed through the years that had adhered to her psyche like lint to Scotch tape. She turned slowly to her husband, awe on her sun-crinkled face, and murmured, "Papa, I can hardly believe this is happening to us."

"Ha!" chortled Fred, leaning over and jostling her hand. "You will when we get there. Hey honey, why don't you go back and make me a peanut butter and jelly sandwich. I'm hungry as hell."

"One Gei-burger coming up," winked Ellen. An inside joke that they cherished with whimsical pride, snatching it out of their grab bag of homemade golf humor at every opportunity. It was Fred who first quipped the double entendre, and he thought it the cleverest pun this side of Henny Youngman, his favorite comic. He used the little *bon mot* to wow them at backyard barbecues and member-guest tournaments, never quite grasping why, in many instances, a feeble, forced smile was all that it garnered when he anticipated uproarious laughter.

Fred and Ellen Whitwam are to golf what an SRO audience is to a Broadway show; what window-shoppers are to windows; what men are to Raquel Welch; what racetrack touts are to Secretariat. Admirers in the purest form. Appreciative, charmed, engrossed, possessed perhaps, authoritative on the subject and slightly intimidated. Some folks in the couple's publinx circle called them fanatics, but Fred and Ellen took that as a compliment. "Fanatic," he would say pompously, "is just another word for elite fan."

The Whitwams met 25 years ago on a pitch-and-putt in Culvar City, Calif. Fred was pitching and Ellen was putting. After Fred executed his famous lob 20 feet from the cup, he noticed a lone woman crouched over her ball on a distant green. He liked her form. And to make a long, pretty dull story short, they fell in love and married a year later, moved to Azusa, where Fred became foreman of a fruit-packing plant, and bought a mobile home only a few blocks from the municipal golf course. Early in their union they decided not to have childen for fear that offspring might interfere with their games. A baby's cry has deterred many a birdie.

And so it was that for 25 years the Whitwams shared a bond that was beautiful, impregnable, and unbreakable. Golf.

On their fifteenth wedding anniversary, while sipping some bubbly over a lavish cake decorated with a likeness of Pinehurst #2, Fred toasted his bride with a promise, "In 10 years, honey, we're going to the Masters."

Thus began a decade of planning, dreaming, and saving. To the Whitwams and legions of devotees, the Masters is the ultimate—the royal event of golf, and Augusta National is Camelot. A realm, not a mere country club. Ellen set aside a cookie jar labled "Masters Money," and Fred brown-bagged it at work every day instead of splurging at Harry's Bar and Grill. They vowed to all the many regulars that they would bring home a bounty of newspaper clippings, slides, and autographs for their viewing pleasure . . . perhaps Fred could emcee a special dinner program recapping the glory of the Great Happening.

As the departure date drew near they dipped into their savings and leased a motor home and shopped for suitable sportswear. Fred got himself three pairs of Hush Puppies, Hawaiian print Bermuda shorts, checked button-down shirts, sunglasses, and straw hats the size of Texas. "If you're going to the Masters," he pronounced, "you might as well go in style."

Ellen indulged herself by purchasing several white canvas caps (for autographs), pastel-colored tennis shoes, stretch capris, and blouses with golf patterns. And of course, there was the investment in spectating paraphernalia.

Fred was cruising at a steady clip now. The road was unraveling and he thought he spotted a freeway junction ahead. A peanut butter and jelly sandwich was jammed in his mouth and he said thickly, "Yep, tomorrow we'll be there."

The next morning the Whitwams showed their gallery badges, which Fred had sent for months in advance, to the guard at the entrance of Augusta National. They were quaking with excitement. A mist fell on the grounds, and Fred's bare legs were prickly with goose bumps. But other than the illogical choice in clothing, he was as well-geared for the occasion as MacArthur was for World War II. Around his neck hung binoculars, an autograph book, a pen, and a bottle opener. His hands clutched a portable seat, an umbrella, and an ice chest stocked with soda pop and Gei-burgers. And from his back pockets sprouted the pairing sheet and the program.

The initial catatonic elation soon wore off, and the Whitwams were on their merry way, ready to explore and discover. The first item on their agenda was the practice tee, a strip of turf backdropped by the hallowed clubhouse—a structure that inspires visions of a graying Bobby Jones rocking on the veranda and Walter Hagen walking jauntily to the upstairs gentlemen-only lounge.

A worshipful crowd stood behind the ropes gazing at a string of pros hitting irons with crisp accuracy. It was Ellen who first viewed Palmer. He was at the far end of the tee, conversing with men in green jackets and pulling a cluster of clubs from his bag. "There he is!" she exclaimed. "Oh! He's hitching up his pants!"

Without breathing a word Fred led her toward Arnie, pushing through a group of miffed onlookers and muttering, "Fore please." They leaned against the rope and stared. After the target of their observations finished warming up, Fred beckoned him with his index finger, hoarsely whispering, "Over here, Arn!" Palmer, puzzled, strode over to Whitwam.

Fred flung his arm around him in a hugging gesture and said, "Jeez, it's good to see you, boy. Ha, ha, how're you doing? You going to win this thing? Listen, while I've got you here, the wife and I would like to ask you a few questions. We're both having problems with the old hook, you know, and I personally think the remedy lies in the grip. Would you mind telling us how to place our hands on the club to. . . ."

Good-natured as he is, Arnie found it difficult to cope with this encounter.

"Uh, well, I'd suggest that you ask your club pro about that. He'll straighten it out for you." He shook their hands and walked away.

"Did you hear that, Mama? We should ask our pro. How 'bout that? Straight from the mouth of Arnold Palmer. A real gem of advice. Hell of a nice guy . . . hell of a nice guy."

They scurried to the first tee and secured a perfect vantage point only five feet from the markers, where the intermittently Merry Mex was taking a few practice swings. When the starter announced his name he took his stance and smothered one down the middle. Above the polite round of applause billowed Fred's ecstatic war whoops. "Go get 'em, Lee! Murder 'em! Pour on some of that hot sauce! Never fear, the enchilada man is here!"

Obviously pleased with his drive, Trevino spouted, "You'd be surprised what this Mexican can do."

Whitwam poked Ellen and several other spectators, chuckling, "Did you hear that? 'You'd be surprised what this Mexican can do.' Ha! What a sense of humor. Terrifically funny guy. He's wittier than I thought. C'mon let's follow him for a few holes and then we can wait for Player and them down the line."

An hour later they were stationed on the knoll leading up to the fourth tee where Nicklaus was getting ready to hit. Fred studied the Bear's dramatic turn off the ball, the slow slide of the head, and the uninhibited right elbow. When Jack completed his swing Whitwam dropped his gear, gripped an invisible club, and tried to imitate the blond bomber's form. He stood there, his arms swishing back and forth, while the throng moved past him.

"Ellen," he intoned, "I'm convinced that the secret is in the pivot. Jack's got it down to a fine science. Man I wish I had his teacher."

Fred and Ellen absorbed as much of the Masters aura as possible. In an authorized picnic area they spread a tablecloth under a sprawling tree, devoured their lunch, and marveled at Ellen's autograph cap, black and blue with hurried signatures.

Toward evening they trooped back to the camper where Ellen did a light wash and prepared dinner while her husband, sublimely content over his panache as a spectator, dozed.

It was a peaceful night, the kind of noiseless eve that precedes calamity. For indeed, the following morning after the sputter of the alarm clock and a quick breakfast, the golf balls would hit the threshing machine, so to speak. The Whitwam's euphoric little world would explode. Ellen would discover that she had accidentally discarded their badges along with other odds and ends while washing. She would report what had happened to Fred. He would let out a glass-shattering "Whhhaaaattttt???!!!" And there would be a mad hunt for the laminated jewels in the trash bins throughout the campsite, to no avail.

"We'll just have to explain the whole situation to the guards at the gate and see if they'll let us in."

So they drove to Augusta National and accosted the first man in uniform they saw. "Hi," greeted Fred weakly. "The name is Whitwam as in wigwam." He began to plead, "Look, we're all the way from Azusa. Over two thousand miles we traveled for the Masters. And we lost our passes. We're honest, decent golf fans. Please. Give us a break. Let us in." Perspiration streamed down his red face and he was constricting the circulation in the guard's forearm.

"You don't know what this means to us, officer," whimpered Ellen.

But the guard shook his head, "Sorry."

"It's no use ," said Fred. "I can tell he won't budge. Our last resort is with the scalpers. You look on this side of the street and I'll search for one on the other side. Pay whatever they want."

They paced up and down the traffic-jammed byway for hours, but the usual parade of rip-off artists had disappeared—the law had no doubt dispersed them.

Finally, at the end of his rope, Whitwam started confronting those privileged weares of badges and proclaiming with the theatrical gestures of a Shakespearean actor, "Please. We're all the way from Azusa. Let me buy a pass for me and the wife. Name your price. I'll pay anything. Here, here's a hundred dollars. Please, I ask only for a drop of your milk of human kindness."

But no one succumbed.

Fred crossed the street and called Ellen. "Mama," he said wearily, "I don't know. It looks pretty hopeless. I've been wracking my brain about what to do. But I can't come up with a solution. We better try and get a room someplace and at least we can watch the rest of the tournament on TV."

There were no vacancies in Augusta, so the Whitwams crossed the state line to Aiken, SC., where they roosted in a motel called the Walk-On Inn with green phosphorescent lights over the doorways. Aside from a few cockroaches and the stench of tobacco in the linen, it was a luxurious room because it had a black-and-white set with a 24-inch screen.

On Saturday and Sunday Fred and Ellen propped themselves up in bed, flanking their ice chest and gazed at the network splendor before them. Fred wore his Hawaiian shorts and straw hat and peered through his binoculars at the action to simulate the feel of actual spectating.

And it wasn't long before they believed that they were in the midst of it all, in the majestic green yonder clapping and laughing and slapping the backs of their favorite pros between shots. Fred swallowed another sandwich and commented, "Yeah, that Jack's got a helluva pivot."

The Whitwams had been to the Masters.

BASEBALL

THE SHORT SEASON

By Jim Brosnan

From Playboy

Spring in Sarasota, 1975. Twelve years since I had taken a contract to camp on the shores of Tampa Bay. Property of the Cincinnati Reds, I had sweated under the west Bay sun at Al Lopez Field, named for the then manager of the White Sox who had had his own pitchers doing 50 laps a day across the way at south Bay's Payne Park. Señor Lopez would, within 60 days, trade one of his pitchers for me, inadvertently foredooming my career. Later that year, the White Sox management declared that I would never go to a spring-training camp at Sarasota if I insisted on writing about baseball while employed as a pitcher. It was in the contract! The silliest of prohibitions. I could have raced thoroughbred horses, operated a saloon, or written advertising copy for a living. That is: I could have gambled, pushed booze, or lied a lot for profit. But publish for laughs an insider's notes on game playing? That was an invitation to blacklisting.

What ego-pleasing irony, then, to be back in the Florida sunshine cruising in a rented LeMans down the west Bay's Gulf Boulevard, headed for a White Sox spring-training camp, where, as a freelancer on assignment, I would catch their pitch about the coming season and put it down.

Driving the Sunshine Skyway triggered heartburn memories of a bus trip to Payne Park with the Reds, who were scheduled for an exhibition game with the American League champion White Sox (they win a pennant every 40 years; you could look it up). I was at a physical peak then, thirty-one and flat-bellied and strong-armed, but there was the prospect of pitching that day. And so the mound fright, the worries over making the right pitches, making points with the manager and his coaches—making the team!—caused acid to rise while the bus wheels rolled.

Tooling down the North Tamiami Trail, I chewed a WinGel and missed the turnoff to Highway 301 that would have taken me right to the Sarasota Motor Hotel, "Winter home of the White Sox." I would be late, something I'd always avoided when pitching for those Sox in 1963, because Lopez fined tardiness at the rate of 10 dollars a minute. Don Gutteridge, a Lopez coach destined to inherit Al's job when the señor developed a stomach ulcer, would stand at the clubhouse door, grinning obscenely at panting players who plunged through just on time, beating the fine-tuned Gutteridge Timex.

Buck Peden, the 1975 White Sox PR man, was upset though powerless to punish me for blowing our 4-o'clock appointment. Buck Peden! A tidy little man, no match in stature for that catcher of the same name who called the signals in the only no-hitter I ever pitched as a professional (Fayetteville vs. Rock Hill, 1948). I asked this Buck for a pressbook, stat sheets, room numbers of selected Sox players, and directions to Arthur Allyn Field, where the club would work out until the Chunichi Dragons appeared for a Friday-afternoon exhibition game at Payne Park.

"You ought to do something on Nyls Nyman," said Buck. "He's the only phenom we have in camp this spring."

Well, now, bad news, indeed! The White Sox had finished a game but pragmatic fourth in the Western Division of the American League. Snobbish fans claimed that those Sox were not in the same aesthetic league with the champion Oakland A's. What's more, the Sox had, during the off-season, lost two true superstars, Dick Allen and Ron Santo, who had retired, taking away their power to hit homers and to draw customers.

How now in the new year could the Sox sell their pennant chances without a marching phalanx of phenoms in the flesh and under contract? For management, that's what spring training is all about—selling illusions to the folks back home.

Nyls Nyman the lone phenom? At least he had some credentials. Minor-league player of the year in 1974. Season's end sensation with the Sox. In five games, Nyls had batted .643, scored five runs, batted in four, and stolen a base. Then, he was drilled in the arm by a hard-throwing left hander, was removed to the hospital, and was through for a year, a bruised but wiser phenom.

My motel room was sandwiched between those of Buck Peden and Johnny Sain, the Sox pitching coach. Five phone calls convinced me that players and coaches alike had taken off for the day, to beach, golf course, movies, anywhere but the Sarasota Motor Hotel. Later, I was to learn that four of the five I wanted to reach were in a four-hour class devoted to Jose Silva's Mind Control Program. What's more, they were paying their own way through the course! Such unprofessional player behavior led me to ponder baseball's new breed. Since it was past five o'clock, I went off to have a martini. First of the season, 1975.

Dusk had already dropped a shroud on the deserted 10-story building that had been called the Sarasota Terrace Hotel when most players in spring training were white and all others were housed elsewhere. When Sox blacks were refused lodging in Sarasota in 1961, Sox owners bought the Terrace, built a motel behind it, and sold their costly mausoleum cheap to the county, which promptly closed it.

A White Sox white elephant, it towered over the two-storied motel lodges surrounding a rectangular courtyard that was half parking lot, half "recreation area." A thick hedge, bounded by palm and sea grape trees, separated automobiles from two shuffleboard courts and a tiny swimming pool shaped like a garbanzo bean and filled to the brim with several gallons of fresh water. Baseball players, for no sound medical reason, are discouraged from swimming during spring training. There was no chance of any Sox player tiring or drowning in the Sarasota Motor Hotel pool.

In the parking lot, a rookie outfielder named Kilpatrick had rolled his Riviera into the space beside my LeMans. On the Buick's front bumper was an extra license plate emblazoned with the owner's first name. In six-inch-high letters. CLEO. A pretty name. No doubt a left hander's name. But what kind of name is that for a phee-nom? The young Sox pitchers had solid jock-type names: Rich. Bart. Skip. Butch. Bugs. But backing them up was a potential lineup of Hugh, Lamar, Cleo, and Nyls.

At Walt's seafood house, the martinis went down well with oyster stew and stuffed shrimp. Burping appreciatively, I gleaned data from Buck's pressbook, a scorecard full of such wondrous achievements by Sox players in 1974 that one had to wonder how the club could have finished nine games out of first. More amused than informed by Peden's prose, I returned to the hotel and spotted Chuck Tanner in the parking lot. His greeting effusive, his heartiness unrestrained, Tanner was gray at the temples but little changed since we'd last been in camp together.

Seventeen years before, Tanner and I had played on the same Chicago team (the Cubs). An outfielder of limited skills, Chuck was a man of infinite bonhomie. Had his prowess at the plate equaled his conversational charm, Tanner would have been a .300 hitter in the

National League, just as he had been in the minors (Southern Association, 1951–54).

What Tanner had lacked in star talent he made up in attentiveness, curiosity, and enthusiasm. His managers liked that. Chuck's arm and legs and instincts were no more than competent, but he had good eyes and good ears and a good line. Good coach material, as they say in the biggies. Maybe too nice a guy to be a manager.

"Things have changed a lot, ol' buddy," said Tanner when I asked him what's new in the training-camp biz. "Not like the old days in Arizona, when you and Moose Moryn and Lee Walls used to stand around in the outfield waiting for the neons to turn on in Phoenix. Wait and see. We start working out at ten. Want to have breakfast at the Waffle Shop about seven?"

Baseball at sunrise! An unhealthy prospect. Might ruin my day. Tanner had been quoted as having been so eager to start this spring training that he had dreamed about baseball the night before the Sox pitchers reported to camp. His pitching staff was not the kind that pleasant dreams are made on, but Tanner's unnatural optimism admits of no nightmares. He greets each dawn with a grin.

I missed Tanner at the Waffle Shop. Watched Sox outfield Carlos May, dressed in a faded-blue-jean leisure suit, wolf down four scrambled and a side of sausage. Chipped my left incisor on a shell lurking in a pecan waffle. Lost my way to Arthur Allyn Field. Reminded myself that a bad start simply makes the adrenaline flow in an old pro. Reached the clubhouse door at the stroke of ten, stopped at the first locker on the left, said hello to Johnny Sain.

Sain is the best pitching coach in baseball, a crusader with a simple credo: The mechanics of pitching can be taught to anyone who can throw a baseball 55 feet.

In a highly conformist profession, Sain is a genius and therefore a maverick. He has refused to coach for a manager he didn't like (Yogi Berra of the Yankees). He resigned rather than work for an owner he didn't respect (Calvin Griffith of the Twins). Yet Sain can have any job he wants off his track record (champion staffs at New York, Minnesota, and Detroit) and because his pitchers speak of him with rare affection. In a sport where "coaches" are more tolerated than admired by players, Sain has received public testimonials from pitchers Jim Bouton, Dennis McLain, and Jim Kaat, all of them mavericks in their own right but all of them stars under Sain.

Hawking a stream of tobacco juice into a paper cup he was carrying, Sain explained what I should have known back when I could have used it.

"I can teach the mechanics and give you ideas and help you learn from experience. But pitching is control and control is subconscious. You can't think about what you're doing and do it the way it should be done. When you're pitching right it looks instinctive, but it's the result of all these things you've learned and selected for yourself and discarded the crap that isn't for you. If I tell a pitcher to go out there and use a certain pitch in a certain situation, hell, it's his ass if it doesn't work. So he has to believe it will work. I can't make him do what he should do."

The most useful thing Sain does for pitchers is to teach them spin mechanics. It is the spin on the ball as it enters the plane of the strike zone that makes it so difficult to hit solidly. Putting the proper spin on the ball so that it sinks, sails, slides, hops, or drops is what the mechanics of pitching is all about. In 1947, Sain invented a simple inexpensive gadget to help pitchers learn the principles of proper spin. Recently, he devised a control target (a three-inch-thick cement block in a pressed form of two-by-fours weighing 300 pounds, with the strike zone painted on its surface) at which anyone can throw a properly spinning ball and learn to pitch.

"There ought to be one in every camp. Hell, in every playground. Teach a boy how to spin the ball and let him practice. Baseball needs something like this. It's tougher now more than it ever was to pitch in the big leagues. I've talked to the commissioner's office, to everybody I can think of about this. Maybe it's too simple. Nobody listens to me but pitchers."

Big John! Where were you when I needed you?

The two-hour workout had started; the first intrasquad game of the spring would follow. I strolled through the clubhouse sniffing familiar smells.

A hundred lockers. Twice what the spring-training roster called for. Less than what would be needed when the minor leaguers reported in a month. Each of the occupied lockers had extra uniforms that were provided by the club, extra shoes and gloves that were free from Adidas and Rawlings, an assortment of personal belongings. No fan mail. But on the top shelf of most lockers was a hair drier!

A hair drier!

Ty Cobb would have cursed. Roger Hornsby would have raged. Christy Mathewson would have let his hair grow long. (Pitchers have always been a progressive breed.)

The sound of calisthenics drifted into the trainer's room. Charley Saad, quartering oranges for the midday break, grinned and agreed that not much had changed in his line of work.

"So what does a trainer need, hah? Good ears to listen to their troubles. Good sense so he can tell 'em what they want to hear. Good hands so he can give 'em a little flesh. That's what they want. That's what they need. Just like anybody else."

A chunky man, quick on his feet, Saad has the soulful eyes and clutching gestures of a Lebanese merchant. Give him an opening and he'd sell you the sheet off the rubbing table. He swept a hand along the wall counter, pointing out his supplies for the camp.

"Two gallons of half-and-half baby oil and Sloan's Liniment to get 'em loose, 36 pounds of Atomic Balm to get 'em warm. Twelve tubes of Capsolin to get 'em hot. Ascriptin with Maalox for hangovers. Geritol, wheat germ, vitamin C. Whatever they want. Can it hurt? They're grown-ups. Bill Melton thinks vitamin B-12 shots help his sciatica. That's OK. If Bill thinks it's good for him, I'll give him one."

Fingering my bicep, Saad leaned over to whisper: "Y' know the thing that worries 'em all? They say to me, 'Charley, will this end up in cancer?' Y' know? Tendonitis. Chipped bone. Pulled muscle. Ankle sprain. Whatever. They worry they're gonna get cancer from some hurt.

"Y' know what you never do? Never, never tell a guy the medical name of the thing that hurts him. God, he's right into the anatomy book looking it up. Saying it wrong. Worrying over it. Driving himself nuts."

Sox players call Saad Uncle Charley. Like most big-league-baseball trainers he is more psychologist than physical therapist.

"Hey, a monkey can tape. Put a bell on the spool. One turn, rring! Two turns, rring! The monkey slaps the guy on the ass and sends him out to play!"

Buck Peden's pressbook didn't even list Uncle Charley's name. Which indicates how little the front office knows about what goes on in the clubhouse. The trainer is usually the first man to know whether or not a player is able—or willing—to play on any given day.

"Hey, big 'un," said Saad, handing me an orange slice to suck, "why don't you check out their heads? We got a lotta good bodies down here this spring. But what kind of heads we got?"

Sain worried about hands that could spin a ball properly. Saad worried about heads. Sox management worried collectively about an arm that might or might not work to their satisfaction.

Roger Nelson, an off-season acquisition from Cincinnati, had a history of arm troubles. What Nelson didn't know was that the Sox had promised a young pitcher to the Reds if Roger made the team in the spring. Was his thirty-two-year-old pitching-savvy head worth a twenty-year-old's hard-throwing arm?

"The Sox make you feel like a human being. They talk to you like you're a person."

Sure, Rog. They tell you all the facts you need to know.

"When I was healthy on the mound, I never caught my lunch, never got belted out of the ball park. But my whole career has been bad luck. I've tore up my shoulder muscles, front and back. Tore up my elbow. Had operations. Used all kinds of stuff to keep down the pain."

Nelson sipped Gatorade from the iced tub filled with the team's two-and-a-half gallon daily ration. Tall, dark-haired, "Spider" Nelson had had a big season in 1972 at Kansas City, where he was equally famous for Tacos a la Nelson, a gustatory delight published in Royals Recipes, the K.C. team's cookbook. Since then, Spider had had two poor years in a row and was obsessed with doubt, an affliction at least as bad as a sore arm to the Sox. John Sain, a disciple of W. Clement Stone, preached Positive Mental Attitude to all his staff. To Sain, self-pity ruins more pitchers than the hanging curveball.

I wished Nelson luck, made a date for dinner with Jim Kaat, a pitcher with no doubts whatsoever, and walked out to diamond number one to watch the intrasquad game. Spring-training games are rarely memorable, their statistics meaningless. In the spring, it's truly not whether the players win or lose but how they play the game that counts. And which bigwig sees them.

In the bright sun, a scattering of fans watched for free. A pair of braless teen-agers measured the pitches and pitchers, the clouts and the clouters. (Wonder if groupies take spring training. Or need it.) Bill Melton hit a grand-slam homer late in the game. Hit it off Roger Nelson. In the tiny manager's room, half filled with team equipment, Chuck Tanner said everybody looked good, everybody was hustling just fine and the Sox would be better than ever in 1975.

"Have a couple of martinis for me tonight, Chuck. Having dinner with Kaat."

"Have a couple, anyway. He'll watch."

"Drinking is not a spectator sport," I reminded him.

Jim Kaat may be the only pitcher in baseball history who has won over 200 games but doesn't smoke, doesn't drink, and doesn't screw around on or off the mound. A leader in the Fellowship of Christian Athletes, a successful investor, "Kitty" Kaat considers pitching satisfactory only if he wins a complete game and finished it in 90 minutes or less. Tall, blond, well-built, he has the arrogance of a dedicated evangelist, a hard-nosed competitor, and a smart businessman. Some people like him, anyway.

We ate Italian, at a local shopping center's only restaurant. Kaat drove his van, an Econoline with the floor boards, inner walls, and ceiling covered in green-and-white shag carpeting. There were color-coordinated curtains. The horn was half a baseball. The tape deck played, not music, but a golf lesson recorded by Jim Flick, a teaching pro from Florida.

"Took up golf a couple of years ago. Want to play to a two by the time I'm through pitching. I listen to the lessons whenever I'm driving the van. Having a goal gets me going in the morning, you see."

We had ordered lasagna, talked about pitching coaches (twice Kaat had won over 20 games in a season, both times under Sain), and switched the conversation over coffee (milk for Kitty) to the Fellowship of Christian Athletes.

"At Minnesota, the Twins had the largest number of nonsmoking teetotalers in the game. We got it together and it spread around. Some managers might be afraid we're trying to separate the good guys from the bad guys, but that's not how it works. For instance, I'd go from locker to locker on Saturday and let everybody know what room we'd have for the Sunday chapel. Everybody's welcome. The FCA doesn't shy away from junkies and drunks and shack-up artists. Last season, every man on the team dropped in at least once."

Some of my fondest Sunday-morning memories are of gentle hangovers that followed Saturday-night victory celebrations. Poor Kitty. He'd never have one.

"I'll tell you," Kaat unexpectedly confessed. "I once had a beer and I puked all over a cigar back behind my family's home in Michigan. But in a strict Christian home, smoking and drinking were the kind of habits that were taboo. I never really got into them and didn't have to give 'em up."

Kaat was thirty-six. At that age, the average athlete regrets even occasional debauching and begins to doubt the purity of his bodily essences. Did Jim Kaat feel any anxiety about spring training?

"No. I've never worried about my job in the spring. Always had one or so I thought. You take Roger Nelson, now. If I ever get into his position, I'll probably hang 'em up and go to coaching. For Nelson, six weeks of spring training is a whole season. Either he makes it or he's out on his can."

I marveled at Kaat, his equanimity, his self-confidence. In profile, his nose was like carved stone, down which he'd slide an ice-blue glance. But I had more empathy with Nelson, whose insecurity was frightening and debilitating but normal. Besides, the Spider wore glasses. I like that in a pitcher.

Dawn came up with thunder and rain and the certainty in my mind that Chuck Tanner would forgo breakfast, sleep in, and dream about World Series rings. In the baseball biz, they are the ultimate status symbols. (Mine is forever falling off my finger at cocktail parties.) In the Sox clubhouse, a couple of young pitchers stood in front of the wall-length mirror, blow-drying their hair into a manageable shape on which to fit the White Sox red-billed caps. I asked Jack Kucek to step outside and tell me some stories. Belying his dark locks, Kucek was the "fair-haired boy of the spring camp." The pitcher's version of phee-nom fair-haired boys of past Sox camps included Rich "The Goose" Gossage and Bill "Bugs" Moran. Kucek had no distinctive nickname. Some people called him "Flaky," but that is a general sobriquet applied to any nonconformist in the game.

"I'm a weird case," Kucek blushingly admitted. "I understand my own mind. Nobody else does."

Kucek was a hot-shot college pitcher who jumped from Miami University (Ohio) to the majors in one season. Nothing unique and mostly due to Tanner and Sain's passion for seeing strong-armed kids in action. Young Jack won a game for Tanner in 1974. He also demonstrated a splendid imagination and a knack for getting ink from the press.

"My Uncle Zeddo's helping me," Kucek would say. "Zeddo had a wooden leg and he died when I was eight. But he is with me on the mound whenever I'm pitching. He was there when I signed my contract. Tanner was smoking this big cigar, turning on the charm, and I was digging it a little but couldn't make up my mind. Zeddo said that if Tanner shifted his cigar from one hand to the other in the next 10 minutes, then I should grab the pen. Chuck did, and I did, and pretty soon I'm humming in the bigs."

During the intrasquad game, I'd seen Kucek warm up on the side lines. It made this old pitcher's arm hurt just watching and listening to the kid's hummer. I wonder if he had any novel theories about getting in shape, because he still had some baby fat on his belly.

"I read," he said, "where a half hour of sex is worth an hour of jogging."

And, with splendid timing and a charming leer, he added: "I'm getting two hours running every night."

The kid's future was so bright it brought tears to my eyes.

"You know," he said, "how guys leave girls mementos of the occasion? A tip, a present, an autograph? I write 'em a poem when I split. Right off the top of my head. Surprising how they never seem to forget me."

He was a natural for the Jose Silva Mind Control Program that many of the young Sox players were attending. Asked by Rich Herro, the program director, to put himself into a Beta state of consciousness (a sort of self-hypnotic spell), Kucek responded with wild will.

"Drove myself right through Beta and down to Delta. Rich

couldn't get me out with the password. Had to bang me on the head about 30 times."

Did Kucek think the program would do him any good, make him a better pitcher?

"I'm twenty-one," he retorted, "nothing's farfetched to me."

Psychological conditioning is not new to big-league baseball. Autosuggestion, or "psyching up," is common: Hypnotism has been tried by many players and by one whole team (the St. Louis Browns); Caribbean-born players have been known to summon a voodoo doctor (brujo) to cast out the spirit (obeah) disturbing their professional performance; psychoanalysis was tried by the Chicago Cubs on a batter (Bob Ramazzotti) who, once beaned, was inordinately afraid of a pitched ball. (The doctor declared his patient perfectly normal and sent him back to the dugout.)

In the spring of 1975, the Silva Mind Control Program had already had 400,000 graduates. They included one big-league pitcher, Bart Johnson of the Chicago White Sox. Handsome, articulate, and hyperactive, Johnson was a bullpen star at twenty-one, a pitching flop at twenty-two, a dropout from the game at twenty-three. In 1974, rejuvenated by his Silva course, Bart made such an impressive comeback that Chuck Tanner figured him to be a regular starter, a potential staff leader, and, at twenty-five, the key to the future championships.

"I used to get by just blowing smoke," Johnson said when I asked him to comment on his whirligig career. "Come in from the bullpen and just throw fastballs. Had a curve but lost it. For two years, I kept looking for it instead of listening to Sain."

We stood just outside the clubhouse. Johnson literally talked in circles, walking around me, chatting and gesticulating, answering one question in the northwest quadrant of his orbit, illustrating a point by swinging a phantom seven iron at an imaginary golf ball, pondering another query in the opposite sector of his interview circuit, delivering his reply as if he were delivering a pitch, complete with follow-through.

"Pitching is really more fun than throwing. It's like I'm carving out a piece of action sculpture on the mound. I program myself to throw strikes, it's that simple. I've got good stuff, so I just put it in the right place and it works. I can do the programming the night before, go over the hitters and how I'll pitch to 'em the next day."

Johnson says the idea of "programming" a game is perfectly natural.

"It sounds like you're making a robot out of yourself, programming your computer—your brain—to pitch. But that's really what every pitcher does, anyway, without thinking about it."

Unlike his conversational style, Johnson's pitching form is right out of the *Spalding Baseball Guide*, smooth and effortless, with little wasted motion. The mind conditioning of the Silva program gave Johnson the needed self-control to harness his talent.

"I used to blow my cool at umpires. Didn't do me any good, couldn't change their call no matter what, right? Now, I know they don't miss a call, because they're fixing the game or because they've got a hard-on for me personally. But I'd yell at 'em, anyway, till I was told it would cost me 250 bucks if I did it. Well, I'm not paying any fine for an umpire's mistakes, right? So I'd stop yelling. Out loud. But I'm still yelling in my mind, see. So I've lost my head, my concentration, my control. It's all gone. Today, I just accept it and forget about it. Wind up and pitch."

Johnson's nervous energy and too-much-too-soon success led to other ego problems and a roisterer's reputation.

"I'm married since I was seventeen," he said, raising an eyebrow, "so I might figure to have missed some of life, right? But I didn't. Right? But I've cut down on that because I really learned to like being responsible. To my kids. To my wife. Hey, I used to have an argument at home, go to the park, and I couldn't even pitch! Now, I just block out the fight. Get on the mound. Let 'er rip. Easy."

Rich Herro sells the mind-control course with the claim that it helped him take seven strokes off his golf score. Bart Johnson went off to see if he could get his down to scratch. Another intrasquad game was on tap, but pitchers sure of their jobs seldom stick around in spring training to watch the Nelsons and Morans and Kuceks fight for theirs.

But if Johnson and Kaat were off playing golf (on separate courses—different strokes for different folks) and Wilbur Wood the knuckleballer was in a boat fishing and not even thinking about the Chunichi Dragons who would be waving at his butterfly pitches within 48 hours, there were 20 other pitchers and six catchers and 11 infielders and 10 outfielders to play the game or watch from the bench just in front of stands half-filled with spectators, most of them connected in some way with the club. Up and down the right-field foul line they'd tramped, from clubhouse to diamond and back.

HARVEY WINEBERG: the player's agent who got outfielder Ken Henderson a $90,000 contract, down from Chicago to sit in the sun and watch his man play ball. "Don't call us an agent," said Harvey. "We're a full-service representative who helps 'em get a contract, lays out a budget, cuts down on their taxes, advises them on investments, and keeps 'em out of financial trouble. None of our players has ever bought a house without seeing us first. Most agents are percentage guys. They take their money and run. We want an ongoing relationship on a mutual 90-day cancellation agreement. If we don't like the way they're living or they don't like our way of doing things, we split. No hard feelings. They don't owe us a dime."

DON UNFERTH: the pale-faced Pale Hose traveling secretary, working so hard that he had no time to tan. "We haven't lost a day to rain in two weeks," said Unferth. "So I guess the players are earning their money. Know what they get in spring training nowadays? Nineteen-fifty a day meal money. Sixty-nine-fifty a week for incidentals. If they live out, don't stay at the hotel they get $10.40 extra per day and $12.50 a week as an additional supplement. Marvin Miller's done some job on fringe benefits since he's been head of your organization."

(Let's hear it for Marvin Miller!)

ROLAND HEMOND: the White Sox general manager, a harried little hustler trying to sell a rundown organization to a quondam fandom that traditionally supported losers and did not believe it would get, or deserved, any better. "We're all into PMA. Clement Stone sends us literature and we distribute it in the clubhouse. We urge our people into psychocybernetics. We're high on the mind-control program. I had to arrange baby-sitters for two of our guys the other night. Heck, I was gonna baby-sit myself, if I couldn't find one."

HARRY CARAY: ruddy, raucous, ribald, the onetime "voice of the St. Louis Cardinals," whose success as the White Sox broadcaster had had a critical influence on the Tanner-Hemond management team. He had trailed by a retinue of paunchy middle-aged men who looked as if they had tried to follow Caray day and night, a challenge even for young men. I asked Caray if I could buy him a drink and he said no.

"We'll have a drink, but no broken-down old relief pitcher is going to pick up my tab. Come out to the beach tomorrow and we'll lift a couple to old times."

In the clubhouse later, puffing on an end-of-the-workout cigar, Tanner fed the press some well-chosen words. Tanner has an inexhaustible supply of hope that offends cynical sports writers. None would buy the message painted on a clubhouse sign: A CHAMPIONSHIP—WHY NOT? The sign hung over a door that opened on a blank brick wall.

"Breakfast at seven, big Jim?" Tanner asked me. Again.

Well, why not? I could program my brain to fool my body into thinking it should be ready to go at dawn.

At Walt's, I chewed on a gin-soaked lemon twist. Scratched the first peeling skin of the spring off my nose. One more day till the exhibition season. Thirty-two games till the regular season began. One hundred and sixty-two scheduled games till the start of the league playoffs. No reason so far to think that the Sox, in their seventy-fifth season, would get to play almost 200 games and earn those World Series rings.

Too many questions unanswered: Melton's back? May's legs? Nelson's arm? Wood's knuckles? Was Nyls Nyman a true phee-nom? (Was Jack Kucek?) Was Johnson's comeback a one-year wonder? Were there tangible benefits to be had from PMA and Silva Mind Control? Could Harry Caray talk enough Sox fans into buying tickets to see Chuck Tanner's new-style club so that Roland Hemond could meet the payroll all year long?

At 7 A.M., the hotel courtyard was dark and silent, the palm fronds fibrillating, the shuffleboad court damp with dew. But Chuck Tanner was all sunny smiles, already turned on by the day's prospects.

"Every spring I expect to win the pennant. Every day I expect to win the game. Call me an incurable optimist, if you like, but that's the way I am."

At the diner, Tanner put his arm around the proprietor's shoulders, chucked the waitress's chin, glad-handed two bleary-eyed customers, waking the place up and cheering the people on to work.

"I'm a salesman. That's what I do best. Getting a chance to be a manager meant one thing to me. I got a chance to sell some young guys on how to get to heaven. 'Cause that's what the big leagues are. Heaven. Took me eight years to make it and I wasn't disappointed. And if I see a kid wants it bad enough, I'm gonna bust my ass to help him make it."

We ate eggs and sausage and grits. Lots of grits.

"My first job. Davenport, Iowa. I tell my kids, 'Listen, goddammit, everyone of you is goin' to the big leagues if I have to bust your asses to do it. But we're gonna do it my way.' This is 1963, see. So I tell 'em, 'Go, get a crew cut. No wearing sweat socks off the field. No goddamn T-shirts on the street!' One kid has this hair drier in his hand. I grab it. Throw it at the wall. Yell at him, 'Go see a barber.' A kid named Sollami comes up wearing Bermuda shorts. I yell, 'Go get some pants on. You can't go to the big leagues in goddamn Bermudas.' Jesus, I was a hard-ass. But we looked like winners and we were winners and a couple of 'em really did make it."

Tanner smiled his top sergeant's smile, let it relax to a softer grin.

"But then I got a triple-A job in 1970 and I had to change my attitude. Hell, I had the raggediest bunch of guys, the misfits, the drunks, guys coming down from the big leagues, playing out the string. Bo Belinsky, Dennis Bennet. That kind of guy. What a crew. They'd ask me, 'What are the rules? Curfew? Things like that.' I'd say, 'The rules are whatever I say they are.' And I had different rules for everybody. If some guy on the way down wants to drink a case of beer every day? OK. Some nineteen-year-old kid, though, I'm all over his ass, 'cause he's going up, not coming down. I'd say, 'I don't give a damn what you do till that game starts, but between those white lines we're gonna have us some fun. And the only way to do that is to win. Losing ain't no fun.'

"Well, hell, we blew that league apart."

That winter, Tanner and Roland Hemond took over the White Sox.

"When Roland and I came up here, this club didn't have shit. No farm system. A team that just lost 106 games. Guys that couldn't play. Guys that didn't want to play. We had to make trades, make plans, start building, start getting the message to the fans. I'm out making appearances everywhere.

"One night, I'm in Appleton, Wisc., snow up to my ass. The next night, I'm in Harvey, Ill., a hell of a long drive. And what kind of reception do I get? I walk into Rube's Sportsmans Club. Bar-restaurant type of place. It's jammed. Guys drinking, cussing, arguing, stuffing themselves with kapusta and kielbasa and all that good Polish food. I ask Rube where's the meeting. He says, 'This is it. This is the business end of the meeting. Sit down and eat. We'll call you when we're ready.'

"So, they're drinking more booze, eating more food, cussing and yelling louder than ever. Finally they call me up and I start walking by the tables. And some guy yells, 'How the hell can you trade Aparicio?' And a guy yells, 'What's your next stupid move?' And another guy screams, 'Manager my ass!' So I'm thinking, What the fuck's going on here? I'm standing up there and a guy yells, 'We're Cub fans. The Sox are shit!'

"Well, hell, I start yelling right back at them. 'You don't have to listen to me. Go on, get your asses on out. I came 60 miles just to talk to you dummies and that's what I'm gonna do.'

"An hour and a half we're screaming at each other. They love it. I love it. At the end, some guy raises his mug and says, 'Next year, White Sox Park.' And they have been coming ever since. By the busloads."

By 1972, the White Sox were making money and Tanner was major-league manager of the year. The fans loved him because he talked their language. The press liked him, because he gave them something worthwhile to write about. The players respected him for crediting them for his success and because they knew that his image of Mr. Good Guy was only partially accurate.

"I've chewed ass. I've fined guys. I've banged heads on the clubhouse wall. But I do it in private. I don't make a big thing over it. And I forget it the next day. Off the field, anybody who knocks any of my players is gonna have to deal with me. I may have ripped a guy off in private, but nobody is going to rip him off in public, because it's not just him that's hurt by the press and radio and TV. It's his family that gets hurt and that's not fair. Hell, I know I'm gonna forget about what's said in 24 hours. But readers and listeners and viewers remember that shit forever.

"I'm a family man. I'm a family manager. We don't have dissension on the White Sox. We have family problems. Just like any fan does. Hell, we have divorces, bankruptcy, hangovers, accidents, disease. Ball players are human, just like fans. Some players don't like others. They cut each other up. And what I do is get 'em to talk to me, so I can straighten everything out. Some groups of players are easier to handle than others. My first two years in the majors were easier than the next two."

For Tanner, triumph and trouble were tied up in the same package, the talented and temperamental Dick "Richie" Allen. In 1972, Allen was the best player in baseball, the key to Chuck Tanner's best record as a major-league manager. In the following two years, Allen was the highest paid but least disciplined player in the game, a man who alienated some Sox fans and who wrecked Tanner's can-do-nothing-wrong reputation. Awed by Allen's talent, Tanner could not control the man's temperament. Eventually, Tanner took responsibility for Allen's failures, the club's disappointing record in 1974, and the necessary shake-up in personnel for the new season.

"Dick Allen is an artistic genius," Tanner insisted, grinding his cigar butt in my grits. "It was my pleasure to be his manager. Now, we go from here."

Tanner deserved kudos for graciousness. Or at least a fresh supply of cigars. What kind?

"I smoke Churchills when they're free. And White Owls when I'm buying."

I bought him one and we went off to the ball park.

Roger Nelson pitched batting practice, gritting his teeth but throwing loosely. Jack Kucek, his arm strong from pitching winter ball in Puerto Rico, humped up on a couple of hitters, grinning as they swung, missed, and groaned. Ken Henderson hit 90-grand line drives. Buddy Bradford clouted cheaper but longer flies into the trees. Carlos May ran and ran, as if his thickly muscled legs never ever had hurt.

Red-faced from the hot afternoon sun, I drove to Lido Beach to see Harry Caray in his natural habitat. Caray is unique among broadcasters, his own man, a fan's fan. He admits that his mouth sometimes has a mind of its own. The Sandcastle's poolside cabana bar was cool, the nearly topless waitress was accommodating and Harry was soon holding court, handing down opinions:

On the Necessity of Spring Training: "Spring training is bullshit. Two weeks is all the players need to get ready. It's the fans that need spring training. You gotta get 'em interested. Wake 'em up. Let 'em know that their season is coming, the good times are gonna roll."

On Chuck Tanner, manager: "Tanner is a great salesman. He could sell anything. Personable, enthusiastic, full of bullshit. And he was a hell of a young major-league manager. One of the best I've ever seen. And I said so. Then he sold his soul to Richie Allen. Which made him a bad manager. And I said so. Chuck will admit privately he was wrong about Allen. But he's afflicted with that old Nixon syndrome—loyalty above integrity."

On His Overly Publicized Feud with Tanner: "Chuck wants to be the big man in town. But, you know, I told him, 'Chuck, there's no way you're going to be as popular in Chicago as I am. No way! You can win 162 games and I'll be cheering all the time. But in the end, there will be a million people who will remember Harry Caray talking about the team.' "

On Silva Mind Control for Ball Players: "Hey, the less a ball player uses his brain, the better he's gonna be. A big-league ball player is a natural, or he should be. If he hasn't got the natural talent, he shouldn't be out there."

On the 1975 White Sox: "I wish I knew what Tanner and Hemond are trying to do. They might have a team on opening day with only one black in the lineup! The team could be pretty good. But it could be pretty bad. So bad, the price will drop and Hemond and his bunch will jump in and buy the team cheap! Pretty wild speculation, isn't it? Well, if I was good at predictions, I wouldn't be working for a living."

On the Necessities of Life: "Booze, broads, and bullshit. If you got all that, what else do you need? I only wish I'd known I was gonna live this long. I'd have taken better care of myself."

I drank to that. Picked up the tab. Paid it. Harry didn't fight too hard. But what the hell, I'm bigger than he is.

The Chunichi Dragons came to play at Payne Park on March 7. As the 1974 major-league champions of Japan, the Dragons won a spring-training trip to Bradenton, Fla. To a man, they were enthusiastic about playing on grass. Grass infield. Grass outfield. Firm, green natural turf. In Japan, the ball-park surfaces are more dirt than sod. Legendary gardeners as they are, the Japanese don't waste much grass on playgrounds.

Politely, most American pros agree that playing on grass is good. It's traditional and it's easier on the feet than plastic carpeting. Still, grass infields can be lumpy and bumpy, full of tricky bounces, and bad hops that lead to errors. In truth, many shortstops lie about the advantages of grass.

In the right-field stands behind the White Sox bullpen I feasted my eyes on the grass of Payne Park and watched the game with the No. 1 White Sox Fan of the spring, Rube Walczak, proprietor of the Sportsmans Club in Harvey. Rube's qualifications as a fan are indisputable. He buys $2,700 worth of tickets for box 77 at White Sox Park every season. He flies a dozen or more fans to Sarasota every spring to check out the club. He sponsors six busloads of fans who make the trip from Harvey to Sox home games. His station wagon bears a license plate: WS 14 (Bill Melton's uniform number).

He takes his role as fan seriously: "In September of 1972, I'm visiting the old country. Mszana Dolna, 50 kilometers outside Krakow. Couldn't get any word on what's happening. I know we're only five games out and I should be back here helping. Finally get to Rome, check the American paper, and we're dead. Oakland's got it sewed up. It's all my fault."

Too often, a fan can't help much. Chunichi whipped Chicago 1–0. It was a dull game. One memorable moment. In the fifth inning, a Japanese batter sliced a hard line drive into the stands. Hit a woman in the face. Splat!

Watch it, Rube! Being a fan can be dangerous to your health.

It was some weeks later when I caught up with the White Sox. Drove up from Indian Shores to Clearwater to watch them play the Phillies. For all intents and purposes, spring training was over. The euphoria and optimism of the first weeks had dissipated. All the managers who had announced that all the players in camp had a chance to make the team were now revising their expectations and settling on a roster to open the season. The Sox had taken 50 men to camp. They would keep 25. Most of them had been with the losers of 1974.

Spring training can be like that. Disappointing to the management. Disillusioning to the fans. Dismaying to players. Trauma was about to hit.

Roger Nelson had pitched well. Had given up two earned runs in 16 innings. Had announced on March 17 that he was ready for opening day. He never made it. The Sox released him.

Jack Kucek had thrown hard but wildly, was inconsistent, and wondered aloud if he'd like pitching in Denver, the 1975 Sox's AAA farm team. Kucek made the final cut of the spring but was, indeed, in Denver by May.

Bart Johnson hurt his back on March 14. He didn't pitch again for three months.

Wilbur Wood's knuckleball was unhittable in the spring, but he lost 10 of his first 12 decisions during the season.

Nyls Nyman was almost phenomenal in Florida, but he was out of the regular lineup by mid-May.

Even in Clearwater's Jack Russell Stadium, back on that hot late-March day, there were signs of anxiety in the Sox's key men. Chuck Tanner and Harry Caray had, in their own estimation, saved the franchise for Chicago. But in this spring of 1975, they had some troubled reservations for the future.

"Spring training," said Tanner, "is too short. There's not enough time for teaching all the mechanics. Not enough time for the players to absorb all we can give them. Not enough time for experiments. The mind-control people say that it's possible for a man to consistently do the best he's ever been able to do. Wouldn't that be something? If we could get just one guy this year to do that. . . ."

"I'm getting married again," said Harry Caray. He'd tried it twice. The second divorce is said to have cost him half a million.

A photographer asked Tanner and Caray to pose together. I left them smiling at each other and went off to find John Sain and talk about pitching. He wanted to talk hitting.

"You know the expression, 'You show me your ass and I'll show you mine?' That's basically what it's all about. Nothing starts unttil the pitcher lifts his front leg to deliver the ball. Then the batter lifts his front leg to step into the pitch. Everybody goes from there."

Depend on Sain to get down to basics.

"You show me your ass and I'll show you mine," eh, John?

I showed him mine and went back to the beach.

For most big-league teams the false hopes of spring are dimmed by June and dead by October. Only one team can be best, 23 end up losers. Occasionally a mediocre team will win a championship—if most players live up to their potential, some players have a phenomenal season and the better team or teams collapse. For the 1975 White Sox, there was no such luck. They were a mediocre team in Sarasota. They looked worse during the summer. They were inept by autumn. Injuries decimated John Sain's pitching staff; Jim Kaat won 20 games, but Wilbur Wood lost 20, and both were put up for sale. Harvey Wineberg's high-priced clients, Melton and Henderson, flopped on the field and were offered for trade. Carlos May looked tired by July, Jack Kucek never came back from the minor leagues, and, though new faces came and went at White Sox Park, there were no phenoms, not even Nyls Nyman. Especially Nyls Nyman.

Chuck Tanner lost most of his charisma and some of his optimism. Harry Caray lost faith in the team, was more bitter than sarcastic in his reporting, and was eventually fired by Sox owner John Allyn. The team was never a contender, the fans lost interest, and Allyn ran out of money.

At season's end, an incredible denouement loomed; the Sox were for sale and the likely buyers planned to move the franchise to Seattle. That's a hell of a long way from Rube's Sportsmans Club. Was there no one to save the Sox for the great South Side of Chicago? Were there no moneyed men to buy the Sox and preserve a tradition three quarters of a century old?

Oh, hell yes, sports fans. This is America, land of business opportunity, home of the freebooter's enterprise system. And isn't that Bill Veeck coming? Ol' peg-legged Bill, the fun-loving pirate from the Maryland shores? The guy who wrote *The Hustler's Handbook,* or "How to Make a Buck Out of Baseball"? The same Bill Veeck who, in 1959, brought the American League championship to Chicago?

Bill Veeck! Baseball fans had learned to love him because he made fun for them. Baseball owners hated him because he made fun of them. But then who understood better than Bill Veeck that in the business of baseball, the name of the game is gamesmanship?

Writing about that 1959 pennant year, Veeck said that they won the pennant too soon. Ideally, he claimed, you should build over a four-year period, go from sixth to fourth to second to first. That's the way to build attendance. It's strictly an engineering problem.

Four more years, eh, Bill?

Now, that's a springtime promise a fan can live with.

BASKETBALL

THE CELTICS SHAKE OFF AGE AND THE SUNS

By John Schulian

From The Washington Post

They were old and tired, but they were also the Boston Celtics. When they felt the Phoenix Suns' hot breath on their necks today, that deceptively simple matter of identity meant more than anyone could imagine.

The Celtics rose up in all their regal splendor in the fourth quarter to snatch away their thirteenth National Basketball Association championship, 87–80, with an effort built of equal parts sweat, pride, and courage.

All of a sudden, the bickering and the bullying that marked the first five games of this frantic series evaporated, and the Celtics were out doing the things that created their heritage.

There was thirty-six-year-old John Havlicek, his aching left foot hurting more by the minute, tossing in the long season's most important free throws. There was Dave Cowens exhibiting one last ounce of ferocity to dominate Alvan Adams, whose youth and skill typify what made the Suns so difficult to overcome.

There was Paul Silas muscling for one of the 10 rebounds he had in the second half. There was Jo Jo White, the most valuable player in the finals, holding the Celtics together when Phoenix took its short-lived 67–66 lead with 7:25 left. There was Charlie Scott, who led all scores with 25 points, showing the Suns they shouldn't have traded him by saving his best game for last.

And when it was all over, when the 13,306 fans filling every inch of Veterans Memorial Coliseum had sung "Auld Lang Syne" to the vanquished but valiant Suns, there was Boston coach Tommy Heinsohn swigging from a bottle of champagne, the overflow running down the front of his shirt.

"It was a question of guts," Heinsohn roared above the happy din in the Celtics' dressing room. "Everybody was tired, but we just kept moving it, moving it, moving it. We've been there before. We knew we could do it again."

Anybody who had doubts before the game had every reason in the world for them. While the Celtics had beaten Phoenix 128–126, Friday to go ahead in the series 3–2, it had taken them three wearying overtimes. The question coming into game six was: Could the old men take it?

"You wouldn't believe how early I was up today," said Havlicek, who played 58 minutes in the fifth game, just 39 hours before today's start. "I wondered how many times I was going to have to shower and brush my teeth before we could play."

But neither the Celtics nor the Suns, with all those eager kids lusting after their first taste of fame, could do anything right in the first half. It looked as if the two teams that had played the NBA's version of the sixth game of the 1975 World Series on Friday had been replaced by two pickup squads from the local YMCA.

Boston made 12 turnovers, but Phoenix was even worse with 17. In the first quarter, the Suns got 16 equalizing points from the backcourt of Paul Westphal and rookie Ricky Sobers.

That brought a 20–20 tie that Phoenix quickly dissipated when Westphal and Sobers were shut out in the next 12 minutes. The Celtics were almost as bad as a team, finishing the half with 30 percent shooting from the field. But the spidery Scott bombed away from 20 feet and beyond for 14 points to provide the makings of a 38–33 half-time edge.

"Charlie was just super," said Silas, "and so was Cowens. Dave got inside and made a lot of key hoops for us along with Charlie when we weren't shooting well."

Indeed, Cowens had 14 of his game high 17 rebounds in those first 24 minutes, and he went right back up with four of them to score baskets while Phoenix's front line of Adams, Curtis Perry, and Garfield Heard watched in bewilderment.

"I hate playing against Dave Cowens more than anybody in this league," Adams admitted later.

The big redhead from Boston didn't put as many bruises on Adams's slender body in the second half because he picked up his fourth personal foul with 5:13 left in the third quarter and his fifth with 10:09 left in the game.

But Cowens avoided the foul that would have put him on the bench, and gave Adams one more thing to remember him by. With the Celtics leading 68–67, and 6:54 left, Cowens stole the ball from the straight-faced Phoenix center as he tried to dribble, then steamed for the basket that may really have finished the Suns.

But the job today was not as easy as it may have seemed when Boston took a 2–0 lead in the finals. "They kept coming back and coming back," said White, who scored 15 points.

For the Suns, who fought from 11 points behind in the third quarter, there was the obvious lure of the $250,000 that went to the winners. (The losers got $185,000.) There was also the matter of proving they belonged.

"It was like a dream, being in the finals," said Heard, who came to Phoenix from Buffalo when the Suns were 20–27.

But the Suns' dream proved to be impossible, not only because of Cowens, but because of the heroics of the other Celtics. When Cowens got in foul trouble, Silas made up for him on the boards and White and former Sun Scott took it upon themselves to go to the basket.

Then Cowens came back to whirl around Adams on the baseline and bank in his twenty-first and final point of the afternoon, and the Celtics were ready to go to the dressing room to salute their reason for being.

It is called the NBA championship trophy.

GENERAL

MISSION IMPOSSIBLE: GETTING A SUPER BOWL TICKET

By Bill Paul

My mission impossible was to get a decent, reasonably priced seat at the Super Bowl.

So here I was last Thursday at the Forge, an ultraposh Miami Beach restaurant. Keith, the bartender—you don't demand last names on missions like this—leaned over the bar and asked if I could use two seats on the 50-yard line. Keith said that Mike, a waiter, could get them for me, and Mike would be in soon.

In no more than 15 minutes, a busboy brought me a folded slip of paper with a message: "Tickets on the 50-yard line—32 rows up—I have them now." I finished up the crab imperial and sauntered back to the bar. Instead of Mike the waiter, a long-haired customer in a cream-colored leisure suit looked me over and handed two tickets to Keith. Keith brought them to me. They were for Section 2, Row 32, smack-dab on the 50-yard line.

Then Keith lowered the boom: $325 for the pair—$300 to the seller, $25 to Keith. "For my time," he said, and smiled.

And thus I had found that anybody, even a nobody like me can get the best seats in the house at the Super Bowl.

But my mission was to get reasonably priced seats, and I decided to keep looking.

The way tickets to the Super Bowl are handled is a scalper's dream. There are only about 80,000 tickets in existence, and none are ever sold directly to just plain fans like you and me.

The National Football League divides about 26,000 tickets between the two competing teams. Each club keeps about 4,000 for its own purposes and sells the rest to season-ticket holders. Another 26,000 tickets are sold to season-ticket holders of the team whose city plays host to the game—this year the Miami Dolphins. An additional 16,000 tickets or so go to other teams, and 12,000 go to newspeople and celebrities. The price for all seats, wherever located, is $20 each.

There are never enough tickets for everybody, not $20 tickets, at least. Two weeks ago in Pittsburgh, season-ticket holders of the Pittsburgh Steelers, who yesterday beat the Dallas Cowboys, 21–17, nearly rioted when told after standing in line in bitter cold all night that there weren't nearly enough to go around.

Scalpers more outrageous than Keith have swapped tickets for mink coats and automobiles. One woman once wrote the NFL that she could land a husband if she could get two tickets for her fellow. The league obliged, and that was the last anyone heard from her.

Had I been willing to spend $300, I could have got tickets in a less hit-or-miss way than at the Forge simply by telephoning a Los Angeles citizen called Mr. Tickets. He is one of a handful of entrepreneurs who specialize in finding hard-to-find tickets to sports events. For the Super Bowl, Mr. Tickets went to Dallas and bought an unknown number of tickets from Cowboy season-ticket holders who had bought their full allotments (up to 10 tickets) for the bowl. Most of these ticket holders planned to use two or four tickets and sell the rest at a profit to finance their trip to the game.

Mr. Tickets says the champ ticket-getter, however, is a Los Angeles travel agent who claims to have obtained 2,000 tickets this year. He says he got some from friends, NFL players who rounded up a hoard from other players. Every player on a team not going to the Super Bowl gets two tickets. "If you're good," the travel agent says, "you can get 40 or 50 from every club." Players for the teams meeting in the Super Bowl each get 25 tickets—some free, some they pay for—and the travel agent says he bought 200 tickets from players on the Dallas team.

The travel agent uses the tickets in package tours including the game, hotel room, and airfare.

I was told that if I could discipline myself to wait until the last minute, my best chance to get a ticket would come outside the Orange Bowl just before kickoff. Knowledgeable fans assured me that scalpers always overestimate their market and usually are eager to liquidate tickets at any price at game time. Tickets sold then are often sold for face value, or so I was told. For one thing, it's against the law to scalp tickets, although the law usually is enforced only at the site of the game.

But how many fans have the cool to risk missing the game altogether? If they are like me, I figured, there wouldn't be many. So I started asking bell captains of hotels on Miami Beach for tickets. A bellman at the Carillon gave me a phone number and said I should ask for Joe. Instead, I found that Jimmy, a bellman at the Deauville, had two tickets around the goal line that he offered at $75 each. I turned him down.

Next I took out an ad in the local newspapers asking ticket sellers to call my hotel room Friday between 5 P.M. and 6 P.M. with "reasonable offers only." The first caller wanted $40 for a seat so far from the field that Pittsburgh's 275-pound defensive tackle Joe Greene would have looked like a midget. The second caller, a Mr. Ramirez, told me he'd rather sit home in front of the television with a quart of Scotch. But his ticket was no better located than the first caller's so we didn't even discuss price.

The third caller, a man who would identify himself only as J.B., offered me a ticket in the end zone just high enough to give me a pretty good view of the game. J.B., who said he was a cable splicer for Florida Power & Light Co., wanted $30. When I told him another caller had asked only $30 for a better ticket (sorry, J.B., I lied), he cut the price to $27.50.

I met J.B. in front of his plant, took his ticket, and rubbed the number on it to see if it smudged, which would mean it was counterfeit. The ticket was authentic. J.B. was a friendly, grey-haired gentleman with a bushy moustache, a Dolphin season-ticket holder who, like Mr. Ramirez, preferred to stay home and watch the game on TV.

Counting $8.10 for the ad, the ticket had cost me $35.60.

With J.B.'s ticket as insurance that I would get into the bowl, I decided to see how well I could do outside the gates before kickoff. I arrived an hour ahead of time and found plenty of people offering tickets at $40 to $100 each. Finally, I bought one for $50—and sold it for $60 two minutes later. I bought two more, one at $40 and one at $35, and sold them, too, a few minutes later, at a profit of $5 each. Five minutes before game time I found a 15-yard-line seat for only $40 and bought it. I immediately sold J.B.'s end-zone ticket for $35.

The net result: I had spent $200.60 for five tickets, sold four of them for $180 and wound up in a nice seat that cost me $20.60—only 60 cents more than its official price. But I sure missed the instant replays.

OUTDOORS

ELK HUNTING THE HIGH LONESOME

By Jack Samson

From Field & Stream

In October, when the bright gold leaves of the aspens have fallen from the stands of trees in the header canyons of the high country, the wind blows chill and clear down from the snow-clad peaks across the line in Colorado. And it is then that the elk hunting is at its best in the tall spruce- and ponderosa-covered mountains of northern New Mexico—when the herds start feeling the urge to move down to winter range before the first heavy snows blast through the passes on the wings of blizzards that can blanket a mountain range in hours.

The bugling is about over and, through the big bulls—necks still swollen with the rut—still watch over herds of cows and yearlings, it is greener grass and not combat the herd bulls seek. Each day the elk move slowly lower, dropping from the sanctuary of fallen spruce timber on the nape of peaks named Purgatory, Baldy, Wheeler, Culebra, Ortiz, Big Costilla, and Ash Mountain. They move into valleys where tiny, meandering streams trickle through grassy parks which were formed by beaver dams in the days when the mountain men from Taos, Cimarron, Clayton, Raton, and Maxwell sought the prized furs for the trade brought in by the wagons on the Santa Fe Trail a few miles to the south.

The land is little different today in the high, lonesome peaks than it was in the days when the elk herds roamed the rolling plateaus of northern New Mexico, northwest Texas, and southeastern Colorado. Perhaps it's a bit more overgrazed by Hereford cattle from the big ranches and by sheep of the small Spanish-American herders than when it was the domain of the mule deer and the bighorn. It was the wagon train hunters, dirt farmers, and ranchers—pursuing the wapiti herds for their wondrous meat as the settlers flooded west—that finally drove the elk herd into the high peaks. And there the few remaining herds struggled for survival against the trappers and the meat hunters seeking food for hungry bellies in the tiny frontier towns and ranches huddled at the base of the big mountains in long-gone days when New Mexico was a territory of distant Spain and Mexico.

And long before New Mexico became part of the United States, the elk had been killed out of the high counry along the Colorado border by men who should have known better (the same way they should have known better about the passenger pigeon and the heath hen and a lot of waterfowl along the heavily populated East Coast), before men of good sense and vision came along. It took men like Muir, Pinchot, Hornaday, Burroughs, Seton, Roosevelt, Merriam, and Leopold—many of them hunters as well as naturalists and conservationists—to see to the restocking and the setting aside of the wild lands and the establishing of bag limits and proper seasons and international treaties that, hopefully, mean we will now always have the game species to hunt properly.

They took the elk from the Yellowstone region, during the days of World War II, and put them back into the high country where I was hunting last year. And the elk took to the ancestral lands from which they had been gone since before the turn of the century and multiplied. And here, where the late afternoon sun silhouetted Ash Mountain to the west and the chill wind sighed through the tops of towering ponderosa, there were elk below me in a stand of thick aspen across a valley. I had been waiting hours for them to come out and feed on the sparse grass of a snow-dusted meadow. My horse stood, hipshot and asleep, 100 yards down the slope below me, the late sun warming its flanks. The temperatures were due to plummet in a matter of minutes, as soon as the orange sun dropped behind Little Costilla Peak towering to the left of Ash Mountain.

The valley floor and the slope opposite had been in shadow for more than an hour, but elk don't feed until the last light and I would have to wait, hoping the bulls would come out with the advance scout cows before too much light had gone for the 3-by-9 scope to gather enough to make a last-minute shot count. I had spotted the small herd entering the aspen stand at 3 P.M. from several miles away, my powerful binoculars enabling me to see that there were at least two good bulls and a couple of younger ones along with about a dozen cows and a few yearlings. It had taken almost two hours to ride from where the guide and I had first sighted the herd—into canyons and over ridges and saddles strewn with rocky outcroppings and dotted with wind-twisted pines—until we had gotten into a fair position to take a shot if the herd came out of the trees at the header canyon before dark. The tracks led in and never led out, so there was little guesswork involved.

There was only the simple fact that elk are about the smartest big-game animals on the North American continent. If they sensed there was the least danger, they would not venture out to graze on the tiny park until after dark and there would be no way to hunt them then. Also there are few hunters alive skillful enough to stalk and kill elk on foot in heavy timber. A huge bull—spreading antlers notwithstanding—can both run at full speed or slip silently away in timber where a man would have trouble making his way on all fours. How? It's just a fact, that's all—like so much of nature we may never fully understand. So it was stay crouched at the base of the big, lichen-covered rock, keep watching the aspen with the glasses, and hope for the best. And the best was going to be a 300-yard shot—and maybe some more if the elk spooked and began to run. The .300 rested against the rock where it had been leaned—the scope left on 4X, a shell in the chamber, three in the clip and the safety on.

The guide and his horses by now should have been stationed on the ridge top to the northeast, to the right and above the aspen grove, just in case the herd had either scented or sighted me and attempted to steal out the top of the valley on the far side of the trees. If that were to happen, three shots in the air were to notify me that the stalk for the day was over and unsuccessful and I would mount and work my way down the mountain until we both rendezvoused near the base camp miles below. If I was lucky and got a shot and made a kill, three shots by me, and then three more, would eventually bring the guide, his riding horse, and pack horse. Hopefully, I would have the elk field-dressed and partly cut up so we could start packing out the meat before too much of the night was gone.

Two ravens swung in slow circles high over a sheer rock wall far up the bigger valley to the north, an occasional hoarse croak carrying clearly in the cold air.

To the north, towering high above the near peaks, climbed the snow-clad crags of the Colorado mountains. Clearly visible and blood-red in the setting sun were both East Spanish Peak and West Spanish Peak, bracketing both Apishapa and Cordova Passes, they and 14,069-foot Culebra Peak reigning over a domain as incredibly beautiful and solitary as it was in the days when Kit Carson led his mount through the same stillness in which I waited.

And down to my right sprawled the Vermejo—approximately

half a million acres of some of the finest elk hunting country in North America. The big ranch—since the days when W. J. Gourley, a Fort Worth, Texas, businessman, bought the land—has been a mecca for those willing to pay a price to hunt carefully controlled elk herds. They are scientifically culled each year to provide excellent hunting and yet not deplete brood stock or leave too many and allow more than nature would herself leave for the carrying capacity of the land. There are those who argue that God's wild creatures are for all to hunt and that charging a fee to hunt wildlife on private land is wrong. There are also the ones who forget the greedy fools who erased the elk, bighorn sheep, pronghorn, and other game species from the Rockies before concerned sportsmen, the game biologists, the federal government, and the state game departments moved in and stopped the carnage before all game went the way of the bison herds.

They are also the ones who think uncontrolled hunting of public and private lands with any and all types of all-terrain vehicles is sport hunting: four men with loaded rifles prowling in the peaks and passes all day in a four-wheel-drive car ready to shoot at anything with four legs—including cattle and horses. This is done each year by those who are making it tough for all of us who believe hunting is a fine, honorable sport and a way to bring home the best eating meat a man can get in this idiotic age of filling commercially raised animals with enough chemicals to poison half the world. There are also those who think no animals should be hunted or killed, and they are as misguided and uninformed—in their antiseptic and plastic-filled world—as is the indiscriminate-killing, fence-cutting, poaching, can- and bottle-tossing, littering slob, who wants it all for himself and doesn't care a tinker's dam if hunting will be here for our great-grandchildren or not.

A movement flickered at the edge of the aspens. The light was fast failing and the glasses picked up a lone barren cow elk with forequarters protruding from among the silver trunks. Her head swung carefully to the right and left as she surveyed the park before her. The familiar pounding of the heart in the temples began as I slowly reached out and slid the rifle across my knees. A moment later she had eased out onto the light snow surface and had begun to scrape away the thin layer of snow to get at the last remaining brown grass of fall. A yearling slipped out behind her and was followed by another cow. In a matter of minutes half a dozen elk were grazing in the dusk where there had been bare snow. Still no bulls showed. The sun had sunk behind the western mountain and in five minutes there would not be enough light to see anything well enough for a shot. The rifle steadied across the boulder and the safety slid off with a barely perceptible sound. The glasses steadied on the grove of trees and the wait began.

When I had begun to think there were no more bulls, there was a movement to the left of the feeding herd and what appeared to be a young bull elk moved inside the fringe of aspen. The scope picked him up and stayed on what could have been his forequarters in the purple and black shadows beneath the jutting aspen limbs. An ear flicked and a neck turned and a foreleg inched a few feet further out into the open. The maze of branches from the animal's shoulders upward was too thick to permit a clear view. My mouth was dry and my heart was pounding. But there was nothing but the partially obscured elk and the cows and yearlings grazing. I swung the scope back to the animal which was still motionless in the trees. The light had faded even more and there was no chance to be sure of the horns—unless the animal stepped out into the open within the next few moments. It never did.

Finally, letting out a long, slow breath and lowering the rifle, I slid the safety back on. There was not enough light for a shot. It might have been a bull and it might have been a cow. I could have shot and I could have killed a cow. I didn't want a cow elk. I wanted a bull elk, but I didn't want a wounded bull I would have to track all the following day and perhaps never catch up with—and have it finally die.

As I stood up in the dusk and flipped the cartridge from the rifle chamber—tottering slightly on cramped, cold legs from the long wait—the herd below me swiftly and silently disappeared into the aspens as the animals saw my outline against the ridgetop. I closed the bolt and slowly began to make my way down to the waiting saddle horse and the long ride back to camp.

I didn't kill a bull elk the next day on the Vermejo, or the next, or the next. I didn't kill a bull elk near Craig, Colo., either last year, hunting for them for five days with Stan Studer and Jim Midcap and outfitter A. C. Ekker of Utah. I could have killed half a dozen cows or spike bulls the first morning out, but I wanted a big bull. I didn't kill the biggest mule deer buck on that hunt I have ever seen in all my decades of hunting the Rockies. I didn't kill it because—even though the ranch owner would never have said anything about it—the deer season was not due to open until the following day.

I didn't kill an elk in a week of beautiful hunting with Nelson Bryant, Harold Mares, three doctors from Chicago, and outfitter Bob Jacob of Lander, Wyo., on a pack trip into the Shoshone Pass country of Wyoming—after a bruising nine-hour horseback ride just to get into the base camp. The weather was too good and the elk were all back in the heavy timber where we couldn't get to them without spooking them. But every man on those fine trips had a wonderful time. We rode all day, day after day, until we were bone-weary and the ills of the cities were long-forgotten. We caught trout and ate steaks and sat around the fire at night and talked the talk of hunters. We slept under the millions of stars, to awaken in the morning cold, and ready to go again.

And when we came out, nobody had got an elk and nobody really cared. We had a wonderful time, shook hands, and went home. The uninitiated and uninformed, the slob hunter and those who condemn hunting, won't understand why. But a true hunter will understand perfectly.

FOOTBALL

THE REVERSAL STORY

By Joe Hendrickson

From the Pasadena Star-News

A young man from Alhambra named John Sciarra, whom many experts said couldn't pass well enough to become a quarterback in professional football, showed the world what he could do as UCLA upset Ohio State 23–10 before 105,464 shocked spectators in the sixty-second annual Rose Bowl game Thursday.

Sciarra completed 13 of 19 passes for two touchdowns and engineered a Bruin offense that completely reversed a first-half shutout to bring about one of the most amazing reversals of football pattern in any season.

Player of the game Sciarra was totally checked along with his pals on the Bruin offensive unit in the first half.

Imagine a team that gained only nine yards rushing and 39 yards passing in the first 30 minutes coming back from intermission to destroy the nation's No. 1 undefeated team with three spectacular touchdowns and a field goal!

When has anyone heard of a football team not making even a first down the first 26 minutes of action coming back to roll up 17 first downs in the second half?

The reversal story doesn't stop there. Ohio State seemed to gain at will the first half when it out-first downed the Bruins 11–2, but in the second half UCLA had a 17–9 edge in first downs. Never again may a team that was outgained 174 yards to 48 in the first half finish with 414 yards to the early oppressors's 298.

Ohio State hit the Bruins with its powerful offense and bruising defense for 30 minutes and was able to score only three points on a 42-yard field goal by the great Tom Klaban. The Bruin defense, although pushed around, made big plays when necessary to hold the

Buckeyes to three points on four scoring chances—to UCLA's 25-, 33-, 32-, and 21-yard lines.

Then the miracle happened! Inspired and encouraged because they were down only 3–0 when they went to the dressing room, Dick Vermeil's fighting Bruins returned to outplay Ohio State in every phase of football—running, passing, catching, blocking, tackling, and plain good old fight.

The Bruins won with a 33-yard field goal by Brett White, a 16-yard touchdown catch of a Sciarra bullet by Wally Henry who then took a sharp pass and ran for a 67-yard touchdown, and, after Pete Johnson battered in for a three-yard tally to keep Ohio State hopes alive, Wendell Tyler killed the Buckeye dreams with a dashing 54-yard scamper to score with three minutes and 42 seconds left to play.

UCLA also missed on another scoring chance on Ohio State's 17 when the Buckeyes recovered an errant Sciarra pitchout. Sciarra also ran 28 yards for a touchdown only to have it nullified by penalty.

General Woody Hayes, like Napoleon at Waterloo, went down to defeat on one of his favorite battlefields. Hayes conceded to Vermeil with eight seconds left to play when he walked across the field to congratulate the young Bruin coach while the teams still had one final effort to run off before the crowd swarmed to the turf to celebrate UCLA's renewal of its 10-year upset plan. It was 10 years ago that another Bruin team tripped No. 1 Michigan State in the Rose Bowl, 14–12.

The most exciting play of a dull first half was Kate Smith's rendition of "God Bless America" and the National Anthem in conjunction with the UCLA choir and band. There wasn't much to write home to ma about in that first half except possibly the opening tackle, if you were a Pasadenan, because it was Muir High School's John Lynn who pulled down Lenny Willis of Ohio State on the 17 after the opening kickoff.

The Buckeyes mauled the Bruins pretty good for 30 minutes after that, but the young men from Westwood, who thought two weeks ago that Coach Vermeil was working them too hard and told him so through a protest committee, found out what Vermeil had in mind. The Bruins came out with a full gas tank in the second half and completely turned the game around. They had legs!

Thus did the Pac Eight win its sixth Rose Bowl game in the last seven years. It was the West that lost 12 of the first 13 games in this series.

The Bruin heroes are many.

Tyler, who played with a wrist that was in a cast until 10 days ago, carried the football 21 times for 172 yards without fumbling once. The UCLA team lost eight fumbles against USC but coughed up the ball only once in two bobbles against Ohio State.

Henry caught five passes for 113 yards. The Bruins had sure hands. Norm Andersen caught three, tight ends Don Pederson and Rick Walker two each and Severn Reece one.

While the Bruin defense rushed Corny Greene into a mere seven-for-18 passing day, Bruin secondary men Barney Person and Pat Schmidt came through with big interceptions.

In the Bruin defensive line action, nose guard Walt Frazier was a major factor once he shook off his early beating from the Buckeye offense and wound up with 13 tackles, high for the game. Manu Tuiasosopo, Jerry Tautolo, Dale Curry, Raymond Burks, and Raymond Bell were other men who got better as the game progressed and wound up in total command as the great Archie Griffin, Greene, and Johnson were solidly checked following their opening dominance.

Griffin gained 93 yards in 17 carries. Archie's name will go in the Rose Bowl record books with these marks career-wise: Most carries, 79, 412 yards rushing, four Rose Bowl starts.

UCLA's Henry undoubtedly enjoyed his records more, however. His two touchdown catches tied him with six other players in Rose Bowl history for most in one game. His 67-yard touchdown pass play tied the modern record.

This victory was a tremendous achievement for Coach Vermeil and his staff. They knew how to change things in the second half. They decided if you can't punch a gorilla in the nose, soar over him. UCLA found out just before half time that it could connect via the air route—and connect Sciarra did in the second half. The Buckeyes were surprised. Then when they got behind, the Buckeyes lost their poise and their game plan. Instead of pounding for yardage, Greene went for the catch-up pass. This made it easier for the Bruin defense as it rushed Cornelius into difficulty.

Coach Hayes had a tough day. He was knocked over on the sidelines when Henry made a catch. Woody ran on the field several times to cheer his men on and to voice his opinions. Finally he had to stand there on the sidelines and suffer his Waterloo. After his most sportsmanlike gesture to congratulate Vermeil, Woody had to spoil everything at the finish by shutting out the sports writers. Yes, the man dies hard.

UCLA reacted and adjusted this day. Ohio State didn't. It was hard to believe, once the Bruins cracked the candidate for the national crown, Ohio State didn't have the perfection that had marked 11 straight conquests. Big Ten commissioner Wayne Duke was impressed by the UCLA job. "We were outplayed," said Duke.

Vermeil's training under four great pro and college coaches, plus the wisdom of a smart staff, paid off in technical adjustments that turned this game around—and also avenged a 41–20 Bruin loss to Ohio State during the regular season.

The punting in this game would make the pros envious. Ohio State's Tom Sklandany averaged 42.2, his U.S. leading pace, with five booming kicks. John Sullivan averaged 39.4, but had a 57-yarder.

Sciarra's super performance was an example of courage. He played much of the game with an injured thigh. He had to shake off tough early hits. If the pros don't draft him early, they are passing up a true athlete.

UCLA missed an early chance to put Ohio State in a hole when a Greene-to-Griffin pitchout went astray. Two Bruins had a shot at it, but Griffin recovered. Soon Greene connected to Willis for a 21-yarder to set up Klaban's 42-yard field goal.

UCLA was mauled severely every time it tried to go on offense for many minutes. The Buckeyes, meanwhile, jabbed them solidly on attack—until it was time to score. Then something usually went wrong for Ohio State. Something that the UCLA defense made go wrong.

Johnson powered for gains in midfield, but he couldn't move—nor could Greene and Griffin move decisively—when near UCLA's goal line, if you can call 20 to 30 yards out near.

Cross was hurt during this stage to further handicap UCLA's chances, but the Bruins went to the dressing room believing.

"Hell," they probably concluded, "they're pushing us around and we're down only 3–0. We can get 'em." That they did in the second half.

After the kickoff, Sciarra pitched to Tyler for 13. John passed to Anderson for 14. Tyler broke through on a trap play for 30 to the 12. White's field goal followed.

Being tied seemed to upset Ohio State's pattern. It couldn't move. It looked like the UCLA of the first half.

Eddie Ayers, Bruin back, didn't make the gains of Tyler, but he made some key ones. He clicked in the next Bruin drive. Walker made a 21-yard catch and Henry went 10 on a flanker end around. From the 16, Sciarra ducked under a rush and carefully picked out a wide-open Henry in the end zone.

With a 9–3 lead, UCLA pulled a sculler at this point. On the extra-point try, Ohio State was offside. UCLA refused it. It seemed with a yard and a half to go, the Bruins could have tried for two points there. They wanted to kick the point, however, and White missed.

The pass-happy Buckeyes were vulnerable now—both ways. The Ohio offense was too anxious and the defense couldn't cover the Bruin air game. The Bruins moved in for another possible score, but Sciarra was hit by Eddie Beamon making a pitch and Ohio State recovered.

Burks came through with an 11-yard sacking of Greene to force the punt that set up the Sciarra to Henry 67-yard touchdown pass play. Henry came in from the right side for a short pass and outraced the secondary. White converted and it was 16–3 with the fourth quarter about to start.

Ohio State had one try left. Griffin, Johnson, and Greene were truly fine in a drive that culminated with Johnson scoring and Klaban converting. The Buckeyes thought they had a chance with UCLA holding a precarious six-point lead with 12 minutes of the game remaining.

However, an exchange of interceptions by Ohio State's Craig Cassady and UCLA's Person, followed by Schmidt's interception on a Greene overthrow led to Tyler's 54-yard touchdown off the left side and down the sidelines that put the game out of reach.

An amazing bit of statistical evidence sums up what happened in the cool but sunny Rose Bowl on January 1, 1976. Ohio State had the football 21 minutes in the first half to UCLA's nine. In the second half UCLA had it 18 minutes to Ohio State's 12. Yes, a reversal . . . a miracle . . . an attainment of Mission Impossible.

HOCKEY

THE CHAMPIONS BITE THE DUST

By Hugh Delano

From the New York Post

They were popping corks from champagne bottles and spraying foamy geysers around the hot, crowded dressing room. Pierre Bouchard was roaring with glee as he emptied the contents of a bottle of beer and a bottle of wine on Guy Lafleur's head. Yvari Cournoyer was lying on his back on the table in the middle of the room in his long underwear, kicking his legs in the air and giggling as he held the shimmering Stanley Cup to his lips. Yvon Lambert, singing in a falsetto voice, was imitating Kate Smith as he led them in rowdy choruses of "God Bless America."

"Oh, this is beautiful . . . just beautiful. This is what this bloody game is all about. I just want to sit here and watch all this and lock it in my mind so I'll never forget it," said Steve Shutt.

He sat hunched over on the bench in front of his small dressing cubicle, the sweat and beer and champagne that had been poured on him by jubilant teammates running down his weary face and forming a puddle at his feet.

"I am so tired . . . so exhausted. I think I'd have ulcers if the season had gone any longer, if the tension had lasted another day," he said.

Shutt winced and laughed as sprays of champagne soaked his face. He raised his fist and shouted as goaltender Ken Dryden was led by teammates to the middle of the room to drink from the Stanley Cup.

"Go, Kenny. Drink it all!" screamed Pete Mahovlich, sloshing beer on his teammates.

The hockey season is over. The Canadiens are No. 1. A remarkable four-game sweep of the Flyers, who had been No. 1 for two seasons, returned the Stanley Cup to Montreal in last night's 5–3 victory.

The line of Mahovlich, Shutt, and Lafleur hammered the final nail in the Flyers' coffin, accounting for three goals and nine points and blitzing goalie Wayne Stephenson for 14 shots. They had a hand in the last three goals which wiped out a 3–2 Flyer lead.

"The difference between the two teams was our defense, our checking," said Shutt, the slender, intense left wing who scored the first goal and set up the last two, the winner by Lafleur and the insurance goal by Mahovlich.

The Flyers all agreed that the Canadiens' checking is what enabled them to sweep the series.

"I think we surprised them with the way we checked," said Shutt.

Shutt insisted he was so excited, so emotionally drained, that he could not honestly remember how he scored his goal or assisted on the last two goals. He scored the tying goal in the first period with a wrist shot from the left circle. He glanced a shot off defense Joe Watson and then Mahovlich took the carom and passed to Lafleur who sent it to Mahovlich in close for the fifth goal.

"Forget about what I did. Write about us as a team. Hey, don't forget speed. Speed wins games and we've got speed. Some of our plays were so fast I thought we were the Harlem Globetrotters," he said laughing.

Bowman could hardly be heard above the dressing-room noise as he talked about his team.

"The last Montreal team that won the cup also won the Vezina Trophy," said the coach. "I sent letters to each of our players last season, explaining to them that I wanted emphasis on defensive hockey and checking this season. I told them I wanted to keep our goals-against at 200. We did better than that; we gave up only 174 goals. I told them that if we could lead the league in lowest goals-against, we could win the cup."

"Give the coach credit," said Mahovlich. "He put in a defensive system and it paid off. Now we have a combination offense and checking team. The guys who can put the puck in the net can also check."

Mahovlich said he was surprised the Flyers could be shot down in flames in four games but stressed the closeness of the games. The tall center confessed that after Montreal had won the first two games many of its players felt a sweep was possible.

"This is the best team I ever played on," said Mahovlich. "We've got size, we've got depth, we've got good older guys and good young guys, we've got great defensemen and a great goalie and lots of skating forwards who can score and check."

Mahovlich was about to head for the bench when the carom of Shutt's blocked shot came to him along the right boards.

"No one was checking me and I saw Lafleur was all alone in front of the net and no one was checking him," said Mahovlich.

The pass was perfect and Lafleur, 12 feet from Stephenson, did not delay his shot; he took the pass from a stationary position and drilled it on the roll high over the defenseless goaltender.

"I was hoping he would pass me the puck," said the shy, introverted Lafleur. He added: "We had good spirit on our team last year but this year the spirit is even better; we are more close together as a team."

Fifty-eight seconds later Mahovlich took Lafleur's crossing pass in front of the net and backhanded the fifth goal between Stephenson's legs.

"The big goal was the one the little guy got," said Mahovlich, referring to Cournoyer's goal with 11 seconds left in the second period and Philadelphia ahead, 3–2. Lafleur shot from the right side. Stephenson sprawled and the puck rebounded. The Road-Runner, standing in front of the net, lifted the puck over the fallen goaltender.

"That put a lot of [bleep] and vinegar into us going into the last period," said Mahovlich.

Dryden, who finished with a 1.91 goals-against average in the Canadiens' 12–1 playoff season, said: "We returned to the style of the great Montreal teams this season."

Larry Robinson, brilliant along with Serge Savard on defense, laughed when asked about Kate Smith's $10,000 personal appearance to sing "God Bless America," the Flyers' good-luck charm.

"They can do what they want before the game but when the game starts it's a matter of which is the best team," said the big defenseman.

And the moral of that story?

"The best team won," said Robinson with a wink.

HORSE RACING

BOLD FORBES PULLS THE RUG OUT

By Blackie Sherrod

From The Dallas Times Herald

Any day now, Gibraltar may crumble. The sun will set down and nap on the Union Jack. Heck, Italy might even pay its World War I debt. The unthinkable has become the thinkable. The colt that couldn't lose the Kentucky Derby lost the Kentucky Derby.

There was no fluke, no erratic pattern of racing luck. Honest Pleasure didn't stumble or buckle or get himself bumped off course. He simply got his valuable legs run off by brash Bold Forbes, an impudent sprinter whose staying power was suspect. Under a brilliant ride by Angel Cordero, the Puerto Rico horse broke quickly from the gate, took immediate command of Honest Pleasure, and the two colts ran single file for the entire mile and a quarter. They could have run this race down a movie aisle.

The winning margin was one length, although Bold Forbes had as much as a five-length advantage a half-mile deep in the race, and Honest Pleasure doggedly wore it down too a half-length turning into the home stretch. His taciturn rider, Braulio Baeza, went to the whip in the final quarter mile, something he has never used on Honest Pleasure. The Panamanian jock hit his mount at least 15 times during the long trip home, but Bold Forbes not only held his advantage, he increased it by a few feet. At the wire, the winner seemed to have more stamina left than the big favorite, who was laboring a little.

There has been no favorite in modern times more pronounced than Honest Pleasure, who had won his last nine races with a minimum of effort. The Churchill Downs crowd of 115,387 bet him down to the overwhelming odds of 40 cents to $1. Only Citation, the great Triple Crown winner of 1948, was so favored by Derby money.

Honest Pleasure did set one dubious record. There was $1,049,461 spent on worthless win tickets. In all, there was a record $3,449,065 bet on this one race alone.

The winner had a pari-mutuel payday of $8, $2.40, and $2.60. He was the second favorite of the betting crowd. Honest Pleasure paid $2.40 to place and $2.20 to show. The third-place finisher, Elocutionist, paid $2.60.

One inane sidelight of the race came when some goof tossed two smoke bombs on the home stretch while the horses were on the back stretch of the track. An alert National Guardsman ran on the track and pitched the grenades to one side, while puffs of green smoke went almost unnoticed by the crowd. Had the bomber waited until the horses entered the stretch, there could have been a tragic bolting of the skittery colts.

The race went almost as forecast. Bold Forbes was expected to take an early lead and Honest Pleasure was expected to ride close herd, although the latter had won his last nine races from wire to wire. The railbirds expected Bold Forbes to run out of fuel in the stretch, with the favorite charging on to win.

Only the pacesetter didn't fold. He ran the first quarter in 22 and two-fifths seconds, fastest ever by a Derby winner. He ran the first half mile in 15 and four-fifths seconds, another Derby record for winning speed. The speed, naturally enough, slackened in the last quarter mile and the Derby winner was clocked in 2:01 and three fifths. Six Derby races have been faster.

Cordero said he was given no special instructions by the trainer, Lazaro Barrera.

"I didn't make no plan of the race. I just waited to see what would happen after the break. I was not worried about how fast he was going," said the jock.

The trainer had a slightly different version of prerace planning.

"I told him to break him on the lead and stay there," said Barrera.

There had been prerace speculation about Bold Forbes's reserve.

"He was ready to go two miles if necessary," said Barrera. "My horse has as much speed as anybody in the country.

"This is a great horse that we beat today. Before I come to the Derby, I got a book with all the charts of past Derbies, and see that 65 percent of winners come from the lead horse or second horse. So I wanted to be there, too."

In truth, it seemed that Barrera used the old backwoods track coach's instruction to get a mile relay team: "Just kick left and get back as fast as you can."

It was an especially sweet day for Barrera. Another of his horses,

Life's Hope, won the Illinois Derby at Sportsman Park Saturday. Also he had a stakes winner on the same day at Aqueduct.

The Puerto Rican owner of the winner, Rodriguez Tizol, a seventy-two-year-old banker, was not at Churchill Downs to see the mights upset. He has been confined to his home after a heart seizure and was restricted to television viewing.

It was a bitter, bitter defeat for LeRoy Jolley, the trainer, and Bert Firestone, the owner of Honest Pleasure. Jolley had been uptight all week, presumably because his animal was such a big favorite that the pressures of losing were much greater than the pressures of winning. There was talk of a rift between trainer and jockey and even a report that Jolley tried to get Willie Shoemaker to fly to Kentucky for a last-minute change of jockeys. Jolley had delayed five hours before naming Baeza as his jockey on Thursday, after all other Derby riders were listed.

After Saturday's race, Baeza said, "We ran a good race but the winner was tremendous today. And gutty." Baeza said his horse made a slight hesitation when he saw the dissipating puff of smoke hanging in the dull gray haze of the stretch, but "we really had no excuses."

"I thought the smoke was coming from my horse," said Cordero with a laugh. Then he added, "No honestly, I did not see any smoke."

The full order of finish was Bold Forbes, Honest Pleasure, Elocutionist, Amano, On the Sly, Cojak, Inca Roca, Play the Red, and Bidson. They were in that exact order when they entered the stretch and that's the way they finished.

The winner was sired by Irish Castle and his mama was Comely Nell. Both he and Honest Pleasure are grandsons of Bold Ruler. Bold Forbes first came to Derby attention when he won the Wood Memorial two weeks ago in New York, winning as easily as Honest Pleasure usually does. But, as the philosophers say, that's the reason they have horse races.

GOLF

ARNIE'S STILL THE MAN

By Art Spander

From the San Francisco Chronicle

His name, his full name, as much of the free world knows, is Arnold Daniel Palmer. But herewith he will be referred to as The Man. Because when professional golf is discussed, when the entire spectrum is considered, the six-figure purses, the television rights, the popularity, there can be no other.

The Man is past his prime. His record proves it. Yet he refuses to capitulate. He keeps plodding on and on toward failure, making us assert The Man should give it up—but secretly making us very happy he doesn't. Golf, sport, indeed the philosophy of the rugged individualist, will not be the same when he quits.

The Man is something special. Even a month from his forty-seventh birthday he possesses the strength, the build, the personality—in sum, the magnetism—he always has had. The double bogey may have replaced the birdie, the scowl of frustration may have replaced the joy of triumph, but very little else has changed.

The practically absurd optimism. The charisma. The penchant for the spectacular. The marvelous ability to laugh at even his own mistakes. The fullback's torso. The lurching swing. The agonizing grimaces when a putt fails to fall. And the indomitable spirit. These will always belong to The Man.

After the first round of the PGA Championship, The Man came surging into the candy-striped press tent. He was wearing a white golf shirt with a pattern of tiny Revolutionary War drums and the date "1776," a subtle celebration of the Bicentennial. He had shot a one-over par 71, but he was relaxed and at peace with himself. Shed no tears for The Man. "Hey," said Arnold Daniel Palmer, "life is super. I'm healthier, I'm very happy. The only thing is I'd like to be playing better, playing like I did 20 years ago. Still, I'm not complaining."

The Man hasn't won a tournament in America for more than three years. He shoots a lot of 75s where he used to shoot 65s—down the stretch. Journalists keep badgering him about retirement. They insist he's doing himself more harm than good. Forget it, Arnie, they write, and let us remember things the way they were.

A great many athletes would get defensive, grouchy. Not The Man. He doesn't mind the suggestions or the question. "When you get to my age and play the way I've been playing," said Arnold Daniel Palmer, "then I think such questions are only natural and fair. But I'm not thinking of retirement."

What is The Man thinking? Well, he's thinking that he doesn't think the way he used to. On the golf course, "I lose my concentration, I forget to keep my mind on what I should be doing. I might look at someone in the gallery, or I hear a truck or an airplane. I wouldn't necessarily say it's because of my outside interests. Maybe it's that nobody can concentrate all those years."

So now, as happened during the opening round of the PGA Championship, The Man blanks out. He hits his drive in the wrong direction, then compounds the error by hitting the wrong club for the second shot. A 439-yard par four that could be a birdie ends up a double bogey. And another round is destroyed.

"I wonder what happens to me at those times? It isn't that I doubt myself as much as that I get a little cautious. You don't take all the chances you used to take. You don't have the cocky feeling you can do anything you want all the time.

"But I still can make the shots. I hit the ball better now than I did 20 years ago. It's just that I don't play as often, so the law of averages is against me. One bad shot knocks me out of a tournament. But I still can play. And I can still win."

And the rest of us still can admire The Man—no matter what he does on the scorecard.

GENERAL

SISTER MARY MUMMY'S CLOSE CALLING

By Greg Hoffman

From womenSports

The silence in the camp cubicle that functioned as Our Lady of Pity's candle storage area and locker room was broken only by the metronomic sound of Dudley Mack's massive right fist slamming into the well-oiled leather pocket of his pitcher's mitt.

A few feet away, Jimmy Sullivan, our feisty shortstop, was gracefully plucking imaginary grounders off the bare concrete floor and firing phantom strikes to first baseman "Fat" Chance. Fat was sitting in front of his locker trying to ignore Sullivan's antics.

I, meanwhile, was thoroughly engrossed in my pregame ritual of stuffing handfuls of Kleenex deep into my flimsy catcher's mitt to provide additional protection against Dudley Mack's blister-producing fastball.

"Look at Sullivan," whispered Marty Shea, as another invisible runner fell victim to the shortstop's arm. "He even closes his eyes when he's pretending."

"Yeah," I replied, "but at least he's consistent. He closes his eyes when he bats too."

"Hey," Marty said, "do you remember the time he actually hit the ball and then ran the wrong way?"

"Right. He was the first player in history to turn an easy triple into a close single."

"I'll never forget the look on the first baseman's face when ol' Sullivan slid into the bag waving his spikes in the guy's face."

A few minutes later, Marty spoke again. "You nervous?" he asked.

"Sure I am," I said. "I've never played in a championship game before. Do you think we have a chance to win?"

"What do you mean? We're undefeated, aren't we? We have a

good coach, Dudley Mack's fireballs, and a shortstop who's capable of making three errors walking from the dugout to the on-deck circle, but no team's perfect. Not even the Yankees."

"I guess you're right," I said.

"We're gonna get massacred," said Marty Shea solemnly. "We have about as much of a chance as a snowball in h-e- double toothpicks."

"I'm not quite that confident," I said.

A lot of people were calling the Pitifuls a miracle team because of our unprecedented seven-game winning streak. Never before in the long history of Our Lady of Pity had any of its athletic teams won even two games in a row, much less a shot at the league championship. Of course, we owed our streak to Dudley Mack's right arm, and more good luck than any team has a right to expect. We were losing our opening game 7–0 when the entire St. Louis School team was placed on academic suspension in the middle of the third inning. We owed our second victory to another forfeit when the St. Stephen squad unanimously voted to stay after school and clean the blackboards rather than face Dudley's pitching. We won our next five narrowly, but legitimately, and in a few hours we would take the field against Our Lady of Perpetual Motion for the league championship.

Suddenly Coach Willis entered the locker room. As usual, his presence snapped us into immediate lethargy. Coach Willis was a jovial, intelligent man with an incredible grasp of the intricacies of the game, but he was incapable of transmitting even the tiniest shred of his knowledge to his players. His own baseball career had been cut short by his complete lack of coordination and ability.

"Men," he said, attempting to clap his hands together but failing miserably, "I have a little surprise for you."

"Our Lady of Perpetual Motion chickened out?" someone asked, hopefully.

"No, nothing like that," said Coach Willis. "Monsignor Munchkin has consented to stop by and say a few words of encouragement to you."

"Thank you, Coach Willis," said Monsignor Munchkin. "Boys, I will keep this very short." He waited for the applause to subside before continuing with his obviously prepared remarks.

"Thank you, Coach Willis." The nervous little priest stopped and crumpled the index card he was reading from and threw it over his shoulder. "Uh, um, oh, yes. Here we are." He cleared his throat and began to read from another card. "I just want to say that everyone at Our Lady of Pity is proud of the tremendous job you boys have done and, as you know, our trophy case always has room for one more. Ha! Ha!" The Monsignor appeared not to notice the absence of laughter, "but," he said, dramatically, "if you should happen to lose, don't be ashamed. After all, no one really expects you to win anyway."

"OK, Monsignor," yelled Coach Willis. "We'll see you at the game."

"I'm afraid not, Coach," mumbled Monsignor Munchkin. "I'm teeing off at two o'clock this afternoon."

Another round of applause greeted that announcement, and he left the locker room with a timid wave.

An hour later the team bus pulled into the parking lot of Elysian Field, Our Lady of Perpetual Motion's home park.

"There she is, right on time," said Marty Shea.

Sure enough, Sister Mary Mummy, our unofficial mascot, official statistician, and only fan, was standing near the chicken-wire backstop intently watching our opponents' batting practice.

The bus's squeaky brakes alerted her to our arrival, and she walked over as we disembarked from the Yellow Peril.

"Hello boys," she said, hefting our equipment bag and carrying it tooard the visitors' dugout. "I've been watching these guys, and they don't look all that tough. I figure their .768 team batting average is a fluke."

"Oh, yeah," said Marty Shea, as a wiry kid belted a pitch over the distant center-field fence. "Check out that little guy's power."

"Anyone can look good in batting practice," replied Sister Mary Mummy, "except possibly Sullivan."

"Maybe," said Dudley Mack, "but he hit that thing one-handed."

Sister Mary Mummy dropped the equipment bag and consulted the roster on her clipboard. "Don't worry about him," she said, "he's third string."

Several months earlier, I had asked Sister Mary Mummy why she attended all of Our Lady of Pity's baseball games.

"I just love baseball," she said, "and since there aren't any real teams around, I have to be content with watching the Pitifuls. And, I might add, seldom has an athletic team been blessed with a more appropriate name."

Her remark came to mind as I watched my teammates struggle through infield practice. Of course, the poor condition of the field contributed somewhat to our general display of incompetence. It had more gouges and ruts than a backcountry road after a long, hard winter. The outfield grass was so high that it looked like the outfielders were playing on their knees.

"C'mon, Shea," Sister Mary Mummy yelled after our normally steady third baseman let a slow grounder roll up his arm and over his shoulder into left field. "I could've handled that one barehanded with my eyes closed. You guys look like an outtake from a Keystone Kops movie."

When it became apparent that we weren't going to improve, Coach Willis whistled the team off the field and began reviewing the starting lineup. A few minutes later, Our Lady of Perpetual Motion's coach approached our dugout. He looked grim.

"I've got some rather disturbing news," he said.

"What's wrong?" asked Coach Willis.

"The umpire called in sick and we don't have a replacement."

"We're Number One!" screamed Dudley Mack, immediately grasping the fact that a forfeit was imminent.

"I'm afraid we'll have to forfeit," said the crestfallen coach.

"Gee, that's a real shame," lied Coach Willis, "but we can't play without an umpire."

"Just a moment, gentlemen," interrupted Sister Mary Mummy. "You can't decide a league championship this way."

"Do you have any other ideas, Sister?" asked Our Lady of Perpetual Motion's coach.

"Certainly," replied Sister Mary Mummy. "I will serve as umpire."

"That's very generous of you, Sister," said Coach Willis hurriedly, "but, but . . ."

"Do you doubt my qualifications, Coach Willis?"

"No, of course not," he sputtered, "it's just that . . ."

"Can you be impartial, Sister?" asked the opposing coach.

Sister Mary Mummy fixed him with an icy glare. "Could Babe Ruth bounce 'em off the upper deck?"

"What about protection?" asked Coach Willis. "The players' equipment is much too small and you can't go behind the plate without adequate protection."

"I'll take care of that," replied Sister Mary Mummy. She began to jog toward the parking lot. "Be back in a minute."

Dudley and I began warming up his pitching arm. He had thrown about a dozen scorchers when he stopped in midwindup and stared disbelievingly past me.

"Oh, my God," he gasped. "Look at that."

Sister Mary Mummy was trotting toward us wearing her hastily improvised umpire uniform. She looked like some kind of surrealistic executioner. A large, faded, graffiti-laden red seat cushion from the Yellow Peril was strapped to her chest. Her face was hidden behind the wire basket that usually decorated the handlebars of the bicycle she rode to the games. She was carrying a full-sized broom in her right hand and when she reached home plate, she began sweeping frantically. Before long, she had raised a dust cloud straight out of *The Grapes of Wrath.*

"Play ball!" she yelled, when the dust finally settled.

The first four innings were scoreless and hitless. It was obvious that a pitcher's duel was in the making.

The other team's pitcher was not quite as fast as Dudley, but we weren't making contact. Dudley's control was superb. He had given only one foul ball while retiring the first 12 batters. Sister Mary Mummy had, as expected, assumed a complete air of neutrality, confirming her conversation to calling the balls and strikes.

Then in the top of the fifth I came to bat with one down and the bases empty. The count went to two balls and two strikes. I dug in for the next pitch. I was so sure that it would be a fast one down the middle that I made no attempt to move. The ball slammed into my ribs. The pain was excruciating, but I tossed my bat away and began to jog toward first base.

"Just a minute," called Sister Mary Mummy. "You can't take first. You let yourself get hit. The count is three balls and two strikes."

"But Sister," I said, "I couldn't . . ."

"Batter up," she said.

Reluctantly, I retrieved my bat and took a pitch that missed the outside corner by a foot. Again I headed for first.

"Strike three!" yelled Sister Mary Mummy. "You're outta there."

"What!"

"You heard me," she said. "If your tail isn't on the bench within five seconds, you're out of the game."

I was sulking in the dugout when Dudley, the next batter, hit a line drive out of the park. We went ahead 1–0 and the score stayed that way until the bottom of the ninth.

Dudley struck out the first two batters with ease and we were only a single away from clinching the championship.

Dudley kicked his left leg higher than a Radio City Rockette and sent the next pitch toward the plate. The ball was traveling so fast that it looked smaller than a golf ball. But the batter stayed with it and unleashed a vicious swing that sent the pitch halfway to the state line. We were tied, and the prospect of extra innings loomed unpleasantly. Nine innings of catching Dudley Mack's fastball, the only pitch in his arsenal, was about all I could endure. My right hand already resembled a half-pound chuck and my ribs were bruised and sore.

I was still cataloging my ills when the next batter accidentally lined one down the left-field line while trying to get away from an inside pitch.

"Fair ball," screamed Sister Mary Mummy, throwing off her wire basket and hustling toward third. The ball and the runner arrived at approximately the same time, but she was right on top of the play.

"Safe!"

The winning run was on third and Our Lady of Perpetual Motion's weakest hitter was in the box.

"Strike!" The ball tore into my glove and set my hand on fire.

"Strike two!" The batter missed on a bunt attempt and the fire in my glove intensified.

The next pitch was in the dirt, but I managed to partially block it. I spun around and threw off my mask.

"Where's the ball?" I screamed.

Dudley Mack charged in from the mound to cover the plate and Sister Mary Mummy was running backward to give me some room, but I still couldn't find the ball. The other team's third-base coach noticed my confusion and waved the runner home.

Then I saw it! It was under the hem of Sister Mary Mummy's habit. I dove toward her feet.

"Throw me the damn ball," Dudley screamed as the runner bore down on him. "Sorry, Sister," he muttered automatically.

I managed a weak underhanded toss in his direction and he met the sliding runner with a perfect tag.

"Safe!" yelled Sister Mary Mummy with the classic palms down sweeping motion and absolutely no hesitation.

We, of course, protested the call that had cost us the league title. But, like all good umpires, Sister Mary Mummy declined to change her mind.

"When I officiate during a ball game," she said, "many are called but none are wrong."

AUTO RACING

MOTHER NATURE JILTS A HANDSOME TEXAN

By Hubert Mizell

From the St. Petersburg Times

Mother Nature jilted one handsome Texan and laid a wet championship kiss on another Sunday in the third rain-butchered Indianapolis 500 in four years.

It was the "Indy 255."

Johnny Rutherford of Fort Worth became a two-time Indianapolis winner in Indianapolis's shortest race ever when thunderstorms, after first giving A. J. Foyt a marvelous break, then destroyed the fabled Houstonian's fading dream of a record fourth victory.

The thirty-eight-year-old Rutherford passed Foyt's swerving red automobile on the eightyieth lap around the two-and-one-half-mile Indianapolis Motor Speedway and was 11 seconds ahead when the Hoosier skies began dripping on a festive multitude of more than 300,000.

Rutherford's payoff wasn't immediately announced, but he is expected to clutch about $215,000 of a total purse of $1 million when figures are announced today. Foytt will get something less than $100,000 for second.

To be official, the scheduled 200-lap race must go a minimum of 101. There were 100 laps on the Indy scoreboard when United States Auto Club people whipped out yellow caution flags because of the weather. Two more laps were run under caution before the 27 remaining cars were red-flagged to a stop.

Just enough.

"It's sweet, any way you can get it," said Rutherford, who won the 1974 Indy 500. "I feel sad for A.J. because if we'd resumed racing

. . . well, old Foyt was repaired and ready . . . loaded for bear and ready to give a charge. I don't know if I could have stayed with him."

Foyt wouldn't talk.

Although he had stuck with Rutherford, the forty-one-year-old Foyt knew his car wasn't functioning properly. It had begun on the fortieth lap. Foyt had wrestled with his steering wheel to keep from scraping the infamous speedway walls.

But, during the two and one-half-hour rain delay, A.J.'s pit crew discovered the machine's ailment. The sway bar was busted. As they were peppered by raindrops, the Foyt mechanics repaired it in 20 minutes.

Soon, sun funneled through the clouds, Foyt sat on the pit row wall, smiling and talking with reporters. "Yeah, I can catch Johnny now," he said. He was philosophical and admitted to being a fatalist about racing fortune.

"This might be just the blessing . . ." he said. "If it's your day, things fall into place. If we're not supposed to finish, we'll blow up. I believe that kind of stuff, I really do. Today might be the day . . . it's a storybook thing. Just like last year wasn't our year here, from start to finish."

Soon afterward, Foyt's car and the other 26 were pushed into a single-file lineup for a restart of racing. The weather, as if by fate, spit on Indianapolis just as the drivers had been ordered to reboard their machines.

It was called 12 minutes later.

Foyt could smile no longer. Nor talk with reporters. He ran for shelter of the Gilmore Racing Team's garage in Gasoline Alley. "A.J. don't wanna talk," said a burly aide, slamming the doors shut. Car owner Jim Gilmore later came out as a spokesman.

"It's very difficult for him . . . A.J. has been such a winner," Gilmore said, seemingly on the verge of tears. "He's in deep thought. Not a mad, snorting type thing. Just thinking about what has happened to us . . . and what's ahead."

Foyt won the last of his three 500's in 1967. Nine years of attempting to become Indy's lone four-timer. Another May that became a month of no-rain.

Rutherford, Foyt, and third-place driver, Gordon Johncock, were the only men in the same two and one-half-mile lap when Mother Nature did her thing. Just as she had done in 1975 when Bobby Unser won the "Indy 435" and in 1973 when Johncock took the "Indy 332½" in other rain-clipped races. Before this 3-for-4 rain problem, Indianapolis had suffered only two rain-shortened events in 56 years.

Trailing Johncock this time was Wally Dallenbach with Duane

"Pancho" Carter fifth, Tom Sneva sixth, two-time champion Al Unser seventh, Mario Andretti eighth, Salt Walther ninth, and last year's hero, Bobby Unser, was tenth.

Rutherford had won the pole position with a qualifying average of 188.957 miles per hour for four laps. He is the first pole-sitter to win at Indianapolis since Al Unser in 1970.

Rutherford averaged a comparatively slow 148.724 miles per hour in the injury-free 102-lapper. Caution flags arose six times for 23 of the laps. Veteran Roger McCluskey had the only serious wreck, smashing the rear of his racer into the wall on the tenth lap.

Actually, it was Sneva who came closest to being hurt on the gray Sunday. While running 90 miles an hour under a caution, a coil spring left on the road by some other car bounced into Sneva. It then broke Sneva's racing helmet and landed in his lap. The twenty-eight-year-old Spokane, Wash., driver suffered cuts inside the mouth, but continued running to finish sixth.

Foyt narrowly missed being penalized a lap by USAC officials. His crew was using an extension wrench after 32 miles to adjust the car's rear wing, allowing an extra pitman to reach and work from behind the wall. When Foyt departed, the wrench was stuck . . . hanging from the rear end of his automobile. If it hadn't fallen off several hundred yards later, Foyt would have been black-flagged into the pits for removal.

Early in the long rain delay, Foyt fumed about Rutherford making up yardage illegally during caution laps. He talked of a protest, but later cooled and decided not to.

"Johnny's a good friend of mine," Foyt said at the time. "But, hell, right's right and wrong's wrong. I started the caution [period] with a 23-second lead and came out of it leading by four. Now, is that legal?"

Rutherford shrugged off the comments after being declared the race's winner. "Yeah, A.J. gave me some . . . well, I guess you'd call it verbal abuse," he said in a mass press interview. "But I wasn't cheating on the yellow [flag]. I certainly wouldn't cheat out there . . . anymore than A.J. would; or Bobby Unser would; or Johncock would."

That drew laughter. Racing is a get-away-with-what-you-can sort of sport. "Only thing is," Rutherford added, "is that you don't do anything too obvious. If you get caught, especially at Indy, it's a terrible price to pay."

Gilmore, the Detroit broadcasting executive who owns the Foyt car, said his team was unhappy at USAC officials for ordering such a long waiting period before deciding to restart the race.

"My personal opinion is that they could've started much quicker," Gilmore said outside his garage. "We feel, as a team, that we have an obligation to the fans. Everybody in the stands could see it was going to rain again. They should've gotten the show on the road."

That is all according to where you sit. Rutherford did, however, say that he "preferred to restart the race." His wife, Betty, said that "Johnny would rather have won going flat-out." Rutherford said he was nervous and edgy during the delay. "I knew it would rain again, too," he said, "so my real fear was that we'd get started again and that A.J. would edge past me after a couple of laps . . . and then we'd get rained on again."

BASEBALL

A SAD STORY

By Maury Allen

This is a sad story. It is a story about a young man, thirty years old, healthy, a professional athlete of enormous skills, a bright man, witty, in total control of his life, his emotions, and a great part of his future.

In a way it may be a story about so many baseball players today, so many professional athletes, different than most in only one respect. Ken Holtzman is a very honest man.

The Yankees are in a World Series that is passing Holtzman by, as he was passed by in the playoffs, as he was passed by in the final days of the season.

Each day, for some 10 days now, Billy Martin has been asked about Ken Holtzman.

"What about Holtzman?" he says. "Uhh, when will he pitch?" Martin looks coldly at the questioner and says, "When I tell him to get up."

Holtzman has been asked if there is bad blood between himself and the manager, if there is a sore arm being hidden, if there is some secret intrigue in his conspicuous absence. He laughs at all the fuss.

"I'm not a romantic about this game," he says. "I play baseball for money. George Steinbrenner is paying me a lot of money, an awful lot of money. I'll take it whether I pitch or not."

The World Series is the time of year when emotion is highest among players, when joy and ego and pleasures of playing overwhelm all the material gains. There is not all that much difference to people making hundreds of thousands of dollars between the winning share of $25,000 and the losing share of $18,000. The joy should be in the playing, in the doing, in the winning.

"If they want to pay me for sitting here I'll sit here," said

Holtzman. "If they want to pay me for pitching I'll pitch. If they want to pay me for being in the bullpen I'll go to the bullpen."

Holtzman came to the major leagues at nineteen with the Cubs of Leo Durocher. The boyhood dreams of baseball, fostered in high school in St. Louis, at college with the University of Illinois, were driven out of him by Durocher's tongue and Charlie Finley's vicious negotiating sessions.

"You can't imagine how that man [Finley] can demean you in negotiations," said Holtzman.

Holtzman's eyes were opened to the hard truths of baseball by Durocher, expanded further by Finley, made, one might say, perfectly clear by a trade this year to Baltimore. If Oakland wouldn't meet his terms, maybe Baltimore would. They wouldn't.

On June 14 he was traded to Kansas City. One condition was imposed on the deal. He had to sign a Kansas City contract. He was offered $1.1 million for four years. He also asked for a no-trade clause and some special deferred payments. The Royals agreed to the money but not to the no-trade and some special covenants.

He dressed again the next day as an Oriole, a man without a team.

Gabe Paul was in Chicago talking with Charlie Finley about Vida Blue. He also began talking to Hank Peters about Ken Holtzman. A whopping 10-player trade was made and Holtzman was a Yankee, an unsigned Yankee, but a Yankee.

Now, Jerry Kapstein, the commissioner of baseball without portfolio but with more than half a hundred players in his stable, stepped in. He went into high gear, the Yankees came up with big numbers and Holtzman signed through the 1980 season, a year past the due date of Catfish Hunter's expired contract.

The contract terms, of course, were never revealed but $1.4 million was given as a ball-park figure, give or take a few hundred though.

"It's a lot of money," said Holtzman. "A great deal of money."

It may or may not be a coincidence but Holtzman's pitching performance since the contract signing has not been of sterling nature. It is the real reason he hasn't pitched in October.

"I don't care," he said. "As long as the checks keep coming."

It's sad that he doesn't care. But this is what has happened to baseball and baseball players. Please don't let any little boys hear this story.

FOOTBALL

CALVIN HILL'S CHOICE: TO PLOW OR PREACH?

By Kathleen Maxa

From the Washington Star

Calvin Hill remembers well the last Cowboys-Redskins game at Texas Stadium in which he figured.

To date: November 28, 1974. And Hill, then Tom Landry's best running back, was suffering from a painfully swollen left foot. The week before the Washington-Las Vegas-Dallas axis buzzed with speculation. Would Hill play or wouldn't he? The oddsmakers were tearing their hair.

But as he stood on the sidelines of palatial Texas Stadium, tossing a football with teammate Robert Newhouse, Hill wasn't thinking about the point spread. And for a brief moment, minutes before the start of the game, he even forgot about his throbbing foot.

"All of a sudden," he recalled, "we heard this 'let's go' echoing out of the tunnel leading to the visiting team's locker room. I remember thinking it sounded like a herd of cattle. Newhouse nudged me with his elbow and said, 'Hey, watch these guys.' It is unbelievable. They were that psyched. I mean in Dallas, we had young guys who were lean and looked the part. But here [in Washington] you had all these old guys with beer guts. It was incredible."

As it turned out, those old guys with beer guts had the game won until a substitute quarterback named Clint Longly heaved a 50-yard touchdown pass to Drew Pearson with 28 seconds left in the game. The young Dallas toughs squeaked by Washington 24–23, a slender victory made no less so by the fact that Hill, the cotter-pin of the Cowboys' offense, never did play.

This Sunday, Calvin Hill will have to wonder whether some young tough in a Cowboy uniform—Scott Laidlaw, who wears Hill's old Dallas number, maybe—will be nudging a teammate with the same incredulous laugh as the Over-the-Hill-Gang stampedes into Texas Stadium once again, this time with Calvin Hill.

It's ironic how things turn out. Yes, even incredible that Calvin Hill is probably even less certain to start in Sunday's game as a perfectly healthy Redskin than he was as a practically crippled Cowboy just two years ago.

Is this the same Calvin Hill?

Earlier in the season, talking about his performance in the Seattle game, Hill said, "When I hit that field, Allen had me so charged up I just wanted to do something. I was tingling. I was so high, I was ready to tear somebody up. I had that feeling when I was a rookie. And I had that feeling when my son was born."

But yesterday, coming off his best performance as a Redskin—73 yards rushing against the Jets—there was no hint of that tingling as he talked of the game that should be the biggest tingler of them all.

What will Calvin Hill be doing the rest of this week to prepare for the Cowboys? "I'll be [Cowboy running backs] Preston Pearson and Doug Dennison," he said, referring to his stand-in role during practices. "I told them I drew the line at being Scott Laidlaw, the guy they [the Cowboys] gave my number [35] to." He laughed.

From the beginning, it has been a frustrating season for Hill.

Even before he donned his Redskin uniform, Hill and his reported salary of between $130,000 and $140,000 garnered the kind of attention he said he didn't want.

"I was trying to maintain a very low profile coming here," he said during an interview at his home, a California-style split-level on a wooded lot in Reston, complete with a garage housing two late-model, gun metal gray Mercedes-Benz sedans. A silver Ford Granada was parked in the driveway.

"And then I see myself on the cover of *Sports Illustrated*. One of the things that bothered me was my name is always preceded by "High-salaried" or "one of the Rich Four." And while I think I'm adequately paid, I'm not high-salaried when you consider [Larry] Csonka, O.J. [Simpson], or [Joe] Namath."

Hill, shoeless and relaxed with shirttails hanging out, was stretched out on the beige shag wall-to-wall carpeting of the paneled family room on his day off. He reached for the control knob on the large color television console, turning off the afternoon talk show he had been watching.

"Every now and then I'll take out my American Express card in the locker room (parodying the commercial) and say, 'Hi, I'm high-salaried Calvin Hill.' When you joke about it, it relieves some of the tension."

Hill jokes about himself a lot. For example, ask him how he met his wife, Janet, and he replies, "I thought she had some dough."

Janet, a striking woman, gives it right back to him. "I was at Wellesley, and at Wellesley you weren't anybody unless you were dating somebody from Harvard," she chided. "During a party after the Harvard-Yale game, Calvin came up to me and asked me to dance. I had no idea who he was. He had a tongue injury at the time, so he could't speak very clearly, and I thought, 'Wow, this guy doesn't even know how to talk.' I had to question whether this was the typical jock.

"When I got back to the dorm, the girls started buzzing about what a big star Calvin Hill was. A few months later, after his tongue had healed, he called me. I was impressed."

"If I had known you were as impressionable as that," said Hill, "I would have written." He then went on to say that the only reason he called her was that he had this free telephone credit card, see . . .

They were married two years later, after she had completed her master's degree in mathematics at the University of Chicago.

Hill seems to delight in retelling anecdotes and parables to illustrate the point he is trying to make at the time. He has a knack for quoting verbatim the words of others—Machiavelli, St. Matthew, Tom Landry, Duane Thomas.

Sometimes, you get the feeling that he has an index of the Top All-Time Hit Quotes which he whips out from time to time, before an interview, for example, to dazzle you.

At other times, you can almost imagine him weaving his parables and quotations from a pulpit, leaving his flock to ponder such profundities as Duane Thomas, Chapter 1, Verse 2: "If the Super Bowl is the ultimate, why are they playing it next year?"

Calvin Hill, you see, once believed he had a "calling" to the church, a church he saw as a vehicle for social change, only to find that his calling was to professional football.

You could say that Hill's youthful idealism fostered by the liberal intellectualism at Yale foundered on the fundamentalist, conservative rocks at Southern Methodist University where he continued his divinity studies for a time after the Cowboys drafted him No. 1 in 1969.

Or you could explain it the way Hill does, with a parable.

"I'm probably like the guy who was out plowing one day and looked up in the sky and saw the letters *G-P*. This fellow then went out and started preaching, got a couple of people to follow him, and went into debt to build a church. Before long, he lost the church, his followers deserted him. One day, he knelt down and prayed, 'Lord, I thought you wanted me to Go Preach.' And the Lord said, 'No, I wanted you to Go Plow.'

Or you could say that Hill was tempted. "When I was drafted, it was just like gravy," he said. "I mean here I was offered a bonus just to sign."

And he succumbed. "I said, 'Well, gee, maybe I could make a little money, buy my parents a house.' I didn't expect to be playing this long."

Now, a house or two, a couple of Mercedes, and a Ford Granada later, Calvin Hill, former Yale divinity scholar, is still playing professional football, still answering questions like, "What is your philosophy of running?" with glib answers like, "I just try to get there as fast as I can," and trying to find a kind of spiritual fulfillment in a game.

"It's a nice feeling to go out to a game and not care which guy makes the touchdown, to root for a guy who you are competing against to start at a position," he said. Team sports, he believes, provide one of the only situations in which people come together to really help each other.

"The thing that makes this team great—you know, the Over-the-Hill-Gang and all of that—is that the Redskins serve one another." Hill said. "Their greatness is from serving. There is a quote in the Bible about that. Let me find it."

With that, he whipped out a dog-eared, paperback Bible, and searched for the quote. Gesturing expansively, he read, "He who is greatest among you shall be your servant.'

"The Bible talks about how when people come together in a covenant they have to die to reach a certain goal. I'm not saying God wants us to win the Super Bowl. But I think there is a morality in a group of guys coming together in some cases to die to reach a common goal, utilizing their God-given talent, giving up some of their humanness, by that I mean selfishness.

"It's an exciting thing, an exciting thing to play and a difficult thing to be on the sidelines. It was especially difficult for me in the opening game. It's difficult to put aside your personal ambition, to root for another guy, even for a moment to rise above the humanness, or selfishness.

"The Super Bowl to me is the Promised Land. Not for a lifetime but for this year. God told the Jews that if they established a covenant among themselves that they would get to the Promised Land.

"I've been there. I've seen it. I've had a taste of the honey. It's an infectious thing."

TENNIS

FOREST HILLS '76: THE YEAR THE CROWD TOOK OVER

By Peter Bodo

From Tennis Magazine

In 1968, tennis became a business—for better or worse. It's just like digging ditches now. All titles are "major" now because they all offer big money. The only difference is a title like Forest Hills has a little arrow going here, saying "You've made it, kid."

—James Scott Connors

At 4:21 P.M. on Friday, September 3, 1976, the U.S. Open hurtled into its own vision of the future, a future so vast and powerful that it took the tournament nine days to recover a composure it may never fully possess again. The following events transpired simultaneously during the next 60 seconds, a minute which ultimately served as a mirror allowing tennis a clear glimpse into its changing face:

At the entrance to the marquee, a dutiful cop stubbornly refused admittance to transsexual Renée Richards, while two-dozen oglers clustered at a safe distance, whispering, "It's her. It's her." In the rest area between the stadium and grandstand, a pair of urchins sat amid the redwood benches and plastic shrubs holding up slightly blurred prints of Bjorn Borg. "We're asking a buck and a half," said the younger boy. "He's the No. 2 seed, right?" Above the stadium, the Goodyear blimp waddled through the sunshine, so close to the ground that its shadow sucked along like a massive storm cloud, blotting out whole sections of the crowd at a time.

And then on the clay floor of the arena, Hans-Jurgen Pohmann took the second set from Ilie Nastase and flung a triumphant fist into the air. The crowd heaved and growled, and Nastase turned to the player's box with a grimace of absolute terror, a small creature cornered by a beast he had helped provoke out of a long slumber.

"You've got to be loose—that's what it's all about," Jimmy Connors had said long before an assassin's nerve and brilliant shotmaking vaulted him past Borg in a stomach-knotting final. "You can be scared of Wimbledon or Forest Hills; sometimes I'm scared out of my mind by these events. But then sometimes I'm scared going from my bedroom to the kitchen and I just say why be scared of a tennis ball?"

Yet in truth there is far more to fear in this Open than the unruly bounce of a ball. Forest Hills this year was a changed event, an event rushing after and finally catching up with boom-time tennis, swallowing or crushing all but Connors and Chris Evert, who were respectively the loosest and coolest players through 12 seething days. Last year's celebrated uprooting of the hallowed grass courts was a change of the most illusory kind. It was merely a prelude to 1976, which may very well be remembered as the year the Open finally entered the brave new world of big-time sport. And it did not enter triumphant. It lurched and staggered like a drunken sailor. It reached the threshold and arrived. But only just.

"I can't find the pulse here," admitted Lesley Hunt early in the tournament. "It's like some big machine; it sends out very strange vibes to me." A heavy dose of those vibes emanated from a little green shack between the corner of the stadium and the marquee, in which were housed the offices of the tournament referee, Charles Hare, and Capital Sports, a bullish firm rerecruited to market the U.S. Open.

While Hare is an able man, his office must be held accountable for the disgraceful officiating which exposed how tennis clings perversely to the habits of a tranquil, amateur past even as the swell of commercial and popular success threatened to crash over and obliterate the whole circus. Capital Sports was responsible for the new water fountains, air-conditioned ladies' toilets, plastic shrubs, widened walkways, bright red Avis banners hanging strategically alongside the scoreboard, bacon and gruyère quiche, Coffe-mate, Dijon mustard made with white wine, public benedictions of Kodel polyester, the decline and fall of Mr. Peanut, and what was advertised as "Strawberries with Devonshire Cream." Actually, they were really strawberries with Reddi-Whip on top. Oh well, that's marketing.

Other strange vibes emanated from the draw, where the conspicuous absence of names long synonymous with Forest Hills announced the emergence of a new generation, ruled by youth with feet of clay. With the exception of Nastase, the important names were young names, like Connors, Borg, Guillermo Vilas, Adriano

Panatta, Harold Solomon . . . no Rod Laver, Ken Rosewall, Arthur Ashe (an early, disinterested loser), John Newcombe, or Tony Roche. For the first time in 35 years, no Australian was seeded.

"I don't feel 35 or anything," said Stan Smith early in the tournament, "but I guess I'm one of the old guys now." Mark Cox put it this way: "The name has grown exponentially. We are in a totally new era of tennis. The old generation was allowed to survive as long as it did because it effected the transition from amateur to pro tennis. Now, they've been pushed out by the first generation raised as complete professionals."

But the strangest vibes poured forth from a crowd weaned on spectacle and too many bogus championships, grown up with Nastase and team tennis, manipulated and encouraged by the frenzied commercial rush to buy a piece of the game. You could sense the beast coiled inside the stadium even through the calm, opening days of the event. You could hear it stirring in the grating, restless shuffle of feet on the clay-dusted walkways and in the chiming of a hundred empty tin cans, animated by the wind in the upper reaches of the stadium at night. For the better part of a decade, this beast had slumbered even as the game changed all around it. When Nastase finally raised it with his own galvanizing personality, it nearly devoured him and the Open as well.

The specifics of Nastase's match against Pohmann have long ceased to matter. What remains disturbing is the misapprehension of those events in the media, particularly *The New York Times*, which callously announced "Ilie Nastase disgraced Forest Hills yesterday" in the lead story. Really, it was the crowd which disgraced tennis.

It was a crowd that lost all semblance of rationality and degenerated into a malevolent, bloodthirsty mob. In its frenzy, the beast further maimed a man it had never really understood but whose presence it lusted after.

Nastase reached into the very heart of the beast, and that is always a terrible, violent place. If he cursed, screamed, berated largely incompetent linesmen and made a public confession of his deepest neurosis, Pohmann urged the mob to judgment and demanded Nastase's head. Carried away by his own emotions, the German played *Parsifal* in the finest Wagnerian tradition. He helped the beast track and crush a terminal delinquent with a deep impulse to be loved and accepted. It was a classic example of mob manipulation; for understandable reasons, Pohmann was moved to bow from the waist when it was all over. A shattered Nastase reached the quarterfinals carrying something dead inside himself, looking as if he would crumble at so much as a touch.

"I want to play, but is not me I have to please, is everybody but myself," droned Nastase after Borg easily decimated him in the quarter-finals. "I have the lowest image in the world now, no matter what I do. I think I will not play this tournament next year. The crowd just want me to be like other players. I think half the people just want to see what Forest Hills look like, to come out in the new clothing. . . . Against Pohmann I was almost crying, I think I kill somebody. I don't take Pohmann racquet. What I do? I don't take Pohmann racquet."

This was the lament of genius, not just another gifted, mercenary jock but a player Fred McNair defended as "a man who cares deeply about his craft. The Einstein of tennis." It is entirely possible that Nastase's grip on existence measures 4⅝ inches around—roughly the size of his racquet handle. Tennis seems less a job to him than a reflection of life itself, which is why he constantly brings moral dimensions and conflicts into the otherwise small world of sports. It is astonishing that he reached the quarters after the mob and media took his racquet.

Yet there was another genius on hand, a kid tough as the steel racquet he swings; bold, shrewd, perfectly adapted to the faint odor of cigars now hovering over the game. Connors is a most deserving champion, and when the baseliner Borg offered him the title, he had both the courage and confidence to seize it. Connors trod easily but carefully throughout the draw, with one eye on his own notorious past and the other on the crowd.

"These people came to see blood and I didn't want to give them any of mine yet," said Connors in retrospect. "I decided to just come here and not say a word. I hate to say anything about this crowd because I have to face them. Let's just put it this way: I'm glad they're out there. I'd get awfully bored playing before an empty house."

So yesterday's rebel is today's regenerate. Unlike Nastase, who has consistently squandered away titles with his compulsion for self-expression, Connors has learned how to play the game both on and off the court. The only scar he bears is a cynicism evident in his evaluation of what the Forest Hills title means. "I figure about two million when you count everything," he said. With such a realistic grip on the sport, it is no surprise that his tennis was both stirring and elevated.

In both the semifinal against Vilas and and the final against Borg, Connors exposed the weakness in the vogue top spin game as he hammered his fluid, flat balls from corner to corner with the kind of pace and depth no topspinner could really match. Said Pancho Segura long before the final: "Jimbo owns this tournament. Borg is the big worry, mainly because he is so mentally tough, tough even as Laver. But all this wristy, over-top-spin s—— is gonna go out soon. Jimbo hits the ball hard, deep, low, clean. All these other guys hit big spinning balls in the middle of the court. Useless. Jimbo gonna kill that stuff."

The final echoed Segura's words even though Borg was "20 percent below fit," according to his coach, Lennart Bergelin. That was attributed to his long layoff after Wimbledon where he injured a stomach muscle. Borg groped through the tournament, playing very patchy tennis, flirting with elimination against Jaime Fillol and Brian Gottfried.

Predictably enough, he played a serene, cool final, unmoved by the hot stream of winners Connors rifled by him in the first and easily most attractive set. He would wait his oppenent out, but Connors succeeded in combining his hunger for smashing winners with an equivalent deliberation and did not become impatient. The title belonged to Connors; he produced the most mentally intense final Forest Hills had seen in a long time with his 6–4, 3–6, 7–6, 6–4 victory.

Lost among all the dramatics in the men's division were the women, for totally understandable reasons. By the middle of the tournament, it was clear that the draw was less like a developing chessboard than one swept over by a rough, careless hand that left it littered with overturned pawns and one queen standing at each end.

Evert and Evonne Goolagong was the matchup everyone had anticipated and it proved no match at all. Allowing her opponent just three games in the final (the score was 6–3, 6–0), Evert proved that she might very well be the greatest competitor the game has ever seen—male or female. Her domination of women's tennis is so thorough that it sometimes seems like the best thing she could do for the game is retire. Until then, she will in all likelihood go on winning and the spectators will continue to take her for granted. It is the unique punishment for her genius.

Before the final, Goolagong calmly said that "there would be more pressure on Chris." She was absolutely correct, but neglected to say that this is precisely the condition under which Evert is motivated to play her best tennis. It was by all standards a tailor-made final for Evert, with her consecutive clay court win streak of 100 matches and the No. 1 world ranking at stake. When it was all over, Evert said, "At 5–3 I felt spacy, like anything would work, like any ball I wanted was a winner." She paused. "I get that feeling on clay a lot."

So the 1976 Open belonged to Evert, Connors, and the crowd, which shows just how far down the road to staggeringly popular success the game has traveled. Although there was precious little to polarize the mob in the women's draw, Nastase had opened the floodgates and demonstrated that unless the game abandons the color and excitement which is so fundamentally responsible for its success, crowds at Forest Hills will never be the same again.

"Team tennis has taken its toll," rued Vitas Gerulaitis after losing to Connors. "If I went up into that crowd now, 50 percent of the people wouldn't even know what the score was. I felt like a gladiator out there tonight. The fans are hungry. They want action."

Polarized, predatory crowds are not new to sports, but they do pose a threat to tennis because of the game's chronic history of woefully inadequate officiating and reliance upon an intelligent, well-informed crowd. Tennis today is a vulnerable sport, dragged into the future by a commercial gold rush but dangerously close to falling back on the stifling authoritarianism which is born of chaos.

The blame does not lie with line judges, who are often overworked, under paid, and unqualified. It belongs with the entire tennis community, whose general greed has driven the game faster and further than its own internal development can keep up with.

The beast is awake now, and more likely than not it will remain with us. Forest Hills 1976 was not the end of something but the beginning—and heaven help anybody who is not holding on tight as the sport careens toward its uncertain future. The game will undoubtedly continue to accelerate; Capital Sports has not been recruited to market the U.S. Open for nothing. This year, Capital eradicated the crowded, hectic street-fair atmosphere that has prevailed at the tournament for years and replaced it with plastic shrubs. Overpriced, lousy food has been replaced by good food that is still overpriced but at least chic. If the general public has benefited from Capital's presence in terms of creature comforts, it has also traded away the accessible, human feeling of the tournament's past.

And the revolution is by no means over. The West Side Tennis Club, long supported by the admission money of tennis fans, has now to start paying off the debt. Standing on the clubhouse sundeck and looking out over the grounds at night, it takes no undue labor to imagine the great stadium of the tennis future (instead of the present intimate, ivy-covered horseshoe) towering and gleaming in the moonlight, its steel walls piercing the sky, bigger than anything envisioned back in 1968, throbbing with the lusty roar of half a million as the new champion wins match point with an atomic ace, and delivers his victory speech from behind a panel of bulletproof glass.

BASKETBALL

THEY REJECTED EMOTION TO WIN

By Betty Cuniberti

From The San Bernardino Sun-Telegram

The mechanical Indiana Hoosiers watched one of thier starters leave the game on a stretcher. They watched the scoreboard as it showed them falling behind—by four, by six, by eight.

Then, like the awesome machine that the Hoosiers have become, they rejected emotion, interchanged a few parts, and mercilessly destroyed Michigan, 86–68, to win the NCAA championship Monday night.

Indiana finished the season computer perfect—32–0. In the first public show of emotion all year, the Hoosiers left the game one by one and hugged and kissed each other.

Indiana forward Scott May, everyone's player of the year, actually danced off the floor, holding his index fingers in the air, departing with a team-high 26 points.

Indiana has been top-ranked from the first preseason poll, but the championship it seemed so destined to attain suddenly fell into jeopardy when Michigan forward Wayman Britt sailed the length of the key for a lay-up and landed with his elbow on Bobby Wilkerson's chin.

The Indiana guard lay stunned for several minutes before he was removed by stretcher and taken to a hospital for treatment of a mild concussion.

Indiana Coach Bobby Knight replaced him briefly with streak shooter Wayne Radford, then changed his mind and alternated between senior Jim Crews, for experience, and Jim Wisman, for quickness.

When Wilkerson left in the opening minutes of the game, Indiana was behind, 6–4.

The Wolverines, who had lost twice by slim margins to a healthy group of Hoosiers early in the year, played what Coach Johnny Orr called "our best first half of the year," running down the Hoosiers and scoring 18 points off the fast break.

Michigan pulled to its biggest lead when guard Steve Grote hit an open 18-footer for an 18–10 lead.

Knight called a time-out and put in Crews for Radford, who looked visibly relieved to sit back down.

Indiana briefly took a lead but Michigan went right back on top with a three-point play from Britt and a back court-press steal and basket, making it 31–27.

All-Tournament guard Rickey Green scored 10 points in the first half as the Wolverines took a 35–29 half-time lead, hitting 61 percent of their shots.

The Hoosiers, meanwhile, had shot just 45 percent—a low figure for them, and the replacements for Wilkerson had combined for just two rebounds and no points.

Things looked dim for the Hoosiers, who had played the extremely physical game that is commonplace in the Big 10 Conference. It was the first time in history that two teams from one conference had met to determine the NCAA championship. And after the first 20 minutes, at least, it looked as if the Big 10's second-place team would become the nation's first-place team.

But Indiana proved it could win in good times and bad, and regrouped at half time.

"When Bobby Wilkerson got hurt, we knew we had to go at it tougher," said the other starting guard, Quinn Buckner. "Bobby's a big part of our team, he's a 6-foot-7 guard!

"We did go at it."

"At half time," said May, "we talked about keeping our game plan and outhustling them. No panic."

Center Ken Benson, who scored 25 points and was voted the outstanding player of the tournament rearranged his mind at intermission.

"In the second half, it was a matter of me going out and gathering myself together," said Benson, who gathers together at 6-foot-11, 245 pounds. "I had to go strong to the hoop and play defense. I played harder in the second half."

Indiana forward Tom Abernethy, who played with a bruised knee, spoke of the players' feeling for the injured Wilkerson—or, the lack of it.

"Once you're in the flow of the game, you can't worry about those things," said Abernethy, who scored 11. "When I looked at him on the floor, I didn't think it was that serious. Then he just laid there and laid there.

"I was worried about him for his own safety but we knew we had to just go and play with him or without him."

Indiana opened the second half with four quick points and tied the game within five minutes. Michigan was not as quick in the second half and had little success with its break. The game's intensity was like "World War III," according to Grote.

May and Benson combined for the Hoosiers' first 10 points of the half to knot the score at 39–39 with 15 minutes left in the game.

Michigan's final undoing came on foul trouble, as center Phil Hubbard and Britt picked up four early, and Indiana went into the penalty-foul shooting situation with a fat 12 minutes left in the game.

The score was tied for the tenth and final time at 51–51 with 10:04 left to play, when Indiana ran off five straight points. It was still anybody's championship with six minutes left, and Indiana leading 63–59.

Then the Hoosiers scored 10 straight points, going to the free-throw line for half of them, to deliver the kayo punch. Hubbard already had fouled out and Britt left midway through the spurt.

May threw in a pair of free throws and suddenly Indiana was in command with a 73–59 lead with four minutes left.

Without Hubbard and Britt, the Wolverines were unable to retaliate.

"It just seemed that when we got into foul trouble, everything slacked off," said Green. "Our game changed. Everything."

And so the hopeful Wolverines were to bow out with a 25–7 record and a second-place finish to Indiana again.

"No question," said Michigan Coach Johnny Orr, "Indiana is the No. 1 team in the country.

"We were superb in the first half, but they were stronger in the second.

"Maybe it was because they wore us down. Down the stretch. They made all the free throws and baskets. Whatever, I don't think I could have done anything different that could have changed the outcome."

Throughout the season, there was nothing any team could do to stop the near perfect Hoosiers.

"There's a pressure we've had," said Abernethy. "We've had just one thing in our minds—to win it all. Once we finally made our goal, we knew it was all over.

"We weren't going to stop until we got it, and we would do anything to get it.

"That's just the way we've done things."

GENERAL

A HOCKEY LESSON FOR DR. KISSINGER

By Dave Anderson

From The New York Times

In their patriotic contribution to the Bicentennial celebration, the Broad Street Bullies, alias the Philadelphia Flyers, alias the Stanley Cup champions, bisected the touring Soviet Central Army hockey team today, 4–1, and upheld the Spectrum's reputation as the cradle of licensed muggings. The triumph of terror over style could not have been more one-sided if Al Capone's mob had ambushed the Bolshoi Ballet dancers. Naturally, it warmed the hearts of the Flyers' followers, who would cheer for Frankenstein's monster if he could skate. Warmth was important because the temperature inside the Spectrum was as chilly as the atmosphere, as if somebody had left a window open in Siberia somewhere. The chill developed into a freeze when the Soviet team returned to its dressing room for 16 minutes during a scoreless first period in a protest of the Flyers' tendency to use their (a) shoulders, (b) elbows, (c) sticks, (d) all of the above. But the National Hockey League president, Clarence Campbell, persuaded the Soviet delegation to accept detente. As it turned out, they also accepted defeat, the Army team's only loss after two victories and a tie. In international policy, perhaps Clarence Campbell should give Dr. Henry Kissinger a few lessons.

"This is no way to terminate a series of this kind," Campbell advised Vyacheslav Koloskov, the Bulganin of Soviet hockey. "You must resume."

Koloskov agreed, and he quickly convinced Konstantin Loktev, the Soviet coach who had removed his red-uniformed team from the bench. Andrei Gromyko never stalked out of the United Nations with more style, or less reason, considering that the Russians knew how the Flyers play before they scheduled this tour. The most honorable thing about the Flyers is that they're not sneaky. Ed Van Impe, an elderly defenseman, proved that when he massaged Valery Kharlamov's brain and the Soviet left wing, who is considered their best player, as a left wing should be, curled up on the ice like caviar on a cracker. Moments later Loktev did his Gromyko imitation.

"I had just come out of the penalty box," said Van Impe, as comfortable there as he is in his easy chair at home. "He was looking down to pick up the puck. And when he looked up, I was there."

To some viewers of the TV replay, it appeared that Van Impe's elbow was mostly there. Some of the Russians later contended that Van Impe had slugged him with his gloved hand. At least nobody indicted his stick.

"It was," Van Impe testified, "my right shoulder."

"Not your elbow," he was asked, "or not your glove?"

"Oh, no," he said with a thin smile, "but I think I hit him, anyway. If he had done that to me, I would've just gone to the bench. It was ridiculous to take the team off the ice. I bumped him pretty good, but not like he was dead. He looked like he was on show-time."

But with the Army team the nucleus of their Olympic squad next month at Innsbruck, the Russians were concerned about injuries.

"In that case," Ed Van Impe said, "they should've played somebody else or they should've stayed home. They know who we are."

In the negotiations the Russians requested that their two-minute penalty for delay of game should be erased, but Campbell remained firm.

"You can't change the rules," said the one-time military attorney at the Nuremberg trials, "in the middle of the game."

Whether the Soviet players had been intimidated is difficult to tell because only seventeen seconds after the game had resumed the Flyers scored on a goal by Reggie Leach, a right wing who leads the NHL with 27 goals. After that the Russians appeared deflated as the Flyers, persistent forecheckers, anyway, kept them pinned at midice most of the time.

"They do a lot of unnecessary skating," said Fred Snero, the Flyers' coach. "They do a lot of retreating, hoping to get one man to leave his position. But we wouldn't be enticed out of position. It takes patience to beat them. Bobby Clarke knew that from having played for Team Canada against the Soviets in the 1972 Series, and he told our forwards."

At his locker Bobby Clarke wore a rosette of blood on his forehead, a souvenir of Viktor Kutergin's stick.

"It was an accident," the Flyers' captain said seriously. "He came right over and apologized when it happened."

That's more than any of the Flyers did, but then they're not hypocrites. They marveled at the Soviet goaltender, Vladislav Tretyak, a spiderman who made 45 saves, almost all of them spectacular. And when the game ended, the Flyers and Russians shook hands, as they had after the introductions when they exchanged gifts.

"Somebody told me we got little pennants and pins," Clarke said, "I don't know. I haven't looked at them."

In keeping with the NHL tradition, the Soviet Army players each received a lucite plaque with the Flyers' crest on it. They can add it to their collection of plaques with the crests of the New York Rangers, Montreal Canadiens, and Boston Bruins, their other opponents. But the Army players had been hoping for a different gift this time. They didn't realize that the Flyers would really give them the business.

BASKETBALL

KAREEM ABDUL-JABBAR GOES WEST AGAIN

By Barry Farrell

From Sport

The PA system at Los Angeles's "Fabulous" Forum sounds mighty like the voice of creation when it declares that the tall fellow in the goggles is "The World's Greatest Basketball Player!"—but this is Hollywood, sweetheart, and that's what we call faint praise. When you've got a myth in motion making hoop history right here in Tinseltown, you can't get by on simple bragging any more than you can with newspaper ads for home games saying

KAREEM!
LAKERS!

in that order, or program notes alleging that number 33 on our side is "THE FORCE in pro basketball." When the standard hype fails to exaggerate the powers of a loved one—especially a loved one returning from a cold northern exile to the comforts of a five-year contract worth between $2.5 and $4 million—the local idea of grandeur requires the boosters' chorus to come up with a new song and dance. That's what I imagined I was hearing last summer, when L.A. began to buzz with a story worthy of daytime TV: Six Milwaukee winters had worked wonders on the Lakers' new dynasty-maker, so that now, besides being the game's greatest player, Kareem Abdul-Jabbar was also the world's nicest guy.

No news could have been more welcome in Los Angeles, where feelings of unrequited fandom were a plague upon the two great houses of basketball. Wilt Chamberlain had stalked off the Lakers to sack the ABA franchise in San Diego and was now pursuing a bizarre obsession with volleyball. Jerry West had retired sooner than expected to become a gentleman golfer and unconvincing television shill. Gail Goodrich and the Lakers were then said to be more than

$100,000 apart in contract talks. But cheers rang particularly thin in memory for the heroes of Westwood, Lew Alcindor and Bill Walton, whose teams in six championship seasons had won 174 games out of 180 for coach John Wooden and UCLA. The enigmatic Alcindor had left town in what many took to be a huff, only to become the sulky Abdul-Jabbar; the embarrassing Walton, meanwhile, had emerged as a left-wing Mortimer Snerd, a Dresden-doll rookie whose more-organic-than-thou approach to life had him leading the NBA only in sick calls.

Kareem's accomplishments were not to be disputed—he was twice the collegiate Player of the Year, three times the NBA's Most Valuable Player, four times a first-team All-Pro, and the league leader in career scoring average, with 30.4 a game. But the impression lingered that Southern California had failed to charm him, that life in Los Angeles had left him feeling, as he once remarked, like a man "on a raft in the middle of the ocean." So while no one doubted that the Lakers had done well to invest in his talents, the town was in need of consolations not to be found on the court alone, and the press was primed to quiz him on his loyalty to Lotusland when it assembled at the Forum for the grand unveiling.

The lights fell dramatically as the master of ceremonies intoned the Arabic words for "Noble and Powerful Servant of Allah," a name that for all its Islamic piety could hardly be better for basketball—"Kareem!" (the sound of a rebound) "Abdul!" (an elbow in the eye) "Jabbar!" (slam-dunk). A pin spotlight clawed its way up the crack in the curtain until it found the smiling, bearded face. Then, to the scribes' loud applause, the prodigal returned, shambling up to the dais like a stretched-out Jimmy Stewart. Kareem made many assurances that he was pleased to be back in L.A., and his calm and cosmopolitan manner was all it took to convince the grateful city that he was just what the Lakers were claiming—"a new super center with a new super attitude."

Sensing that the demands of folklore had somehow got the best of the principles of psychology, I made arrangements to meet Kareem one afternoon after a Lakers' practice. The team had looked ragged winning at the Forum the night before, and coach Bill Sharman was running the players through what seemed to be an intense and spirited scrimmage. Kareem worked hard in the thick of it, wrestling down rebounds, passing smartly, paying special attention to the rookies, laughing and hustling like a man with a new super attitude. The few times he took a shot himself, his teammates whooped it up for him, glad to be a part of Sky Hook Enterprises. Kareem scrimmaged for 10 or 15 minutes, then went over to a hoop at the side of the court to practice shooting free throws. He made 42 out of 49 and I was waiting for number 50 when he left the gym, beckoning me to follow.

I had to skip to keep up with his antelope stride as we made our way out into bright sunshine. We were on the Loyola Marymount University campus in southwest Los Angeles, a place of palm trees and succulents and hard green lawns, flat and interchangeable. Kareem walked to his car and leaned on the right front fender of the Mercedes. We had hardly exchanged a word, but now I saw that his eyes were flashing an ON THE AIR sign.

"Everybody's been saying what a changed man you are," I began. Watching the scrimmage had cast some doubt on my assumption that the story was a hype, and I could hear new uncertainty entering in my voice. "Can this be true? Are you going to have to come up with a bright and sunny disposition to live up to all your clippings?"

"No, not really," Kareem said after a moment's silence. "I'm just going to be myself, and in doing that, I think they might realize that the other ideas they've had about me were pretty far off. There's no way you can add me up to some of the things that have been printed."

"So your attitude isn't 180 degrees different from what it was this time last year."

"No, no, there's no way. This is the first time I've been in Southern California when I've been able to speak freely to the press. Also, when I was in L.A. before, I was an adolescent. Now I'm a man. That makes a whole new way of relating."

"So you do expect to relate to L.A. better than you could to Milwaukee?" I asked.

"Definitely. The Southern California life-style is completely different from what you find in the Midwest, I mean look. . . ." His arm swept across the semitropical tableau, a scene more like Marrakesh than Milwaukee. "See, I'm from Harlem. That means I'm from the cultural capital of Afro-America. Truly. People like W.E.B. Du Bois, Dizzy Gillespie, Charlie Parker, Nikki Giovanni, LeRoi Jones, they all derive from Harlem. In Milwaukee, there was just very little for me to relate to. This is not to put Milwaukee down, by no means, but it can be a pretty lonely life if you've got nothing to relate to."

The conversation proceeded along these lines, guarded, perhaps, but pleasant and cordial. We discussed matters of mutual interest in a friendly manner. We enjoyed a frank exchange of views. Overhearing us, you might have guessed that he was the Saudi ambassador and I the protocol man from the State Department. I had gleaned a list of adjectives used to describe Jabbar in newspaper articles over the years and, with his indulgence, I tried them out on him one by one.

"How about 'reclusive'?"

"No, not at all. I'm not hiding from anybody. Definitely not. I spend time alone, but reclusive I'm not. I've got a lot of friends. I spend time with people I like and who I'm pretty sure like me."

" 'Aloof'?"

"I can be aloof. But I think that has to do with meeting people who come at me as if I'm an object. Forgive this example, but I guess I might have a lot in common with a beautiful woman. A beautiful woman has to meet people who don't care anything about her, who just want to see her up close. And for me, I meet a lot of people who want to ask me how tall I am. Actually. That's their first and only remark to me. After a while, you see them coming, and you become what they call aloof."

"How about 'skeptical' and 'suspicious'?"

"I'm not . . . no, maybe I am a little suspicious. That might be true. It is true. I think it comes from growing up in this world. It's a tough world. A little suspicion can put you on a good survival track."

" 'Quiet'?"

"Initially, I am kind of quiet. I lay back at first and watch. That's a New Yorker's way. You do a lot of people-watching in New York, and I think I do that still."

"What about 'mentally hyperactive'?"

Kareem raised his eyebrows and looked far away. "I'm very curious about a lot of things. You talk about something new and I'll be all ears. But 'mentally hyperactive' sounds like a psychiatrist's term. I know I don't have to make any effort to clear my mind to play, not after doing it so long. It's my living, it's my blood. I suppose if my mind were hyperactive that might be a problem. Last year, when my hand was broken and I wasn't playing, that was the first time since I was in the fourth grade that my basketball season didn't start in the late summer. I had a chance to think about a lot of things. I might have been a little hyperactive then, I guess." He shook his head in a kind of baffled amusement.

"Would you say you're 'short-tempered'?" I asked, choosing another description from the list.

"No. Definitely not."

"Didn't you break your hand by getting so mad you smashed it against the backboard?"

"Against the backboard standard, yes. I punched it. The guy who drove me to the hospital told me that one time he was working in his basement shop and he put a drill bit through his thumb. It made him so mad that he kicked the wall and broke his foot. People do these things. It happens. That was my only consolation."

He stood up and jingled his car keys, agreeing to meet at the Forum before the game the following night. Before I could gather my belongings, he was gone. It occurred to me that even though our meeting had been perfectly pleasant, Kareem would have had a hard time picking me out of a police lineup if I had snatched those keys and made off with his Mercedes.

The sports writers of Milwaukee—authors of most of the words on my list—did not seem to be mourning Kareem's departure.

"Kareem was inaccessible a lot of the time," Rel Bochat, the basketball writer for the *Milwaukee Sentinel,* told me when I called. "We had confidential home numbers for all the players except him. That's just an example. Then a lot of times if you asked what he thought was a dumb question, he'd just give you the 'look.' Or else he'd say, 'Excuse me,' and barge right past, leaving you standing there with your pencil. On the road he was better. We'd go into New York, and those guys could ask all the dumb questions they wanted. They'd ask him about his Islamic faith and all that, and he'd sit there talking to them.

"The press here didn't ride him or anything like that. Once about three years back he made an obscene gesture on the floor, raised his finger, and the *Journal* ran a picture the next afternoon. He got pretty corked off about that. And then once I did a piece in which I mentioned Lew Alcindor had set some record, and Kareem didn't like that one little bit. I tried to explain that I didn't mean to offend him, that Lew Alcindor was his name at the time he set the record. But he gave me a big lecture about it anyhow. When he left, the town was divided, but as far as I'm concerned he won't be missed. The team's making money, we're getting some full houses, and we're going to win some games. Give my regards to Lew Alcindor."

Kareem patted the chair beside him when he saw me enter the Lakers' locker room. He was trying to work some comfort into a new basketball shoe, and he didn't speak or look up while I settled down beside him. I had been forewarned that he didn't enjoy talking about basketball much, feeling that his idea of the game is adequately expressed on the court, but still I began our second talk by asking him if he had any further personal objectives as a player.

"No, no," Kareem said, not lifting his eyes from the shoe. "I've accomplished everything anybody could hope to accomplish as a basketball player. I just want to continue to play like I've been playing, and that's enough. It's put me at the top of the profession."

He continued to knead the shoe, calm and deliberate in motion as well as word. His matter-of-fact answer left no room for elaboration. I asked him about his attempt to break the NBA gag rule last season, when he said after a game that referee Jerry Loeber "sets a standard for ineptitude that is unequaled," adding that he would, if necessary, ask the American Civil Liberties Union to defend his right to speak his mind.

"Oh, that ended up pretty well diffused," he said. "They fined me. I refused to pay. My team paid for me. And that was it. I think it might have shook a few people up, but I didn't expect any immediate change to come out of it. The pro basketball official has the roughest job of any sports official. We couldn't play the game if it wasn't for them. There'd be fights out there, one after another.

"It's just that the officiating has to be more consistent. If they're going to allow some roughness, they should make it the same for all players all over the court. They allow a lot more roughness under the basket than anywhere else. To the point of bloodshed, literally. The bigger you are, the taller you are, the more they allow people to do to you. They all blow calls, they're human, but the good officials will at least blow the whistle. It's the officials who don't blow the whistle at all, who just watch the game, that make it hard on you. The game just gets out of hand."

Kareem's teammates were assembling in the locker room, a roomful of well-paid athletes whose quiet manner produced an atmosphere more like the haughty downtown athletic club than the grab-ass locker rooms common to basketball. Kareem had a nod or a greeting for all of them, but, as in a decorous gentlemen's club, no one came over to intrude on his conversation. Kareem had shown immediate enthusiasm for the team, missing no practices and making no complaints, "as dedicated as a rookie," coach Sharman said. Kareem was glad to be free of the pattern-bound game of Larry Costello, whose Bucks playbook is said to be as thick as the Manhattan Yellow Pages. The Lakers' style is more like a city game, a pickup game, and that's the way Kareem likes to play.

As he dressed for the game, Kareem was recalling an important summer in his life, the summer before he graduated from high school. He was putting out a newspaper for a community project in Harlem, and his work took him often to the Schomburg Center for Research in Black Culture, on 135th Street in Manhattan. At Power Memorial Academy, where his teams won 71 games in a row, he was not only a superstar but also a 7-foot black at a midtown Catholic school; Jack Donohue, his high-school coach, had said to him, "Lewie, let's face it, you're a minority of one." But at the library,

Kareem discovered a larger context for his sense of being a person apart, and that led him to open his eyes to what was going on in Harlem. That summer, he became aware of black nationalist groups, of the Black Muslims, of various Yoruba groups, and of Malcolm X.

"My father always knew about our family history," he said, "back to the man who brought us over. We knew that we were Yoruba, that we'd gone from the Yoruba country straight to Trinidad. I really have to credit my father with giving me some knowledge of my roots. All of us are supposed to have roots, but the Afro-American's roots have been just . . . crushed out, you know. I wasn't in that position. I knew things about my family history which gave me some pride, and that was a good thing, because I was going to a school with a lot of Irish kids, and they could be sort of unkind. Then that summer came along, and I became aware of many new things."

Three months after Malcolm X was assassinated in Harlem on February 21, 1965, Ferdinand Lewis Alcindor appeared at a press conference to announce his decision to attend UCLA; the summer he arrived in Los Angeles was the summer Watts burned. His freshman team beat the UCLA varsity in his first appearance at Westwood, and Lew Alcindor was at once the toast of the town. But Kareem's reaction to Los Angeles was colored by dismay at the bland vanilla grins that greeted him on campus, the idle chatter that went no further than "How ya dune?" He turned inward, kept company with foreign students, read *The Autobiography of Malcolm X* and Frantz Fanon's *The Wretched of the Earth* and *Black Skin, White Masks.*

"Malcolm X had a big influence on me," Kareem said, now in his uniform and ready to play. "The contrast he made between Islam and Christianity was very concrete to me. Then I read the Fanon books. There were some Algerians at school, and they were telling me things, and one of them was teaching me a little about Islam. So in that atmosphere I absorbed it very deeply. Frantz Fanon—what struck me most about his thinking was the way he put down any kind of racism. We're dealing with human beings, so humanism is the only answer. . . ."

Sharman moved around behind Kareem and made eyes at the clock, signaling me to scoot. When Kareem saw me looking past him to the coach, he stopped talking at once. "Come on back after the game if you feel like it," he said as I departed.

The Lakers looked slewfooted beating the Atlanta Hawks that night. The free-lance game was out of whack, and with only one starter back from last year's squad, the team was forced into a patterned offense which no one played with any assurance. Although Kareem has an outlet pass as quick and strong as any in the league except, perhaps, Wes Unseld's, the Lakers weren't giving him much of chance to use it, with the guards breaking too fast or not at all and the forwards chugging downcourt late on offense.

But Kareem's play was superb, marked by what the hometown fans took to be a new exuberance. He dribbled the ball, loped downcourt for lay-ins, raised a power fist after satisfying baskets, and behaved as though he was having a wonderful time. His ideas on how to play the game of basketball were all there to be seen in the way he planted himself and looked toward the action, waving for the ball, passing into thickets of movement for many sharp assists. And when he went up for his patented sky hook, his arm described an arc of supremacy that was his alone, the dimension of his game that makes his presence on the court the most dominant in basketball. His performance seemed part game, part recital, and when it was announced that he had scored 39 points, taken 23 rebounds, and blocked 10 shots, the crowd reacted with a giant whew!, as though unaware of how much Jabbar had been doing.

Outside the locker room, Sharman was like a movie-star's manager, a smiling man with a luxurious problem. "Fellas, like I say, I hate to keep picking him out all the time, but what can I tell you?" he told the crowd of reporters. "He just did it all. He made us win a game we might not have deserved. It's going to take some time for the team to come together, two or three months, maybe longer. The thing about Kareem is that he can help us win some of these subpar games."

Sharman had said that he was "a little apprehensive about the guy" before Kareem arrived, but that as soon as practice started his worries vanished. "Some stars, you know, they're a little bit special, but not Kareem. He's not that way. He wanted to play, and that's a great big inspiration for the others, that someone as great as he is will practice with such dedication. And he's a very unselfish player. He's got great vision, he looks to pass before he shoots. He's great for a team with rookies, because he's going to give you the ball if you get open, and he's got such great hands that he can catch a bad pass and make you look good. I just can't say enough about him. He's a serious man, a reader, a good conversationalist, good company, a pleasure to be around. He's just a super player with a super attitude."

The first Laker road trips had produced some anecdotes about Kareem—small stories that made his teammates feel attached to him. He'd said something funny on the bus, told a good story in the locker room, got mad playing against Seattle's Tom Burleson (the only man in the NBA taller than he is), and declared a 12-minute *jihad,* scoring 15 points in the first quarter. Ted Green, who covers the Lakers for the L.A. *Times,* said that once you comprehend the ordeal of passing through public places at Kareem's altitude, his reputation as distant and aloof comes into focus. "I couldn't believe what happened just going through the L.A. airport," Green said. "I was walking with him, and I counted, and between the ticket counter and the boarding ramp he was stopped seventeen times by people who actually said, 'How's the weather up there?' and 'How tall are you?' And Kareem just kept walking as though he didn't hear. It's sad. He has to run away from the world so much of the time."

Kareem patted the chair next to him and picked up where we'd left off, talking about *The Wretched of the Earth.* It was only 10 minutes after the game, but he didn't seem the least bit flushed or fatigued. He maintained a dignified reserve, even in the course of applying a generous amount of powder to his peninsula-sized feet. Talking about Fanon led him back to the practice of Islam.

Kareem's sense of privacy, his reticence about his home life, his caution, derive in large part from the dangers that attach to speaking out as an orthodox Muslim in America. Threats have come his way, and three years ago seven members of the Nanafi, a division of his Sunnite faith, were murdered by intruders in a house he owned in Washington, D.C. The four persons convicted of the killings were all Black Muslims. There was, Kareem said, "the same mentality" about the killings as in the assassination of Malcolm X—"people trying to quiet down those who expose the lies.

"What the so-called Black Muslims believe is not Islam. Heaven and Hell are not on Earth. Any Muslim knows this. So that means these people are lying, or what they believe in is a lie, even if they accept it sincerely. They want to quiet the fact down. I don't see them as a danger, just something to test my faith. I have to live it. There have always been obstacles to test Muslims. There've been other false prophets. These people just aren't Muslims. They use Islamic trappings, but that's all."

"How about Muhammad Ali?"

"Cassius Clay is not a Muslim. He's just sowing confusion. If you asked the average American in Waukegan about the Muslims, he'd probably think first and foremost of Cassius Clay.

"You don't call him by a Muslim name. If he should choose to become a Muslim, I'll call him by whatever name he wishes to use."

Kareem, who has studied Arabic at Harvard, said, "I want to become completely bilingual by the time I'm through playing, because there's a great deal of anticipation and speculation as to our dealings with the Arab world and after I'm finished playing I definitely would like to respond to that."

The locker room was just about empty, Kareem was dressed, and his car keys were beginning to jingle. He said he still enjoyed the basketball life, didn't mind the road trips, tried not to let his interests be thwarted by the impossibility of being anonymous in public.

"I've been this height since I was fourteen or fifteen, you know, so I've learned how to deal with it. I've learned a whole lot about stealth, about how to sneak in and out, to walk fast, to watch people and know when their attention is going to be misdirected so I can go right on by. It can be hard to deal with, but I've always had positive identities about my height. When I've thought about what I am, I've identified with the Empire State Building and redwood trees. Seriously. That's exactly the truth. If you're going to be different, make yourself really different. Make it a mark of excellence."

BASEBALL

"IT WAS A WEDDING THAT MOVIES ARE MADE OF?"

By Hal Bodley

From The Wilmington News Journal

It was a wedding that movies are made of. She, the beautiful model whose smile and vivaciousness made watching toothpaste commercials on television exciting.

He the greatest catcher in baseball, the game's most eligible bachelor, the player who had done more for the sport in the past 10 years than anyone.

The wedding in February of 1975 was the social event of the sports year. Johnny Bench and Vicki Chesser were married with all the trimmings and dashed off to Tampa, Fla., for spring training with their faces on the cover of just about every magazine in America.

Johnny Bench doesn't know exactly when it started to go sour.

"We were both to blame," he told people. "I wanted her to be the perfect wife, the best of all worlds. It just didn't work."

The split came late last year and weighed heavily on Bench's mind when he reported to spring training last March.

Johnny Bench will tell you injuries and other problems caused his dismal 1976 season, a year in which he hit just .234 with only 16 homers and 74 runs batted in. He had shoulder problems and other nagging injuries. He played in just 135 games as the Reds' catcher.

But the most important problem Johnny Bench carried to the plate every day were those involving the divorce. He repeatedly got calls from Vicki's attorneys and the demands became high.

When you realize what Johnny Bench has gone through the past nine months, you can better appreciate how important his performance in the just-completed World Series was.

Bench, who will be twenty-nine on December 7, blasted two home runs good for five RBI as the defending world champion Reds ripped the New York Yankees last night 7–2 to win the World Series in four straight games.

Bench, who batted .533 in the four games with eight hits in 15 at bats, was named the Most Valuable Player for the seventy-third Series and will receive a trophy as well as an automobile.

"There were times when I wondered," said Bench in the midst of the wild and wet Reds' clubhouse celebration. "I didn't help my team too much this year because of the injuries and other problems. I was happy at last to contribute. I think this game tonight is the best I have ever played as a professional."

"This team will get a lot better than it was this year," predicted giddy Cincinnati manager Sparky Anderson. "The reason is because of Johnny Bench. He is all the way back. He's healthy now. He's had some problems I won't go into, but he seems to be over them now. I've never seen a better ball player, and I really believe the Good Lord meant for him to be a great baseball player."

Bench began to regain his batting stroke the last month of the season and proved he had it completely in the playoffs when he cracked a dramatic ninth-inning home run in the third game at Riverfront Stadium to tie the Phillies 6–6.

"I knew he was back then," said Anderson.

"I'm the kind of person who feels things are always going to be great," said Bench, "but when I had to have four cortisone shots in my back during the month of May and the spasms I had after the All-Star Game had me wondering. That was the low point for me, but things began to get better and better. Honestly, I'm relieved."

Bench, who is normally not an emotional person, showed excitement when told he was the MVP.

"It's the greatest thing that ever happened to me," he said. "This performance tonight was my best. I've hit three home runs in a game before, but this was my best. I was emotionally high in that I did not play well near the end of the season.

"I read where my biorhythm was supposed to be high for the Series. I guess it was. I kept trying to do better each day. Tonight, I feel I did and it makes me very happy."

Bench said there were lots of problems both on and off the field in 1976.

"I actually found my stroke between the end of the season and the end of the playoffs. This was the time to do it."

Bench did not have that beautiful model waiting for him as he left Yankee Stadium last night, but it didn't seem to bother him. Not one bit.

As he walked out of the dressing room, clad in an expensive suit, complete with vest, he said, almost like a little boy: "I can't believe this is happening to me. Not after all the things that have happened to me this year. Next year has to be better."

BASKETBALL

"THE MAN": REALITY VERSUS THE LEGEND

By Tony Kornheiser

From The New York Times

Thoroughly unfamiliar with the terrain, he moved his car slowly to the rear entrance of the Spectrum, looking for an attendant to guide him to the players' parking area. The directions were brief, but as he was pulling away he noticed the attendant staring into the car at him—a deep, searching stare of the kind usually reserved for persons of rare celebrity—and he paused.

"Hey," the attendant said hopefully, "are you The Man?"

And Julius Erving just smiled. The man, The Man, indeed.

He had been a Philadelphia 76er less than one day and already the word had spread, saturating the city with feverish expectation of what he would do, what he could do. Local newspapers had bannered his acquisition across their front pages. Local radio and television stations had announced it with bulletins on their news reports. Local cab drivers had all but canonized him to their fares.

His reputation as basketball's greatest natural resource had preceded him. His teammates awaited his coming with awe and wonder, questioning the 76er who knew him best, George McGinnis, as to the reality versus the legend.

"A couple of the guys don't know him," said McGinnis, indisputedly the team's best forward until Erving signed on Thursday. "They saw some film clips of Doc's best dunks on TV"—McGinnis began rotating his arms like a windmill, faster and faster—"and they asked me, 'Can he really do that stuff in the game?'"

"I said: 'You ain't seen nothing yet. I've seen him do that number over 7-foot-2 Artis Gilmore.' I'll tell you, there's gonna be a lot of guys in this league standing around watching him when he gets started."

Other 76ers treated Erving's signing as if it had been a bonus payment for them, perhaps an unlimited charge account at the bank of their choice.

"When I heard that Doc was coming," said Caldwell Jones, "I just fell down on my knees and cried. At least I don't have to worry about him going to the hoop on me."

Said Doug Collins: "I'm just so excited, I just can't imagine playing on the same team with George and Julius. The thought of the excitement we could create on the court is beyond my imagination right now."

Last year—even last week—Erving was a New York Net, a charter member of the American Basketball Association. He was the player most responsible for effecting the merger with the National Basketball Association; he created the demand for it. Then, suddenly, because of a bizarre combination of money and pride, he was sold to the 76ers. And though his uniform colors are still red, white, and blue, the number is 6, not 32; the shirt says, "Sixers," not "Nets."

"I'm a 76er now," Erving said simply. "I was as soon as I signed the contract. Everybody might as well get used to it."

But it will take time, mostly for the others.

"I know he played in Virginia," said Mike Gale, who once was Erving's teammate on the Nets and now plays for San Antonio. "But it seems like he's been in New York the whole time he's been playing. He almost always relates to New York. It seems he should be there. Automatically. It's strange seeing him play for Philly."

For Erving, the only adjustment was learning where to exit on the New Jersey Turnpike for Philadelphia. He spent most of Thursday and Friday driving up and down the road, from his home in Upper Brookville, L.I., to his job in the city they call the Little Apple. He hadn't had time to think about what it meant to be a 76er for the duration of his contract—the next six years.

"When I'm settled in," he said, "then I'll start thinking."

He was the first 76er to arrive in the team locker room on Friday night for the NBA opener against the Spurs. As he was getting taped, the first of his teammates straggled in, saying their hellos.

"Doctor," exclaimed Collins, "how you doing, man!"

"Julius, welcome to the Sixers," said Steve Mix, the starter Erving will replace as soon as he gets in shape.

More reporters than Erving had ever remembered watched him dress, recorded his movements, and noted his mutterings. They sensed they were privy to the making of history.

He slowly put on his uniform.

"Too big," he decided. "Gotta get a taper job."

He spoke deliberately, careful not to antagonize his new teammates, who were amazed at the crush in the room, realizing Erving's attractiveness to the press.

"I haven't played in competition for months," he said. "In my mind, I feel I can do anything I want on the court. But I don't think my body can do what my mind wants it to do. My body will tell me when it's ready. It'll take time."

He was in the shower area when McGinnis walked in; this would be the crucial greeting, the confrontation of perhaps the two best forwards in the game, suddenly teammates. McGinnis, who wants no part of "hyped" rivalries, spotted Erving and grinned widely. Extending his hand, he said loudly, "You sure look funny in that uniform, man."

The spectrum was dark when Erving's name was announced to the crowd of 17,196, except for lights on an overhead message board that spelled, "Is There a Doctor in the House." The announcement was brief:

"From Massachusetts. Number Six. Julius Erving."

The announcer's voice was swallowed by a tidal wave of cheers cascading down the solitary figure bathed in a spotlight on the floor. The crowd stood and clapped for two minutes, going wild when a fan gave Erving a doctor's bag.

"Outstanding," said Erving. "Probably the greatest ovation I ever received. I almost didn't know what to do."

Even his teammates were moved.

"That was a real touching thing, the way they cheered Julius," McGinnis said. "A real touching thing."

The game started with Erving on the bench. He remained there with a teammate, Fred Carter, trying to learn the Sixer patterns, which resembled a demolition derby until five minutes 51 seconds remained in the first half. Then Coach Gene Shue pointed at Erving and said, "Get in for Steve Mix."

Erving played the remainder of the half. His first pass was stolen. His first shot, a short jumper from the right side, missed. He got one rebound and blocked two shots. But he missed all four of his foul shots. Had he been a fringe player fighting for a job, he might have been cut at half time.

"When was the last time you saw Julius Erving miss four free throws in a row?" asked the 76er general manager, Pat Williams. "You can tell he's under intense pressure."

But Erving, who couldn't remember ever having missed so many fouls in a row, said the reason was conditioning more than pressure. He admitted to nervousness, but said his shooting was so crooked because he hadn't played in five months.

"My rhythm was off," he said. "I knew it."

The second half was much better. He went in with 3:17 left in the third period and scored the first two points of his NBA career on a shovel lay-up with 2:41 remaining in the period.

"I never worried about not scoring," he said.

Although the 76ers, the acknowledged team to beat in the 22-team league, were beaten, 121–118, Erving made a reasonable debut. He scored 17 points in 16 minutes. He didn't know the plays and he didn't look great. But greatness wasn't demanded, not even in a city that takes pride in booing dogs and children.

"Good start, Julius," said Fitz Dixon, the millionaire owner of the 76ers, who paid almost six of his millions to buy Erving. "We have 81 games to go. We'll win them all."

Erving said, "Yeah." He knew it was impossible, but he was in no hurry to offend his owner; he had learned the error of that way recently, and painfully.

"This is going to be a good situation for me," he said. "I see potential here. Give us some time. We won't be losing many more games this season."

There was something about the way he said "we."

He is a 76er now. People might as well get used to it.

FOOTBALL

A GAME TO REMEMBER

By Vito Stellino

From the Pittsburgh Post-Gazette

Forget the Monsters of the Midway. Forget Run to Daylight. Forget the No-Name Defense.

Forget the 1958 Baltimore-New York overtime game. Forget last year's Oakland-Miami playoff game.

Remember, instead, the Pittsburgh Steelers. And remember their 21–17 victory over the Dallas Cowboys in Super Bowl X.

It was a game to remember. And the Steelers are a team to remember. They've now won two straight Super Bowls. Only Green Bay and Miami have matched that. Now they're going for three straight.

The Steelers showed they're champions yesterday. They showed they can win any way they have to. They showed a sellout crowd of 80,187 at the Orange Bowl and millions more on television that they're a team for the ages.

They showed the Super Bowl doesn't have to be a conservative, defense-oriented game. The Steelers and the Cowboys both came to stage a shoot-out. The loser was going to go down with guns blazing.

The Steelers passed for a touchdown on third and one. They tried another pass that failed on fourth and two.

It wound up with Roger Staubach firing into the end zone on the final play of the game with everything up for grabs. But Glen Edwards intercepted it to end the most exciting Super Bowl ever and one of the most dramatic championship games of all time.

In the end, the Steelers proved they deserve to be champions. They're champions because Lynn Swann came back from a concussion to show he still has those hands that would make a pickpocket seem clumsy.

They're the champions because Roy Gerela, whose ribs hurt so badly that he sighed as he drew each breath after the game, came back from missing two earlier fields goals to kick a pair of pressure-packed ones in the final period.

They're the champions because Terry Bradshaw again proved he's a winning quarterback who was able to throw the winning touchdown pass even though he was clobbered as he released the ball and didn't even know it went for a score.

They're the champions because all 43 guys play an important role, even the unsung special team guys like Reggis Harrison, who blocked a punt that turned the game around in the fourth period.

They're the champions because Chuck Noll, a guy who usually plays it tight to the vest, seemed like a swashbuckling riverboat gambler as he took several big chances and came out on top.

They're the champions because Randy Grossman caught a touchdown pass on a play the club hadn't used since the College All-Star Game.

Yes, the Steelers are the champions.

How good are they now? Do they rank with the great teams?

"Those other great teams are gone and we're still trying to reach our peak," grinned Mel Blount.

"I don't like the word 'dynasty,' " said Andy Russell. "We don't win things for that. We win for today. But I'll say one thing. The pro football being played today is the best that's ever been played. It's a lot better than when I came into the league 13 years ago. And we're the champions. So draw your own conclusions."

The Steelers played their usual tough physical game and Jack Lambert became quite upset when Cliff Harris taunted Gerela after a missed field goal. Lambert stepped in to jaw with Harris and tempers flared. But mostly, it was just a sound game. The Steelers, who sacked Roger Staubach seven times for a Super Bowl record, didn't have a single penalty called on them.

But they weren't exactly super at the start. They got fooled on a reverse on the opening kickoff and Gerela bruised his ribs making the tackle that probably was responsible for his missed field goals.

Then Bobby Walden fumbled a snap on a punt and the Steelers' defense then got caught by a Dallas shift. Half the defense was playing one defense, the other half was playing another and the result was a 29-yard touchdown pass by Staubach to Drew Pearson for a 7–0 lead in the first period. It was the first time all year the Steelers have given up a touchdown in the first period.

The Steelers came right back to tie it up, thanks largely to the first circus catch by Swann and a surprise play when Bradshaw flipped the seven-yard touchdown pass to Grossman on a third-and-one call when the Steelers were in their right-end, short-yard running offense.

Toni Frisch's 36-yard field goal with 36 seconds elapsed in the second period was the next score and it stayed that way until the final period. By this time, there were a lot of nervous Steeler fans in the stands and back in front of their TV sets in Pittsburgh.

The Steelers seemed to be dominating the game, but Gerela had missed two field goals and the Steelers couldn't crack the goal line.

Then came the big play. The Steelers had Dallas in a fourth-and-13 situation on the Cowboy 16 and they decided to try and block the punt, Dave Brown played up close to create a 10-men rush instead of dropping back, and Dallas didn't adjust its blocking.

The path opened for Harrison to crash through and he blocked Mitch Hoopes's punt out of the end zone for the safety that made it 10–9. "I just wish that ball hadn't bounced out of the end zone and I could have fallen on it for six," Brown said.

The game seemed to turn around. After Dallas kicked off, the Steelers march back to the Dallas 20. Gerela came in to try a 36-yarder with 8:41 left in the game.

A lot of Pittsburgh people were thinking about Carson Long as Gerela went to try the third one after missing two. The fact that his ribs were aching didn't help, either.

"I wasn't worried," Gerela said in the locker room with the pain openly showing in his face. "I hadn't missed the other two by much. It wasn't like I was way off."

Gerela got it through and the Steelers were ahead 12–10 for the first time in the game. He added an 18-yarder and Bradshaw hit Swann on the 64-yard touchdown strike as Dallas gambled on a safety blitz that failed.

Bradshaw went down on the play and was still dazed after the game, but the score was 21–10 as Gerela's extra point attempt hit the crossbar.

Then came the Dallas charge, Staubach's touchdown pass to Percy Howard cut the deficit to 21–17, and their last attempt came after they took over on their own 39 with 1:22 left.

Noll's decision to run the ball on the fourth down instead of trying to punt drew a lot of questions after the game.

"We already had botched one punt and they can score a touchdown on a blocked punt," Noll said. "I had confidence in our defense. We were giving them the ball with no time-outs and I figured our defense could do it."

It did.

Mike Wagner had already intercepted a pass that set up Gerela's second field goal when he recognized a Dallas formation out of the shotgun and stepped in front of Drew Pearson.

Staubach scrambled once and tossed a few passes but the best he could do was to get to the Steeler 3.

Those 38 yards looked like a short distance to the writers who were standing in the end zone on the way to the dressing room for interviews with the Steelers ahead by 11.

But Glen Edwards intercepted a pass to end the game. On the play before that, Howard was hit at about the five and as the ball went over his head he protested to no avail that interference should have been called.

"It was tough at the end with no time-outs left," Staubach said.

But as Lee Roy Jordan said, "I'm proud of the way this team played."

The Steelers could be proud, too.

Franco Harris said, "I'm very happy, more excited than last year. We're No. 1 two times . . . we have championship blood in us."

The Steelers certainly do.

BASKETBALL

ONCE IN A LIFETIME?

By Hal Lebovitz

From The Cleveland Plain Dealer

It was Thursday night . . . the fifth playoff game between the Cavaliers and the Bullets, deadlocked at two.

You meet your companions for the evening, Buddy Bell and Duane Kuiper, the Indians' two bright young infielders, outside the Coliseum.

"Never saw a basketball game here," says Buddy. "How is it?"

"You're in for an experience."

"How do you mean?"

"You'll see."

We go inside. Most of the sellout crowd already is seated. The noise hits like a sudden wave.

"Don't you wish the Indians had this kind of cheering?"

"We did. Opening Day," says Kuiper.

"You like it?"

"Love it. Makes you want to go."

"This is going to help baseball, too," says Buddy. "You'll see. The enthusiasm will carry over to our club."

You mention the previous Saturday's game. "Nineteen standing ovations for the Cavs. It should go into the *Guinness Book of Records.* Friend of mine who recently had open-heart surgery had a three-day headache after that game. Gave up his ticket for tonight. Couldn't take another."

The noise grows. Mostly whistling and clapping, and clapping. Chanting begins, "GO Cavs." A few stupes, probably new to basketball, have bullhorns, common to hockey but never heard at Cavs' games before.

One fan, with a bullhorn bellowing in his ear, glowers at the blower. You think, "Every goof with a bullhorn should be put in a closet with the horn blowing constantly. Then when he yells, 'Enough,' break it over his head." Bullhorns should be banished from the land, to be used only at sea.

The announcer introduces the Bullets. Cavs' fans boo, mostly good-natured boos.

"Might as well get with it," says Kuiper. He boos, too.

The Cavs are announced. The fans jump up. Standing ovation. Bell and Kuiper are on their feet shouting. Two supposedly sophisticated professional athletes caught in the enthusiasm, the anticipation, the excitement, the frenzy.

"The frenzy," Bill Fitch, the Cavs' coach, is to say later. "You can feel it on the bench."

The din reaches a crescendo of encouragement as the Cavs take positions for the opening tap.

You, the blasé expert, try to fight off the emotions. It's just a game. You must concentrate, think clearly, analyze. Maybe in an isolation chamber. Not in this fury, in this electricity. The fan in front of you tries to read a magazine, *Minnesota Hunting*. Either a flake, or he can't take the excitement.

You think back. Was it like this in 1948, with the Indians? Or in those big years with the Browns? Not precisely. Not the same intensity as in this playoff series. Not as frenetic. Almost, but not quite. Maybe it's the enclosed building, the closeness to the floor, and the players. The familiarity. The smaller squad. The love affair, beginning with the bumbling but adorable infants who never quit no matter how great the odds, to the same grown-up battlers, at last in the playoffs. A love affair between fan and team.

The game begins. The intensity increases, never lets go. Take the greatest prizefight you ever saw, two men of equal strength and skill, pounding each other relentlessly. Take that palm-sweating chase scene in *The French Connection* and expand it for a full 48 minutes. The good guys are behind, they catch up, they go ahead, they fall behind, they catch up. Pulse pounding, fist-clenching, teeth grinding.

Only once before can you remember the same apprehension, similar tension on the faces around you. Dick Bosman's no-hitter. You sat in the stands that night. Fans nearby kept muttering. "I can't stand it. I can't stand it." The worry the doubt the hope the deliciousness of approaching glory the God-awful fret of approaching doom. It was there for Bosman. It's here tonight.

Buddy Bell stares ahead. The spring tan is gone. His face is white.

"Anything wrong?"

"No, I'm wrapped up."

Kuiper's lips are pressed tightly.

The two major leaguers exclaim and applaud a spectacular play. The Cavs have become THEIR team. The fan in front puts down his magazine. He can't read. He can't even fake it.

It is now approaching the final minute. The Cavs lead by one point. Now they trail by one. Less than one-half minute . . . 20 seconds the Cavs try to find an open man, Dick Snyder passes, the ball is intercepted. Fifteen seconds—the Bullets have the ball and the lead.

Some fans start to leave. It's all over. Beat the crowd. Not this time, pal. You did it once before against the same Bullets. The Cavs were four behind and little time to go. Two quick steals and the Cavs won. It can't happen again, you say, but this time you stay.

You see Bill Fitch on his feet in front of the bench. He's yelling to his men as the Bullets bring the ball down the floor. You think with him, "Foul somebody, grab somebody. Grab a poor foul shooter. Anybody."

He's shouting but his players can't hear above the noise. The seconds drop away . . . precious seconds . . . Seconds the Cavs need if they should get the ball again . . . 10 seconds . . . eight . . . Elvin Hayes gets a pass near the Cavs' bench. Campy Russell sees Fitch gesturing. He grabs Hayes. . . . Foul. . . . Six seconds to go.

Hayes! A great one. He had made nine of his 12 free throws. He had played 46 minutes. More than any other player. Forty-six unrelenting, bruising minutes, up and down, under both boards. If any player had to be fatigued it would be Hayes. Fatigue . . . concentration-blunting . . . the fine little making and missing.

Hayes faces the hoop . . . he tries to get his rhythm . . . he can't . . . he stops . . . starts his rhythm again . . . and misses. . . . But he needs only one and the Bullets can't lose in regulation time. . . . And he sets . . . again he tries to regain his rhythm. He shoots, the ball falls off, directly into the hands of a praying Cav. Time-out.

Bill Fitch has his men around him . . . diagramming. He knows the Bullets have only three team fouls. They aren't in a penalty situation. They can waste one foul before the Cavs try to shoot. Fitch thinks ahead. You try to read his mind. He must talk fast. He must be telling his men, "Get the ball inside to Chones, at the key. They'll have to grab him before he tries to shoot. That uses up their fourth foul. But we've got to get it to make them foul right away. Every second counts. Then when we get the ball out again . . ."

In that time-out he has to set up two plays. Anticipate, think ahead, think with the Bullets, think ahead of them.

Time in. The ball goes to Chones at the pivot. Wes Unseld doesn't dare let Chones try to hook toward the basket. Can't foul him in the act of shooting. He grabs Chones. Foul. The Bullets' fourth team foul. Cavs get the ball out of bounds. One second gone . . . five left.

Now comes the second out-of-bounds play Fitch had diagrammed. Ball should go into Snyder. He's got the hot hand. If he's not free, get it to Bingo Smith, and go with the same play that beat the Bullets in the final seconds last week on the Bullets' home court.

The Bullets know the strategy too. They come out. Snyder is blanketed. Smith gets the ball with Mike Riorden hounding him. Bingo fakes Mike, shakes him, gets a step ahead . . . doesn't realize it . . . hurries his shot . . . maybe figuring to get fouled . . . shoots off his right foot . . . off-balance. No leverage . . . the ball is in the air . . . everybody watches transfixed . . . it's short . . . hits nothing. . . . It's over . . . no miracle this time.

Underneath Jim Cleamons moves toward the ball, grabs, spins it up . . . ball hangs on the rim . . . hangs . . . hangs . . . undecided . . . falls in. Bullets stand around paralyzed. . . . fans are stunned. Momentarily they fail to comprehend.

"What happened?"

"Who shot it?"

"Did it count?"

"Did the buzzer sound?"

"What? What? What?"

The Cavs start jumping for joy. They have won, 92–91.

It sinks in . . . 20,000 fans get the message at once. . . . Bedlam. . . . Pandemonium. . . . Buddy Bell is on his feet shouting. Duane Kuiper is shouting. . . . A normally conservative attorney is screaming. Later he wonders why he is hoarse.

You think: In 15 seconds the Cavs did three things wrong: lose the ball, foul too late, take a shot that doesn't hit the hoop and they win. . . . If Bingo's shot hits the rim or the backboard it doesn't fall into Cleamons's eager hands and the game is over.

Luck, sure, pure luck. Who says wrongs don't make a right? Three wrongs made a right.

"Unbelievable, fantastic," says Buddy.

"Super game, super, super," says Kuiper.

It's a mob scene on the floor. A fan, the blood completely drained from his face, sits limp in his seat. His wife says, "Promise me you'll never go to another playoff game."

You go down to the dressing room to replay the game with Fitch and the players. Frank Duffy, the Indians shortstop, joins our group.

"It's nothing," says an enervated Fitch in mustering a grin. "It's like the bottom of the ninth. Your pitcher is throwing a no-hitter and there are two outs. The batter hits you a slow grounder. Before you get that ball and begin your throw your whole life flashes in front of you."

"Yeah," says Duffy with a shudder. "It's nothing."

You think about Bosman's no-hitter again. This game topped it. In tension, apprehension, in fury, in frenzy, in drama, in unreality, in tempo, in noise, in climax, it topped every sports event you ever had seen.

You say good-bye to Bell and Kuiper and Duffy, who are still caught up in the game, and you go home. You are still perspiring. You take a shower. You go to bed emotionally exhausted. You keep asking yourself, "How much more can you expect from this team. It already has given so much."

Three hours later you finally fall asleep.

For The Record

CHAMPIONS OF 1976

ARCHERY

World Champions

Freestyle—Tommy Persson, Sweden.
Women's Freestyle—Anne-Marie Lehmann, West Germany.

National Agvtery Assn. Champions

TARGET

Amateur—Darrell Pace, Cincinnati.
Women's Amateur—Luann Ryon, Riverside, Calif.
Women's Crossbow—Carol Pelosi, Greenbelt, Md.

FIELD

Freestyle—Darrell Pace, Cincinnati.
Women's Freestyle—Luann Ryon, Riverside, Calif.
Barebow—Franklin Ditzler, Lebanon, Pa.
Women's Barebow—Eunice Anderson, Tijeras, N.M.

National Field Archery Assn. Champions

FREESTYLE

Open—Kenneth Cranberg, Dallas, Tex.
Women's Freestyle—Janet Boatman, Alden, N.Y.

AUTO RACING

World—James Hunt, England.
USAC—Gordon Johncock, Phoenix, Ariz.
USAC Stock Car—Butch Hartman, So. Zanesville, Ohio.
NASCAR—Cale Yarborough, Timmonsville, S.C.
Formula 5000—Brian Redman, England.
IMSA Camel GT—Al Holbert, Warrington, Pa.
IMSA Goodrich—Carson Baird, Laurel, Md.
Trans-American—George Follmer, Huntington Beach, Calif.
Bosch Gold Cup—Tom Bagley, State College, Pa.
Indy 500—Johnny Rutherford, Fort Worth, Tex.
U.S. Grand Prix—James Hunt, England.
Daytona 500—David Pearson, Spartansburg, S.C.
24 Hours of Le Mans—Jacky Icks, Belgium–Gijs Van Lennep, Netherlands.

BADMINTON

United States Champions

Singles—Chris Kinard, Pasadena, Calif.
Women's Singles—Pam Bristol, Flint, Mich.
Doubles—Don Paup, Vienna, Va.–Bruce Pontow, Chicago.
Women's Doubles—Pam Briston, Flint, Mich.–Rosine Lemon, New York.

United States Open Champions

Singles—Paul Whetnall, England.
Women's Singles—Gillian Gilks, England.
Doubles—Roland Maywald–Willie Braun, West Germany.
Women's Doubles—Sue Whetnall–Gillian Gilks, England.

BASEBALL

World Series–Cincinnati Reds.

American League—East: New York; West: Kansas City; playoffs: New York.
National League—East: Philadelphia; West: Cincinnati; playoffs: Cincinnati.
All-Star Game—National League.
Most Valuable Player (AL)—Thurman Munson, New York.
Most Valuable Player (NL)—Joe Morgan, Cincinnati.
Leading Batter (AL)—George Brett, Kansas City.
Leading Batter (NL)—Bill Madlock, Chicago.
Cy Young Pitching Award (AL)—Jim Palmer, Baltimore.
Cy Young Pitching Award (NL)—Randy Jones, San Diego.

BASKETBALL

National Association—Boston Celtics.
American Association—New York Nets.
National Collegiate—University of Indiana.
NCAA Division II—Puget Sound.
NCAA Division III—Scranton.
NAIA—Coppin State.
Women's Collegiate (AIWA)—Delta State.
National Invitation—Kentucky.
East Coast—East: St. Joseph's; West: Layafette; tournament: Hofstra.
Ivy League—Princeton.
Yankee Conference—Massachusetts.
AAU—Athletes in Action.
Women's AAU—Fullerton, Calif.

BILLIARDS

World Open—Larry Lisciotti, Manchester, Conn.
U.S. Open—Tom Jennings, Edison, N.J.
Women's Open—Jean Balukas, Brooklyn.

BOWLING

American Congress

Singles (Regular)—Mike Putzer, Oshkosh, Wis.
Singles (Classic)—Jim Schroeder, Buffalo.
Doubles (Regular)—Fred Willen, Sr.–Gary Voss, St. Louis.
Doubles (Classic)—Don Johnson, Las Vegas, Nev.–Paul Colwell, Tucson, Ariz.
All-Events (Regular)—Jim Lindquist, Minneapolis.
All-Events (Classic)—Gary Fust, Des Moines, Iowa.
Team (Regular)—Andy's Pro Shop, Tucson.
Team (Classic)—Munisingwear No. 2, Minneapolis.

Women's International

Singles—Bev Shonk, Canton, Ohio.
Doubles—Tie between Eloise Vacco–Debbie Rainone, Cleveland Heights, Ohio and Gerogene Cordes–Shirley Sjostrom, Bloomington, Minn.
All-Events—Betty Morris, Stockton, Calif.
Team—PWBA No. 1, Okalhoma City.

BPAA Open

Men—Paul Moser, Medford, Ore.
Women—Patty Costello, Scranton, Pa.

National Duckpin Congress

Singles—Bob Atkins, Baltimore, Md.
Women's Singles—Doris Shortt, Baltimore.

Doubles—Tony Adams–Mike Piersanti, East Haven, Conn.
Women's Doubles—Lorraine Watts–Kathy Cahoon, Williamantic, Conn.
All-Events—Mike Piersanti, New Haven.
Women's All-Events—Susan Slattery, Baltimore.
Team—Conn. Frozen Food, Hamden, Conn.
Women's Team—Overlea Exxon, Baltimore, Md.

BOXING

World Professional Champions

Heavyweight—Muhammad Ali, Chicago.
Light Heavyweight—Victor Galindez, Argentina, recognized by World Boxing Association; John Conteh, England, recognized by World Boxing Council.
Middleweight—Carlos Monzon, Argentina.
Junior Middleweight—Miguel Castellani, Argentina, WBA; Eckard Dagge, West Germany, WBC.
Welterweight—Jose Cuevas, Mexico, WBA; Carlos Palomino, Westminster, Calif., WBC.
Junior Welterweight—Saensak Muangsurin, Thailand, WBC; WBA vacant after stripping Wilfredo Benitez of title for failing to defend.
Lightweight—Roberto Duran, Panama, WBA; Esteban de Jesus, Puerto Rico, WBC.
Junior Lightweight—Samuel Serrano, Puerto Rico, WBA; Alfredo Escalera, Puerto Rico, WBC.
Featherweight—Danny Lopez, Los Angeles, WBC; WBA vacant after Alexis Arguello, Nicaragua, retired in October.
Junior Featherweight—Yum Dong Kyun, South Korea, WBC.
Bantamweight—Alfonso Zamora, Mexico, WBA; Carlos Zarate, WBC.
Flyweight—Guty Espadas, Panama, WBA; Miguel Canto, Mexico, WBC.
Junior Flyweight—Yoko Gushiken, Japan, WBA; Luis Estaba, Venezuela, WBC.

National AAU Champions

Heavyweight—Marvin Stinson, Philadelphia.
178 Pounds—Leon Spinks, St. Louis, Mo.
165 Pounds—Keith Broom, Charlotte, N.C.
156 Pounds—J.B. Williamson, Honolulu.
147 Pounds—Clinton Jackson, Nashville, Tenn.
139 Pounds—Pete Seward, Columbus, Ohio.
132 Pounds—Howard Davis, Glen Cove, N.Y.
125 Pounds—Davey Armstrong, Puyallup, Wash.
119 Pounds—Bernard Taylor, Charlotte, N.C.
112 Pounds—Leo Randolph, Tacoma, Wash.
106 Pounds—Brett Summers, Marysville, Wash.

CANOEING

KAYAK

500 Meters—Steve Kelly, Inwood CC, Bronx, N.Y.
Women's 500—Ann Turner, St. Charles, Ill.
1,000 Meters—Steve Kelly.
10,000 Meters—Brent Turner, St. Charles, Ill.
Women's 5,000—Ann Turner.
500-Meter Tandem—Steve Kelly-Brent Turner.
Women's 500-Meter Tandem—Ann Turner–Linda Dragan, Oxon Hill, Md.
1,000-Meter Tandem—Steve Kelly–Brent Turner.
10,000-Meter Tandem—Bruce and Greg Barton, Horton, Mich.
Women's 5,000-Meter Tandem—Linda Dragan–Jackie Scribner, Alexandria, Va.

CANOE

500 Meters—Andy Weigand, Arlington, Va.
1,000 Meters—Andy Weigand.
10,000 Meters—Andy Weigand.
500-Meter Tandem—Weigand–Roland Muhlen, Cincinnati, Ohio.
1,000-Meter Tandem—Weigand–Muhlen.
10,000-Meter Tandem—Weigand–Muhlen.
1,000-Meter Flurs—John, Robert and Richard Diebold, Glen Ellyn, Muhlen, Ill.

WHITEWATER-SLALOM

Kayak—Eric Evans, Mountain View, Calif.
Women's Kayak—Linda Harrison, Newark, Del.
Canoe—David Hearn, Garrett Park, Md.
Women's Canoe—Cathy Hearn, Garrett Park, Md.
Mixed Canoe—Steve and Susan Chamberlain, Philadelphia.
Masters Kayak—David Kurtz, State College, Pa.

CASTING

World Champions

Inland All-Around—Steve Rajeff, San Francisco, Calif.
Surf All-Around—J. Engelbrecht, South Africa.
Aggregate All-Around—J. DeKock, South Africa.

United States Champions

All-Around—Steve Rajeff, San Francisco, Calif.
Women's All-Accuracy—Mollie Light, New Albany, Ind.

COURT TENNIS

World Open—Howard Angus, Britain.
U.S. Singles—Gene Scott, New York.
U.S. Doubles—William Shettle–Peter Clement, Philadelphia, Pa.

CROSS-COUNTRY

National AAU—Rick Rojas, Los Alamos, N.M.
National AAU—Jamul Toads, San Diego, Calif.
Women's National AAU—Janice Merrill, Waterford, Conn.
Women's National AAU Team—Los Angeles TC.
NCAA Division I—Henry Rono, Washington State.
NCAA Team—Texas-El Paso.
NCAA Division II—Ralph Serna, California-Irvine.
NCAA Division II Team—California-Irvine.
NCAA Division III—Dale Kramer, Carleton.
NCAA Division III Team—North Central Illinois.
NAIA—John Kebiro, Eastern New Mexico.
NAIA Team—Edinboro State.
Women's Collegiate (AIAW)—Julie Brown, Cal State-Northridge.
Women's Collegiate Team—Iowa State.
IC4A—Curt Alitz, Army.
IC4A Team—Harvard.

CURLING

World—United States.
United States—Hibbing, Minn.
United States Women—Highland Park, Ill.

CYCLING

World Champions

Road (pro)—Freddy Maertens, Belgium.
Pursuit (pro)—Francesco Moser, Italy.
Sprint (pro)—John Nicholson, Australia.
Women's Sprint—Sheila Young Ochowicz, Detroit.
Women's Road—Kornelia Van Oosten-Hage, Netherlands.
Tour de France—Lucien Van Impe, Belgium.

United States Champions

ROAD RACING

Senior (114 miles)—Wayne Stetina, Indianapolis, Ind.
Women (37 miles)—Connie Carpenter, Madison, Wis.
Veterans (41 miles)—Jim Meyers, Costa Mesa, Calif.
Junior (49 miles)—Larry Shields, Santa Barbara, Calif.
Junior Women—Francesca Saveri, San Francisco, Calif.

TRACK RACING

Sprint—Leigh Barszewski, West Allis, Wis.
Women's Sprint—Connie Carpenter, Madison, Wis.
Kilometer—Bob Vehe, Mount Prospect, Ill.
10 Miles—Ron Skarin, Van Nuys, Calif.
Pursuit—Leonard Nitz, Sacramento, Calif.
Women's Pursuit—Connie Carpenter.

DOGS

Major Best-in-Show Winners

Westminster (New York)—Ch. Jo-Ni's Red Baron of Crofton, Lakeland terrier, owned by Virginia Dickson, La Habra, Calif.; 3,098 dogs entered.
Boardwalk (Atlantic City)—Ch. Bel Tor Blissful, black standard poodle, owned by Mary Peacock, Chester Springs, Pa., and Pamela Hall, Mahopac, N.Y.; 3,494.
Westchester (Tarrytown, N.Y.)—Ch. Oaktree's Irishtocrat, 2,762.
International (Chicago, fall)—Ch. Aryee Dominator, wire fox terrier, owned by Michael Weissman and Mrs. Florence Weissman, Yonkers; 3,651.
Santa Barbara (Calif.)—Ch. Dersade Bobby's Girl, Sealyham terrier, owned by Mrs. Dorothy Wimer, Churchtown, Pa.; 3,995.

FENCING

United States Champions

Foil—Lt. Ed Donofrio, U.S. Marines.
Epée—George Masin, New York AC.
Saber—Thomas Losonczy, New AC.
Women's Foil—Ann O'Donnell, Salle Santelli, New York.
Foil Team—Wauwatosa, Wis.
Epée Team—New York AC.
Saber Team—Fencers Club, New York.
Women's Foil Team—Salle D'Asaro, San Jose, Calif.

National Collegiate Champions

Foil—Greg Benko, Wayne State.
Epée—Randy Eggleton, Pennsylvania.
Saber—Brian Smith, Columbia.
Team—New York University.
Women's Foil—Stacey Johnson, Cal State-San Jose, Calif.
Women's Team—Cal State-San Jose, Calif.

FOOTBALL

Intercollegiate Champions

Eastern Division I (Lambert Trophy)—Pittsburgh.
Eastern Division II (Lambert Cup)—Delaware.
Eastern Division III (Lambert Bowl)—C. W. Post.
Yankee—New Hampshire.
NCAA Division II—Montana State.
NCAA Division III—St. John's (Minn.).
NAIA Division I—Texas A&I.
NAIA Division II—Westminster.

National League

AMERICAN CONFERENCE

Eastern Division—Dallas Cowboys.
Central Division—Minnesota Vikings.
Western Division—Los Angeles Rams.
Wild Card—Washington Redskins.
Conference—Minnesota Vikings.

NATIONAL CONFERENCE

Eastern Division—Baltimore Colts.
Central Division—Pittsburgh Steelers.
Western Division—Oakland Raiders.
Conference—Minnesota Vikings.
Wild Card—New England Patriots.
Conference—Oakland Raiders.

Super Bowl

Oakland Raiders.

Canadian Professional

Grey Cup—Ottawa Rough Riders.

GOLF

MEN

U.S. Open—Jerry Pate, Pensacola, Fla.
U.S. Amateur—Bill Sander, Kenmore, Wash.
Masters—Ray Floyd, Miami, Fla.
PGA—Dave Stockton, Westlake Village, Calif.
British Open—Johnny Miller, Napa, Calif.
British Amateur—Dick Siderowf, Westport, Conn.
Canadian Open—Jerry Pate.
U.S. Public Links—Eddie Mudd, Morehead, Ky.
USGA Senior—Lou Oehmig, Lookout Mountain, Tenn.
USGA Junior—Madden Hatcher, Columbus, Ga.
U.S. Senior GA—Dale Morey, High Point, N.C.
NCAA Division I—Scott Simpson, So. Calif.
NCAA Division II—Mike Nicollette, Rollins–Winter Park.
NCAA Division III—Dan Lisle, Calif. State–Stanislaus.
NAIA—Will Brewer, David Lipscomb.
World Series of Golf—Jack Nicklaus, North Palm Beach, Fla.

WOMEN

U.S. Open—JoAnne Carner, Fort Worth, Tex.
U.S. Amateur—Donna Horton, Jacksonville, Fla.
LPGA—Betty Burfeindt, Palm Springs, Calif.
USGA Senior—Mrs. Ceil MacLaurin, Savannah, Ga.
USGA Girls—Pilar Dorado, Hayward, Calif.
U.S. Senior G.A.—Dot Porter, Cinnaminson, N.J.
Collegiate—Nancy Lopez, Tulsa.
Curtis Cup—United States.
LPGA Earnings Leader—Judy Rankin.
LPGA Player of the Year—Judy Rankin.

GYMNASTICS

AAU Champions

MEN

All-Round—Coje Saito, Mobile, Ala.
Floor Exercise—Ron Galimore, Tallahassee, Fla.
Horizontal Bar—Coje Saito.
Parallel Bars—Coje Saito.
Pommel Horse—Ed Paul, Penn State.
Vault—Mike Carter, Louisiana State.
Rings—Tie between Vic Randozzo, New York AC, and Todd H. Kuoni, Baton Rouge, La.

WOMEN

All-Round—Roxanne Pierce, Philadelphia.
Uneven Parallel Bars—Ann Carr, Philadelphia.
Balance Beam—Roxanne Pierce.
Floor Exercise—Janice Baker, Syracuse, N.Y.
Vault—Ann Woods, Red Bank, N.J.

NCAA Champions

All-Round—Peter Kormann, Southern Connecticut.

Floor Exercise—Bob Robbins, Colorado State.
Rings—Doug Wood, Iowa State.
Pommel Horse—Ted Marcy, Stanford.
Parallel Bars—Gene Whalen, Penn State.
Horizontal Bar—Tom Beach, California.
Vault—Sam Shaw, Cal. State-Fullerton.
Team—Penn State.
AIAW All-Round—Connie Jo Israel, Clarion State.
AIAW Team—Clarion State.

HANDBALL

United States Handball Assn.

FOUR WALL

Singles—Vern Roberts Jr., Lake Forest, Ill.
Doubles—Gary Rohrer, Minneapolis–Dan O'Connor, St. Paul.

National AAU Champions

ONE WALL

Singles—Ruben Gonzalez, New York.
Doubles—Artie Reyer–Al Torres, Brooklyn.

HARNESS RACING

Horse of the Year—Keystone Ore.
Trotter of the Year—Steve Lobell.
2-Year-Old Trotter—Jodevin.
2-Year-Old Pacer—Jade Prince.
3-Year-Old Trotter—Steve Lobell.
3-Year-Old Pacer—Keystone Ore.
Aged Trotter—Keystone Pioneer.
Aged Pacer—Rambling Willie.
Leading Driver (Heats)—Herve Filion.
Leading Driver (Earnings)—Herve Filion.
Hambletonian—Steve Lobell.
Little Brown Jug—Keystone Ore.
Adios—Armbro Ranger.
Cane Pace—Keystone Ore.
Colonial Trot—Armbro Regina.
Empire Trot—Tropical Storm.
Dexter Cup—Soothsayer.
Roosevelt International—Equileo.
Kentucky Futurity—Quick Pay.
Messenger—Windshield Wiper.

HOCKEY

Stanley Cup—Montreal Canadiens.
National League—Norris Division: Montreal; Adams: Boston; Patrick: Philadelphia; Smythe; Chicago.
NHL Most Valuable Player—Bobby Clarke, Philadelphia.
NHL Leading Scorer—Guy Lafleur, Montreal.
World Association (Avco Cup)—Winnipeg Jets.
World Association—Canadian Division: Winnipeg; East: Indianapolis; West: Houston.
WHA Most Valuable Player—Marc Tardif, Quebec.
WHA Leading Scorer—Marc Tardif.
World Amateur—Czechoslovakia.
Canada Cup—Team Canada.
NCIA—Minnesota.
ECAC—Division I: Boston University; Division II: Bowdoin. Division III: Amherst.
WCHA—Michigan Tech.
Allan Cup—Spokane Flyers.
Memorial Cup—Hamilton Fincups.

HORSESHOE PITCHING

World Champions

Men—Carl Steinfeldt, Rochester, N.Y.
Women—Ruth Hangen, Getzville, N.Y.

HORSE RACING

Eclipse Awards

Horse of the Year—Forego.
2-year-Old Colt—Seattle Slew.
2-Year-Old Filly—Sensational.
3-Year-Old Colt—Bold Forbes.
3-Year-Old Filly—Revidere.
Older Horse—Forego.
Old Filly or Mare—Proud Delta.
Sprinter—My Juliet.
Turf Horse—Youth.

Stakes Winners

Kentucky Derby—Bold Forbes.
Preakness—Elocutionist.
Belmont Stakes—Bold Forbes.

Quarter Horse

All-American Derby—Mito Wise Dancer.

HORSE SHOWS

American Horse Shows Assn.

Hunter Seat—Frances C. Steinwedell, Pasadena, Calif.
Saddle Seat—Virginia Cable, Lima, Ohio.
Stock Seat—Lisa Acquire, San Juan Capistrano, Calif.
Dressage—Overall: Bodo Hangen, Wayne, Ill.; Senior Medal: London Gray, Dixmont, Me.; Junior Medal: Kris Bobo, Cohasset, Mass.

National Horse Show Equitation

ASPCA Trophy (Maclay)—Colette Lozins, Skokie, Ill.
Saddle Seat (Good Hands)—Virginia Cable, Lima, Ohio.

ICE SKATING

Figure World Champions

Men—John Curry, Britain.
Women—Dorothy Hamill, Riverside, Conn.
Pairs—Irina Rodnina–Alexandr Zaitzev, Soviet Union.
Dance—Ludmila Pakhomova–Alexandr Gorshkov, Soviet Union.

United States Champions

Men—Terry Kubicka, Cypress, Calif.
Women—Dorothy Hamill, Riverside, Conn.
Pairs—Tai Babilonia–Randy Gardner, Los Angeles.
Dance—Colleen O'Connor–Jim Millns, Colorado Springs.

SPEED

World Champions

Men—Piet Kleine, Netherlands.
Women—Sylvia Burka, Canada.
Sprint—Johann Granath, Sweden.
Women's Sprint—Sheila Young, Detroit.

United States Champions

Outdoor—John Wurster, Ballston Spa, N.Y.
Women's Outdoor—Connie Carpenter, Madison, Wis.
Indoor—Alan Rattray, Los Angeles.
Women's Indoor—Tie between Celeste Chlapaty, Skokie, Ill., and Peggy Hartrich, St. Louis, Mo.

JUDO

National AAU Champions

139 Pounds—George Cozzi, Chicago.
154 Pounds—Pat Burris, Anaheim, Calif.
176 Pounds—Teimoc Jonstonono, New York.
205 Pounds—Irwin Cohen, Chicago.
Heavyweight—Dean Sedgwick, River Forest, Ill.
Open—James Wooley, Houston, Tex.
Grand Champion—Pat Burris.

WOMEN

110 Pounds—Lynn Lewis, Revere, Mass.
120 Pounds—Diane Pierce, Minneapolis.
130 Pounds—Becky Tushek, Fort Lee, N.J.
142 Pounds—Delores Brodie, Barstow, Calif.
154 Pounds—Amy Kublin, Arlington, Mass.
166 Pounds—Frances Watkins, New York.
Over 166 Pounds—Debbie Fisher, Concord, Calif.
Open—Maureen Braziel, Brooklyn.
Grand Champion—Maureen Braziel.

LACROSSE

NCAA Division I—Cornell.
Division II—Hobart.
Club—Mount Washington LC, Baltimore.
North-South Game—North.

LAWN BOWLING

National Open

Singles—Harold Esch, Clearwater, Fla.
Doubles—Irving Paschell–Willis Tewksbury, Clearwater, Fla.

Eastern Division

Singles—John Durant, Quincy, Mass.
Doubles—David Liddell–Jim Gardner, Greenwich, Conn.

MOTORBOATING

President's Cup—Olympia Beer, Billy Schumacher, Driver.
Gold Cup—Miss U.S., Tom D'Eath.
Unlimited Champion—Atlas Van Lines.
Champion Unlimited Driver—Bill Muncey, La Mesa, Calif.
U.S. Offshore Champion—Joel Halpern.

MOTORCYCLING

National Champion—Jay Springsteen, Flint, Mich.
125 Motocross—Bob Hannah, Whittier, Calif.
250 Motocross—Tony DiStefano, Morrisville, Pa.
500 Motocross—Kent Howerton, San Antonio, Tex.
Supercross—Jim Weinert, Laguna Beach, Calif.

POLO

National Champions

Open—Willow Bend, Dallas.
18–22 Goals—Willow Bend, Dallas.
16 Goals—Boca Raton, Fla.
14 Goals—Jay Farm, Milwaukee.

RACQUETS

National Champions

Singles—Bill Surtees, Chicago.
Doubles—Surtees–Richard Lightfine, Chicago

RODEO

World Champions

All-Round—Tom Ferguson Miami, Okla.
Saddle Bronc Riding—Tie between Monte Henson, Mesquite, Tex., and Mel Hyland, Surrey, British Columbia.
Bareback Bronc—Chris Ledoux, Kaycee, Wyo.
Bull Riding—Dan Gay, Mesquite, Tex.
Steer Wrestling—Rick Bradley, Burkburnett, Tex.
Calf Roping—Roy Cooper, Durant, Okla.
Team Roping—Ronnie Rasco, Lakeside, Calif., and Bucky Bradford Jr., Sylmar, Calif.
Women's Barrel Racing—Connie Combs, Comanche, Okla.

ROLLER SKATING

World Champions

Singles—Thomas Nieder, West Germany.
Women's Singles—Natalie Dunn, Bakersfield, Calif.
Pairs—Ron Sabo–Darlene Wates, Columbus, Ohio.
Dance—Kerry Cavazzi–Jane Puracchio, East Meadow, L.I.

United States Champions

Singles—Paul Jones, Flint, Mich.
Women's Singles—Lisa Bergin, Fort Worth, Tex.
Figures—William Combs, Columbus, Ohio.
Women's Figures—Donna Kiker, Decatur, Ga.

ROWING

United States Champions

Singles—Sean Drea, Ireland.
Singles, Dash—Jim Dietz, New York AC.
Double Sculls—Dietz–Dr. Larry Klecatsky, NYAC
Pairs with Coxswains—John Matthews-Mark Norelius–Ken Dreyfuss, Coxswain, Vesper BC, Philadelphia.
Pairs—Bob Blakely–Mike Borchelt, Potomac BC, Washington.
Quads—New York AC.
Eights—Vesper, Philadelphia.

Intercollegiate Champions

IRA—California; second varsity: Penn; freshmen: Syracuse.
IRA Team Trophy—Penn.
Women's Eastern Sprints—Wisconsin.

RUGBY

World—British Lions.
Europe—Wales.

SHOOTING

Grand American Trapshooting Champions

Men—Frank Crevatin, Tecumseh, Ontario.
Women—Judith Whittenberger, Fort Wayne, Ind.

Skeet Shooting

Men—Charles Parks, Alliance, Ohio.
Women—Valerie Johnson, San Antonio, Tex.
Senior—Tom Hanzel, San Antonio, Tex.
Veteran—Tom Sanfilipo, Fairfield, Calif.

United States Pistol Champions

National—SFC Bonnie D. Harmon, Fort Benning, GA.
Women—SP4—Ruby Fox, Parker, Ariz.

United States Rifle Champions

Small-bore Rifle, Prone—David Weaver, Oil City, Pa.
Small-bore Rifle, Position—Lones Wigger, Carter, Mont.
High Power Rifle—Gary Anderson, Axtell, Neb.

SHUFFLEBOARD

United States Champions

Winter Open—Merritt Gordon, Millington, Md.
Women's Winter Open—Mary Eldridge, Lake George, N.Y.
Summer Open—Dave Karaska, Detroit.
Women's Summer Open—Dorcas Donelson, Carey, Ohio Champions—37.

SKIING

World Cup Winners

Men—Ingemar Stenmark, Sweden.
Women—Rosi Mittermaier, West Germany.

National Alpine Champions

MEN

Downhill—Greg Jones, Tahoe City, Calif.
Slalom—Cary Adgate, Boyne City, Mich.
Combined—Cary Adgate.
Giant Slalom—Geoff Bruce, Corning, N.Y.

WOMEN

Downhill—Susie Patterson, Sun Valley, Idaho.
Slalom—Cindy Nelson, Lutsen, Minn.
Combined—Viki Fleckenstein, Syracuse.
Giant Slalom—Lindy Cochran, Richmond, Vt.

National Nordic Champions

JUMPING

Class A—Jim Denney, Duluth, Minn.
Junior—John Broman, Duluth, Minn.
Veteran—Earl Murphy, Brattleboro, Vt.

CROSS-COUNTRY
MEN

15 Kilometers—Devin Swigert, Sun Valley, Idaho.
30 Kilometers—Devin Swigert.
50 Kilometers—Stan Dunklee, Brattleboro, Vt.

WOMEN

5. 10 and 20 Kilometers—Jana Hlavaty, Chicago.

National Collegiate Champions

Slalom—Mike Meleski, Wyoming.
Giant Slalom—Dave Cleveland, Dartmouth.
Alpine Combined—Mike Meleski.
Cross-Country—Stan Dunklee, Vermont.
Jumping—Kip Sundgaard, Utah.
Nordic Combined—Jack Turner, Colorado.
Team—Tie between Colorado and Dartmouth.

SOCCER

United States Champions

North American Soccer League—Toronto Metros-Croatia.
Challenge Cup—San Francisco AC.
Amateur Cup—Bavarian Blue Ribbon, Milwaukee.
Junior Cup—Annandale (Va.) Cavaliers.

Collegiate Champions

NCAA Division I—University of San Francisco.
NCAA Division II—Loyola, Baltimore.
NCAA Division III—Brandeis.
NAIA—Simon Fraser.

Other Champions

European Federation Cup—Liverpool.
European Nations Cup—Czechoslovakia.

SOFTBALL

Amateur Softball Assn. Champions

Fast Pitch—Raybestos Cardinals, Stratford, Conn.
Slow Pitch—Warren Motors, Jacksonville, Fla.

WOMEN

Fast Pitch—Raybestos Brackettes, Stratford, Conn.
Slow Pitch—Sorrento's Pizza, Cincinnati.

SQUASH RACQUETS

Singles—Peter Briggs, New York.
Doubles—Ralph Howe—Peter Briggs, New York.
Women's Singles—Mrs. Gretchen Spruance, Wilmington, Del.

SQUASH TENNIS

National Champions

Singles—Pedro Baccallao, New York.
Veterans Singles—Bill Lordi, New York.

SWIMMING

Men's National Long-Course Champions

100-Meter Freestyle—Jonty Skinner, Jacksonville, Fla.
200-Meter Freestyle—Mark Greenwood, Fresno, Calif.
400-Meter Freestyle—Casey Converse, Mission Viejo, Calif.
1,500-Meter Freestyle—Casey Converse.
100-Meter Backstroke—John Naber, Ladera Oaks, Calif.
200-Meter Backstroke—John Naber.
100-Meter Breast-Stroke—John Hencken, Santa Clara, Calif.
200-Meter Breast-Stroke—John Hencken.

100-Meter Butterfly—Greg Janenberg, Newtown Square, Pa.
200-Meter Butterfly—Bill Forrester, Jacksonville, Fla.
200-Meter Ind. Medley—Steve Furniss, Long Beach, Calif.
400-Meter Ind. Medley—Jesse Vassallo, Mission Viejo, Calif.
400-Meter Freestyle Relay—Central Jersey AC.
400-Meter Medley Relay—Santa Clara.
800-Meter Freestyle Relay—Mission Viejo, Calif.

Women's National Long-Course Champions

100-Meter Freestyle—Jill Sterkel, El Monte, Calif.
200-Meter Freestyle—Kim Peyton, Portland, Ore.
400-Meter Freestyle—Rebecca Perrott, New Zealand.
1,500-Meter Freestyle—Evie Kosenkranius, Seattle.
100-Meter Backstroke—Linda Jezek, Santa Clara, Calif.
200-Meter Backstroke—Linda Jezek.
100-Meter Breast-Stroke—Dawn Rodighiero, Mission Viejo, Calif.
200-Meter Breast-Stroke—Dawn Rodighiero.
100-Meter Butterfly—Wendy Boglioli, Ocean City, N.J.
200-Meter Butterfly—Alice Browne, Mission Viejo, Calif.
200-Meter Ind. Medley—Kathy Heddy, Summit, N.J.
400-Meter Ind. Medley—Donnalee Wennerstrom, West Valley JC, Calif.
400-Meter Freestyle Relay—El Monte (Calif.) AC.
400-Meter Medley Relay—Central Jersey AC.
800-Meter Freestyle Relay—Central Jersey AC.

National Outdoor Diving

MEN

One-Meter—Jim Kennedy, Knoxville, Tenn.
Three-Meter—Jim Kennedy.
Platform—Kent Vosler, Eaton, Ohio.

WOMEN

One-Meter—Cynthia McIngvale, Dallas.
Three-Meter—Cynthia McIngvale.
Platform—Barbara Weinstein, Cincinnati.

National Collegiate Champions

50-Yard Freestyle—Joe Bottom, Southern California.
100-Yard Freestyle—Jim Montgomery, Indiana.
200-Yard Freestyle—Jim Montgomery.
500-Yard Freestyle—Tim Shaw, Long Beach State.
1,650-Yard Freestyle—Tim Shaw.
100-Yard Backstroke—John Naber, Southern California.
200-Yard Backstroke—John Naber.
100-Yard Breast-Stroke—John Hencken, Stanford.
200-Yard Breast-Stroke—David Wilkie, Miami (Fla.).
100-Yard Butterfly—Matt Vogel, Tennessee.
200-Yard Butterfly—Steve Gregg, N. Carolina State.
200-Yard Ind. Medley—Lee Engstrand, Tennessee.
400-Yard Ind. Medley—Rod Strachan, Southern California.
400-Yard Freestyle Relay—Southern California.
400-Yard Medley Relay—Southern California.
800-Yard Freestyle Relay—Southern California.

TABLE TENNIS

United States Champions

Open Singles—Dragutin Surback, Yugoslavia.

Closed Singles—Ray Guillen, Los Angeles.
Women's Open Singles—Kim Soon Ok, South Korea.
Women's Closed Singles—In Sock Bhusan, Columbus, Ohio.
Doubles—Surback Milivoj Karakesevio, Yugoslavia.
Women's Doubles—Kim Soon Ok-Son Hye Soon, South Korea.
Mixed Doubles—Desmond Douglas–Jill Hammersley, England.

TENNIS

International Team Champions

Davis Cup (Men)—Chile.
Wightman Cup (Women)—United States.
Federation Cup (Women)—United States.

Wimbledon Champions

Singles—Bjorn Borg, Sweden.
Women's Singles—Chris Evert, Fort Lauderdale, Fla.
Doubles—Brian Gottfried, Fort Lauderdale, Fla.–Raul Ramirez, Mexico.
Women's Doubles—Chris Evert–Martina Navratilova, Palm Springs, Calif.
Mixed Doubles—François Durr, France–Tony Roche, Australia.

U.S. Open Champions

Singles—Jimmy Connors, Belleville, Ill.
Women's Singles—Chris Evert.
Doubles—Marty Riessen, Amelia Island, Fla.–Tom Okker, Netherlands.
Women's Doubles—Linky Boshoff –Ilana Kloss, South Africa.
Mixed Doubles—Billie Jean King, New York–Phil Dent, Australia.

Other United States Champions

Team—New York Sets.
Indoor—Ilie Nastase, Romania.
Women's Indoor—Virginia Wade, Britain.
Clay Court—Jimmy Connors.
Women's Clay Court—Kathy May, Beverly Hills, Calif.
Junior—Larry Gottfried, Fort Lauderdale.
Junior Women—Lynn Epstein, Miami.
NCAA—Division I—Bill Scanlon, Trinity (Tex.); Division II; Tim Monroe, California-Davis; Division III; John Blomberg, Claremont.
NAIA—Kari Personen, Mercyhurst.
Women's Collegiate—Barbara Hallquist, Southern California.

Other Foreign Opens

Australian Men—Mark Edmondson, Australia.
Australian Women—Evonne Goolagong, Australia.
French Men—Adrianno Panatta, Italy.
French Women—Sue Barker, England.

TRACK AND FIELD

Men's National Outdoor Champions

100-Meter Dash—Chris Garpenborg, Los Angeles.
200-Meter Dash—Millard Hampton, San Jose, Calif.
400-Meter Dash—Maxie Parks, Los Angeles.
800-Meter Run—James Robinson, Oakland, Calif.
1,500-Meter Run—Eamonn Coghlan, Ireland (Villanova).
5,000-Meter Run—Dick Buerkle, New York, AC.
10,000-Meter Run—Ed Leddy, Knoxville, Tenn.
3,000-Meter Steeplechase—Randy Smith, Striders.
110-Meter Hurdles—Thomas Hill, U.S. Army.
400-Meter Hurdles—Tom Andrews, Southern California.
5,000-Meter Walk—Ron Laird, New York AC.

Pole Vault—Earl Bell, Arkansas State, Jonesboro, Ark.
High Jump—Dwight Stones, Los Angeles.
Long Jump—Arnie Robinson, Los Angeles.
Triple Jump—Tommy Hayes, U.S. Army.
Hammer Throw—Larry Hart, New York AC.
Javelin—Fred Luke, Seattle.
Discus—Mac Wilkins; Portland, Ore.
Shot-put—Terry Albritton, U. of Hawaii.

Other Champions

USTFF Decathlon—Bruce Jenner, San Jose, Calif.
Boston Marathon—Jack Fultz, Arlington, Va.

Women's National Outdoor Champions

100-Meter Dash—Chandra Cheeseborough, Tennessee State.
200-meter Dash—Brenda Morehead, Tennessee State.
400-meter Dash—Lorna Forde, Atoms TC, Brooklyn.
800-Meter Run—Madeline Jackson, Cleveland.
1,500-Meter Run—Francie Larrieu, Long Beach, Calif.
3,000-Meter-Run—Jan Merrill, Waterford, Conn.
100-Meter Hurdles—Jane Frederick, Los Angeles.
400-Meter Hurdles—Arthurine Gainer, Prairie View, Tex.
Javelin—Kathy Schmidt, Los Angeles.
Shot-put—Maren Seidler, Chicago.
Discus—Lynne Winbigler, Eugene, Ore.
Long Jump—Kathy McMillan, Raeford, N.C.
High Jump—Joni Huntley, Sheridan, Ore.
AAU Pentathlon—Jane Frederick, Los Angeles.

National Collegiate Outdoor Champions

100-Meter Dash—Harvey Glance, Auburn.
200-Meter Dash—Harvey Glance.
400-Meter Dash—Ken Randle, Southern California.
800-Meter Run—Tom McLean, Bucknell.
1,500-Meter Run—Eamonn Coghlan, Villanova.
5,000-Meter Run—Josh Kimeta, Washington State.
10,000-Meter Run—John Ngeno, Washington State.
3,000-Meter Steeplechase—James Munyala, Texas-El Paso.
110-Meter Hurdles—Dedy Cooper, San Jose State.
400-Meter Hurdles—Quentin Wheeler, San Diego State.
High Jump—Dwight Stones, Long Beach.
Triple Jump—Phil Robins, Southern Illinois.
Long Jump—Larry Myricks, Mississippi College.
Hammer Throw—Scott Neilson, Washington.
Shot-put—Dana Leduc, Texas.
Javelin—Phil Olsen, Tennessee.
Discus—Borys Chambul, Washington
Pole Vault—Earl Bell, Arkansas State.
Team—Southern California.

VOLLEYBALL

U.S. Volleyball Assn. Champions

Open—Maccabi Union, Los Angeles.
Women's Open—Pasadena (Texas) VC.
Collegiate—Penn State.

Other National Champions

AAU—Outrigger Canoe Club, Honolulu.
AAU Women—Nick's Fish Market, Santa Monica, Calif.-Honolulu.

WATER POLO

National Outdoor Champions

Men—Concord (Calif.) WPC.
Women—Fullerton, Calif.

WATER SKIING

United States Champions

Open Overall—Chris Redmond, Canton, Ohio.
Open Slalom—Bob LaPoint, Castro Valley, Calif.
Open Tricks—Tony Krupa, Jackson, Mich.
Open Jumping—Bob LaPoint.

WOMEN

Open Overall—Cindy Todd, Pierson, Fla.
Open Slalom—Cindy Todd.
Open Tricks—Cindy Todd.
Open Jumping—Linda Giddens, Eastman, Ga.

WEIGHT LIFTING

National AAU Champions

114 Pounds—Joel Widdell, Dewar, Iowa.
123 Pounds—John Yamauchi, Honolulu.
132 Pounds—Dane Hussey, St. Louis.
148 Pounds—Dan Cantore, Pacifica, Calif.
165 Pounds—Fred Lowe, East Lansing, Mich.
181 Pounds—Sam Bigler, Lancaster, Pa.
198 Pounds—Lee James, Manchester, Pa.
242 Pounds—Mark Cameron, Middletown, R.I.
Super Heavyweight—Bruce Wilhelm, Los Altos, Calif.

WRESTLING

National AAU Freestyle Champions

105.5 Pounds—Bill Rosado, Arizona WC.
114.5 Pounds—Jim Haines, Madison, Wis.
125.5 Pounds—Jan Gitcho, Hawkeye WC.
136.5 Pounds—Kiyoshi Abe, New York AC.
149.5 Pounds—Lt. Lloyd Keaser, U.S. Marines.
163 Pounds—Stan Dziedzic, New York AC.
180.5 Pounds—Brady Hall, Los Angeles.
198 Pounds—Ben Peterson, Comstock, Wis.
220 Pounds—Russ Hellickson, Madison, Wis.
Heavyweight—Mike McCready, Hawkeye WC.
Outstanding Wrestler—Keaser.

National Collegiate AA Champions

118 Pounds—Mark diGiralamo, Cal Poly-San Luis Obispo.
126 Pounds—Jack Reinwand, Wisconsin.
134 Pounds—Mike Frick, Lehigh.
142 Pounds—Brad Smith, Iowa.
150 Pounds—Chuck Yagla, Iowa.
158 Pounds—Lee Kemp, Wisconsin.
167 Pounds—Pat Christenson, Wisconsin.
177 Pounds—Chris Campbell, Iowa.
190 Pounds—Evan Johnson, Minnesota.
Heavyweight—Jimmy Jackson, Oklahoma State.
Outstanding Wrestler—Yagla.
Team—University of Iowa.

YACHTING

U.S. Yacht Racing Union Champions

Men (Mallory Cup)—David Crockett, Los Alamitos, Calif.
Women (Adams Trophy)—Ellen Gerloff, Galveston, Tex.

Junior (Sears Cup)—Potomac River, CA, Washington.
Prince of Wales Bowl (Club)—Coronado (Calif.) YC.
O'Day Trophy (Single-Handed)—Buzz Reynolds, Notre Dame.

Distance and Ocean Races

Trans-Atlantic Single-handed—Pen Duick VI, Eric Tabarly, France.
Newport-Bermuda—Fleet; Running Tide.

Olympic Champions

SUMMER GAMES

ARCHERY

Men—Darrell Pace, Cincinnati.
Women—Luann Ryon, Riverside, Calif.

BOXING

106 Pounds—Jorge Hernandez, Cuba.
112 Pounds—Leo Randolph, Tacoma, Wash.
119 Pounds—Young Jo Gu, North Korea.
126 Pounds—Angel Herrera, Cuba.
132 Pounds—Howard Davis, Glen Cove, N.Y.
140 Pounds—Ray Leonard, Palmer Park, Md.
147 Pounds—Jochen Bachfeld, East Germany.
156 Pounds—Jerzy Rybibki, Poland.
165 Pounds—Mike Spinks, St. Louis.
178 Pounds—Leon Spinks, St. Louis.
Heavyweight—Teofilo Stevenson, Cuba.

CANOEING

CANADIAN

500 Meters—Aleksandr Rogov, Soviet Union.
1,000 Meters—Matija Ljubek, Yugoslavia.
500-Meter Pairs—Sergei Petrenko and Aleksandr Vinogradov, Soviet Union.
1,000-Meter Pairs—Sergei Petrenko and Aleksandr Vinogradov, Soviet Union.

KAYAK-MEN

500 Meters—Vasile Diba, Romania.
1,000 Meters—Rudiger Helm, East Germany.
500-Meter Pairs—Joachim Mattern and Bernd Olbricht, East Germany.
1,000-Meter Pairs—Sergei Nagorny and Vladimir Romanovsky, Soviet Union.
1,000-Meter Fours—Soviet Union.

KAYAK-WOMEN

500 Meters—Carola Zirzow, East Germany.
500-Meter Pairs—Nina Gopova and Galina Kreft, Soviet Union.

CYCLING

1,000 Meters—Klaus-Jurgen Grunke, East Germany.
Sprint—Anton Tkac, Czechoslovakia.
Pursuit—Gregor Braun, West Germany.
Team Pursuit—West Germany.
Road Race—Bernt Johansson, Sweden.
Team Road Race—Soviet Union.

EQUESTRIAN

Dressage—Christine Stueckelberger, Switzerland.
Dressage Team—West Germany.
Jumping—Alwin Shockemoehle, West Germany.
Team Jumping—France.
3-Day Event—Tad Coffin, Strafford, Vt.
Team 3-Day Event—United States (Tad Coffin, Mike Plumb, Mary Ann Tauskey, Bruce Davidson).

FENCING

Foil—Fabio Dal Zotto, Italy.
Team Foil—West Germany.
Epée Alexander Pusch, West Germany.
Team Epée—Sweden.
Saber—Victor Krovopouskov, Soviet Union.
Team Saber—Soviet Union.
Women's Foil—Ildiko Schwarzenberger, Hungary.
Women's Team Foil—Soviet Union.

GYMNASTICS—MEN

All-Round—Nikolai Andrianov, Soviet Union.
Floor Exercises—Nikolai Andrianov, Soviet Union.
Horizontal Bar—Mitsuo Tsukahara, Japan.
Long Horse—Nikolai Andrianov, Soviet Union.
Parallel Bars—Sawao Kato, Japan.
Rings—Nikolai Andrianov, Soviet Union.
Side Horse—Zoltan Magyar, Hungary.
Team—Japan.

GYMNASTICS—WOMEN

All-Round—Nadia Comaneci, Romania.
Balance Beam—Nadia Comaneci, Romania.
Floor Exercises—Nelli Kim, Soviet Union.
Uneven Bars—Nadia Comaneci, Romania.
Vault—Nelli Kim, Soviet Union.
Team—Soviet Union.

JUDO

Lightweight—Hector Rodriguez, Cuba.
Light Middleweight—Vladimir Nevzorov, Soviet Union.
Middleweight—Isamu Sonoda, Japan.
Light Heavyweight—Kazuhiro Ninomiya, Japan.
Heavyweight—Sergei Novikov, Soviet Union.
Open Class—Haruki Uemura, Japan.

MODERN PENTATHLON

Individual—Janucz-Peciak, Poland.
Team—Britain.

ROWING—MEN

Singles—Pertti Karppinen, Finland.
Doubles—Frank and Alf Hansen, Norway.
Pairs—Jorg and Bernd Landvoigt, East Germany.
Pairs With Coxswain—Harold Jahrling, Friedrich Ulrich and Georg Spohr, East Germany.
Fours—East Germany.
Fours With Coxswains—Soviet Union.
Quadruple Sculls—East Germany.
Eights—East Germany.

ROWING—WOMEN

Singles—Christine Scheiblich, East Germany.
Doubles—Svetla Otzetova and Zdravka Yoradanova, Bulgaria.
Pairs—Siika Kelbetcheva and Stoyanka Grouitcheva, Bulgaria.
Fours With Coxswains—East Germany.
Quadruple Sculls—East Germany.
Eights—East Germany.

SHOOTING

Free Pistol—Uwe Potteck, East Germany.
Rapid Fire Pistol—Norbert Klaar, East Germany.
Small-Bore Rifle, Prone—Karlheinz Smieszek, West Germany.
Small-Bore Rifle, 3 Positions—Lanny Bassham, Bedford, Tex.
Rifle, Running Game Target—Alexandr Gazov, Soviet Union.
Trap—Don Haldeman, Souderton, Pa.
Skeet—Josef Panacek, Czechoslovakia.

SWIMMING—MEN

100-Meter Freestyle—Jim Montgomery, Madison, Wis.
200-Meter Freestyle—Bruce Furniss, Long Beach, Calif.
400-Meter Freestyle—Brian Goodell, Mission Viejo, Calif.
1,500-Meter Freestyle—Brian Goodell, Mission Viejo, Calif.
100-Meter Backstroke—John Naber, Menlo Park, Calif.
200-Meter Backstroke—John Naber, Menlo Park, Calif.
100-Meter Breast-Stroke—John Hencken, Santa Barbara, Calif.
200-Meter Breast-Stroke—David Willkie, Britain.
100-Meter Butterfly—Matt Vogel, Fort Wayne, Ind.
200-Meter Butterfly—Mike Bruner, Stockton, Calif.
400-Meter Individual Medley—Rod Strachan, Santa Ana, Calif.
400-Meter Medley Relay—United States (John Naber, John Hencken, Matt Vogel, Jim Montgomery).
800-meter Freestyle Relay—United States (Mike Bruner, Bruce Furniss, John Naber, Jim Montgomery).

DIVING—MEN

Springboard—Phil Boggs, Akron, Ohio
Platform—Klaus Dibiasi, Italy.

SWIMMING—WOMEN

100-Meter Freestyle—Kornelia Ender, East Germany.
200-Meter Freestyle—Kornelia Ender, East Germany.
400-Meter Freestyle—Petra Thumer, East Germany.
800-Meter Freestyle—Petra Thumer, East Germany.
100-Meter Backstroke—Ulrike Richter, East Germany.
200-Meter Backstroke—Ulrike Richter, East Germany.
100-Meter Breast-Stroke—Hannelore Anke, Germany.
200-Meter Breast-Stroke—Marina Koshevaia, Soviet Union.
100-Meter Butterfly—Kornelia Ender, East Germany.
200-Meter Butterfly—Andrea Pollack, East Germany.
400-Meter Individual Medley—Ulrike Tauber, East Germany.
400-Meter Medley Relay—East Germany (Ulrike Richter, Hannelore Anke, Andrea Pollack, Kornelia Ender).
400-Meter Freestyle Relay—United States (Kim Peyton, Wendy Boglioli, Jill Sterkel, Shirley Babashoff).

DIVING—WOMEN

Springboard—Jennifer Chandler, Lincoln, Ala.
Platform—Elena Daytsekhovskaia, Soviet Union.

TRACK AND FIELD—MEN

TRACK EVENTS

100-Meter Dash—Hasely Crawford, Trinidad.
200-Meter Dash—Don Quarrie, Jamaica.
400-Meter Dash—Alberto Juantorena, Cuba.
800-Meter Run—Alberto Juantorena, Cuba.
1,500-Meter Run—John Walker, New Zealand.
5,000-Meter Run—Lasse Viren, Finland.
10,000-Meter Run—Lasse Viren, Finland.
3,000-Meter Steeplechase—Anders Garderud, Sweden.
20,000-Meter Walk—Daniel Bautista, Mexico.
Marathon—Waldemar Cierpinski, East Germany.
110-Meter Hurdles—Guy Drut, France.
400-Meter Hurdles—Edwin Moses, Dayton, Ohio.

400-Meter Relay—United States (Harvey Glance, Johnny Jones, Millard Hampton, Steve Riddick).
1,600-Meter Relay—United States (Herman Frazier, Benny Brown, Fred Newhouse, Maxie Parks).

FIELD EVENTS

Long Jump—Arnie Robinson, San Diego, Calif.
Triple Jump—Victor Saneyev, Soviet Union.
High Jump—Jacek Wszola, Poland.
Pole Vault—Tradeusz Slusarski, Poland.
Shot-put—Udo Beyer, East Germany.
Discus—Mac Wilkins, Portland, Ore.
Javelin—Miklos Nemeth, Hungary.
Hammer Throw—Yuri Sedyh, Soviet Union.
Decathlon—Bruce Jenner, San Jose, Calif.

TRACK AND FIELD—WOMEN

TRACK EVENTS

100-Meter Dash—Annegret Richter, West Germany.
200-Meter Dash—Baerbel Eckert, East Germany.
400-Meter Dash—Irena Szewinska, Poland.
800-Meter Run—Tatyana Kazankina, Soviet Union.
1,500-Meter Run—Tatyana Kazankina, Soviet Union.
100-Meter Hurdles—Johanna Schaller, East Germany.
400-Meter Relay—East Germany (Marlis Oelsner, Renate Stecher, Carla Bodendorf, Baerbel Eckhert).
1,600-Meter Relay—East Germany (Doris Maletzki, Brigitte Rohde, Ellen Streidt, Christina Brehmer).

FIELD EVENTS

Long Jump—Angela Voigt, East Germany.
High Jump—Rosemarie Ackermann, East Germany.
Shot-put—Ivanka Christova, Bulgaria.
Discus—Evelin Schlaak, East Germany.
Javelin—Ruth Fuchs, East Germany.
Pentathlon—Siegrun Siegl, East Germany.

WEIGHT LIFTING

Flyweight—Alexander Voronin, Soviet Union.
Bantamweight—Norair Nurikyan, Bulgaria.
Featherweight—Nikolai Kolesnikov, Soviet Union.
Lightweight—Zhigniev Kacsmarek, Poland.
Middleweight—Yordan Mitkov, Bulgaria.
Light Heavyweight—Valery Shary, Soviet Union.
Middleheavyweight—David Rigert, Soviet Union.
Heavyweight—Valentin Khristov, Bulgaria.
Super Heavyweight—Vasily Alexseiev, Soviet Union.

WRESTLING, FREESTYLE

Paperweight—Khassan Issaev, Bulgaria.
Flyweight—Yuji Takata, Japan.
Bantamweight—Vladimir Umin, Soviet Union.
Featherweight—Jung Mo Jang, South Korea.
Lightweight—Pavel Pinigin, Soviet Union.
Welterweight—Date Jiichiro, Japan.
Middleweight—John Peterson, Comstock, Wis.
Light Heavyweight—Levan Tediashvili, Soviet Union.
Heavyweight—Ivan Yarygin, Soviet Union.
Unlimited—Soslan Andiev, Soviet Union.

WRESTLING, GRECO-ROMAN

Paperweight—Aleksei Schumakov, Soviet Union.
Flyweight—Vitaly Konstantinov, Soviet Union.
Bantamweight—Pertti Ukkola, Finland.
Featherweight—Kazimier Lipien, Poland.
Lightweight—Suren Nalbandy, Soviet Union.
Welterweight—Anatoly Bykov, Soviet Union.
Middleweight—Momir Petkovic, Yugoslavia.
Light Heavyweight—Valery Rezantsev, Soviet Union.
Heavyweight—Nikolay Bolboshin, Soviet Union.
Unlimited—Aleksandr Kolchinsky, Soviet Union.

YACHTING

Finn—Jocken Shumann, East Germany.
Flying Dutchman—Joerg Diesch, West Germany.
470 Class—Frank Huebner, West Germany.
Soling—Paul Jensen, Denmark.
Tempest—John Albrechtson, Sweden.
Tornado—Reginald White, Britain.

TEAM CHAMPIONS

Basketball—United States.
Field Hockey—New Zealand.
Soccer—East Germany.
Handball, Men—Soviet Union.
Handball, Women—Soviet Union.
Volleyball, Men—Poland.
Volleyball, Women—Japan.
Water Polo—Hungary.

WINTER GAMES

BIATHLON

Individual—Nikolai Kruglov, Soviet Union.
Relay—Soviet Union.

BOBSLEDDING

2-Man—East Germany (Meinhard Nehmer and Bernard Germeshausen).
4-Man—East Germany.

ICE SKATING, FIGURE

Men—John Curry, Britain.
Women—Dorothy Hamill, Riverside, Conn.
Pairs—Irina Rodnina and Aleksandr Zaitsev, Soviet Union.
Dance—Ludmilla Pakhomova and Alexander Gorschkov, Soviet Union.

ICE SKATING, SPEED—MEN

500 Meters—Evgeni Kulikov, Soviet Union.
1,000 Meters—Peter Mueller, Mequon, Wis.
1,500 Meters—Jan Egil Storholt, Norway.
5,000 Meters—Sten Stensen, Norway.
10,000 Meters—Piet Kleine, Netherlands.

ICE SKATING SPEED—WOMEN

500 Meters—Sheila Young, Detroit.
1,000 Meters—Tatiana Averina, Soviet Union.
1,500 Meters—Galina Stepanskaya, Soviet Union.
3,000 Meters—Tatiana Averina, Soviet Union.

HOCKEY

Team—Soviet Union.

LUGE

Men—Detlef Guenther, East Germany.
Doubles—Hans Rinn and Norbert Hahn, East Germany.
Women—Margit Schumann, East Germany.

SKIING, ALPINE—MEN

Downhill—Franz Klammer, Austria.
Slalom—Piero Gros, Italy.
Giant Slalom—Heini Hemmi, Switzerland.

SKIING, ALPINE—WOMEN

Downhill—Rosi Mittermaier, West Germany.
Slalom—Rosi Mittermaier, West Germany.
Giant Slalom—Kathy Kreiner, Canada.

SKIING, NORDIC—MEN

Jumping, 70 Meters—Hans-Georg Aschenbach, East Germany.
Jumping, 90 Meters—Karl Schnabl, Austria.
Combined—Ulrich Wehling, East Germany.

CROSS-COUNTRY

15 Kilometers—Nikola Bajukov, Soviet Union.
30 Kilometers—Sergei Saveliev, Soviet Union.
50 Kilometers—Ivar Formo, Norway.
40-Kilometer Relay—Finland.

SKIING, NORDIC—WOMEN

CROSS-COUNTRY

5 Kilometers—Helena Takalo, Finland.
10 Kilometers—Raisa Smetanina, Soviet Union.
20-Kilometer Relay—Soviet Union.

WHO'S WHO IN BEST SPORTS STORIES—1977

WRITERS IN BEST SPORTS STORIES—1977

THE PRIZE WINNERS

SHIRLEY POVICH (The Great Yankee Stadium Holdup), winner of the *Best Sports Stories* news-coverage award for the second time, attended Georgetown University, chose journalism as his profession, and at the age of twenty became sports editor of *The Washington Post,* perhaps the youngest sports editor of any metropolitan daily. He won the *Best Sports Stories* news-coverage prize in 1957 with his story on Don Larsen's perfect World Series game against the Dodgers. His other prizes for fine writing have included the National Headliners Award and the Grantland Rice Award. His book, *All These Mornings,* was published in 1969 by Prentice-Hall. He has appeared in *Best Sports Stories* on many occasions.

JANE GROSS (Tennis Isn't the Only Issue), winner of the *Best Sports Stories–1977* news-feature award, is a sports reporter for *Newsday* on Long Island. Her regular beat is the New York Nets, the NBA professional basketball team. A 1969 graduate of Skidmore College in Saratoga Springs, N.Y., she was a researcher and reporter for *Sports Illustrated* for six years before coming to *Newsday,* where she has been for the last two years. This is her first contribution to this anthology, and she is one of the few winners on her first try. She is also the third woman winner in the 33 years of these annuals. Previous distaff winners were Carol Hughes and Joan Flynn Dryspool. This is the second time in her short newspaper career that she has won a prize for her efforts. She took second in the New York State Associated Press competition, also with a feature story. She is twenty-nine years old and unmarried. She is the daughter of Milton Gross, the late sports columnist of the *New York Post.*

MARK JACOBSON (Rebound for Glory), winner of the *Best Sports Stories–1977* magazine award, was born in Manhattan in 1948. He attended the University of Wisconsin, New York University, the University of California at Berkeley and the San Francisco Art Institute. Jacobson produced psychedelic light shows at the Whiskey a Go-Go on Sunset Strip and drove a cab in New York City from 1972 to 1974. He has made two underground feature-length films—*The Birds Coit Tower* and *The Fool Killer*—and has written two plays—*Arnie Con Carne* and *Shaving Cream Fight in Madison.* He has been a free-lance writer since 1974, publishing articles in *New York* magazine, where his current article appeared, the *Village Voice, High Times, Monster Times,* and *Crawdaddy.*

OTHER CONTRIBUTORS *(In Alphabetical Order)*

MAURY ALLEN (A Sad Story), winner of the *Best Sports Stories* news-coverage award in 1976, has been a sports reporter for the *New York Post* since 1962. He began his newspaper career with the *Seymour* (Ind.) *Times* after Army service, went to the *Levittown* (Pa.) *Times,* and then worked for *Sports Illustrated.* He then went to the sports desk of the *New York Post.* He has authored many sports books and his latest, *Where Have You Gone, Joe DiMaggio?,* was warmly received by the critics. Because of his perceptive, interesting sports analysis, he is much in demand by many of the nation's better periodicals.

DAVE ANDERSON (A Hockey Lesson for Dr. Kissinger) is a sports columnist for *The New York Times* and was the winner of the news-feature award of *Best Sports Stories* in 1972. He also won the 1965 magazine award with his profile of Sugar Ray Robinson. He was born in Brooklyn and began his newspaper career with the now defunct *New York Sun.* After his graduation from Holy Cross in 1951, he went to work with the *Brooklyn Eagle,* which is also defunct, and then to the *New York Journal,* likewise out of business. As a columnist and reporter for the *Times,* he covers the entire range of sports.

PETE AXTHELM (Baseball's Money Madness) joined *Newsweek* in 1968 as an associate editor in the magazine's sports section and became general editor in 1970. Since 1974 he has also contributed a biweekly column to the magazine. Before coming to *Newsweek,* he was a writer for *Sports Illustrated* for two years and, before that, was a reporter and horse racing columnist for the defunct *New York Herald Tribune.* He is a graduate of Yale, class of 1965. Besides contributing to numerous magazines, he is the author of four books, all of which have received warm critical acclaim. One book in particular, *The City Game* (Harper's Magazine Press) is regarded as the definitive work on Harlem basketball. His honors include a Schick Award from the Professional Football Writers of America and an Eclipse Award from the Thoroughbred Racing Association.

HAL BODLEY ("It Was a Wedding That Movies Are Made Of?") has been sports editor of the News-Journal Papers, Wilmington, Del., since 1971. He joined the *News-Journal* after serving as sports editor of the *Delaware State News,* Dover, for one year in 1960. He served as writer, columnist, night sports editor, and assistant sports editor before assuming his present position. He attended the University of Delaware. His column has won many regional awards and has appeared in *Best Sports Stories* in 1966 and 1970. He is currently treasurer of the Associated Press Sports Editors Association and Philadelphia chairman of the Baseball Writers Association of America.

PETER BODO (Forest Hills '76: The Year the Crowd Took Over) lives in New York City. He writes frequently about tennis and soccer and is a contributing editor of *Tennis* and coauthor of the book *Pele's New World.* His work has appeared in numerous newspapers and magazines, including *New York,* the *New York Daily News, Sport,* the *Star,* and the *Australian.*

THOMAS BOSWELL (The Deadly Combination) has been a sports reporter with *The Washington Post* since 1971. His major beats are major-league baseball (World Series and playoffs), tennis (Forest Hills), and general assignment coverage of the Washington Redskins, Washington Bullets, college football and basketball. He is a graduate of Amherst College, class of 1969. He won a Baltimore-Washington Newspaper Guild Front Page Award honorable mention in 1974. This is his second appearance in *Best Sports Stories.*

JIM (BROZ) BROSNAN (The Short Season) is a former major-league baseball pitcher who turned to writing and broadcasting after his baseball career was ended. A native of Cincinnati, Ohio, he was born in 1929 and signed his first pro baseball contract with the Chicago Cubs of the National League in 1947. He entered the U.S. Army in 1951, then pitched in the majors for the Cubs (1954–58), St. Louis Cardinals (1958–59), Cincinnati Reds (1959–63), and Chicago White Sox (1963). He was a sports commentator for radio and TV (1964–65) and has been a free-lance journalist since then. He is the author of seven books, 97 magazine articles (*Atlantic, Boy's Life, Esquire, Playboy, Sport,* and *Sports Illustrated,* among others), various newspaper columns and features (*Chicago Daily News, Chicago Sun-Times, St. Louis Post-Dispatch, Los Angeles Times, The Milwaukee Journal,* and *The New York Times*). This is his first appearance in *Best Sports Stories.*

LOU CHAPMAN (The Reds Are Making a Joke of the Series) has been with the *Milwaukee Sentinel* for more than 28 years. He has covered two major-league sports—the baseball Braves and Brewers and the pro basketball Hawks and Bucks. He is a graduate of Marquette University and won six writing awards from the old Hearst organization. He contributed to the *Saturday Evening Post* and the *American Weekly* and is presently a correspondent for *The*

Sporting News. He also coauthored a paperback book on the Milwaukee Braves. He has twice earned the award as Wisconsin Sports Writer of the Year and has appeared in *Best Sports Stories* on a number of occasions.

MURRAY CHASS (A Historical Precedent) has been writing for the sports desk of *The New York Times* for the past seven years and is currently specializing in baseball with an intense interest in the labor and legal aspects of the sport. Prior to coming to the *Times,* he spent nearly 10 years with the Associated Press in Pittsburgh and New York. He has three children of his own and two stepchildren who must keep things pretty lively at the Chass home in Paramus, N.J.

DOUG CLARKE (Parade of the Elephants) was born in Philadelphia in 1940. He is a graduate of Kent State University (1964). Following internship at the *Cleveland Plain Dealer,* he worked as assistant sports editor for the *Poughkeepsie* (N.Y.) *Journal* (1966–67) and as police beat and general assignment reporter for the *Cincinnati Inquirer* (1967–69). He has been writing features, columns, and covering both pro and amateur sports for the *Cleveland Press* since 1969. He is married and has two children.

BUD COLLINS (That Hatchetwoman Called Chrissie) is one of America's best-known tennis writers because of his television exposure on NBC and PBS tennis broadcasts. He is also one of the most respected reporters in sports. His informal jocular "mike" manners amuse and delight his audiences. As a columnist for *The Boston Globe* he has received warm critical acclaim and has authored books on Rod Laver and Evonne Goolagong as well as being a regular contributor to *World Tennis* for five years.

BETTY CUNIBERTI (They Rejected Emotion to Win) was graduated in 1973 from the University of Southern California and started working for the *San Bernardino Sun-Telegram,* where the reprinted story appeared. In 1976 she went to the *San Francisco Chronicle,* first woman sports writer on the staff. That year she won the Moses Grant Award at USC for being the most promising woman writer. Other honors include two best sports stories of the year awards from the Twin Counties Press Club and two second places in the Associated Press Sports Writing Contest.

HUGH DELANO (The Champions Bite the Dust) covers hockey and baseball for the *New York Post* and has been a newspaperman for 20 years. He is the president of the New York chapter of the Professional Hockey Writers Association and is the author of two hockey books: *Eddie Giacomin: A Goalie's Story* and *Power Hockey.* A Marine Corps veteran, he lives in Cranford, N.J., with his wife and four sons.

JOLEE EDMONDSON (The Whitwams Go to the Masters), who began her career in golf journalism in 1974 when she set out to cover the PGA tour as a free-lance writer with a Volkswagen camper and a portable typewriter, is now associate editor of *Golf Magazine.* In 1976, she was the first woman in the history of the Golf Writers Association of America to win first place in its annual writing contest for her portrayal of a fading tour star—"The Flamboyant Twilight of Doug Sanders." She is twenty-seven, a graduate of San Diego State University with a degree in journalism, and her previous posts include being feature editor of two Southern California daily newspapers.

BARRY FARRELL (Kareem Abdul-Jabbar Goes West Again) was born in Seattle, Washington, and attended the public schools there, trying, but failing, at making the basketball teams. He has written for several newspapers, for *Time, Life, Sports Illustrated, Sport, New York, New West, Playboy,* and a number of other magazines, including *Harper's,* of which he is presently a contributing editor. He has lived in a dozen cities while working as a journalist, and in all but New Delhi he filled many good hours playing basketball. He lives with his wife and daughter in Los Angeles, where the courts are always dry, but at 42 has abandoned hope of being able to touch the rim. This is his first appearance in *Best Sports Stories.* The current story appeared in *Sport.*

MIKE GONRING (An Easy Victory, If Not an Artistic One) has worked for *The Milwaukee Journal* on and off since 1968. For three years, from July 1971 to April 1974, he was Sports Information Director at Marquette University. At the *Journal,* Gonring has covered a variety of amateur and professional sports and is currently the *Journal's* baseball writer. He is a 1969 graduate of Marquette. This is his first appearance in *Best Sports Stories.*

TED GREEN (Connors Puts It Right on the Line) is twenty-eight years old and a graduate with a master's from UCLA. he has been with the *Los Angeles Times* for four years, covering pro basketball, tennis, and many major events and personalities for the paper. Included have been pieces on Jerry West, John Wooden, Kareem Abdul-Jabbar, Bill Walton, Julius Erving, George McGinnis, Jimmy Connors, Ilie Nastase, Bjorn Borg, and more. The *Times* has gone to more of a magazine format and he is one of three or four writers who do the magazine pieces. He is married, lives near the beach in Santa Monica, and plays plenty of tennis and basketball.

WILL GRIMSLEY (Where Have You Gone, Joe DiMaggio?) has covered the globe in pursuit of stories for The Associated Press. He has reported on five Olympic Games, made 12 trips to Australia for Davis Cup tournaments, and has had numerous reportorial chores in every major world capital. He also has had time enough to write three books—*Golf: Its History, People and Events; Tennis: Its History, People and Events; and Football: Greatest Moments of the Southwest Conference.* He also was supervising editor of *Century of Sports,* a popular book that sold close to 100,000 copies in 1971. This marks his seventh appearance in *Best Sports Stories.*

JIM HAWKINS (Funny and Fantastic: That's Fidrych) has covered the Detroit Tigers for the *Detroit Free Press* for the past seven seasons. A native of Superior, Wis., and a 1966 graduate of the University of Wisconsin, he began writing sports for the *Milwaukee Sentinel* while in school. Later he wrote for the *Wilmington* (Del.) *News-Journal* and the *Baltimore Evening Sun,* concentrating there on golf as well as college football and basketball. In 1969 he was selected Sports Writer of the Year in the state of Maryland. He is also a regular contributor to *The Sporting News* and, along with Jim Benagh, coauthored the best-selling paperback, *Go Bird Go!* He was the winner of the magazine award in *Best Sports Stories* of 1974. This is his sixth appearance in this anthology.

JOE HENDRICKSON (The Reversal Story) is the author of *Tournament of Roses,* a complete history of the Tournament and Rose Bowl games. He is the former sports editor of *Esquire* magazine as well as the *Minneapolis Tribune* and a former Minneapolis public relations executive. He has been the sports editor of the *Pasadena Star-News* since 1962. He was president of Southern California Football and Baseball Writers Associations and a director on the board of the National Football Writers Association. He graduated from the University of Minnesota school of journalism in 1935. His sports sections were adjudged best in California seven times by California publishers in a 10-year period.

STAN HOCHMAN (Nadia Is a Perfect Angel) is one of the fine writers of the East Coast. He is habitually concerned with the athlete as a human and as a societal adjunct, rather than just with the score of the game. After 12 years as a baseball writer and columnist for the *Philadelphia Daily News,* he became the sports editor of the paper in 1971. Much of his sensitive writing is undoubtedly inspired by his wife, Gloria, who is a successful free-lancer and his daughter, Andee, who is the editor of her junior high school paper.

GREG HOFFMAN (Sister Mary Mummy's Close Calling) started as an accountant at *womenSports Magazine* who became an associate editor of that magazine and then concentrated on writing, mainly on tennis. He has functioned as editor for the World Team Tennis national program and on The Virginia Slims Tennis Association national program. Most recently he has been editor of a biweekly newsletter, *Inside Women's Tennis.* He has also been writing comedy material for Phyllis Diller. His first book, *The Art of World Tennis,* was published by the San Francisco Book Company, Inc.

DAVE KINDRED (King of the Decathlon) is thirty-five and has worked for the Louisville newspapers since 1966. He became sports editor of the *Louisville Times* in 1969, spent a year in the paper's Washington bureau in 1972, and has been sports editor of *The Courier-Journal* since. Four times Kentucky Sports Writer of the Year, he won a National Headliner Award for general-interest columns in 1971. He is the author of a book, *Basketball: The Dream Game in Kentucky.* His stories have appeared in *Best Sports Stories* four times.

TONY KORNHEISER (The Man: Reality Versus the Legend) has worked at *The New York Times,* where this story appeared, for the last two years. Before that he was at *Newsday* in Long Island as a sports reporter, a rock music critic, and the life-style specialist for the daily magazine section. His stories have appeared in *Rolling Stone, New York,* and *Sport Magazine.* He also has been a regular contributor to the *Street & Smith Basketball Annual* and a story from this publication was reprinted in *Best Sports Stories–1976.* This is his fifth appearance in *Best Sports Stories.*

HAL LEBOVITZ (Once in a Lifetime?) is a graduate of Western Reserve University who started his career as a high-school chemistry teacher but then became a sports writer because of his avid interest in athletics. He started writing for the *Cleveland News* and then went to the *Cleveland Plain Dealer,* where he is now the sports editor. His popular column "Hal Asks" has earned him numerous writing honors. He is a past president of the Cleveland chapter of the Baseball Writers Association of America and has been included in *Best Sports Stories* many times.

BARRY LORGE (Ilie Nastase: The Side You Never See), a native of Worcester, Mass., is a 1970 graduate of Harvard College, where he majored in government. He started writing sports for the *Worcester Telegram & Gazette* while he was in school, happened on the tennis beat and since 1971 has been a free-lancer, specializing in tennis. He has covered the sport in more than a dozen countries for a number of publications. In 1975 he achieved the grand slam, covering the Australian, French, Wimbledon, and U.S. opens. He is a contributing editor of *Tennis Magazine* and his stories appear frequently in *The Washington Post.*

WILLIAM A. MARSANO (How We Blitzed the British), formerly the rewrite man in *TV Guide*'s New York national programming office, transferred to the magazine's Radnor, Pa., headquarters in 1970 to become associate editor and then sports editor of that publication. Once content only to edit, he says, he was "driven to writing by the switch from New York to Radnor's eerie rural silence." This is his second appearance in *Best Sports Stories.*

KATHLEEN MAXA (Calvin Hill's Choice: To Plow or Preach?) joined the sports staff of the *Washington Star* in 1972 as a general assignment reporter. Prior to that, she wrote magazine pieces for the *Star's* Sunday supplement. Ms. Maxa graduated from Ohio University in 1971 with a bachelor of arts degree and English major. Currently, she lives in Washington with her husband, Rudy, who is a staff writer for *The Washington Post,* and daughter, Sara.

HUBERT MIZELL (Mother Nature Jilts a Handsome Texan) is thirty-seven and sports editor of the *St. Petersburg* (Fla.) *Times* and a former feature sports writer for The Associated Press in Miami and New York. He has covered almost all of the world's great sports events, including the Olympic Games, and was included in *Best Sports Stores* in 1974 and 1976. Mizell, who is also a contributing editor of *Golf Digest,* began his career on the *Florida Times-Union* in Jacksonville at age seventeen.

MONTY (MAURICE R. JR.) MONTGOMERY ("This Was a Night for Perfection") is thirty-eight years old and has been what he calls a professional student with a B.A. from Stanford, an M.A. from the University of Oregon, and "two utterly useless degrees from the Harvard Graduate School of Education." He wanted to spend the rest of his life writing about trout but he is occasionally required to cover snow sports, including skiing and ice skating, for *The Boston Globe.* He has been employed there for five years and "works there frequently," he says. He was once Home and Gardens editor of the *El Cajon* (Calif.) *Valley News,* a biweekly.

WILLIAM PAUL (Mission Impossible: Getting a Super Bowl Ticket) grew up in Leonia, N.J. He joined the staff of *The Wall Street Journal* in 1970 after graduation from Princeton, and this story appeared in *The Wall Street Journal.* He was assigned to the Philadelphia bureau and remained there until he transferred to Atlanta in 1975. Paul is twenty-eight and single.

EDWIN POPE (The Anticlimactic End of the Masters Golf) was born in Athens, Ga., and maintains he fumbled his way through the University of Georgia. Nevertheless he has established a warm readership as a columnist and reporter with his paper, the *Miami Herald,* of which he became the sports editor in 1957. His former newspaper work was with the *Atlantic Constitution,* the *Atlanta Journal* and United Press International. He is the author of four books: *Football's Greatest Coaches, Baseball's Greatest Managers, Encyclopedia of Greyhound Racing,* and *Ted Williams: The Golden Years.* He has merited many appearances in this anthology.

COOPER ROLLOW (Good as Gold Again), a native of Kansas, has been a member of the *Chicago Tribune* sports staff since 1953 and sports editor since 1969. His coverage of the 1972 Munich Games, including the Israeli massacre, brought him national attention. This is his first appearance in *Best Sports Stories.*

JACK SAMSON (Elk Hunting the High Lonesome) is the editor of *Field & Stream.* His outdoor writing career has spanned 26 years and almost as many countries. He wrote an outdoor column for The Associated Press for nine years and his stories have appeared in all the major outdoor magazines. He is the author of numerous books, ranging from trap and skeet shooting to big game fishing. This is his first appearance in *Best Sports Stories.*

JOHN SCHULIAN (The Celtics Shake Off Age and the Suns) of *The Washington Post* specializes in prose portraits of athletes. But he has also been known to write about touchdowns, home runs, stuff shots, and left hooks. Before coming to the *Post* in 1975, Schulian, who has a B.A. from the University of Utah and an M.S. from Northwestern, spent five years as a cityside reporter and rock-and-roll columnist at the *Baltimore Evening Sun.* His free-lance work has appeared in a variety of magazines ranging from *Sports Illustrated* to *American Film.*

NICK SEITZ (Overemphasis or Hungry Hill Pride?) is one of the few writers who has hit the over 10-time mark in this sports anthology. He is now the editor of *Golf Digest.* His alma mater was the University of Oklahoma, where he majored in philosophy. Then, at the age of twenty-two, he became editor of the *Norman* (Okla.) *Transcript.* His majoring in philosophy was excellent background for his golf articles, which not only concern themselves with the techniques of the game but also with the frustrations and tribulations of ordinary mortals who are constrained to watch the epic golf events on the tube and then attempt to emulate them. He has won numerous prizes in golf and basketball writing contests.

LEONARD SHAPIRO (Little League Umpire) was born in Brooklyn in 1947, raised in Syosset, N.Y., and schooled at the University of Wisconsin, with a B.S. in journalism and the University of Missouri, where he received an M.A. in journalism. He joined *The Washington Post* in 1969 and has covered all sports from the high-school to professional level. His main assignment now is beat man on the Washington Redskins. He also covered Winter Olympics in 1976 at Innsbruck. He coauthored a book with *Post* columnist Kenneth Denlinger, *Athletes for Sale,* an investigation into college recruiting. He was named sports writer of the year in Washington in 1974. He lives in Haymarket, Va., with his wife, Diane, three-year-old daughter, Jennifer, and two dogs.

BLACKIE SHERROD (Bold Forbes Pulls the Rug Out), the executive sports editor of *The Dallas Times Herald,* has garnered just about every important sports-writing prize in the country. To name a few: the National Headliners Award; seven citations as the outstanding sports writer by newspapers, radio, and TV colleagues; and over a dozen inclusions in *Best Sports Stories.* As a master of ceremonies and banquet speaker he has made a reputation almost equal to his reputation for writing. He also has his own radio and TV programs.

ART SPANDER (Arnie's Still the Man), a 1960 UCLA graduate with a B.S. in political science, has been on the *San Francisco Chronicle* for 12 years after periods with the *Santa Monica Evening Outlook* and Los Angeles bureau of UPI. He has specialized in golf and pro basketball but has also covered every other sport from ballooning to volleyball. Spander has won numerous writing awards, including one for best news-coverage story in the 1971 edition of *Best Sports Stories.* He has appeared in this anthology six times. He also won the San Francisco Press Club first prize for best sports story and twice took first place in the Golf Writers Association of America writing contest.

VITO STELLINO (A Game to Remember), thirty-five, has written for the past three years for the *Pittsburgh Post-Gazette,* specializing on the Steeler beat. A native of Grand Rapids, Mich., he worked for nine years before that for UPI in their Detroit and New York bureaus. He has also done extensive writing for sports magazines, concentrating on baseball and football. This is his first appearance in this anthology.

WELLS TWOMBLY The death of Wells Twombly, author of "The End of an Era," at forty-one, occurred just before this anthology went to press. His family and sportsworld have been bereft of a man who had a beautiful way with words. They flowed from his pen and accounted for his meteoric rise. Since coming to the *San Francisco Examiner*, he had published more than six books, contributed to many magazines, and written a daily column in his paper. His work was usually involved with the sportsworld but he had no hesitation in going beyond his particular arena to write about a slice of life that delighted or disturbed him. But whereas a bright meteor quickly disappears without a trace, Twombly left behind him a legacy of marvelous and exciting talent that will be remembered. The only thing is that he left us much, much too soon.

DICK YOUNG (The Barbie Doll Soap Opera) joined the *New York Daily News* in 1941 and appeared in the first edition of *Best Sports Stories* in 1944. He was at that time one of the youngest sports reporters in New York City. Since then he has become one of the two most consistent winners in this series, with five *Best Sports Stories* awards—two in news-coverage (in 1959 and

1960), two for news-features (1957 and 1966), and one in the magazine category (in 1955). He writes a daily column for the *Daily News* entitled "Young Ideas," and baseball is his major sport.

PHOTOGRAPHERS IN BEST SPORTS STORIES — 1977

THE PHOTO WINNERS

MIKE ANDERSEN (Now Girls, Let's Not Have a Row), winner of the feature award, is one of the young talented New England photographers who has earned many appearances in *Best Sports Stories* with his dramatic shots. He has been associated with *The Boston Herald American* for the past eight years after stints with papers in Kansas, Iowa, and Texas. He has been named New England Press Photographer of the Year twice and has won over 140 other prizes, including this book's feature award. He is an ardent supporter of the National Press Photographers Association and has held many offices with that group. He is a graduate of the University of Missouri.

CHARLES R. PUGH, JR. (Grandstand Hails Headstand) is the winner of the actio-photo award in *Best Sports Stories–1977*. He won another action-photo award in this anthology in 1969. He began his distinguished photographic career with the *Johnson City* (Tenn.) *Press-Chronicle* and is now with the *Atlanta Journal-Constitution,* where this photo appeared. He has garnered many state and national prizes for his talented work and has earned a number of appearances in this sports anthology.

OTHER PHOTOGRAPHERS (In Alphabetical Order)

JOHN E. BIEVER (No Tongue-Tied Tennis Here) is employed by *The Milwaukee Journal.* He has a B.A. in business administration from the University of Wisconsin and has won a number of prizes. He has been in *Best Sports Stories* on five different occasions. In 1973 he won the award this series offers for the best action shot.

DON BOORSE (Face Up To It!) is a newcomer to *Best Sports Stories* competition. He has been a photographer for the *Perkasie* (Pa.) *News-Herald* for 10 years and has won regional and state awards. He covers all kinds of events—news, sports, and society—for his paper.

CRAIG R. BORCK (MVP vs. Rookie of the Year) is thirty-one years old, a graduate of the University of Minnesota's School of Journalism and Mass Communications, and is in his seventh year as a general assignment photographer for the *St. Paul Dispatch & Pioneer Press.* This marks his debut in this anthology.

RICHARD DARCEY (Yes, The Doctor Is In) has a reputation of being one of the most talented and versatile news photographers in the nation. He is director of photography at *The Washington Post,* where he has worked since 1948. His past honors include *Look*'s Sports Picture of the Year competition and prizes in national press association competitions. He has won two prizes for his action shots in this anthology.

BARRY EDMONDS (Caught in a Crunch) has been chief photographer of *The Flint Journal* since 1955 and also is a past president of the National Press Photographers Association. His fine work merited four prizes and three runners-up as Michigan's Press Photographer of the Year.

JOHN P. FOSTER ("Ride 'Em Cowboy! Oh Yeah?") is a stringer for *The Seattle Times* and has taught photojournalism for 10 years at Central State College, Ellensburg, Wash. He was promoted to associate professor this year.

DAVE GOGAN (Perils of a Puckish Puck) has been active in photography since childhood. His first news picture was published while he was a teen-ager. At present he is free-lancing in Atlanta, Ga. His current photo appeared in the *Jonesboro* (Ga.), *News/Daily,* an area county newspaper. This is his freshman appearance in *Best Sports Stories.*

CLETUS M. HOHN (Something Old, Something New) was the feature winner last year for his amusing shot of Patty Berg clowning a golf lesson. He has been a photographer for the *Minneapolis Tribune* for 20 years. As a graduate of the University of Minnesota in 1953 he majored in photojournalism and began his career with the *Rochester* (Minn.) *Post Bulletin.* This is his third appearance in this anthology.

ABE ISAAC (Head and Tail) was formerly a photographer for 20 years on the *Newark Evening News,* now defunct. At present he is associated with the *Elizabeth* (N.J.) *Daily Journal.* This is his second appearance in *Best Sports Stories.*

DERRICK ZANE JACKSON (Look Ref, No Hands!) has played a dual role as a sports writer and photographer for *The Milwaukee Journal* and The Associated Press in Kansas City. The photography is a hobby, but good enough to be picked up by his editors. He is twenty-one years of age and has just been graduated from the University of Wisconsin. This is his first appearance in this series.

ROBERT JOHNSON (Ye Gods, Is There No Justice?) is a staff photographer for *The Nashville Tennessean.* He attended the University of Tennessee and broke into photography by taking pictures to accompany sports articles written by his father. This is his fourth appearance in *Best Sports Stories.*

CHARLES G. KIRMAN (The Sandman Cometh) received a B.S. with honors in professional photography from the Rochester Institute of Technology in 1972. Since then he has been employed as a staff photographer for the *Chicago Sun Times.* He has won over 50 photojournalism awards since joining his present paper, and in 1975 he won the Illinois Press Photographer of the Year Award. His pictures have been published in this sports anthology three times before.

JOHN LONG (Net Gain) has been a photojournalist with *The Hartford Courant* for five years. Previously he taught high-school English. This is his second appearance in *Best Sports Stories.* He is now president of the Connecticut News Photographers Association and lives in Manchester, Conn.

CHUCK LYONS (Basketball Karate) recently started his third year as a photographer and correspondent sports writer for Foothill Intercity Newspapers and the *Pasadena Star-News.* He became sports editor of the Foothill Newspapers while attending junior college and continues to work part-time with his present papers while attending a local university. This is his freshman appearance in this series.

RICHARD MACKSON (Names in the News) is a staff photographer at the *San Jose Mercury-News* and has a penchant for shooting interesting photos of personal features at the sports events he covers. He started as a student in photography at City College of San Francisco, then went to International News Photos. Upon the merger with United Press, he spent a couple of years in industrial photography.

FRED MATTHES (Carping Coach) at forty-six is a veteran who has been for 15 years a staff photographer of the *San Jose Mercury News.* He is a member of the National Press Photographers Association, the Bay Area Press Photographers, and a student chapter chairman of the National Press Photographers Association. He has garnered a host of national and regional awards, has been sponsored for permanent display in the Pro Football Hall of Fame, and makes his fifth appearance in this anthology.

WILLIAM MEYER (One in Hand, Two in Cheek) is a twenty-seven-year-old staff photographer for *The Milwaukee Journal* and *Sentinel.* He is a graduate of the University of Wisconsin-Milwaukee. His talents have merited four appearances in *Best Sports Stories.*

JAMES ROARK (Baseball's Bicentennial Boomerangs) is a Chicagoan who completed the Famous Photographers School course and then joined the *Los Angeles Herald-Examiner* as a copyboy. He then became a staff photographer there and for the past three years has been staff sports lensman. His shots have made this sports anthology for the last three years in row.

JOHN ROUSMANIERE (Letting It All Hang Out There) is an associate editor of *Yachting* magazine with writing, photographic, and editing responsibilities that cover the entire sport of boating. He has B.S. and M.A. degrees from Columbia with some Ph.D. work in history. He taught American history for three years at the United States Military Academy before coming to work for *Yachting* in 1972. For two years he was the magazine's West Coast editor, living in Newport Beach, Calif. He now lives in Stamford, Conn., and is the author of a glossary of modern sailing terms, published last year.

DUANE M. SCHEEL (Choose Your Partners) began as a staff photographer with the *Ann Arbor News* and went to the *Fort Lauderdale* (Fla.) *News* in 1968. He also did some free-lance work and then went to work for the *Kalamazoo Gazette.* He has been a member of the Michigan Press Photographers Association for many years and now is the secretary of that group.

BILL SERNE (One Version of Demolition Derby) is one of those rare young lensmen who win a first prize on their initial attempt. His entry in 1974, "Innocent Bystander," showing a referee socked squarely on the nose, won first prize in the action photo division of *Best Sports Stories.* After graduation from Kent State College with a degree in photojournalism, he went to the *Tampa Tribune* and has been there since. This is his third appearance in this anthology.

JIM VINCENT (No Bull Market Today) has a penchant for working with nature, animals, and rodeos. In 1975, he won the action award in this anthology with his picture "Sit Down Strike," depicting a horse that is sitting straight upright with a cowboy clinging and urging him forward. He was with the *Portland Oregonian* for eight years and after that with the *Oregon Journal* for 20 years. This marks his eighth appearance in this sports anthology.

THE YEAR'S BEST SPORTS PHOTOS

GRANDSTAND HAILS HEADSTAND

by Charles R. Pugh, Jr., *Atlanta Journal-Constitution.* It is hard to figure out just what the stands are cheering in this action-winning picture as Florida State tailback Larry Key scored this touchdown against Auburn. Is it for the TD or the miraculous balancing act... or for both? Well anyway, Florida lost, 31-19, but Mr. Pugh's picture will never let the spectators forget this astonishing play. Copyright, ©, 1976, Atlanta Newspapers.

NOW GIRLS, LET'S NOT HAVE A ROW!

by Mike Andersen, *The Boston Herald American.* This feature winner shows a female crew of MIT in complete disarray as they struggle to regain their composure after collision with another boat at the start of their heat in Head-of-the-Charles Regatta. The mixture of resignation, advice, helplessness, and confusion evokes such mirth that it makes this shot into a winner immediately. Copyright, ©, 1976, *The Boston Herald American.*

FACE UP TO IT!

by Don Boorse, Perkasie (Pa.) *News-Herald.* It's difficult to tell whether the action is a face-lift or a face-stuff, but in any event it is a most unusual gesture. The hapless gent to whom the ball is being applied plays for the Lehighton (Pa.) High School Indians. The player in white who is administering the operation is from Pennridge High School in Perkasie, Pa. The referee looks as though he doesn't know what type of infraction to call. Copyright, ©, 1976, Don Boorse.

NO TONGUE-TIED TENNIS HERE

by John E. Biever, *The Milwaukee Journal.* A disputed line call by a linesman evoked this tender gesture from naughty Ilie Nastase in an exhibition match at Milwaukee. Bjorn Borg, his opponent, did not return the compliment. Copyright, ©, 1976, *The Milwaukee Journal.*

YES, THE DOCTOR IS IN

by Richard Darcey, *The Washington Post.* Julius Erving goes up and over Elvin Hayes to slam dunk a two-pointer against the Bullets at Capital Centre. The 76ers blew away the Bullets on successive nights, 143-104 and 114-109. The Doctor totaled 50 points in the two games. Copyright, ©, 1976, *The Washington Post.*

MVP vs. ROOKIE OF THE YEAR

by Craig R. Borck, *St. Paul Dispatch & Pioneer Press.* In this sequence Yankee catcher Thurman Munson, chosen by the AP, as the American League's Most Valuable Player, makes a valiant effort to tag sliding Twins catcher Butch Wynegar, named Rookie of the Year by *The Sporting News.* Umpire Bill Deegan called Wynegar safe. Yankees won, 9-4, at Metropolitan Stadium. Copyright, ©, 1976, *St. Paul Dispatch & Pioneer Press.*

Twins

CAUGHT IN A CRUNCH

by Barry Edmonds, *The Flint Journal.* Motocross racer Danny Wright, Saginaw, Mich. looses control of his dirt bike, goes over the handlebars, and the bike crashes down on him. In the meantime two more racers are making the jump behind him, trying desparately to avoid Wright, who ended up dazed in the middle of the track. Slightly bruised, he returned to race again that night. Copyright, ©, 1976, *Booth Newspapers, Inc.*

PERILS OF A PUCKISH PUCK

by Dave Gogan, *Jonesboro (Ga.) News/Daily.* Atlanta Flames center Tom Lysiak (12) tries to maintain control over a vagrant puck after being up-ended in the third period of Flames' 8-3 win over New York Rangers. Copyright, ©, 1976, Dave Gogan.

HEAD AND TAIL

by Abe Isaac, *Elizabeth Daily Journal.* This unusual tumble ended in a rather peculiar face-off or end-off. The action happened in New Jersey and was the only action of its type during the Bicentennial celebration throughout the country. Copyright, ©, 1976, Abe Isaac, for *The Daily Journal,* Elizabeth, N.J.

THE SANDMAN COMETH

by Charles G. Kirman, *Chicago Sun Times.* The sandman was merely knocking, but the blow that finally put our grimacing boxer to sleep was the one that followed. It happened in the Chicago Junior Boxing Championship.

SOMETHING OLD, SOMETHING NEW

by Cletus M. (Pete) Hohn, *Minneapolis Tribune.* Bill Andberg, "who just turned sixty-five," and holds many national records for senior groups, paces seven-year-old Andrea Vogel of Roseville (Minn.) to the finish line. Andrea had missed the race for her age group, so joined the older group in the last race of the day. Andberg had already finished in five minutes 27 seconds and then ran with Andrea for her final lap. Her time was 8:03. Copyright, ©, 1976, *Minneapolis Tribune.*

YE GODS, IS THERE NO JUSTICE?

by Robert Johnson, *The Nashville Tennessean.* Charles Black of Tennessee makes like Sir Lawrence Olivier appealing to the fates after having been called out on an attempted steal at Vanderbilt's McGugin Field. Vanderbilt's second baseman, Kenny Scholl, nonchalantly flips the ball away after having made the tag. Copyright, ©, 1976, *the Tennessean.*

NET GAIN

by John Long, *The Hartford Courant.* Alan Hangsleben of the New England Whalers takes the net off its pins as he crashes into it during a game at the Hartford Civic Center. Copyright, ©, 1976, *The Hartford Courant.*

BASKETBALL KARATE

by Chuck Lyons, Foothill Intercity Newspapers. Duarte High's Beno Lee seems to be thrusting his foot into the face of a Bell Gardens opponent. Lee is merely grabbing a carom that enabled him to capture the Rio Hondo League's rebounding title. Copyright, ©, 1976, *Star-News* (Pasadena, Calif.), *The Duartean.*

BASEBALL'S BICENTENNIAL BOOMERANGS

by James Roark, *Los Angeles Herald-Examiner.* A flag just about to be burned by two young men at Dodger Stadium is rescued by Rick Monday of the Chicago Cubs. He returned it to the grounds keeper. When asked about his views of this strange event, Monday said that his motivation was historical.

NAMES IN THE NEWS

by Richard Mackson, *Santa Monica Evening Outlook.* Two undistinguished Culver City, Calif., High School football team candidates were sitting on the bench when there was a power failure, postponing the game between the Centaurs and visiting Mira Costa. If Greg Carter and Ezell Ford were at a loss for words when the lights went out, they should have contacted their famous namesakes. Copyright, ©, 1976, Richard Mackson, United Western Newspapers.

CARPING COACH

by Fred Matthes, *San Jose Mercury News.* During an Oakland Raider-Green Bay Packer game, John Madden, the Oakland coach, pointed to the spot where the ball should be set down by the line judge Jack Johnson. He didn't use nice words. Regard how the judge continued to "bleep" back. Copyright, ©, 1976, *San Jose Mercury News.*

LOOK, REF, NO HANDS!

by Derrick Zane Jackson, *The Milwaukee Journal.* Ordinarily, this would have called for a holding penalty but since hands are not involved, it might also have been called for face mask holding. Anyway, Al Beauchamp of the St. Louis Cardinals owns the arm and Bart Smith of the Green Bay Packers has full rights to the mask. Copyright, ©, 1976, *The Milwaukee Journal.*

ONE IN HAND, TWO IN CHEEK

by William Meyer, *The Milwaukee Journal.* Jeff Braun, a shot-putter from the University of Wisconsin, huffs and puffs his face to a size rivaling the shot he has in hand. He pushed the 16-pounder 56 feet to win the Big Ten indoor title on his last throw. His face returned to normal a bit later. Copyright, ©, 1976, *The Milwaukee Journal.*

"RIDE 'EM COWBOY! OH YEAH?"

by John P. Foster, *The Seattle Times.* Cowboy Jordie Thompson was in big trouble but kept on trying at the Othello Rodeo, following the rules by holding on with one hand. His right hand was waving around in the air out of sight. He kept his seat for eight seconds before the horse fell over backward, bruising the cowboy's hips. The effort was good enough for a third prize. Copyright, ©, 1976, *the Seattle Times Co.*

LANE
GAS SERV
OTHELLO
WASH.
T.V

LETTING IT ALL HANG OUT THERE

by John Rousmaniere, *Yachting Magazine.* San Diegan Robbie Haines looks well in charge as his crew, Rodney Eales and Lowell North, "hike out" in their Soling Class sailboat. They were second at the U.S. Olympic Yachting Trials. Copyright, ©, 1976, John Rousmaniere.

CHOOSE YOUR PARTNERS

by Duane M. Scheel, *Kalamazoo Gazette.* This merry party took place on January 2, 1976. Seems as though the guys missed out on their New Year's Eve dance and held each other instead...but at bay. The stars were Kenny Mann of the Kalamazoo Choreographers (white leotard), and Sid Vesey of the Fort Wayne Ballet Danse Macabres. The recital took place under the auspices of the International Hockey League. Copyright, ©, 1976, *Kalamazoo Gazette* Photo.

ONE VERSION OF DEMOLITION DERBY

by Bill Serne, *The Tampa Tribune.* Topping this heap is Miami Dolphin Ben Malone, who is about to score a touchdown against Tampa Bay, which lost this game 20-23. Copyright, ©, 1976, *The Tampa Tribune.*

NO BULL MARKET TODAY

by Jim Vincent, *Portland Oregonian.* John Gloor of West Columbia, Texas, flies out in front while caught in rigging of brahma bull named "Snuffy" on July 5, 1976, at St. Paul (Ore.) Rodeo. Copyright, ©, 1976, *Portland Oregonian.*

HETERICK MEMORIAL LIBRARY
3 5111 00358 0697